BAD  KITTY
SCHOOL DAZE

NICK BRUEL

SQUARE
FISH

ROARING BROOK PRESS
New York

For all teachers everywhere

Page 83, *The Battle at Bunker's Hill*, George Edward Perine after John Trumbull, courtesy of Emmet Collection, Miriam and Ira D. Wallach Division of Art, Prints and Photographs, The New York Public Library, Astor, Lenox and Tilden Foundations

SQUARE FISH

An Imprint of Macmillan
175 Fifth Avenue, New York, NY 10010
mackids.com

Square Fish books may be purchased for business or promotional use. For information on bulk purchases, please contact the Macmillan Corporate and Premium Sales Department at (800) 221-7945 x 5442 or by e-mail at specialmarkets@macmillan.com.

Library of Congress Cataloging-in-Publication Data
Bruel, Nick.
    Bad Kitty school daze / Nick Bruel.
        p. cm.
    Summary: "When Kitty's owners have finally had enough of her bad behavior, it's time to ship her off to obedience school"— Provided by publisher.
    ISBN 978-1-250-03947-7 (Square Fish paperback)
    ISBN 978-1-59643-944-3 (Scholastic edition)
    [1. Cats—Fiction. 2. Pets—Training—Fiction. 3. Humorous stories.] I. Title.
    PZ7.B82832Bao 2012   [E]—dc23   2012015359

Originally published in the United States by Neal Porter Books/Roaring Brook Press
First Square Fish Edition: 2014
Square Fish logo designed by Filomena Tuosto

17 19 20 18 16

AR: 3.3 / LEXILE: GN630L

• CONTENTS •

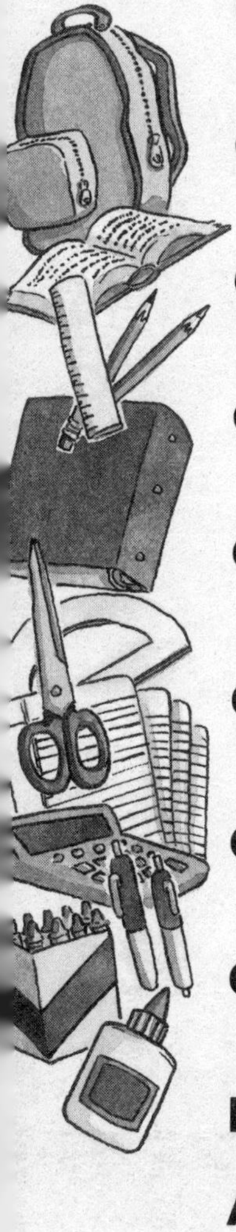

CHAPTER ONE
ONE FINE DAY 5

CHAPTER TWO
THE NEXT FINE DAY 17

CHAPTER THREE
WELCOME 31

CHAPTER FOUR
CIRCLE TIME 42

CHAPTER FIVE
ARTS + CRAFTS 68

CHAPTER SIX
SHOW + TELL 86

CHAPTER SEVEN
STORYTIME 106

CHAPTER EIGHT
GRADUATION 118

EPILOGUE 144

A BONUS 152

•CHAPTER ONE•

ONE FINE DAY

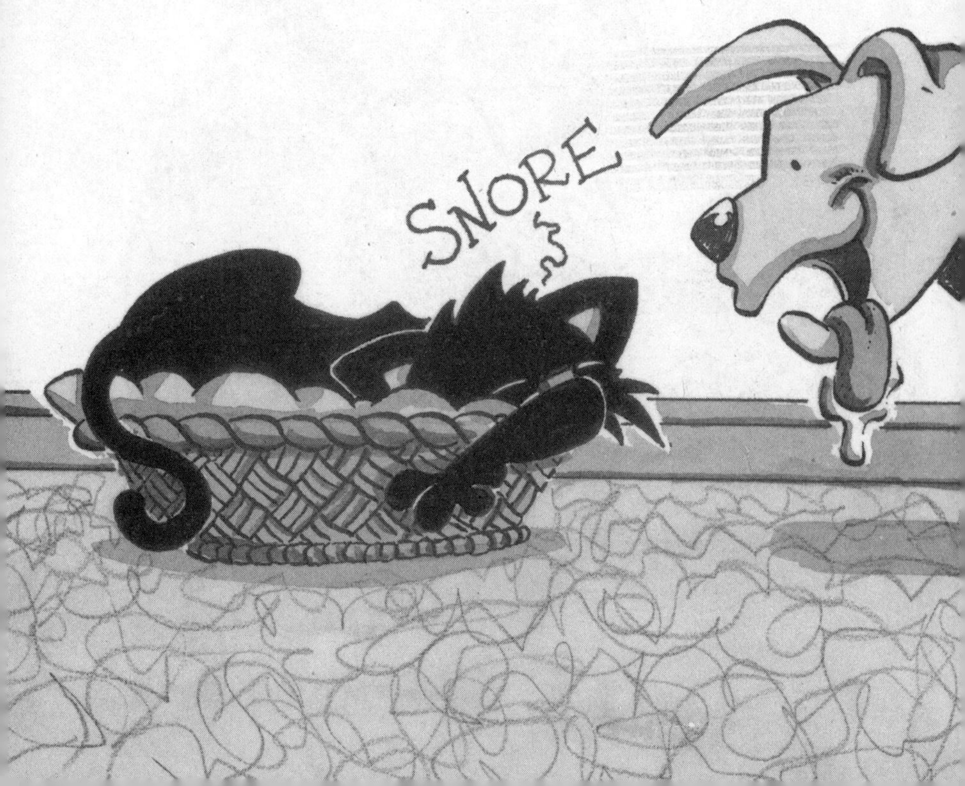
SNORE

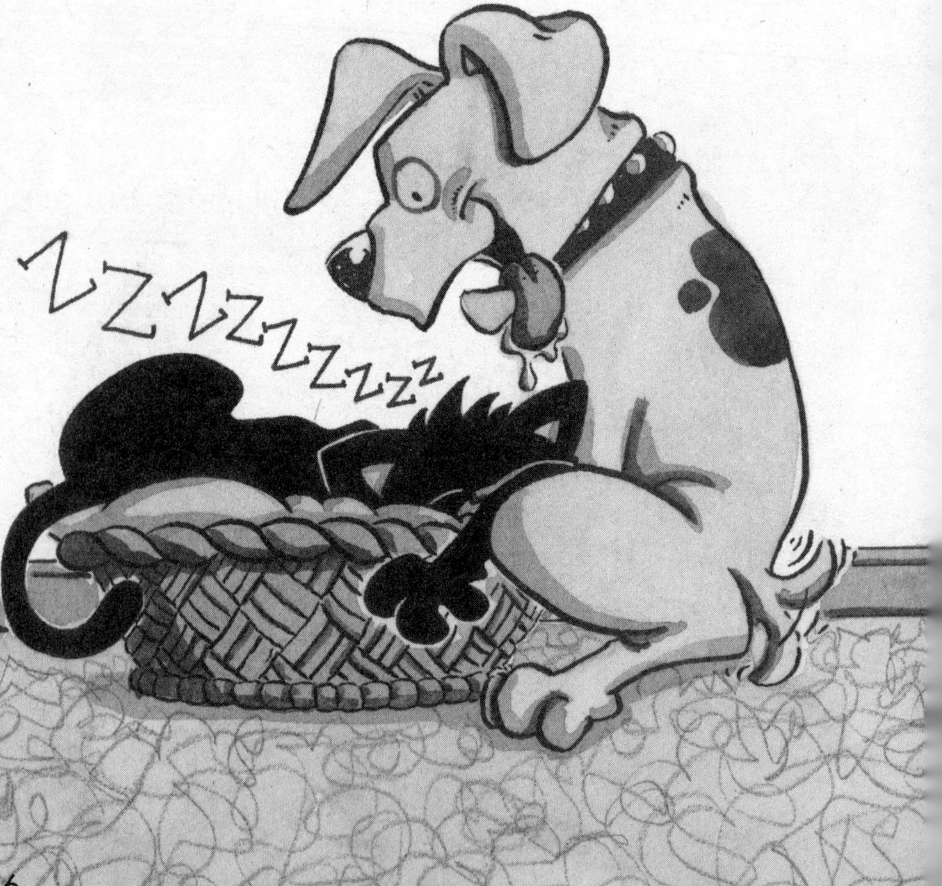
ZZZZZZZZZZ

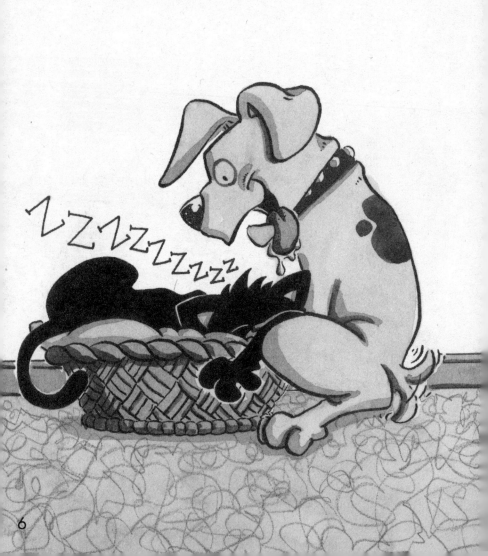

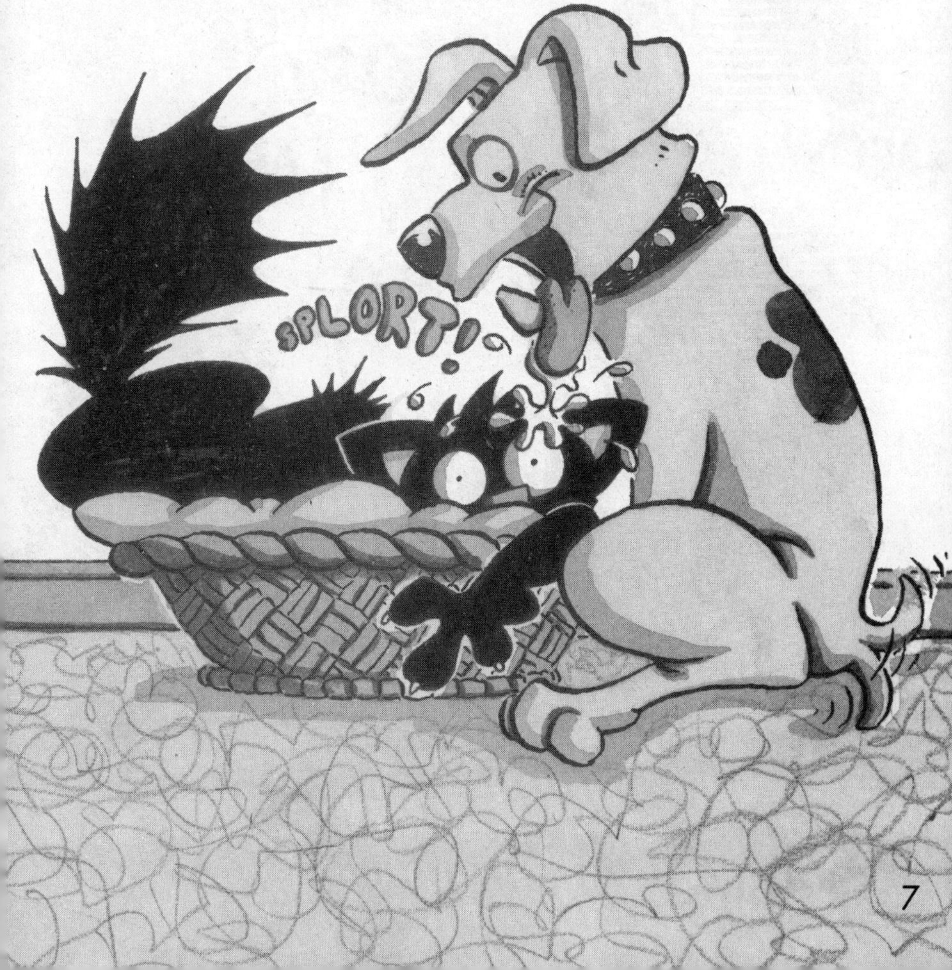
SPLORT!

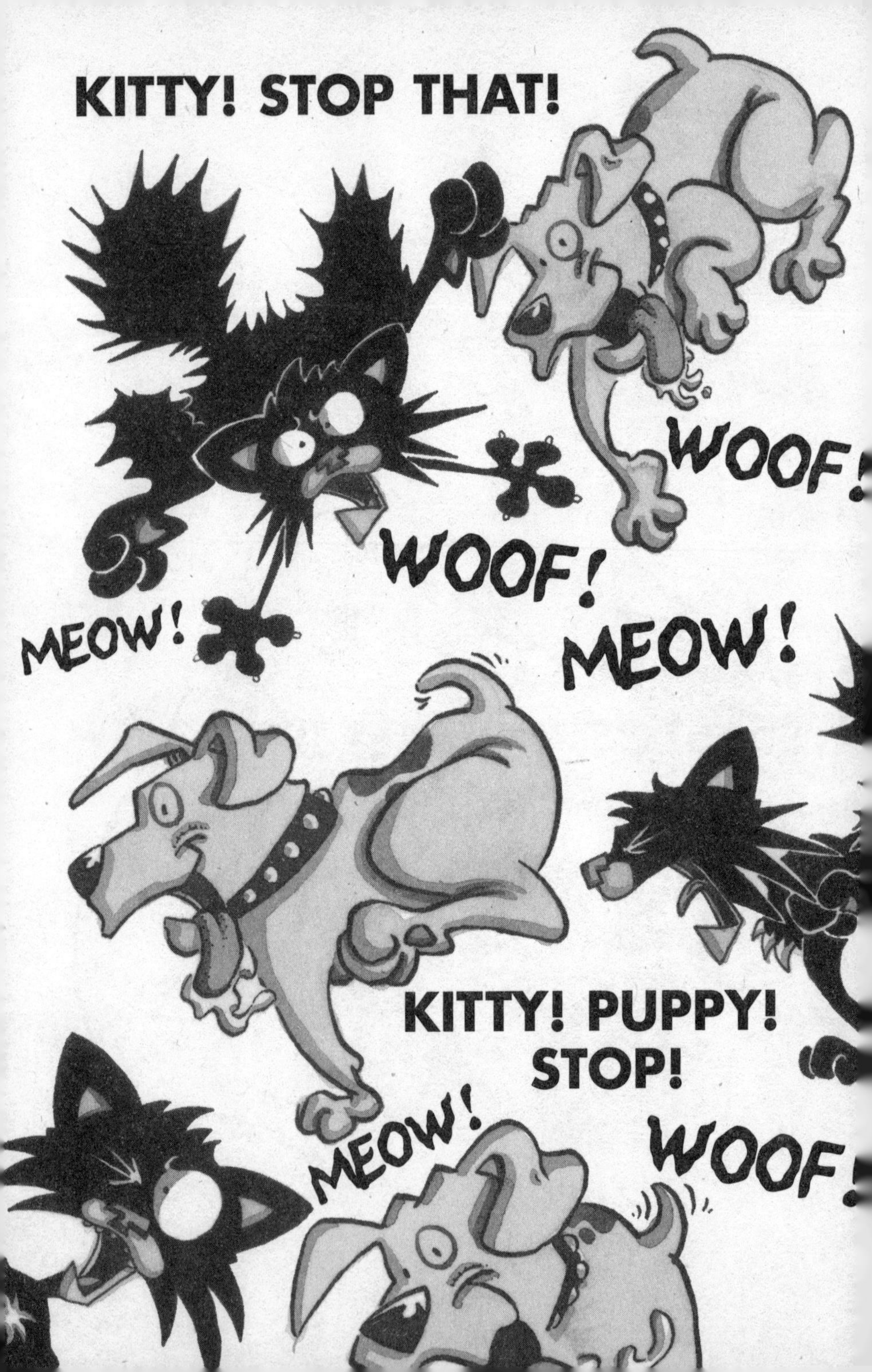
KITTY! STOP THAT!
WOOF!
WOOF!
MEOW!
MEOW!
KITTY! PUPPY! STOP!
MEOW!
WOOF!

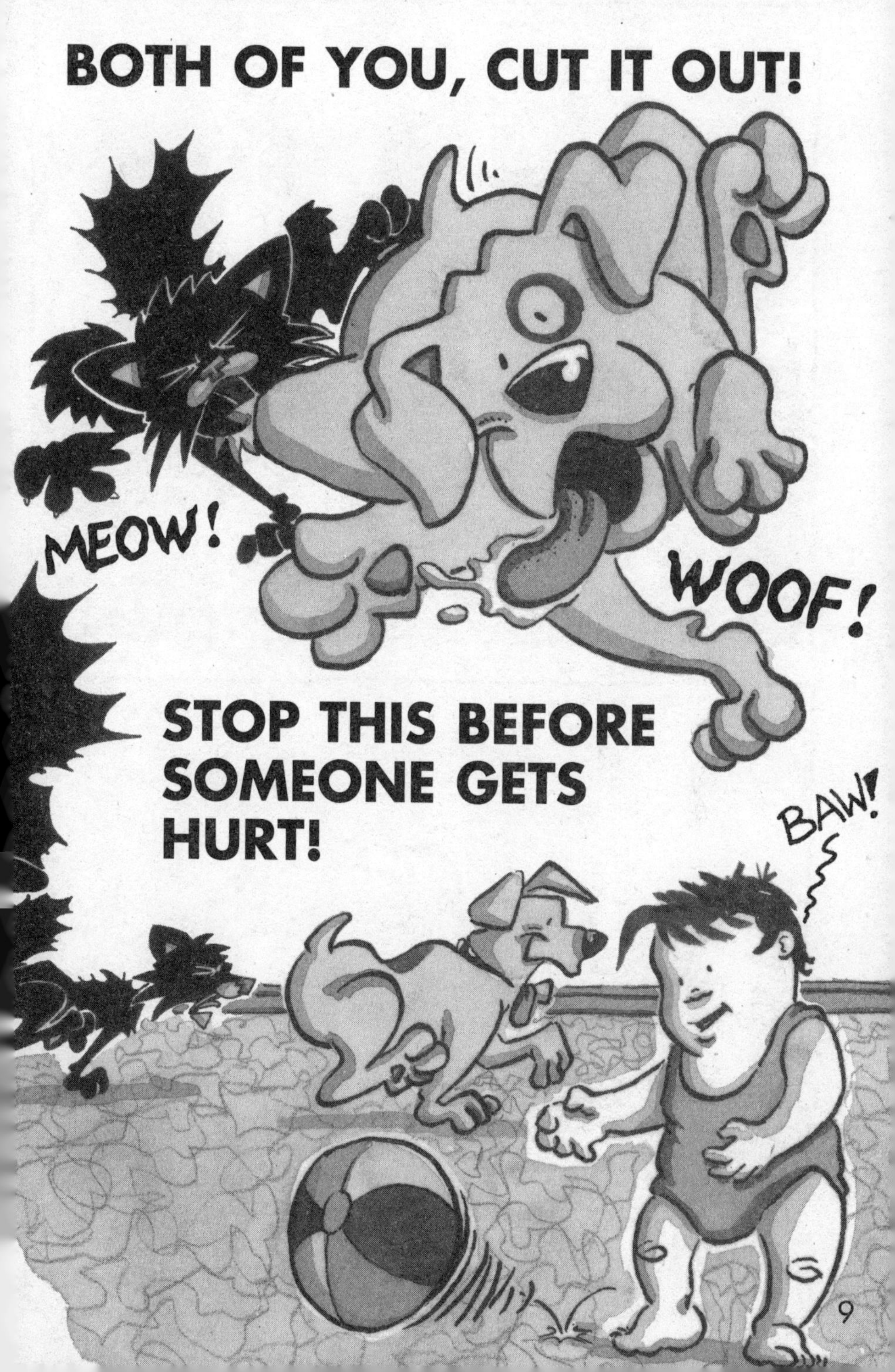
BOTH OF YOU, CUT IT OUT!
MEOW!
WOOF!
STOP THIS BEFORE SOMEONE GETS HURT!
BAW!

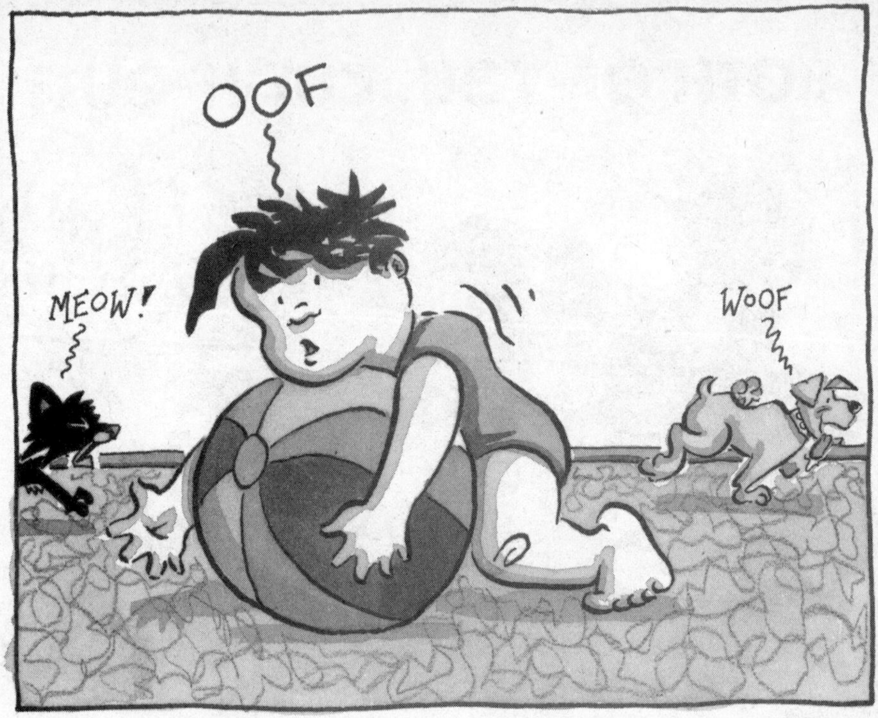
OOF
MEOW!
WOOF

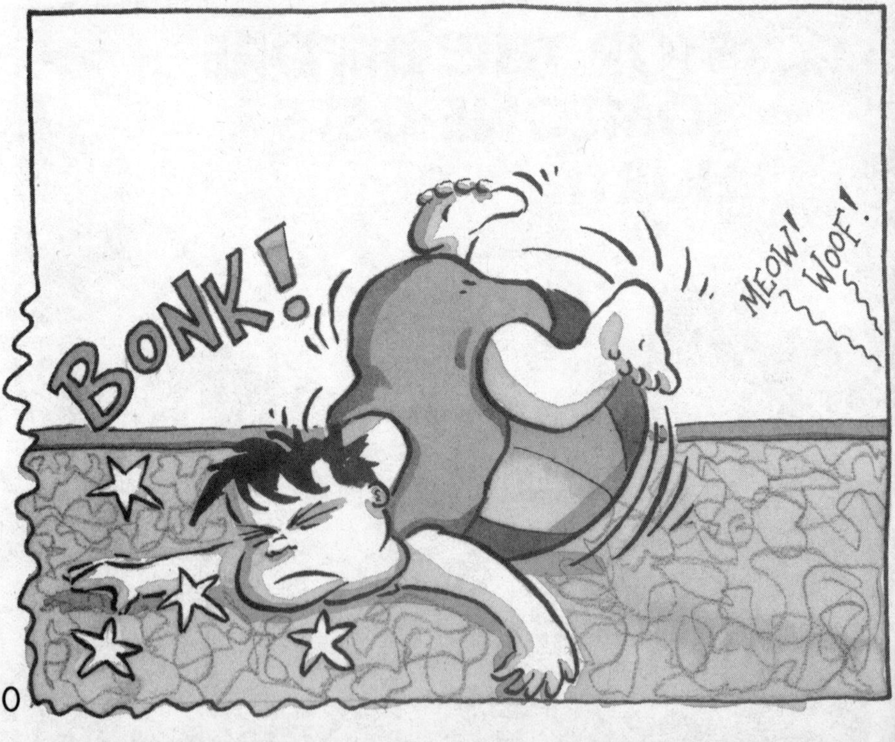
BONK!
MEOW!
WOOF!

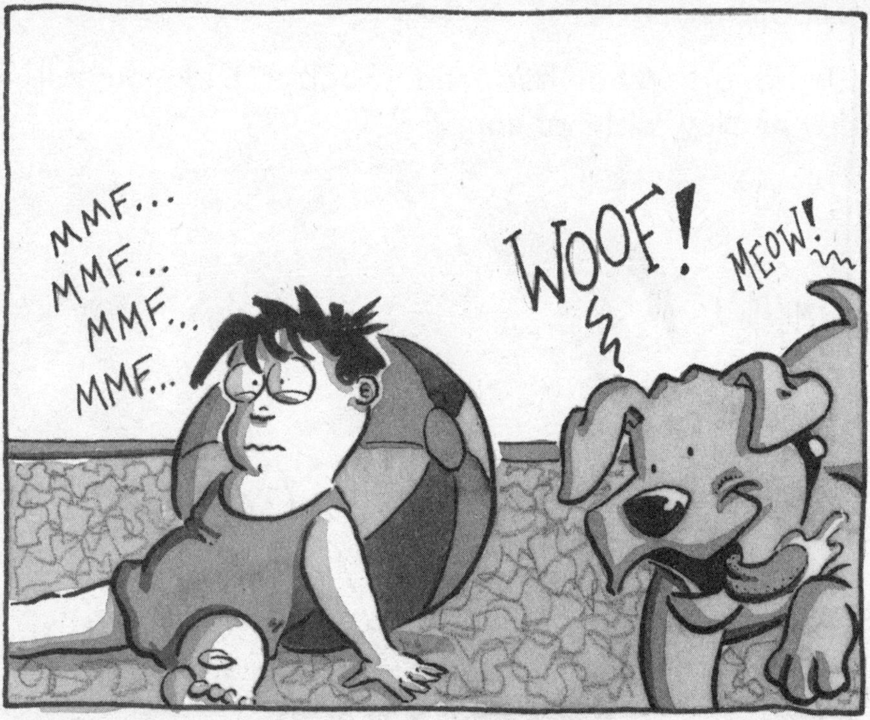
MMF...
MMF...
MMF...
MMF...
WOOF!
MEOW!

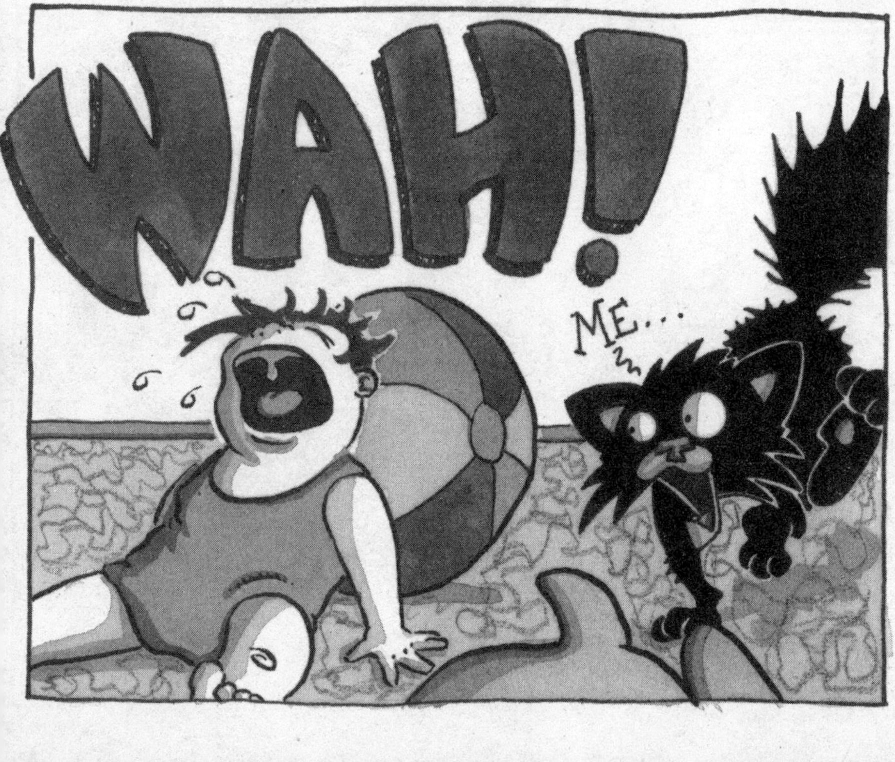
WAH!
ME...

Oh, dear! What happened, Baby? Did you fall down? How did that happen?

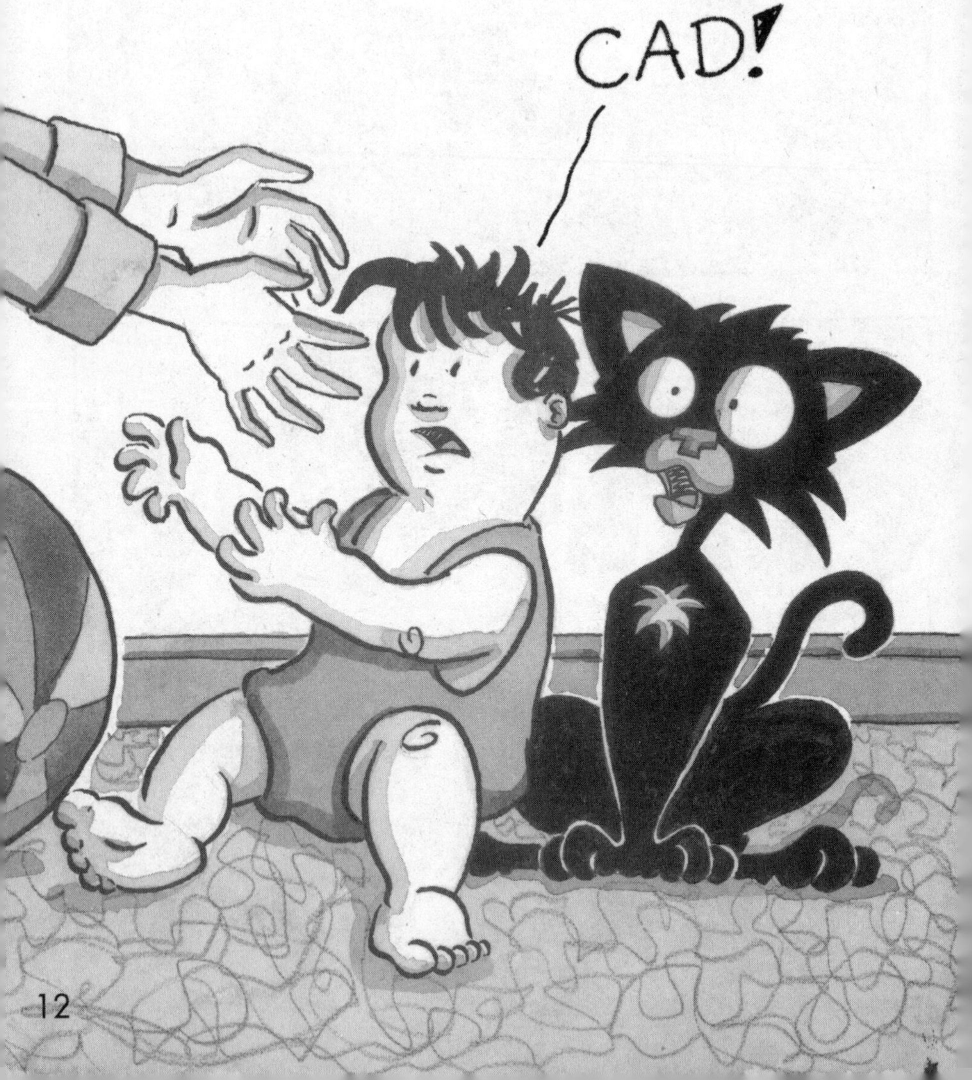
CAD!

The cat did this? Well, I'm not surprised. Tsk, tsk, tsk. The way those two were running and horsing around. But I'm sure it was an accident.

Kitty, it's time for us to have a little talk.

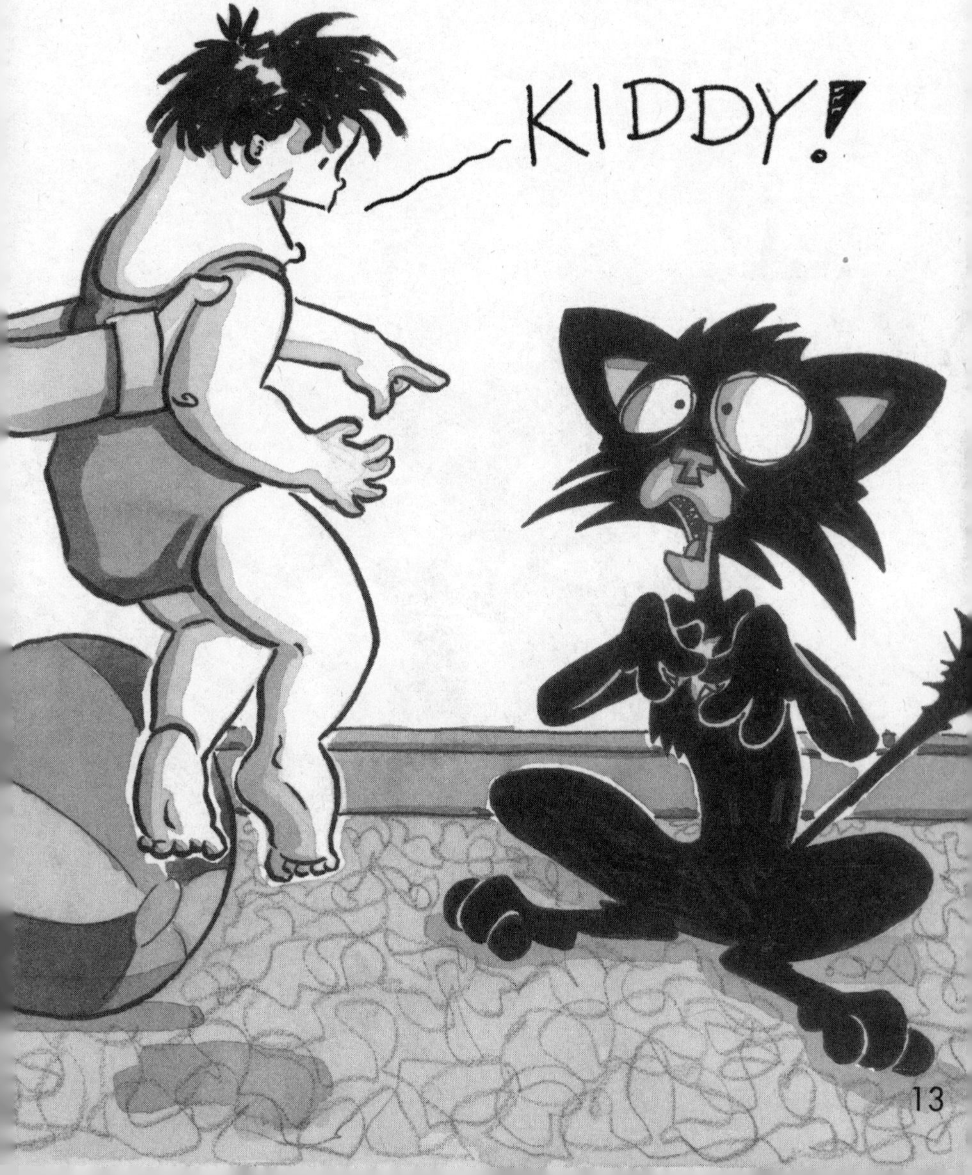
KIDDY!

Kitty, I've had enough of your SCREAMING and HISSING and FIGHTING. It's time we did something about your behavior, your nasty temper, and the fact that you never seem to listen.

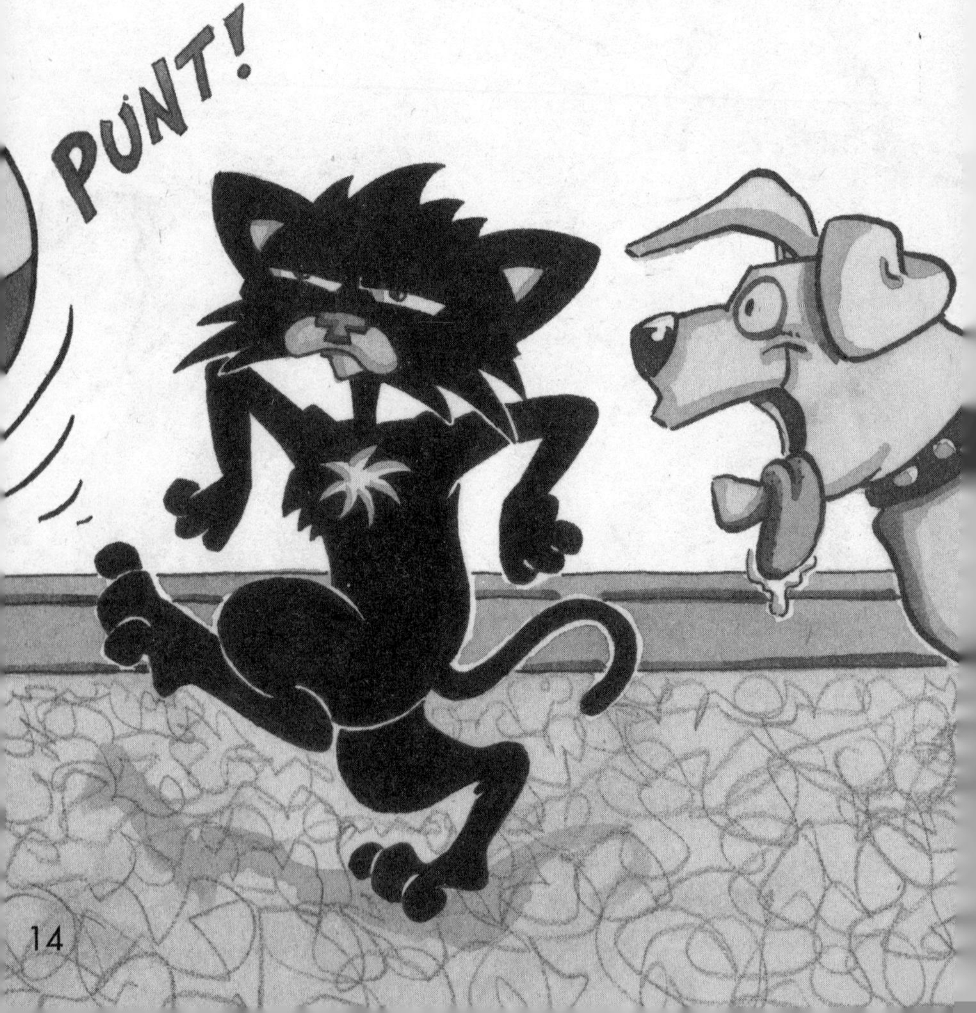
PUNT!

And that goes for you too, Puppy. That drooling problem of yours started all of this.

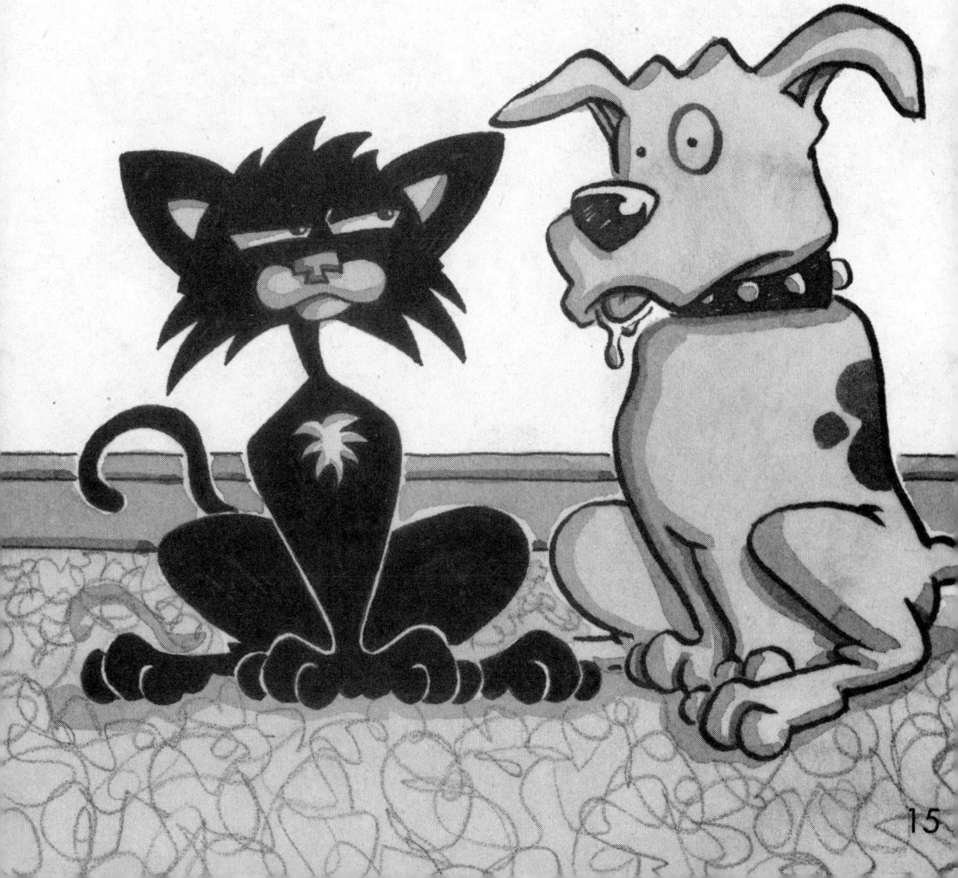

That's why I've decided it's time for both of you to go to . . .

SCHOOL.

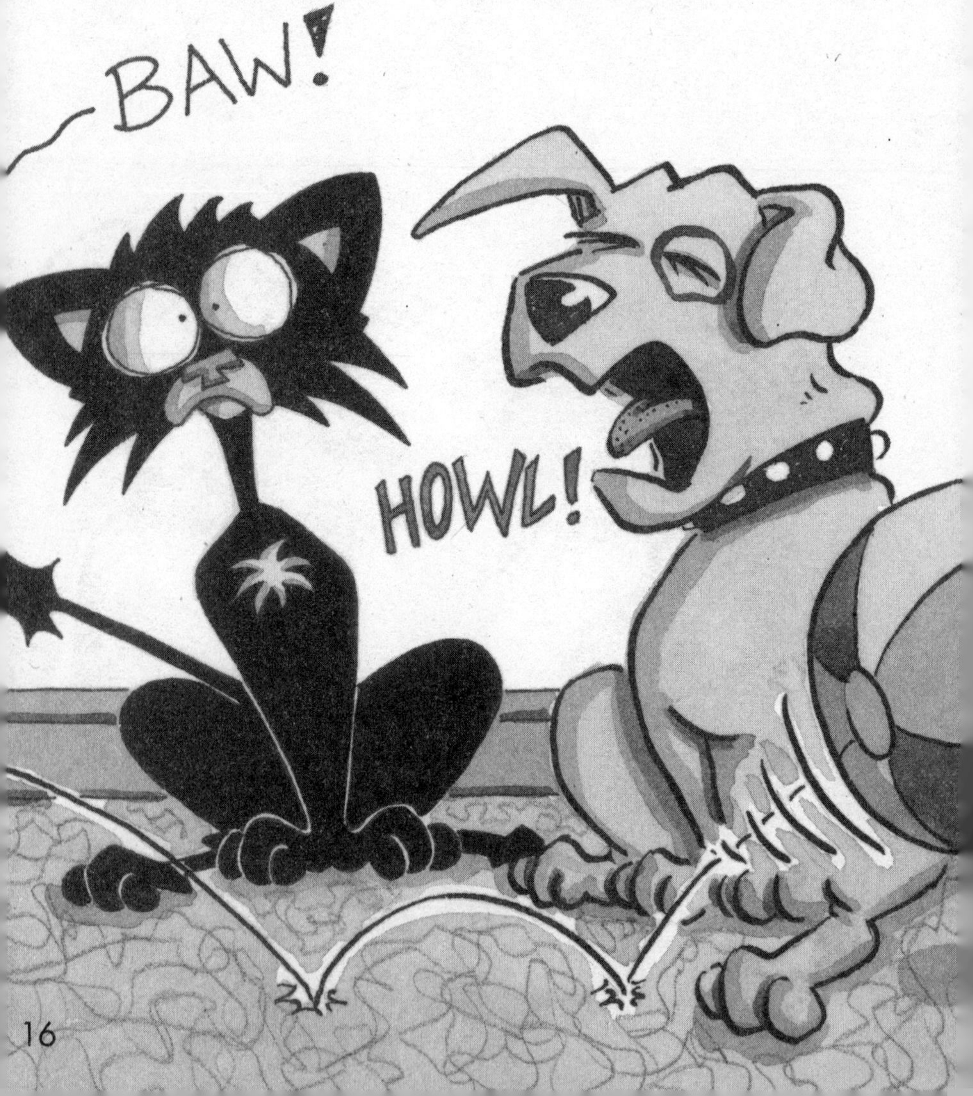

BAW!
HOWL!

•CHAPTER TWO•

THE NEXT FINE DAY

HEY, KITTY! I just got back from the store, and look at all of the super-cool school supplies I bought for you! They all feature your absolute FAVORITE . . .

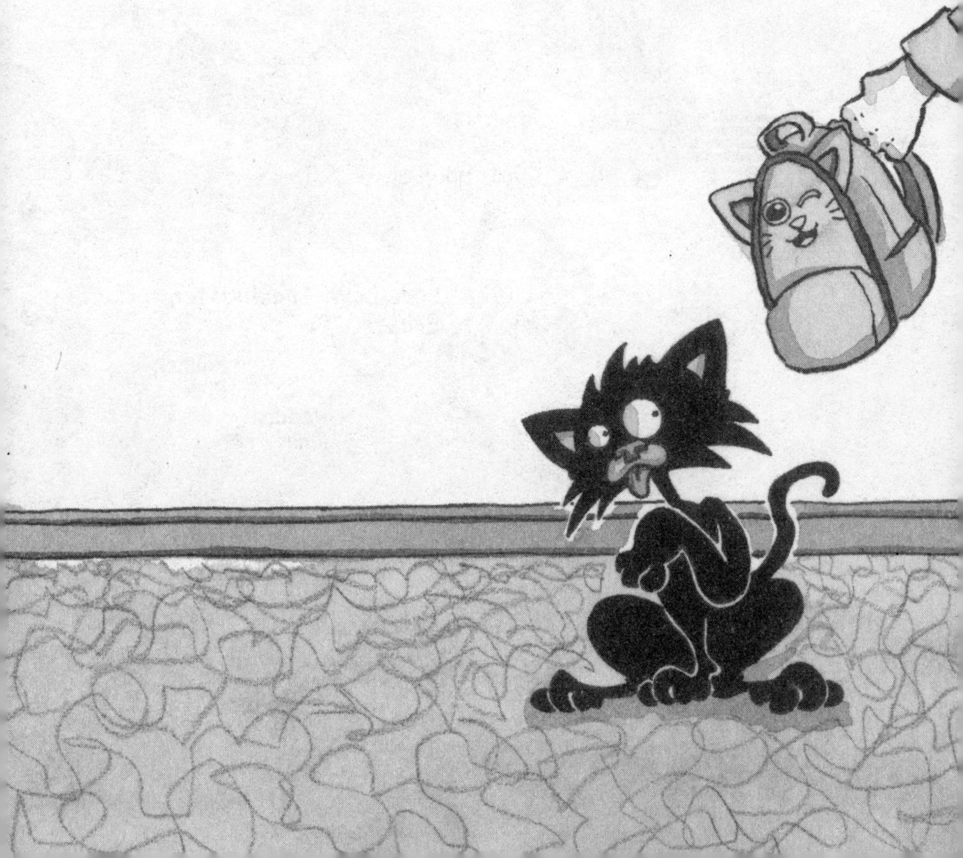

Love Love Angel Kitten

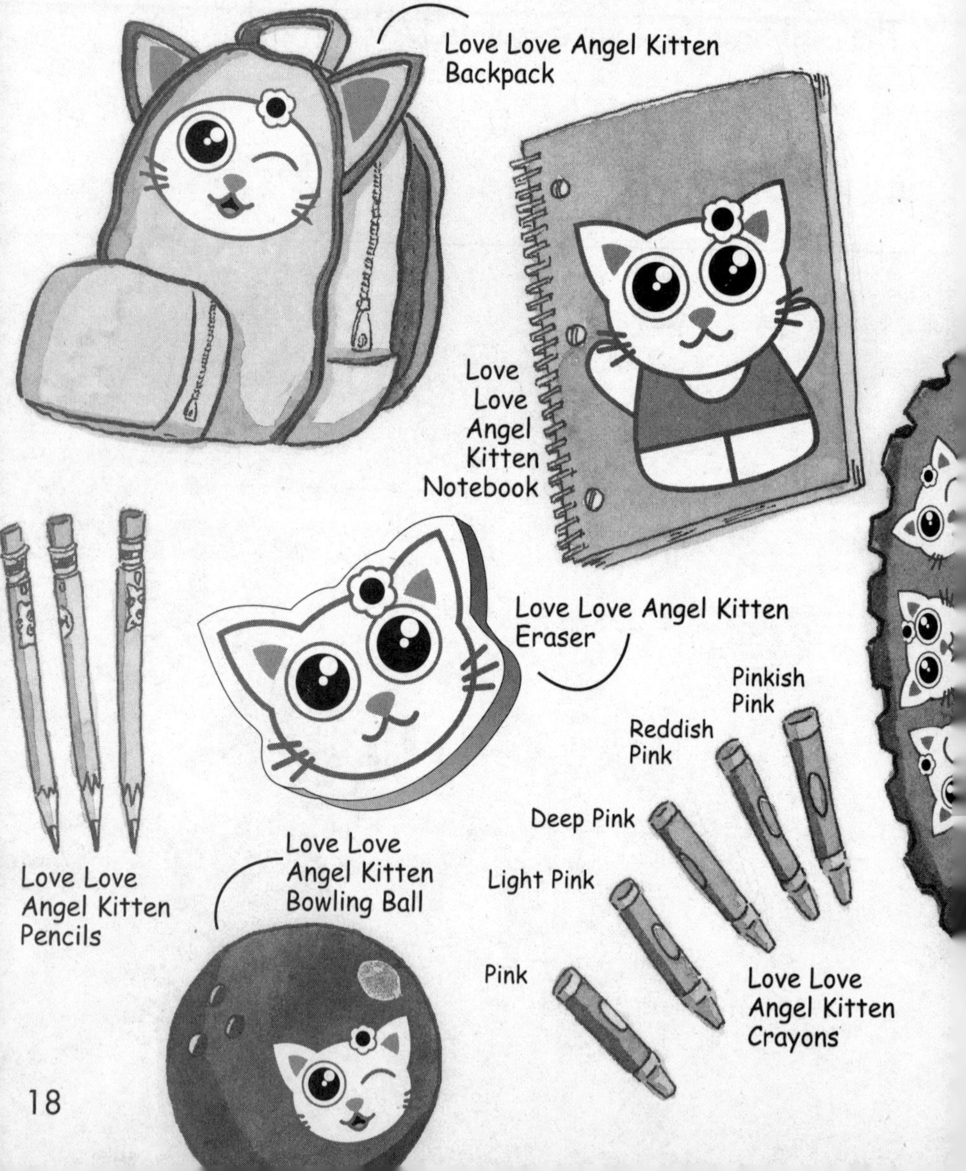

Love Love Angel Kitten Backpack
Love Love Angel Kitten Notebook
Love Love Angel Kitten Eraser
Love Love Angel Kitten Pencils
Love Love Angel Kitten Bowling Ball
Pinkish Pink
Reddish Pink
Deep Pink
Light Pink
Pink
Love Love Angel Kitten Crayons

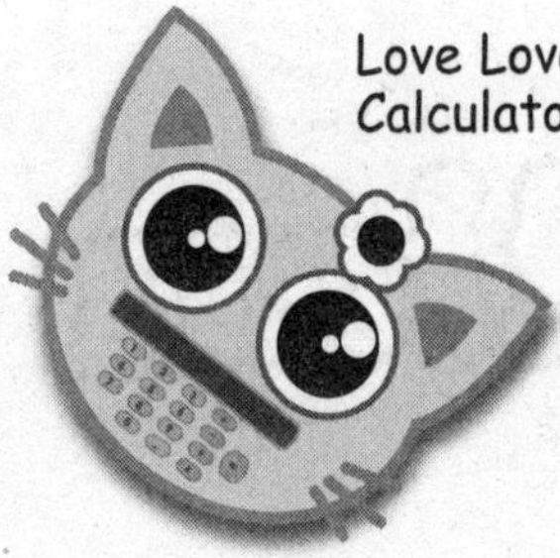

Love Love Angel Kitten
Calculator

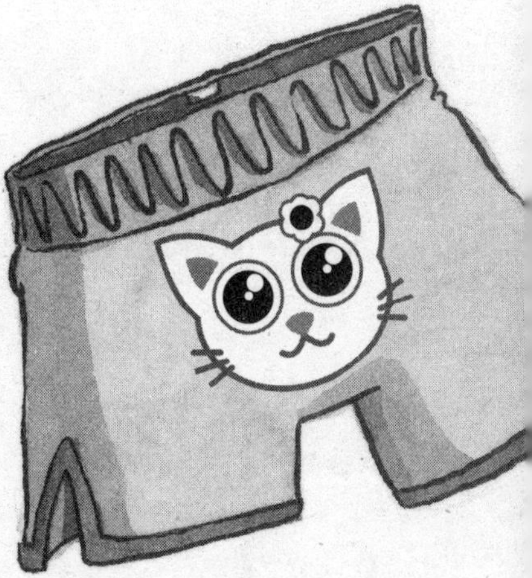

Love Love
Angel
Kitten
Gym Shorts

Love Love
Angel Kitten
Tractor
Tire

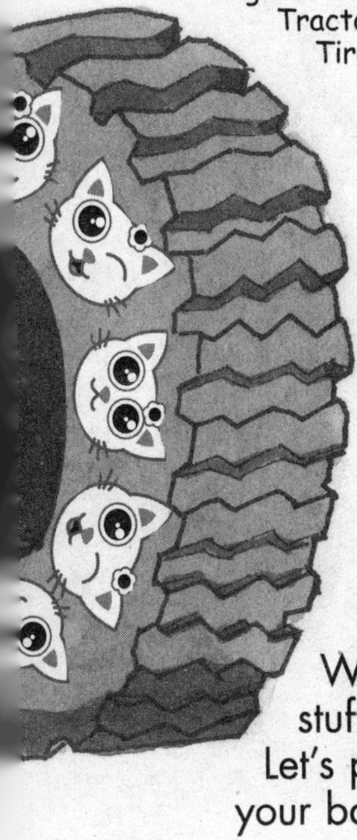

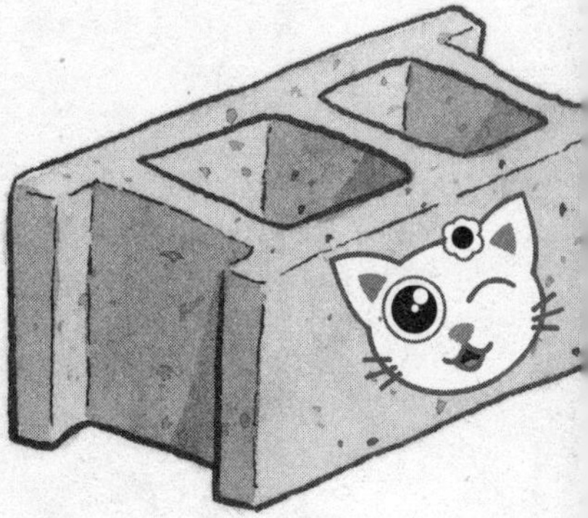

Love Love
Angel Kitten
Cinder Block

Love Love
Angel Kitten
Ruler

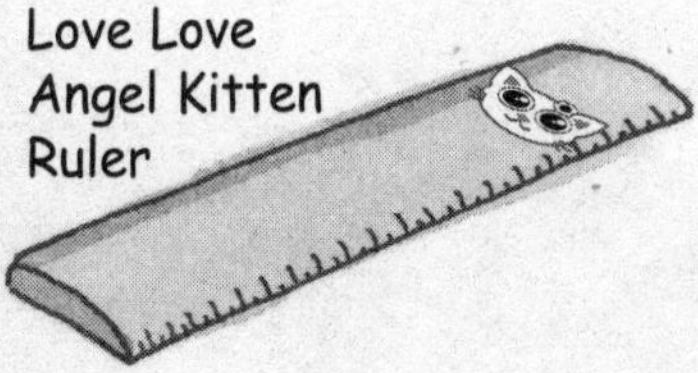

Whew! That's a lot of stuff! Oh well . . . Let's put it all into your backpack.

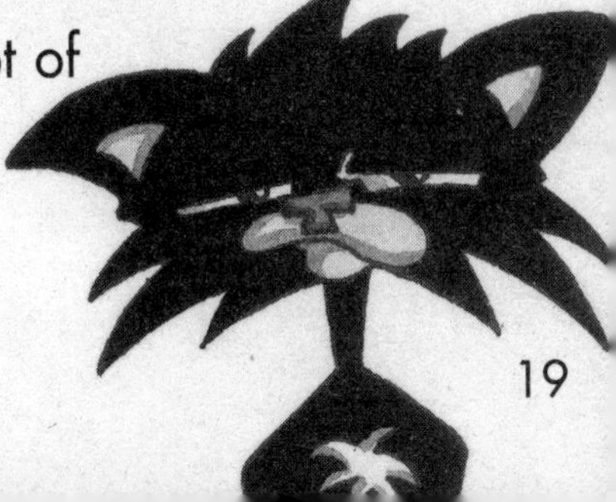

Awww, look at you! All ready for school.

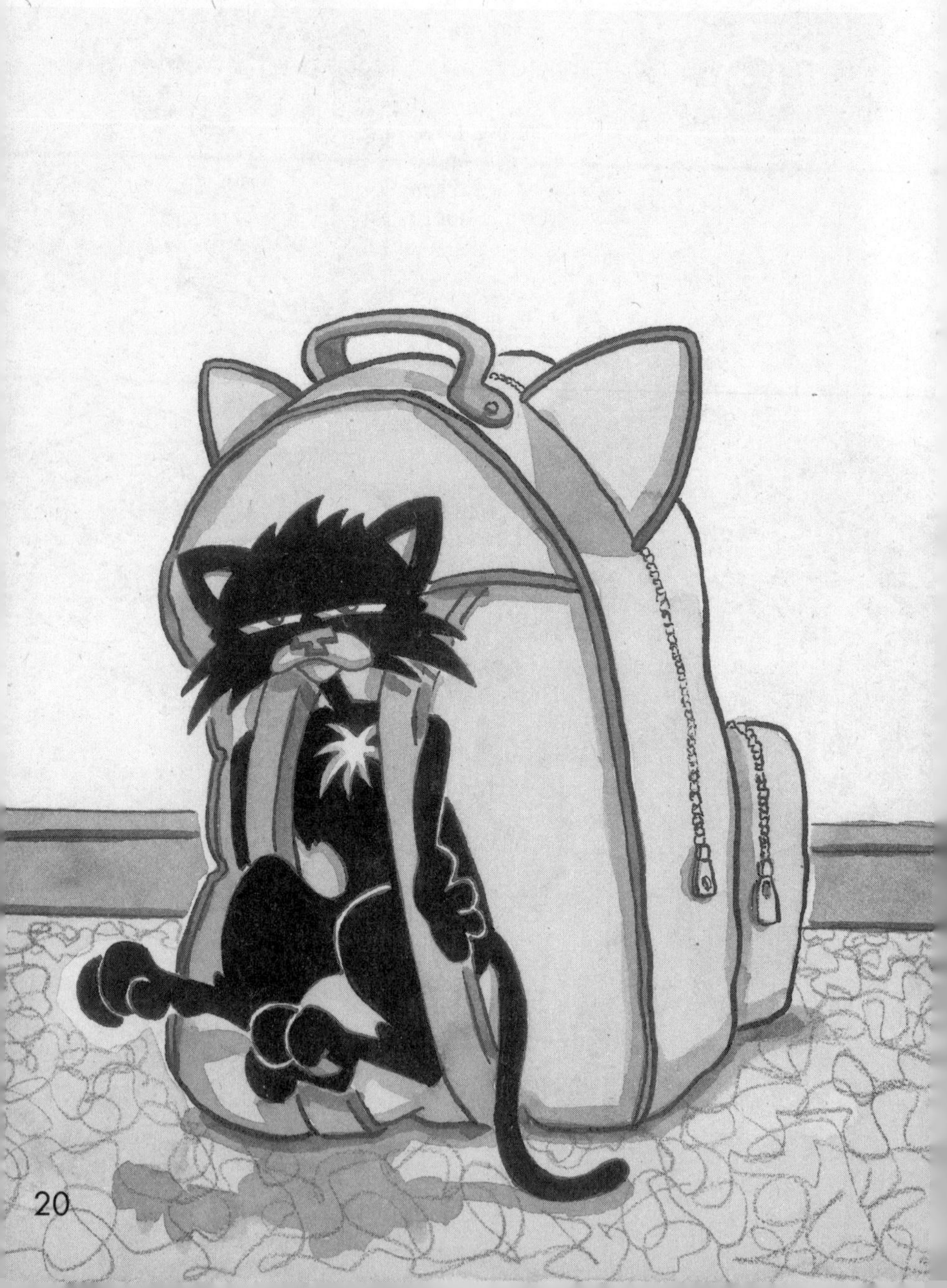

And so is Puppy! Did you pack your bandana, Puppy? I hope so, because you'll need it if you start drooling again.

We better hurry. You guys don't want to be late for the school bus!

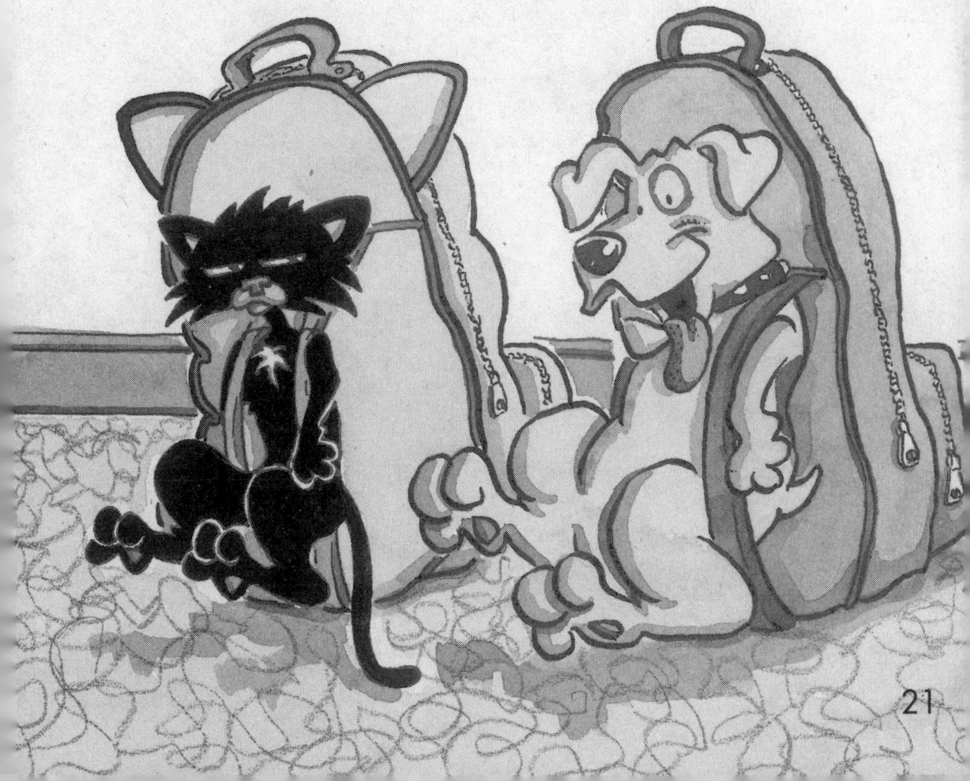

HERE IT COMES!

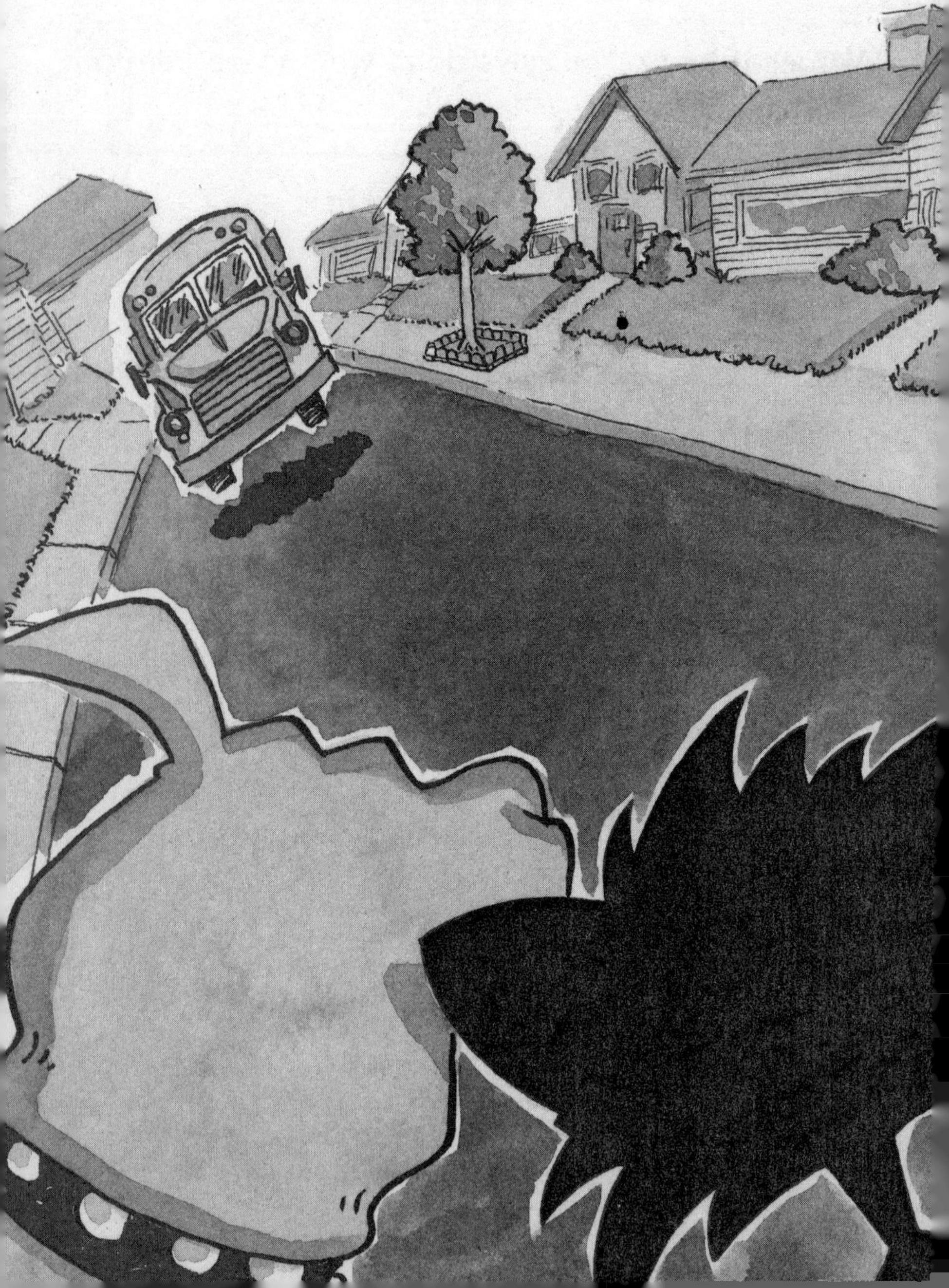

And look who's driving! It's good ol' Uncle Murray!

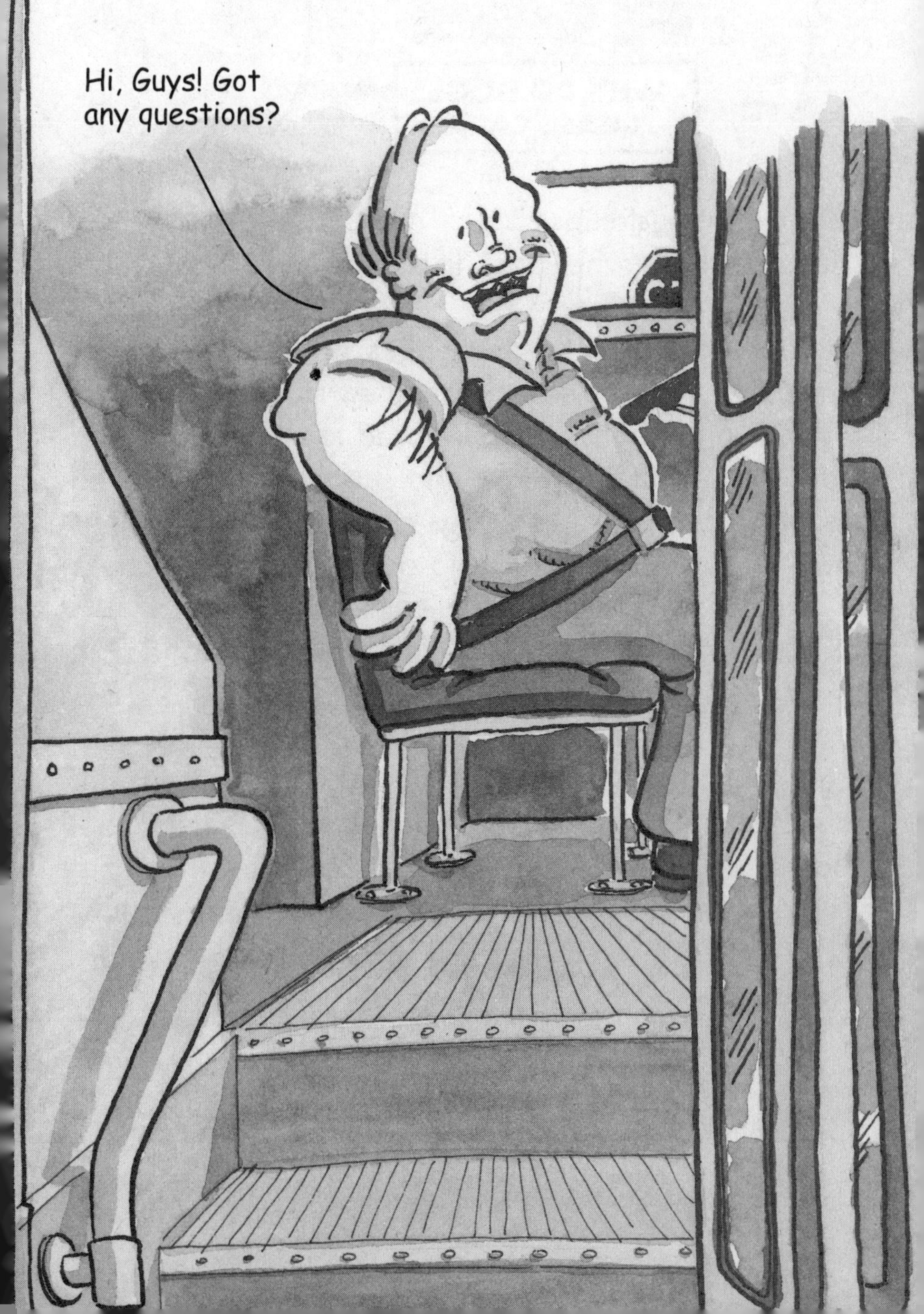

UNCLE MURRAY'S FUN FACTS

WHY DO DOGS CHASE CATS?

Hey, don't blame the dog for this!

Dogs don't just chase cats. They chase lots of things, because that's what dogs like to do most.

Herder dogs like border collies are bred to chase sheep and keep the flock together. Hunting dogs like hounds and dachshunds are bred to chase foxes and rats. Police dogs like German shepherds are trained to chase criminals. And dogs chase all of these things not just because they like to do it, but also because they're so very, very good at it.

When a dog chases a cat, it's not chasing because it's being mean. It's chasing the cat because of instinct. "Instinct" is that part of an animal's brain that controls how an animal is going to act. Birds can fly because their instinct

MEOW*

*Albert Einstein once said that "Peace cannot be kept by force; it can only be achieved by understanding."

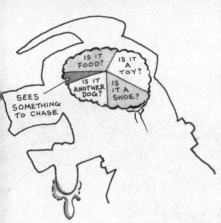

IS IT FOOD? IS IT A TOY? IS IT ANOTHER DOG? IS IT A SHOE? SEES SOMETHING TO CHASE

tells them how. Fish can swim because their instinct tells them how. And dogs chase other animals because their instinct tells them it's an important thing to do.

So when a dog sees a strange cat for the first time, his brain tells him that he MUST begin chasing the cat. It doesn't help that dogs are also very territorial, which means that if the cat is anywhere near something the dog thinks he owns, like his bone or his backyard or his house or even YOU, then he will feel compelled to chase that poor cat away.

Cats, by the way, have the same instinct as dogs. Cats are extremely good at chasing other animals, only they chase animals much smaller than they are, like mice and rats. Most dogs are bigger, sometimes MUCH bigger, than cats. So cats do not generally chase dogs.

Dogs, however, do not have the same sense of caution as cats and will often chase things much, much bigger than them. That's why they'll sometimes chase cars.

I like dogs, but they better not chase my school bus!

All right, ya goofy cat, move on to the back of the bus and you can meet some of your new classmates!

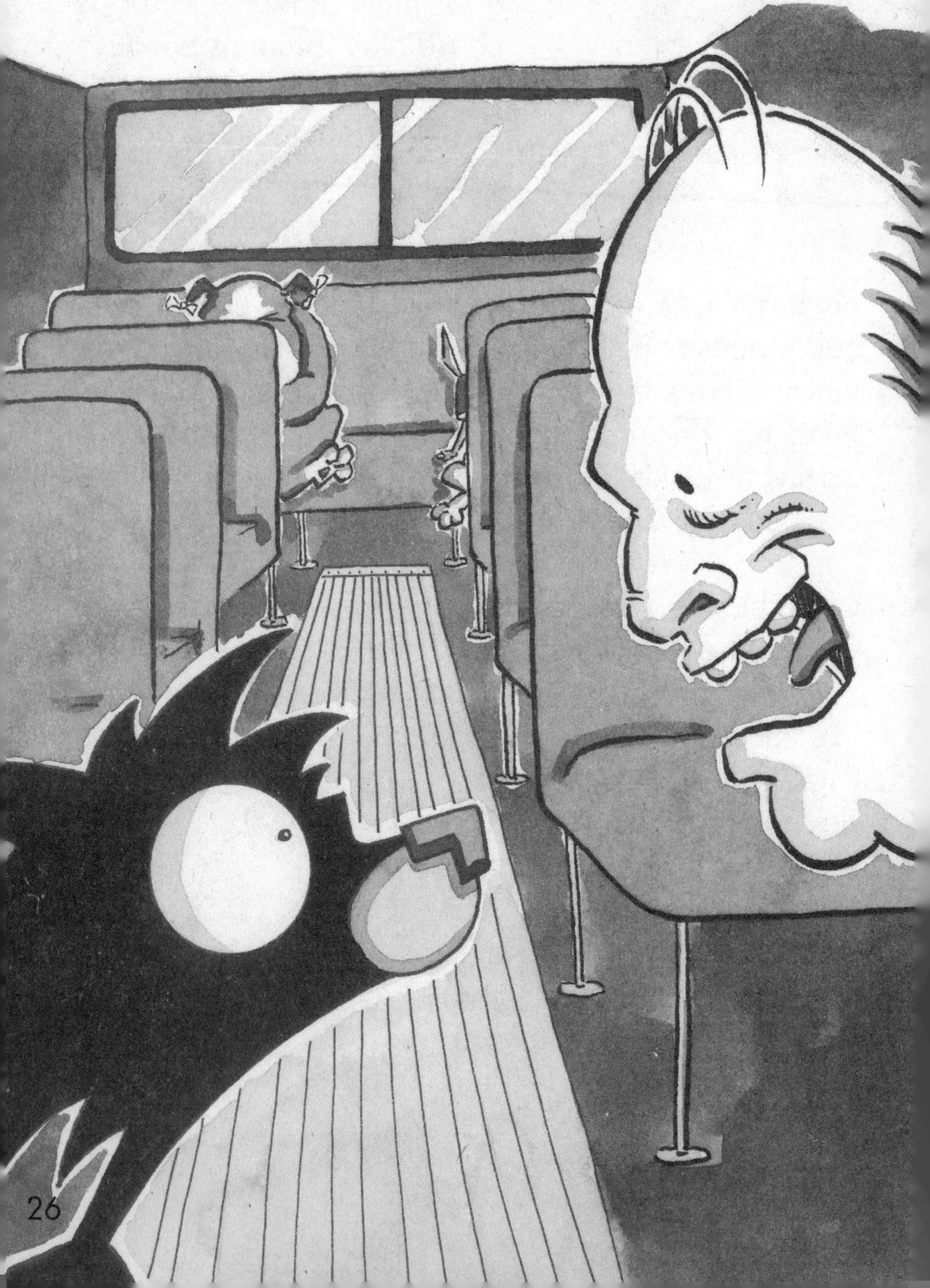

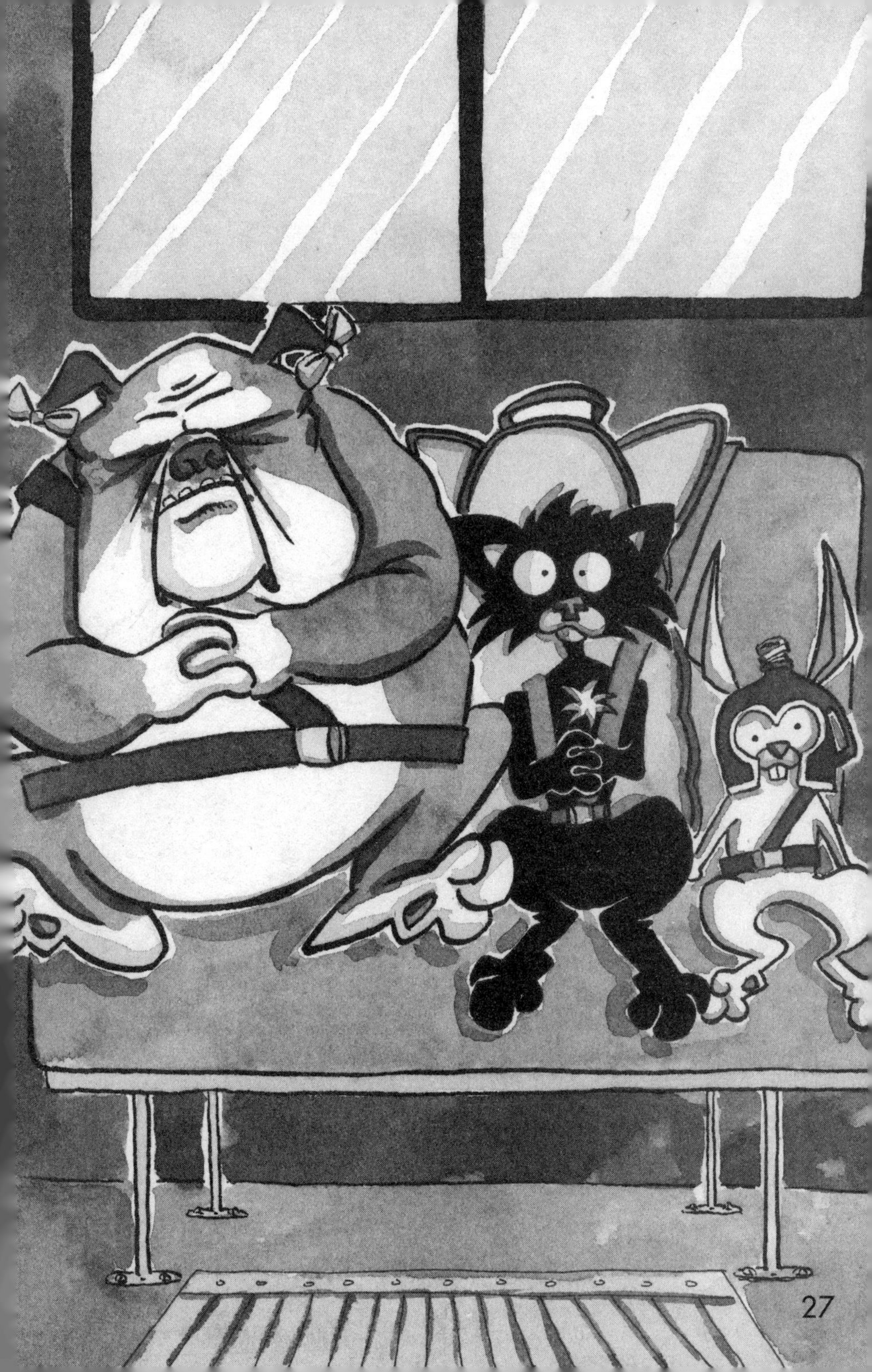

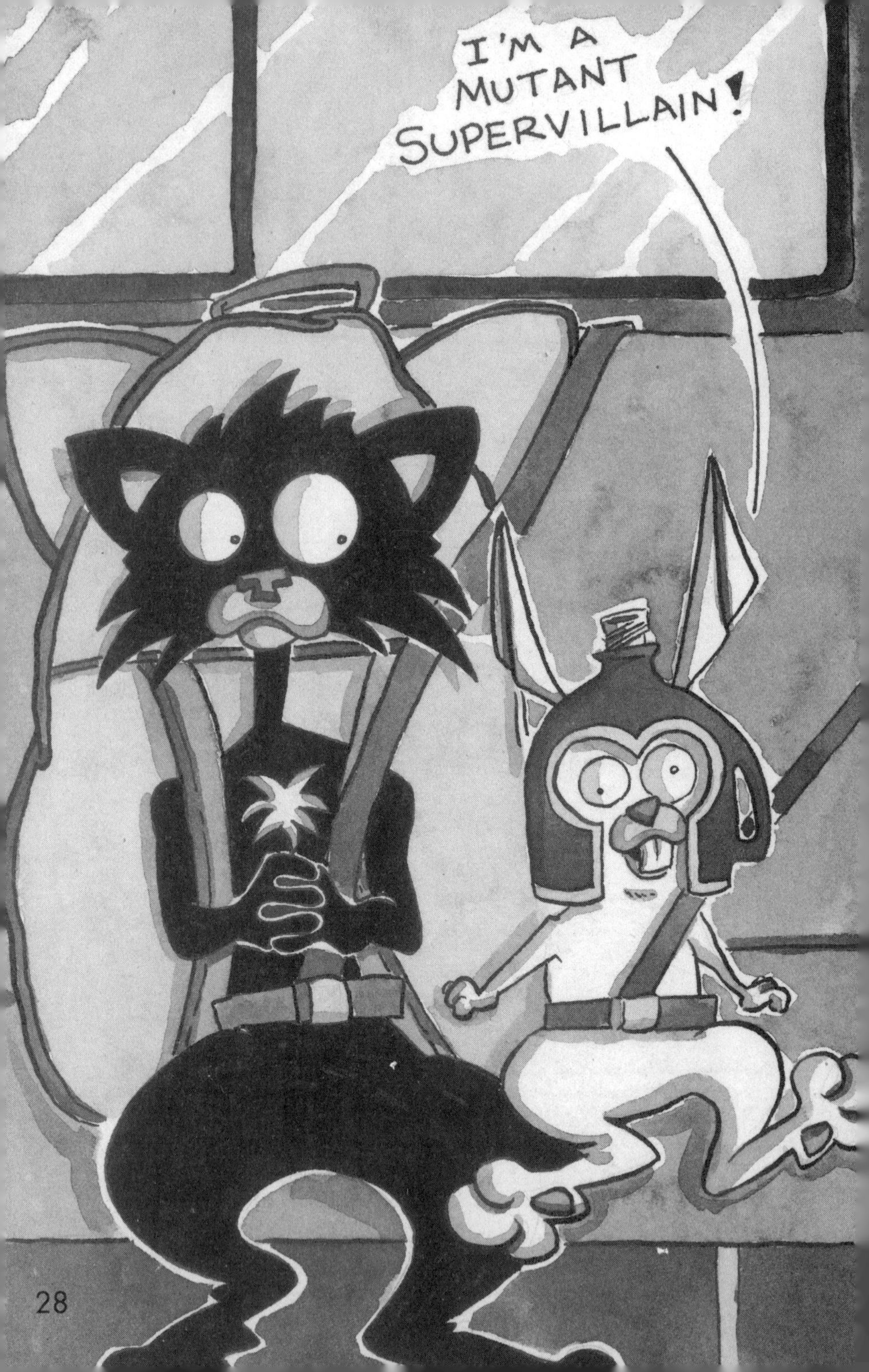
I'M A MUTANT SUPERVILLAIN!

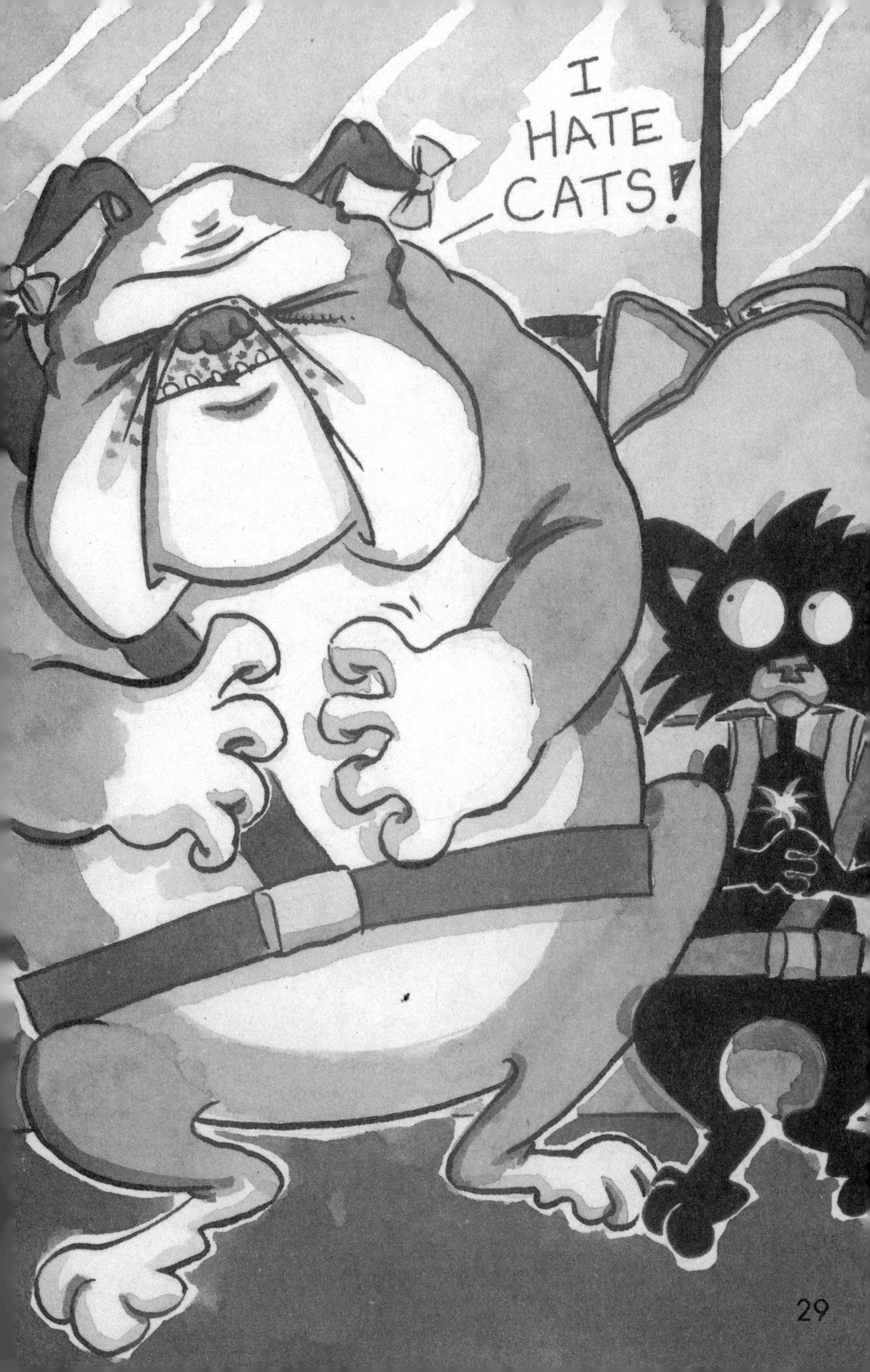
I HATE CATS!

Bye, Kitty! Bye, Puppy! I'll see you at the end of the day!

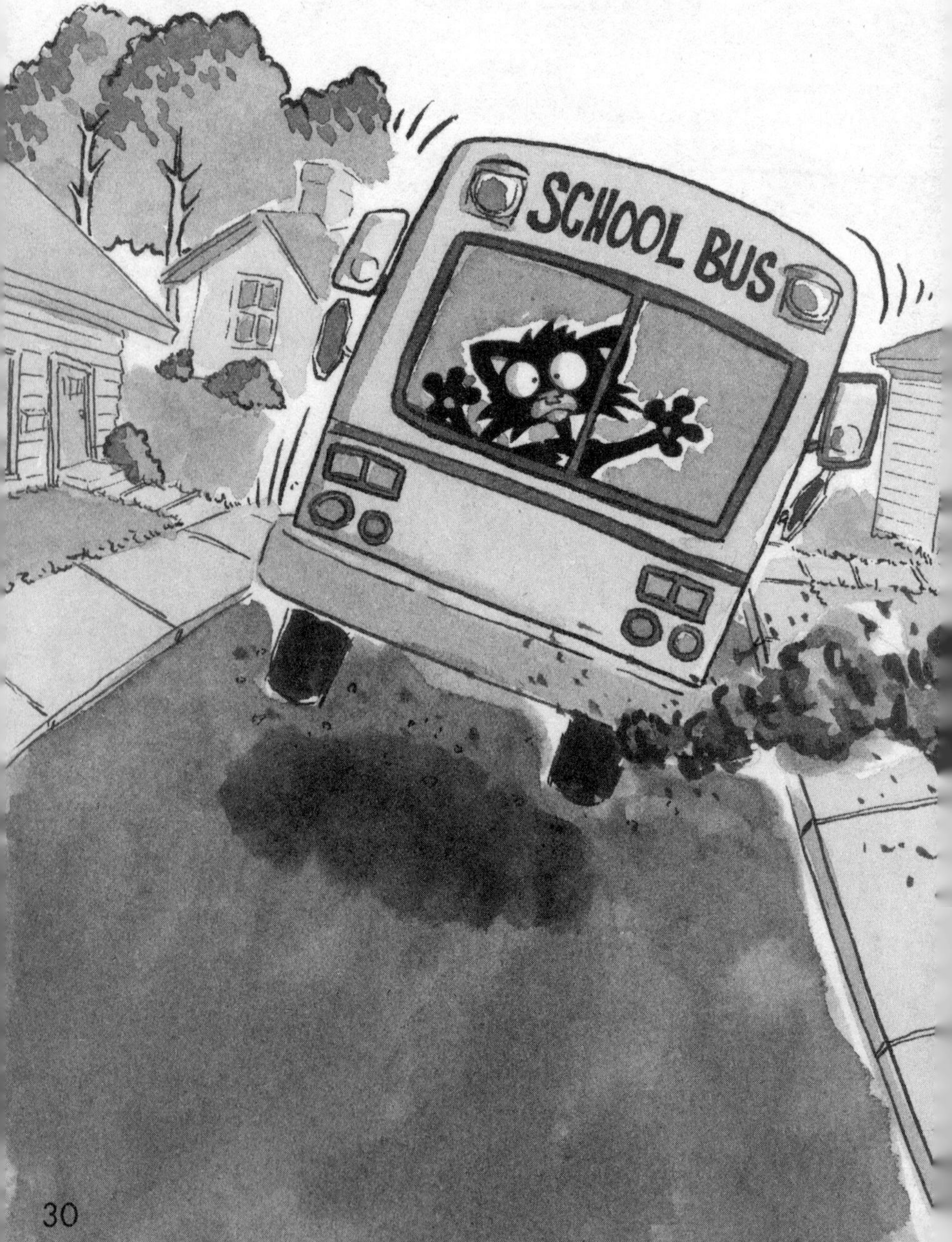
SCHOOL BUS

•CHAPTER THREE•

WELCOME

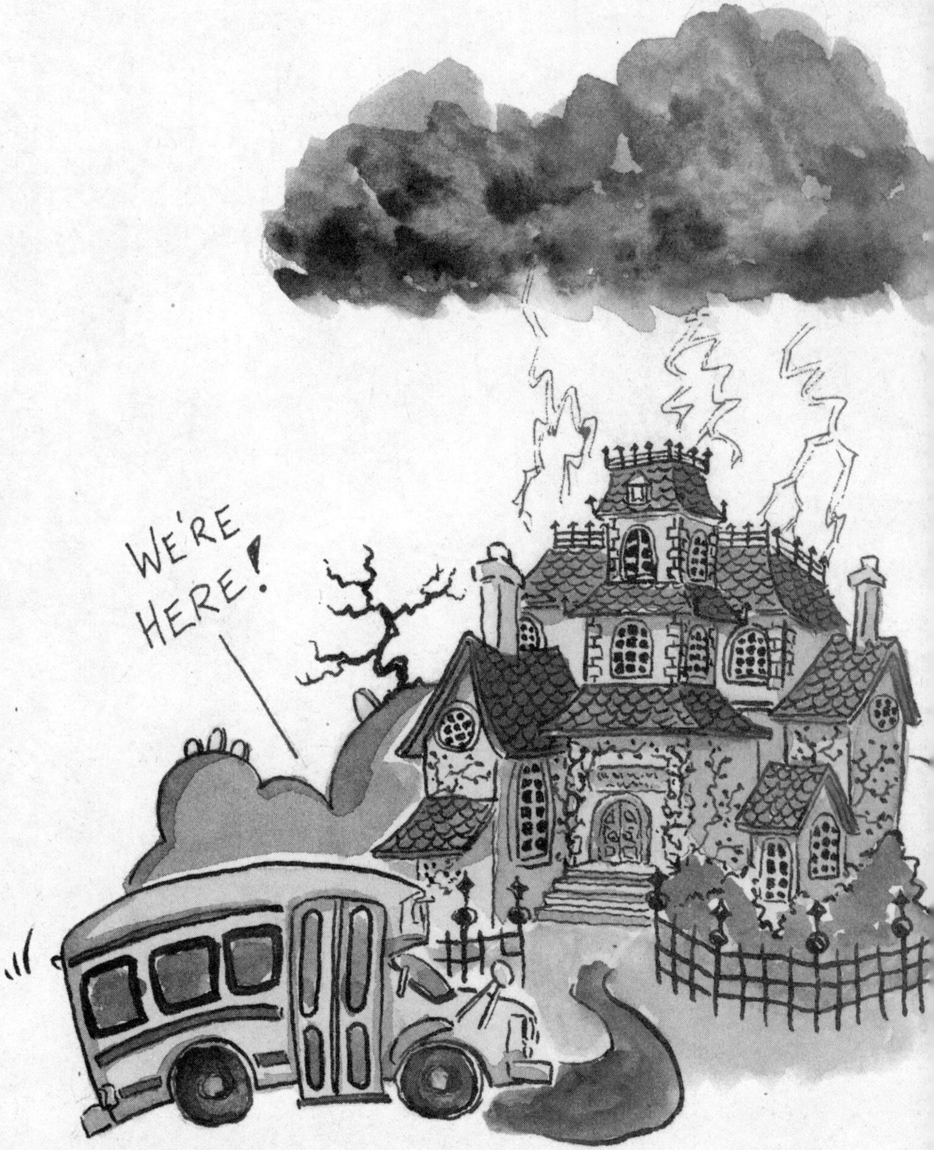
WE'RE HERE!

All right, you guys! Everybody off the bus and welcome to . . .

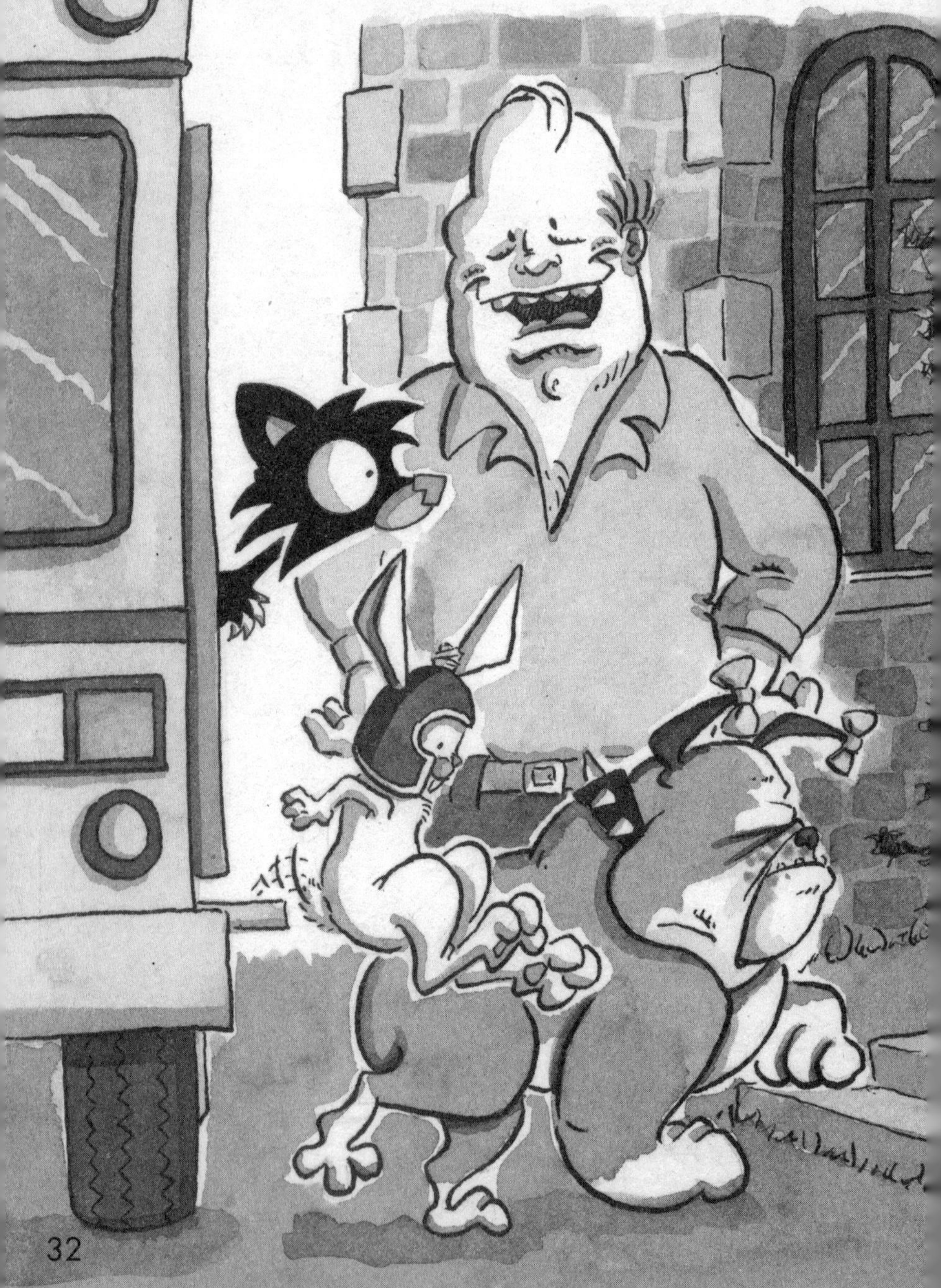

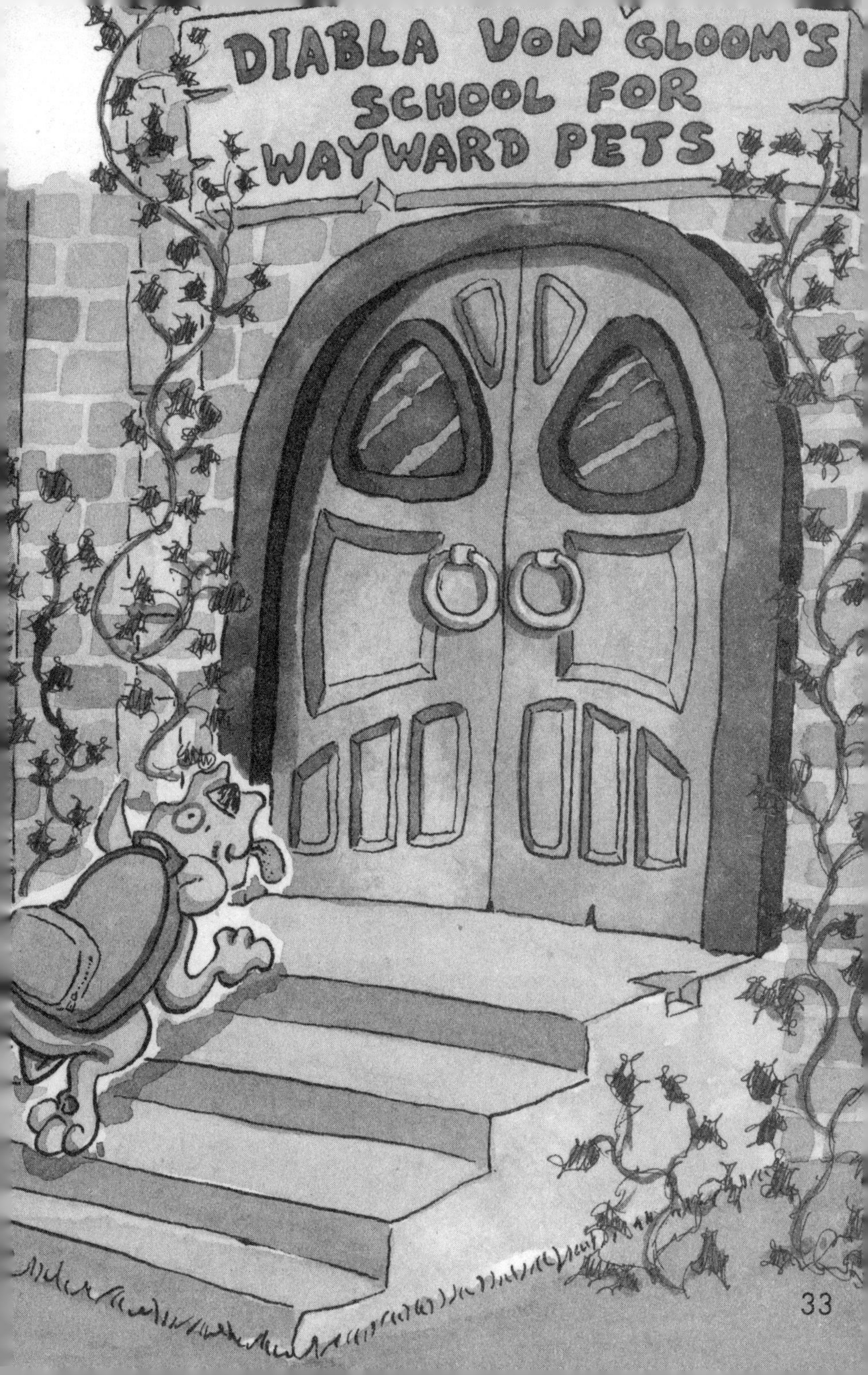
DIABLA VON GLOOM'S
SCHOOL FOR
WAYWARD PETS

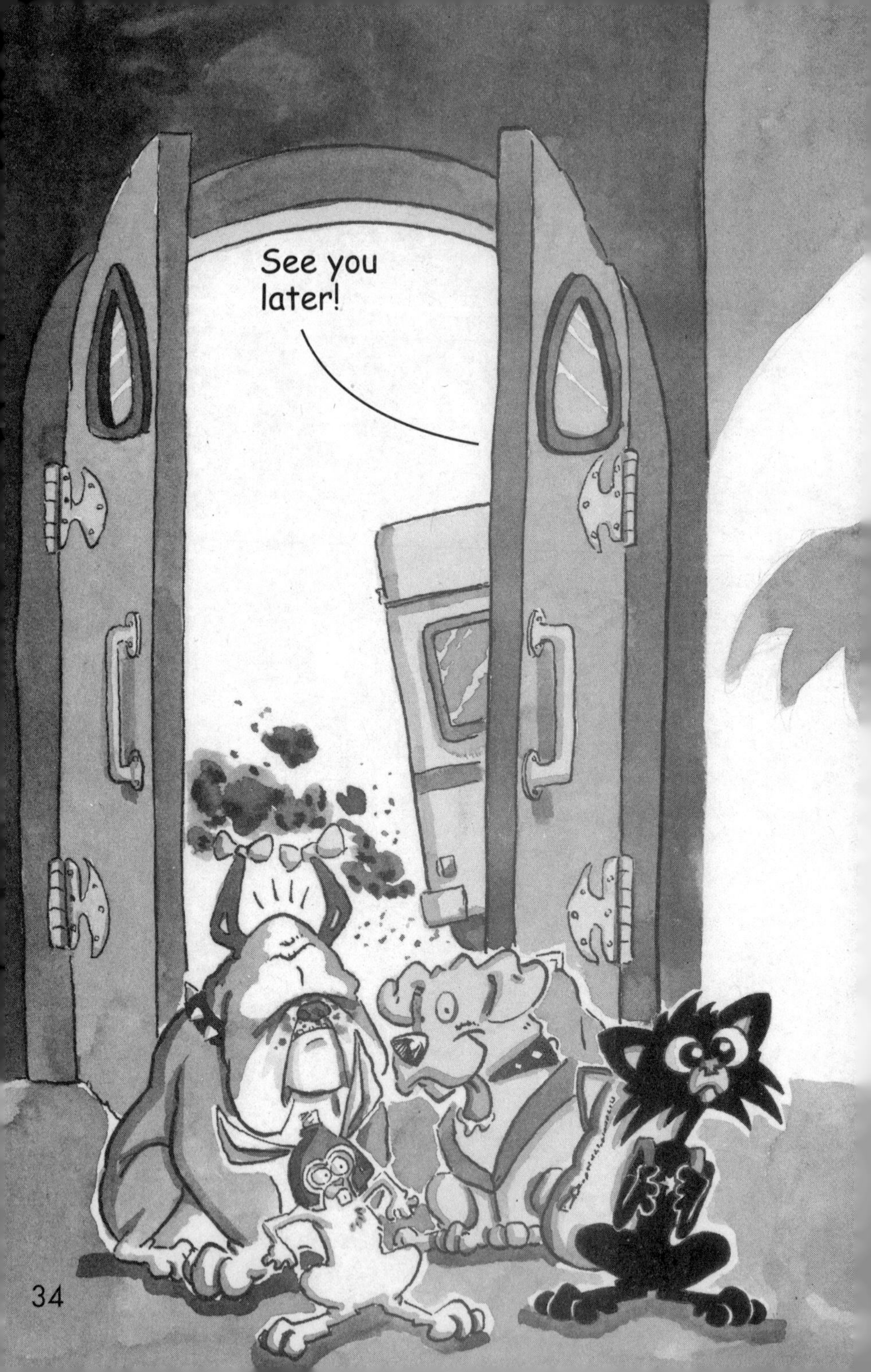
See you later!

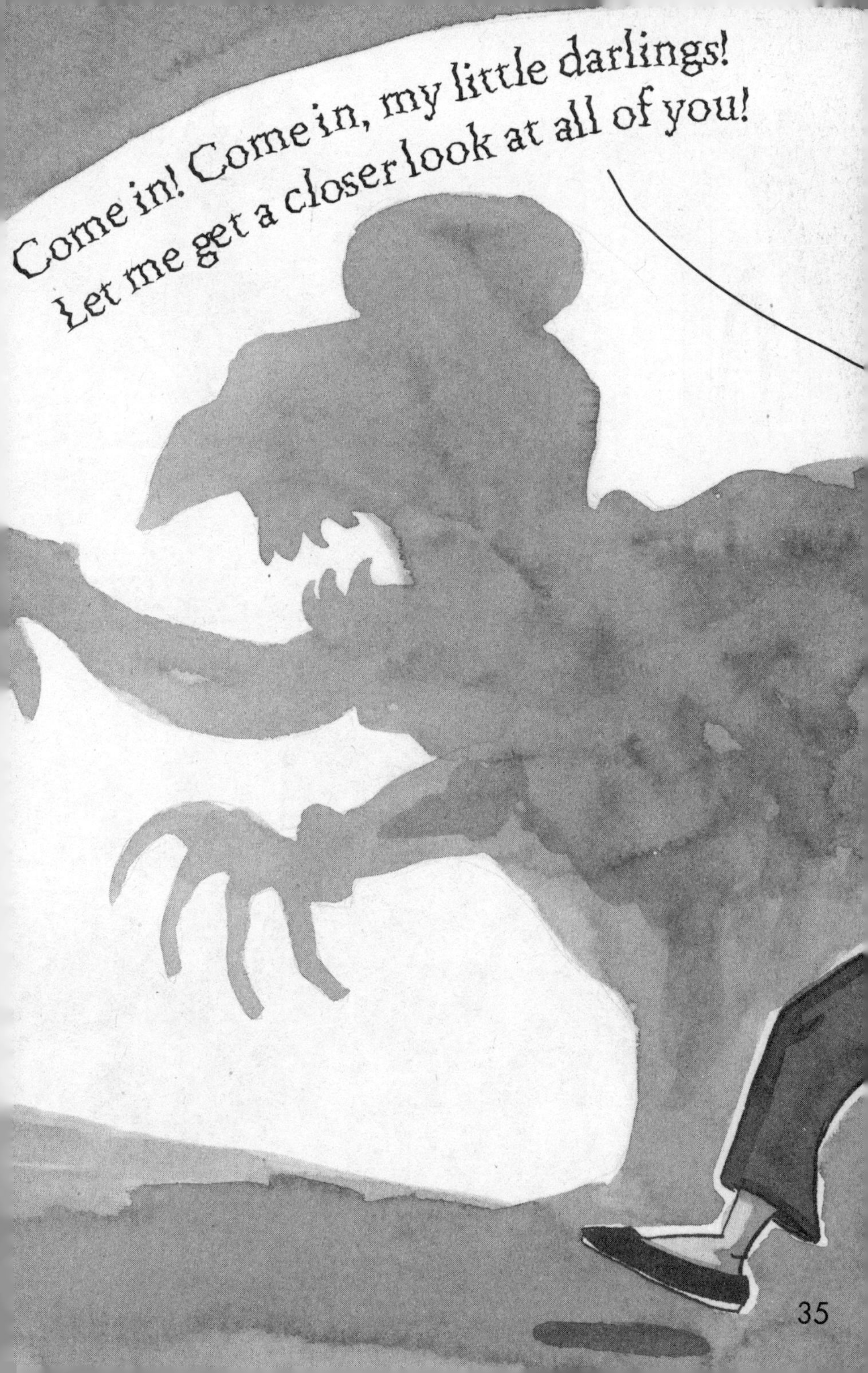
Come in! Come in, my little darlings!
Let me get a closer look at all of you!

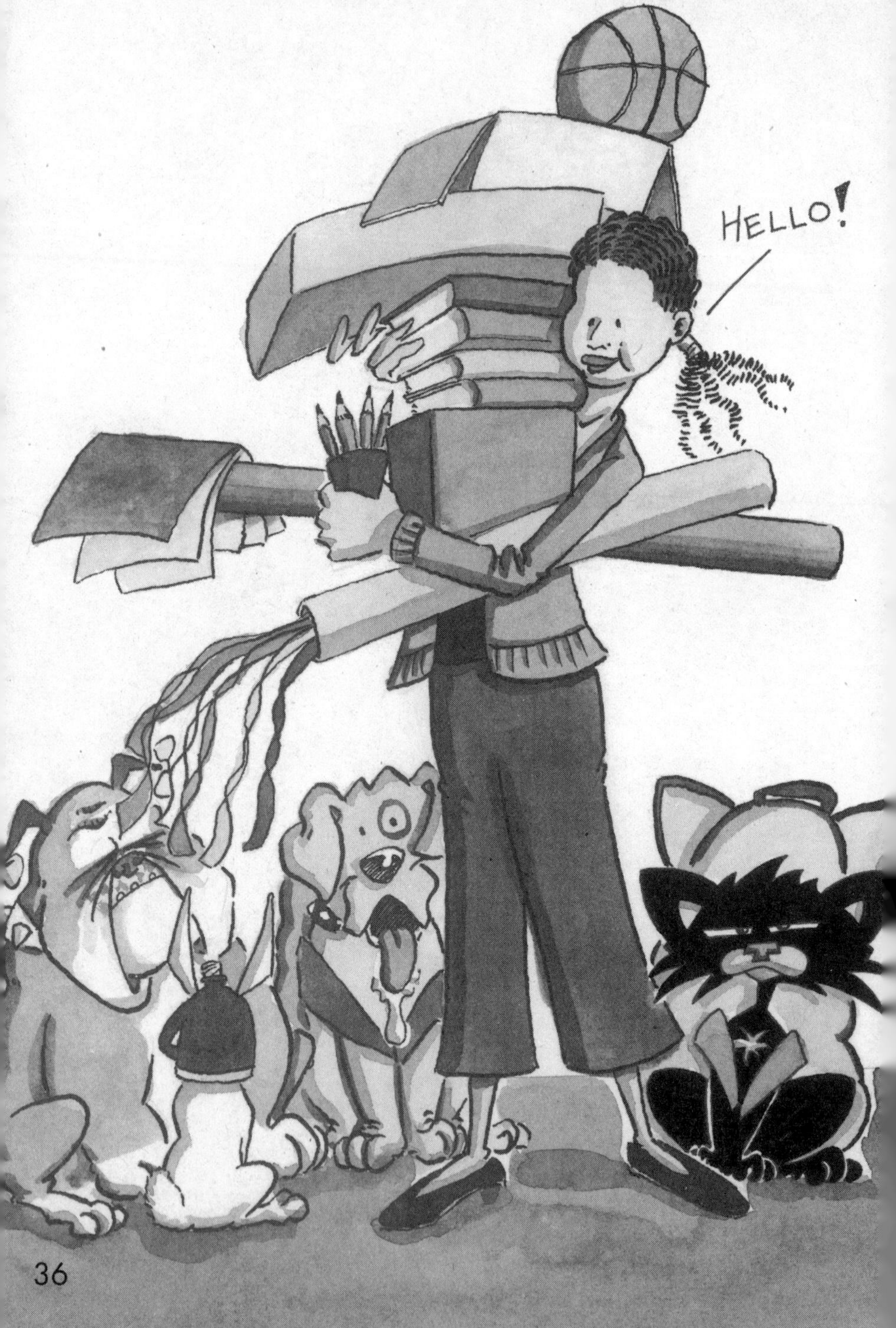
HELLO!

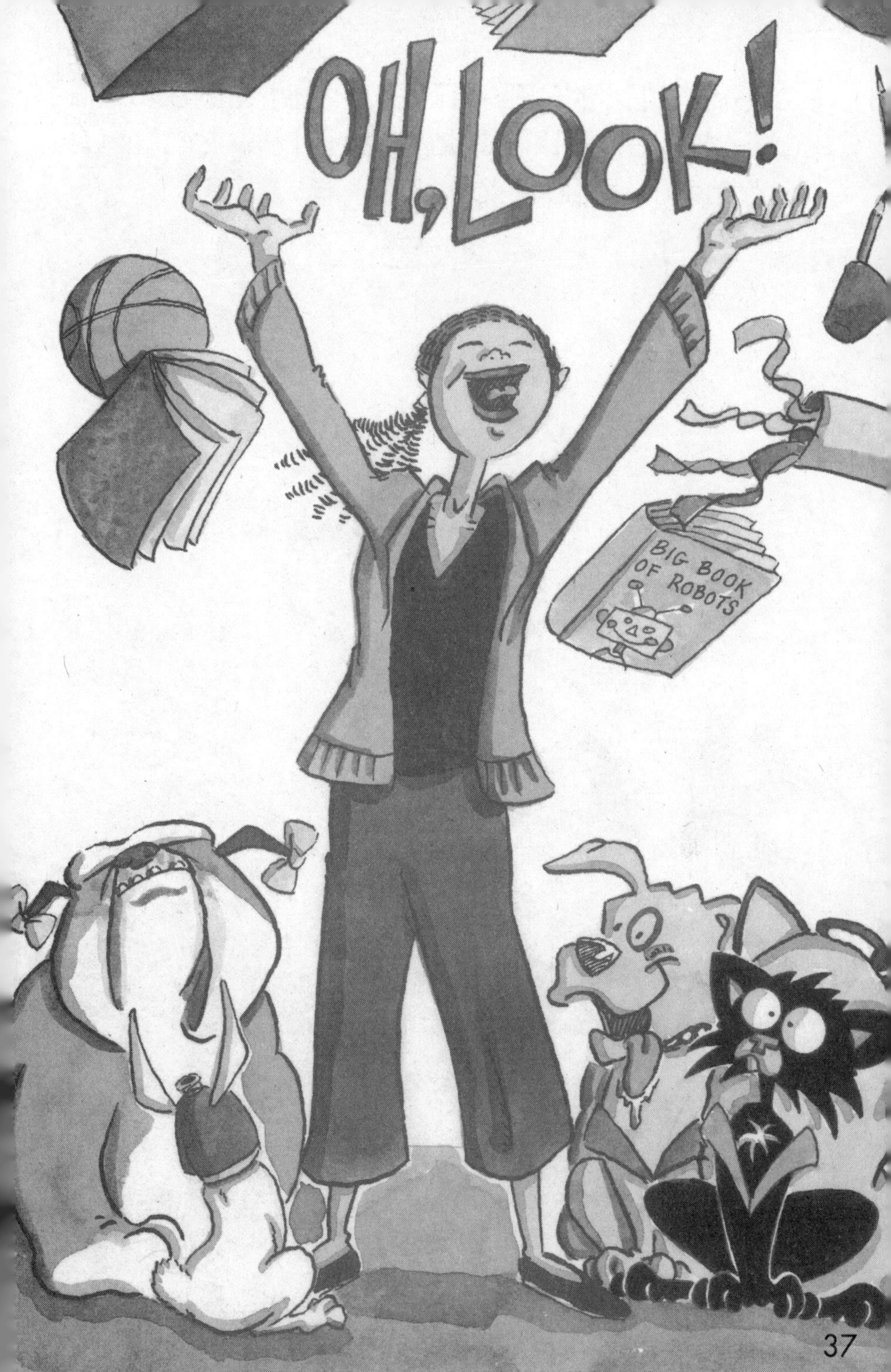
OH, LOOK!
BIG BOOK OF ROBOTS

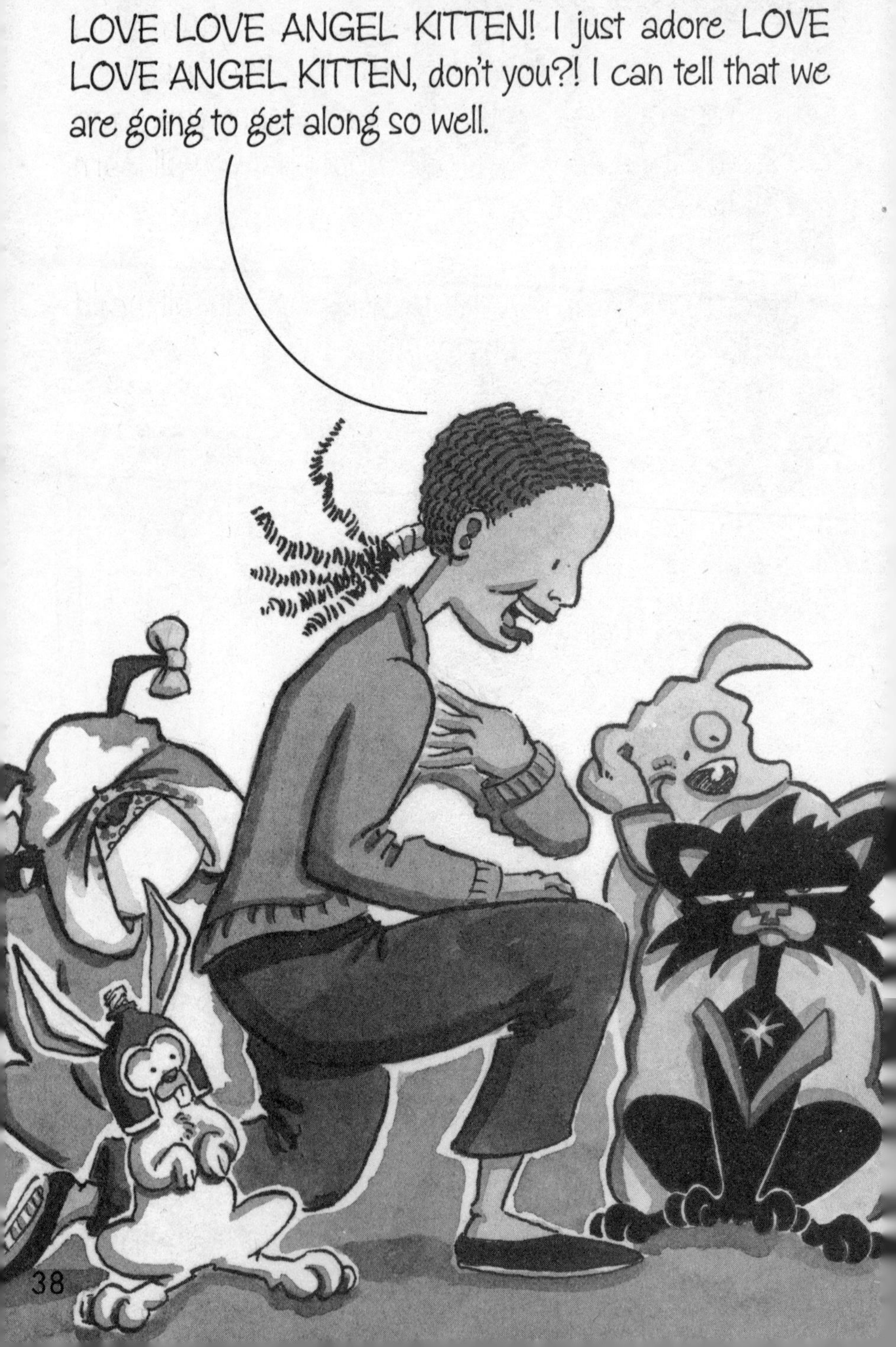
LOVE LOVE ANGEL KITTEN! I just adore LOVE LOVE ANGEL KITTEN, don't you?! I can tell that we are going to get along so well.

Well, pets, my name is Diabla von Gloom. But I want you all to call me Miss Dee. Welcome to my school! School, as you may know, is a place where you go to learn something new. So, I really hope that you all learn something new today.

Let's step into the classroom! And as you all head inside, I want you to understand one thing . . .

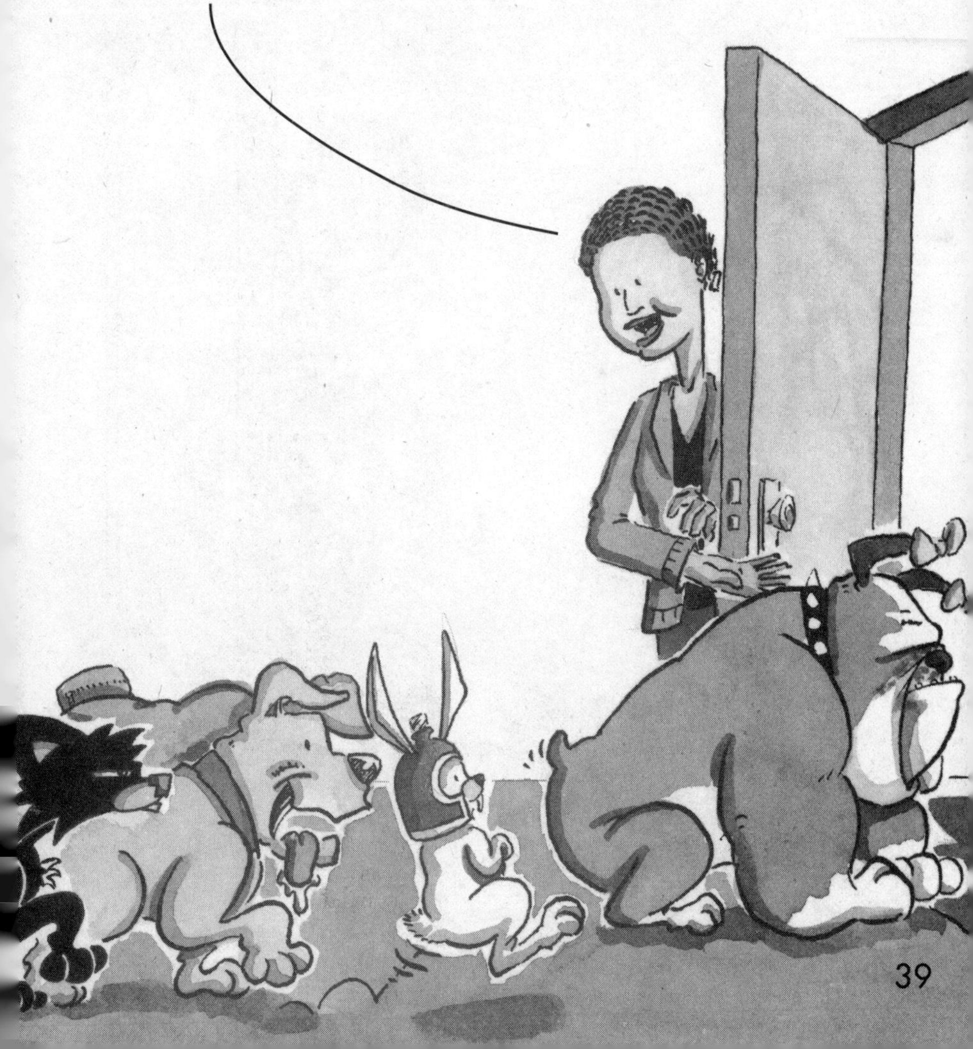

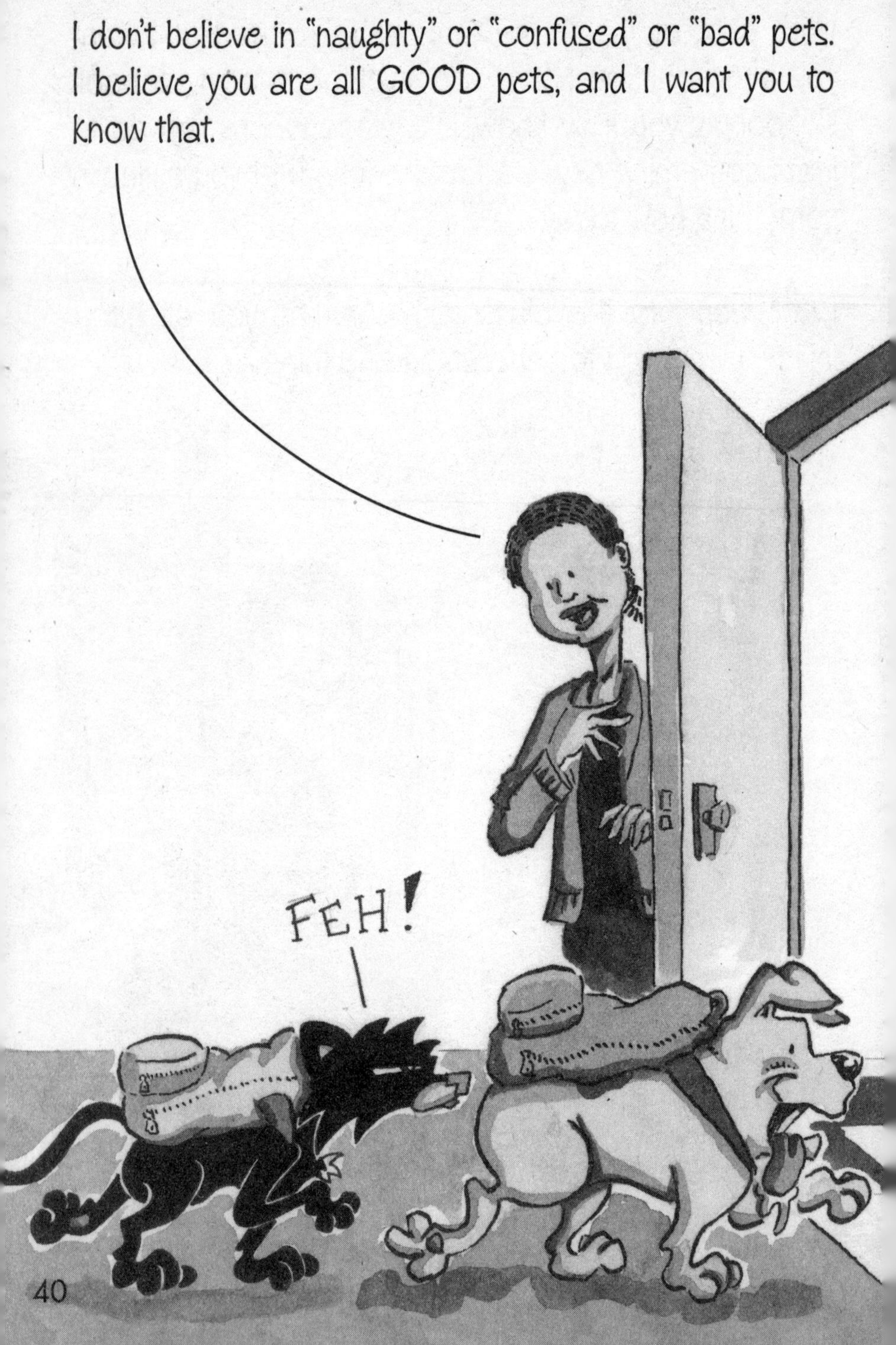
I don't believe in "naughty" or "confused" or "bad" pets. I believe you are all GOOD pets, and I want you to know that.
FEH!

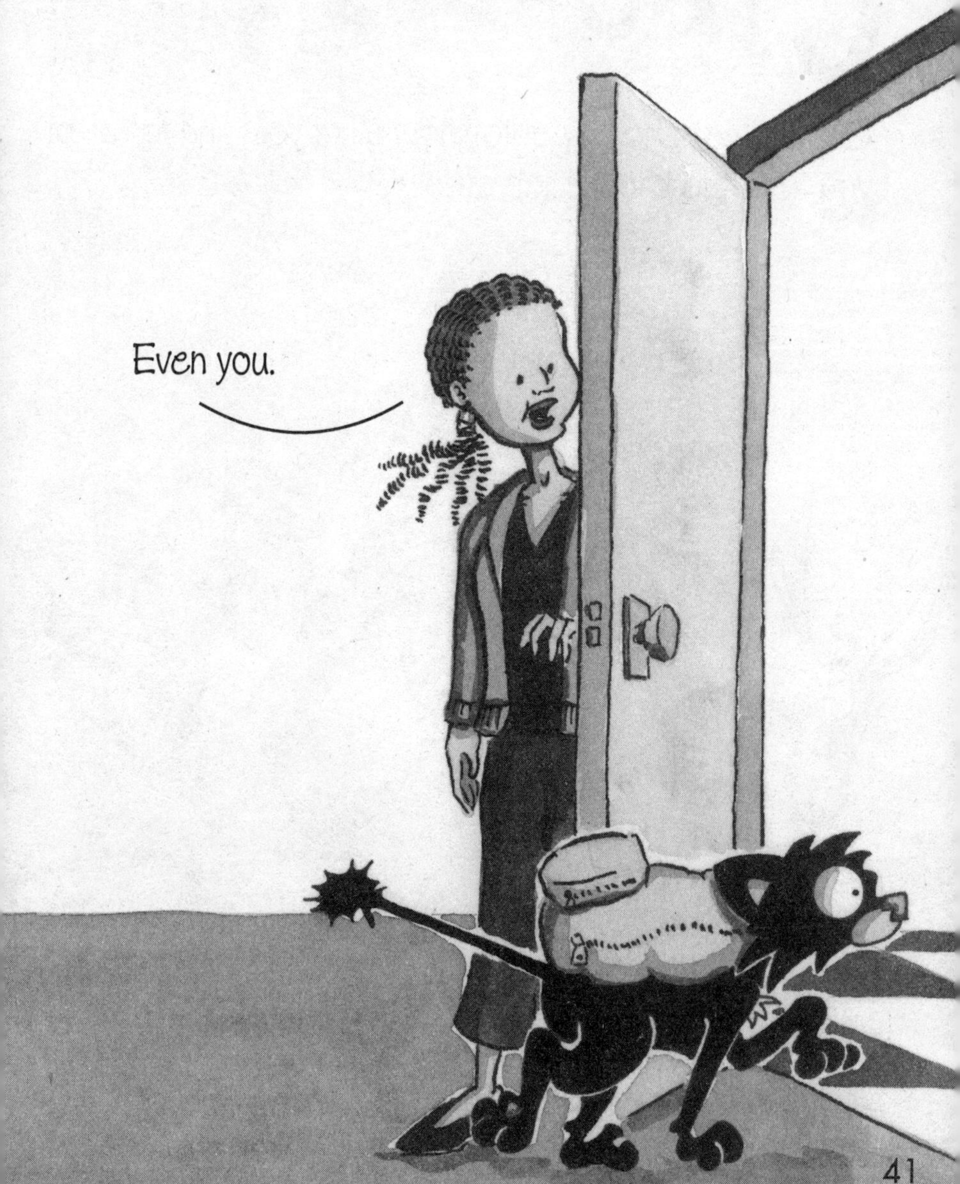
Even you.

•CHAPTER FOUR•

CIRCLE TIME

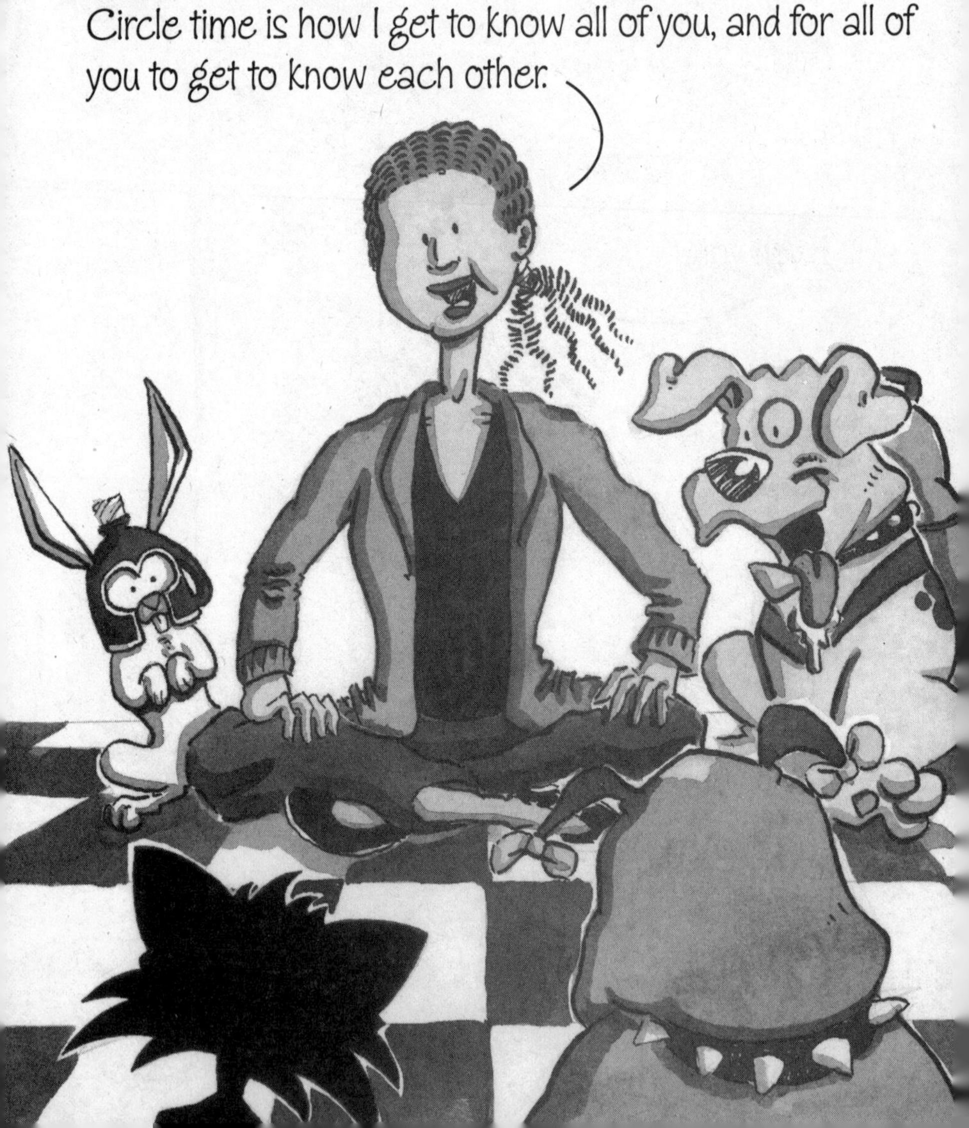
Circle time is how I get to know all of you, and for all of you to get to know each other.

Let's start with you, Petunia. Tell us what's on your mind.

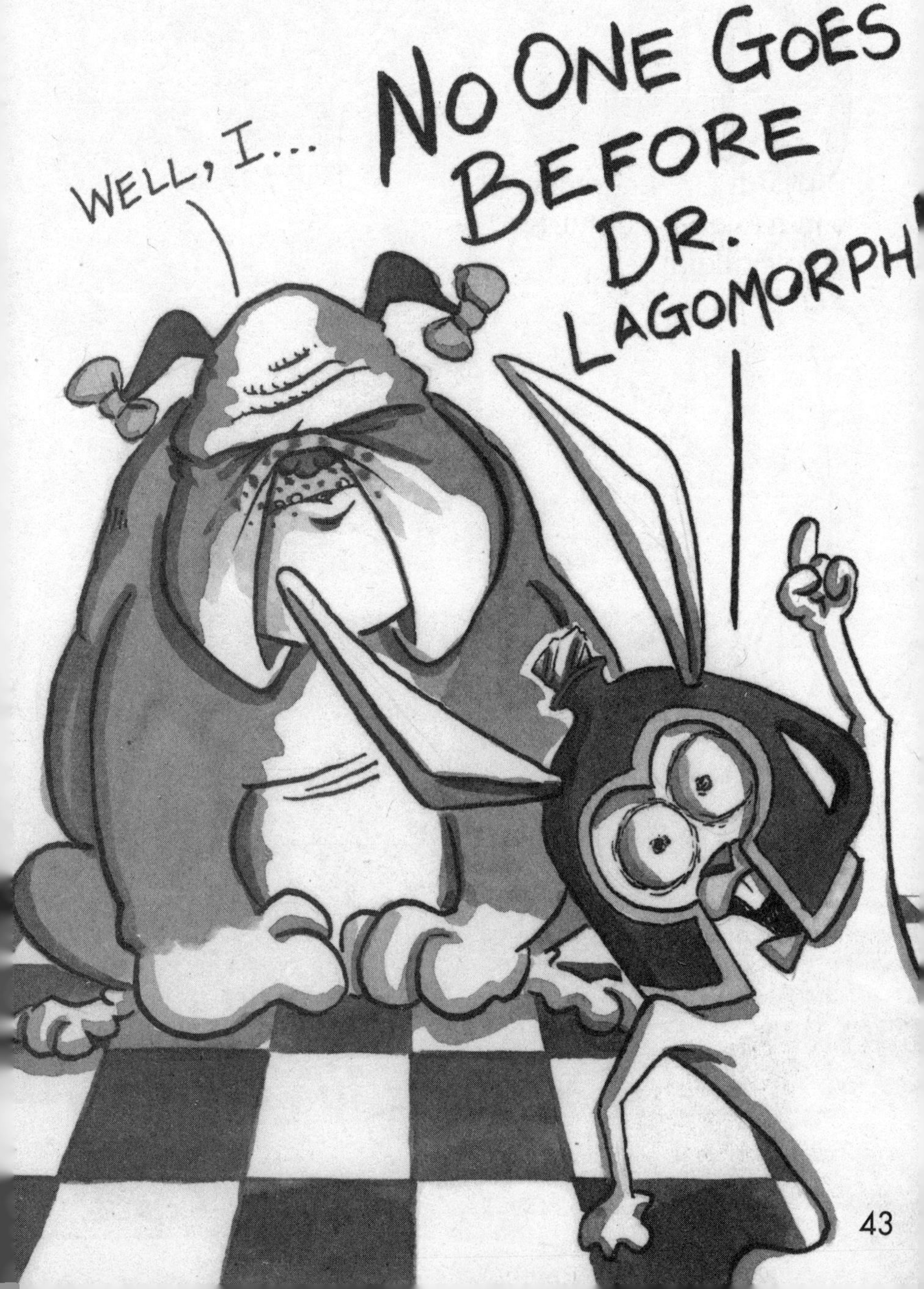
WELL, I...
NO ONE GOES BEFORE DR. LAGOMORPH!

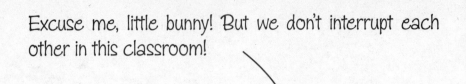

Excuse me, little bunny! But we don't interrupt each other in this classroom!

But I'm Dr. Lagomorph! I'm a diabolical mutant supervillain!

That's no excuse. Sit down, please!

Go ahead, Petunia.

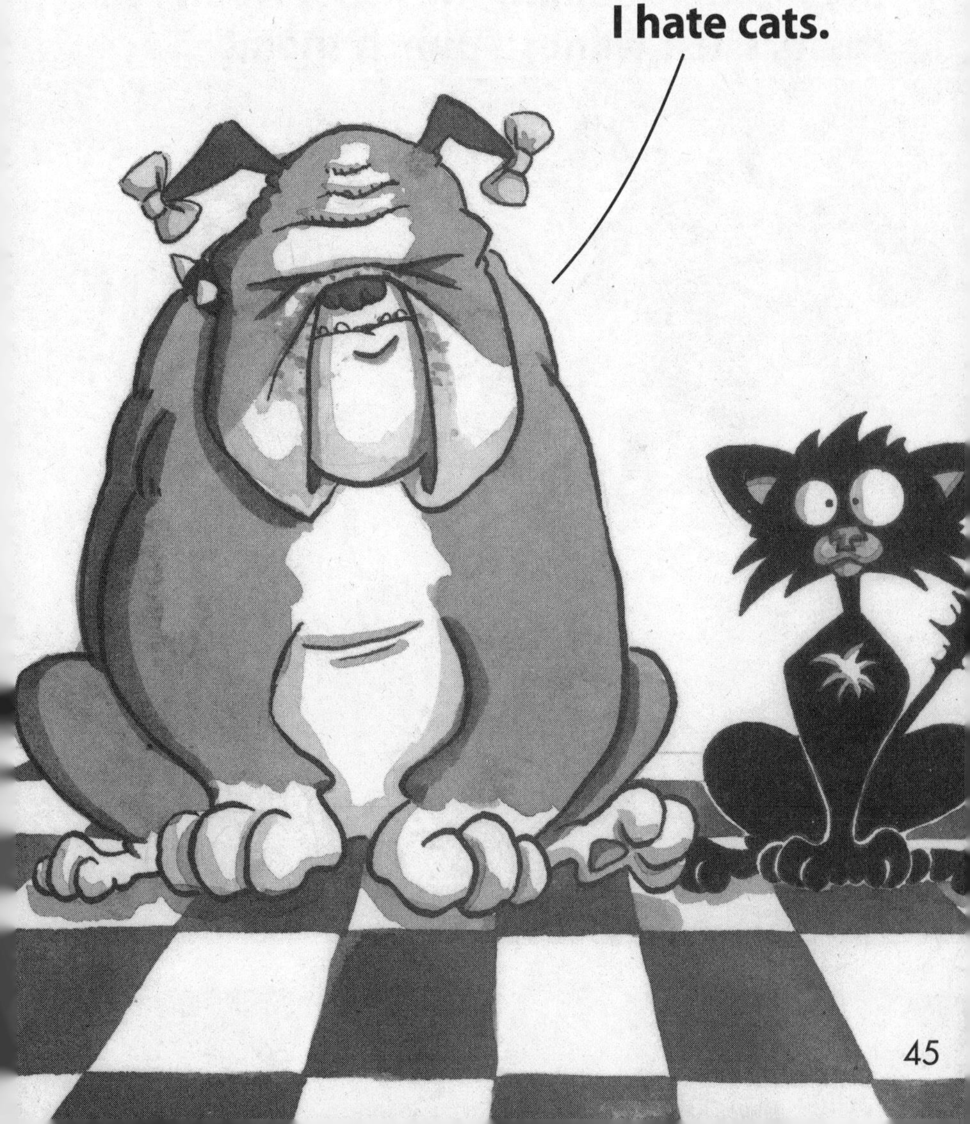
I hate cats.

I just hate them! I hate them so much! I hate their eyes! I hate their noses! I hate their goofy-looking whiskers! When I see them, I just want to punch them!

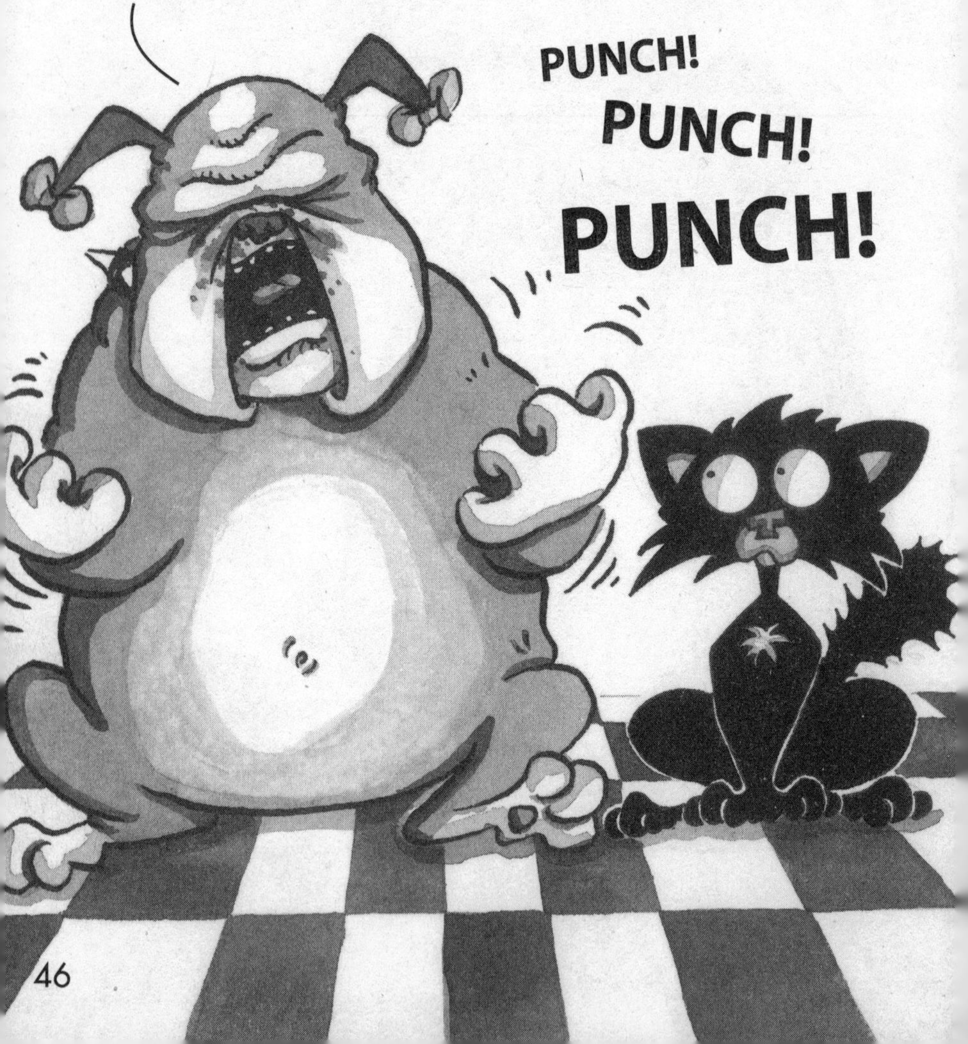
PUNCH!
PUNCH!
PUNCH!

I . . . I . . . just want to bite their heads off and chew their faces like gum! CHEW! CHEW! CHEW! I want to pick them up and throw them all into active volcanos!

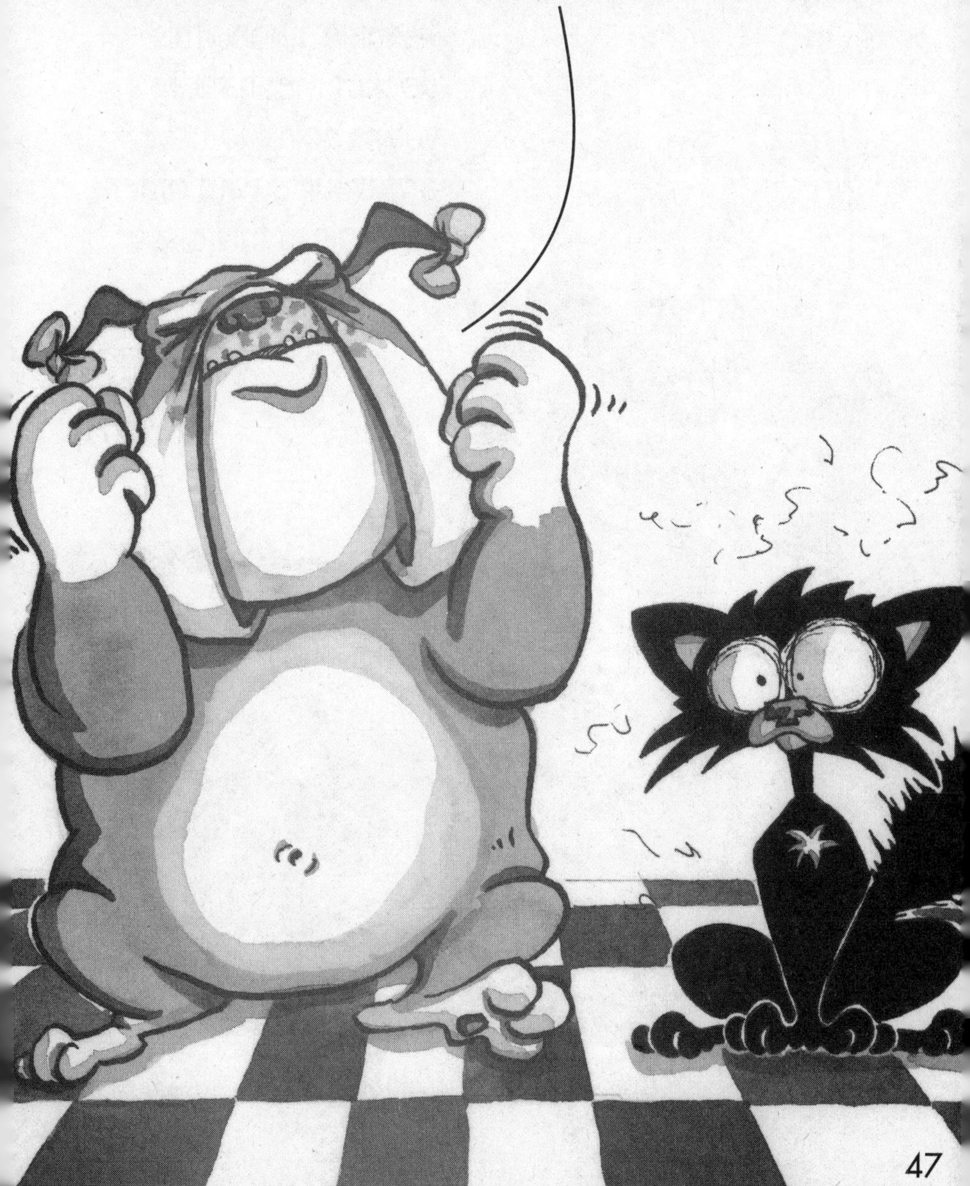

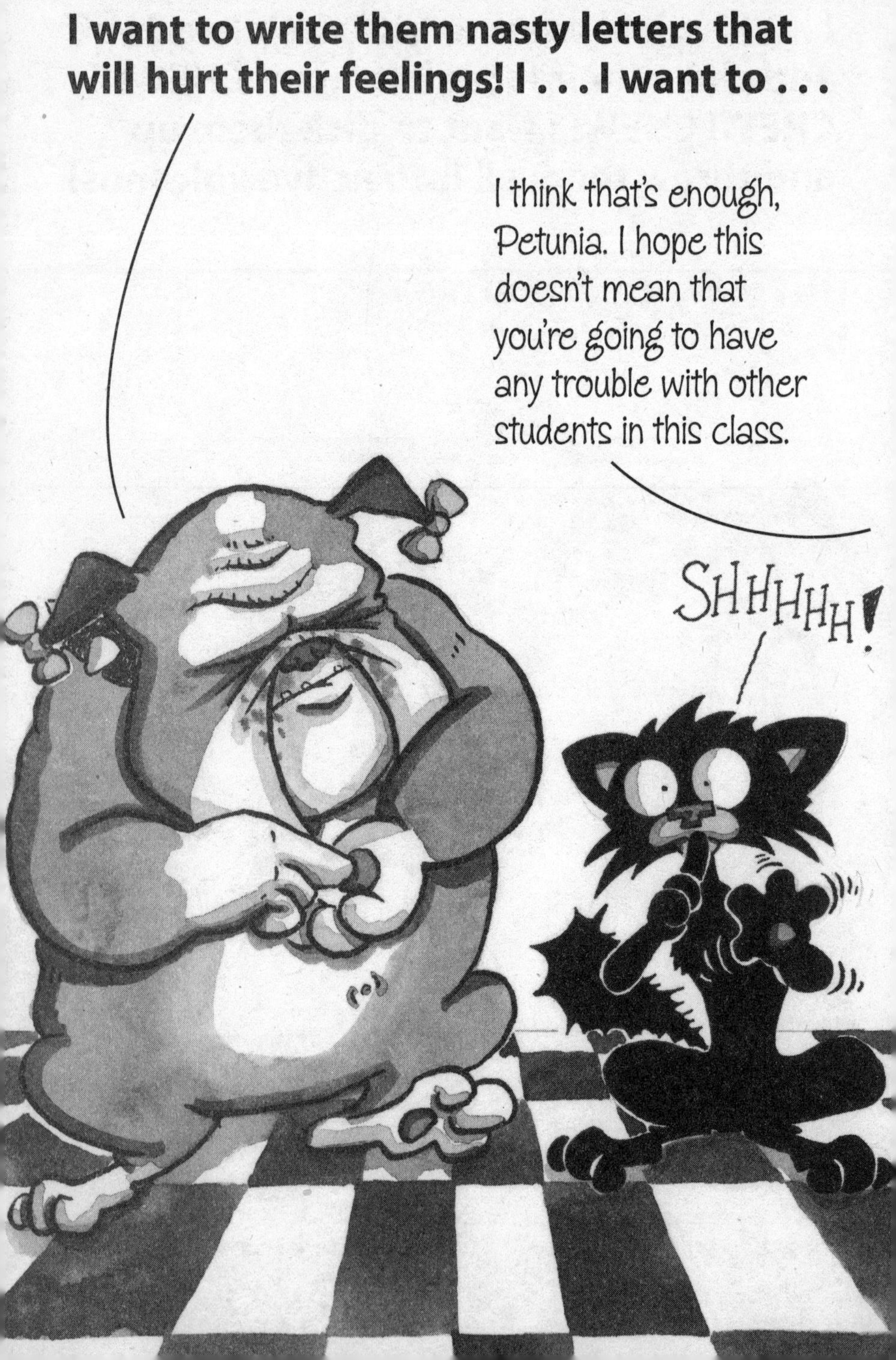
I want to write them nasty letters that will hurt their feelings! I . . . I want to . . .
I think that's enough, Petunia. I hope this doesn't mean that you're going to have any trouble with other students in this class.
SHHHHH!

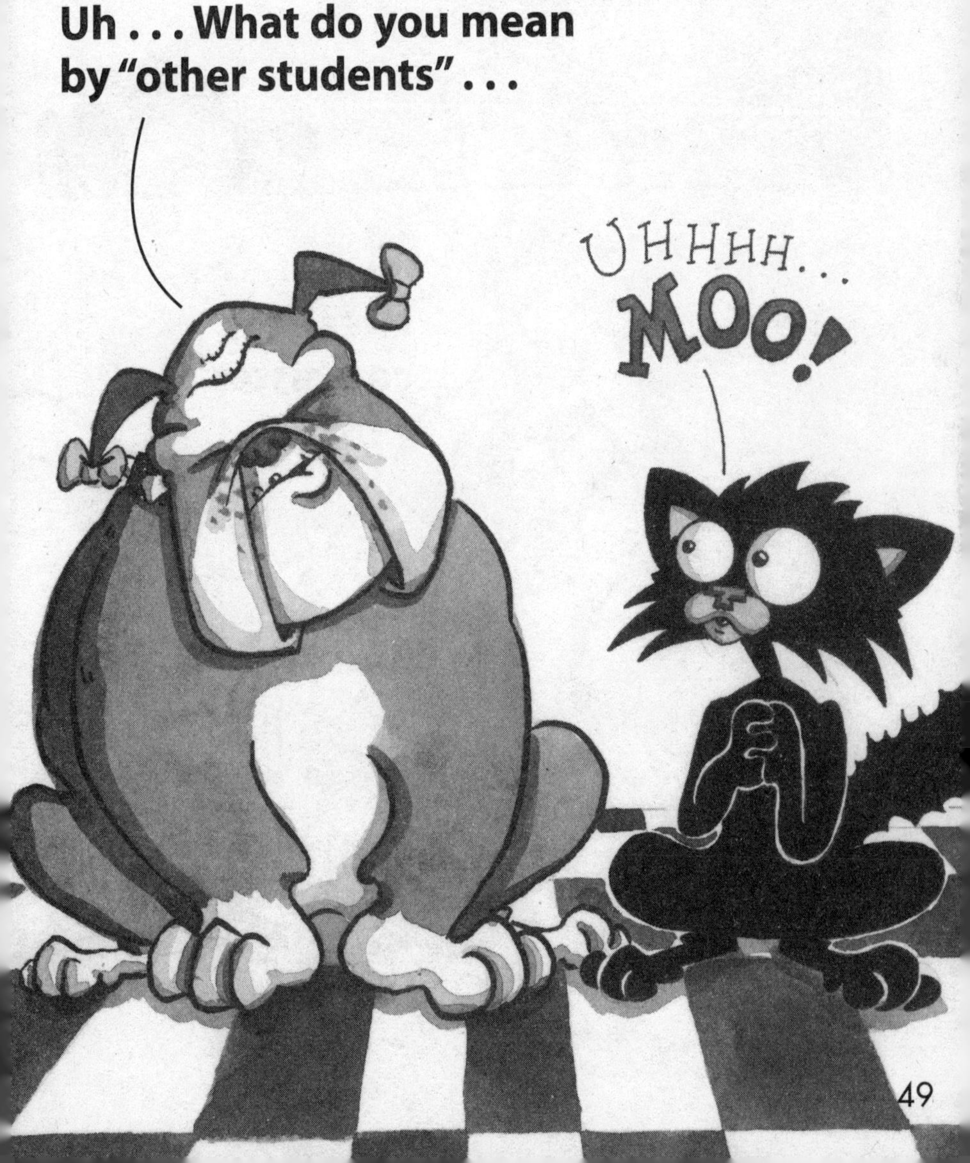
Uh . . . What do you mean by "other students" . . .
UHHHH. . .
MOO!

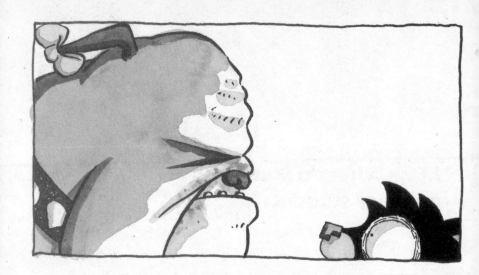

I hear ya,
cow sister.

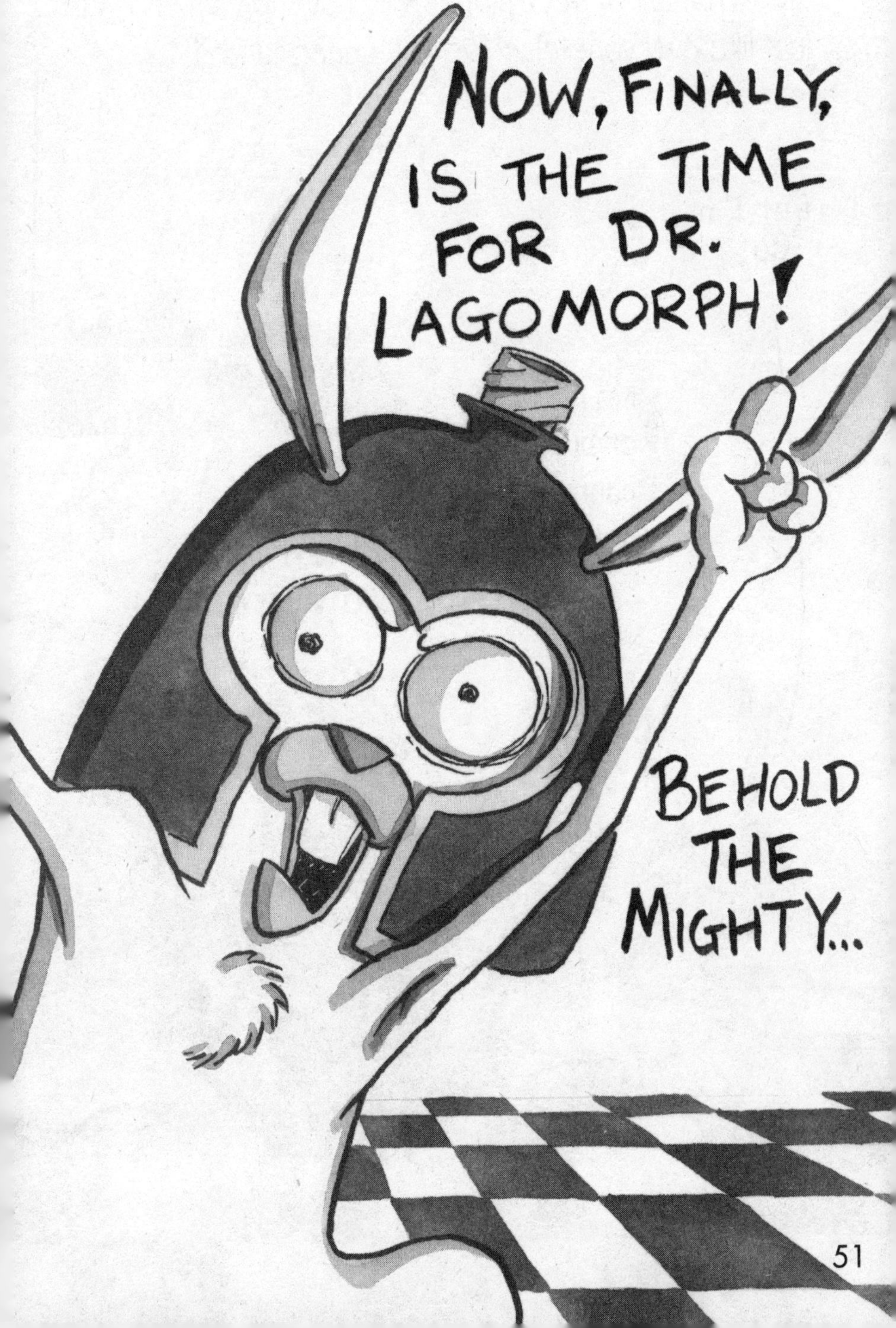
NOW, FINALLY, IS THE TIME FOR DR. LAGOMORPH!
BEHOLD THE MIGHTY...

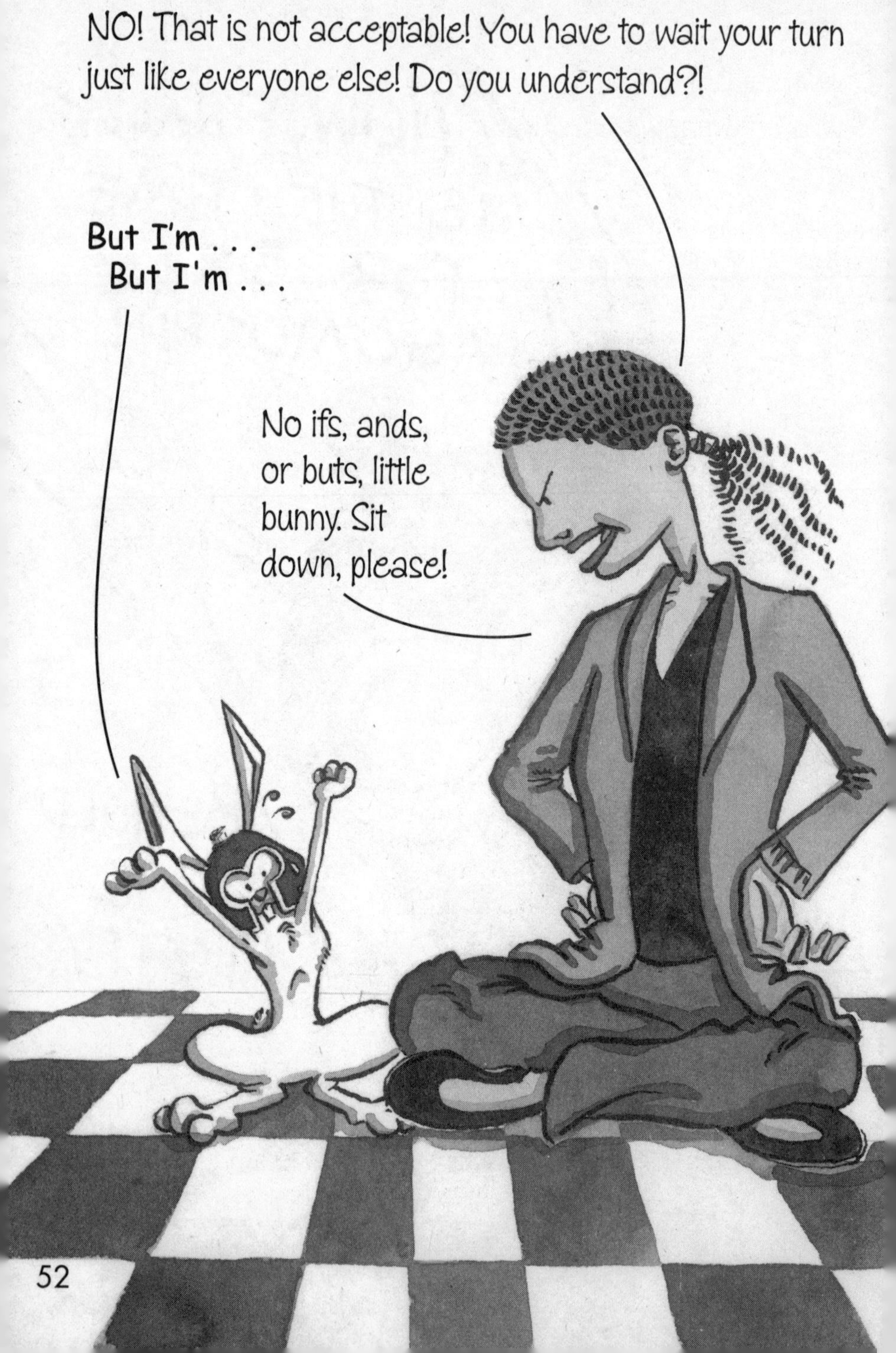
NO! That is not acceptable! You have to wait your turn just like everyone else! Do you understand?!
But I'm . . .
But I'm . . .
No ifs, ands, or buts, little bunny. Sit down, please!

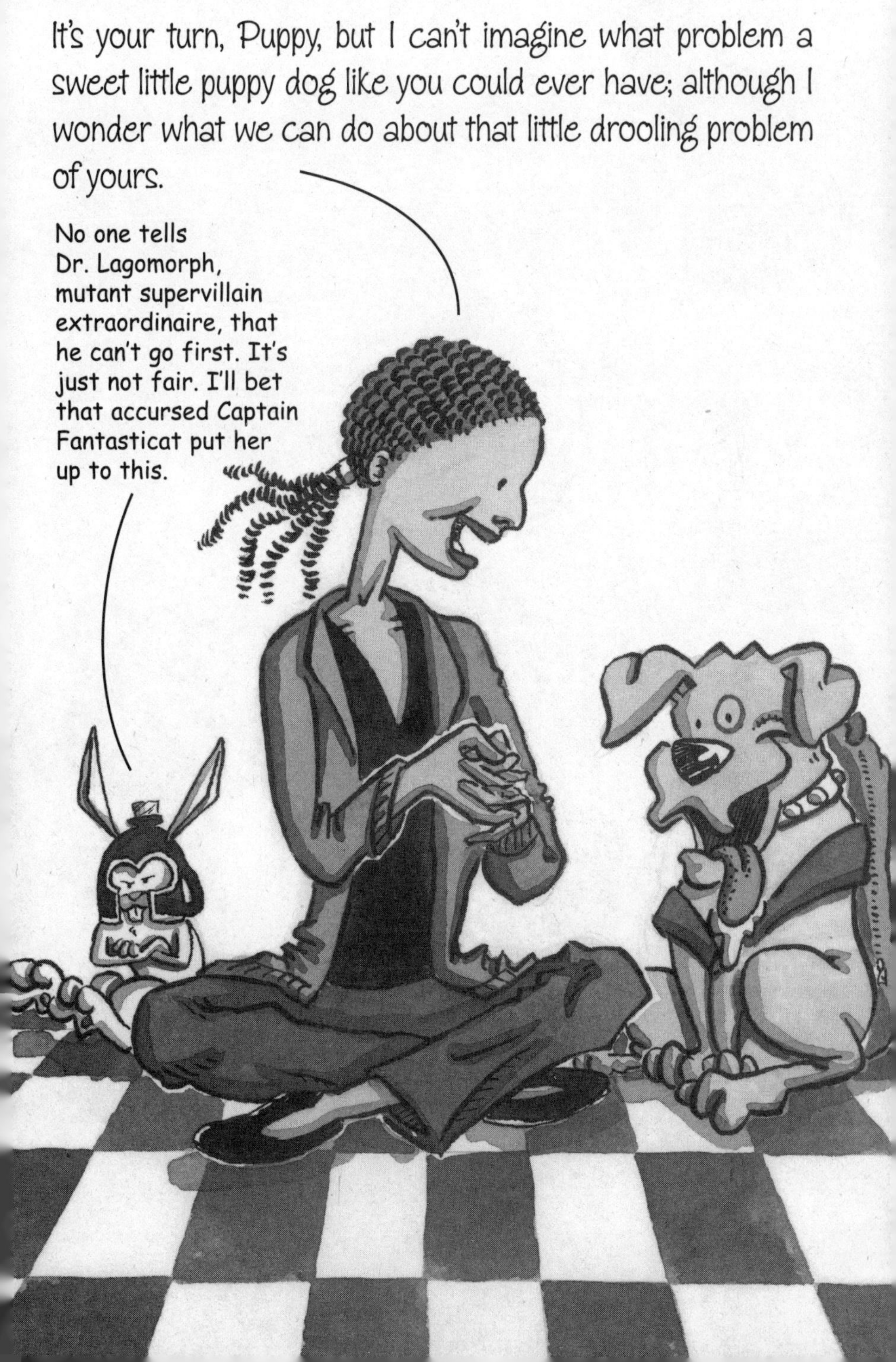
It's your turn, Puppy, but I can't imagine what problem a sweet little puppy dog like you could ever have; although I wonder what we can do about that little drooling problem of yours.
No one tells Dr. Lagomorph, mutant supervillain extraordinaire, that he can't go first. It's just not fair. I'll bet that accursed Captain Fantasticat put her up to this.

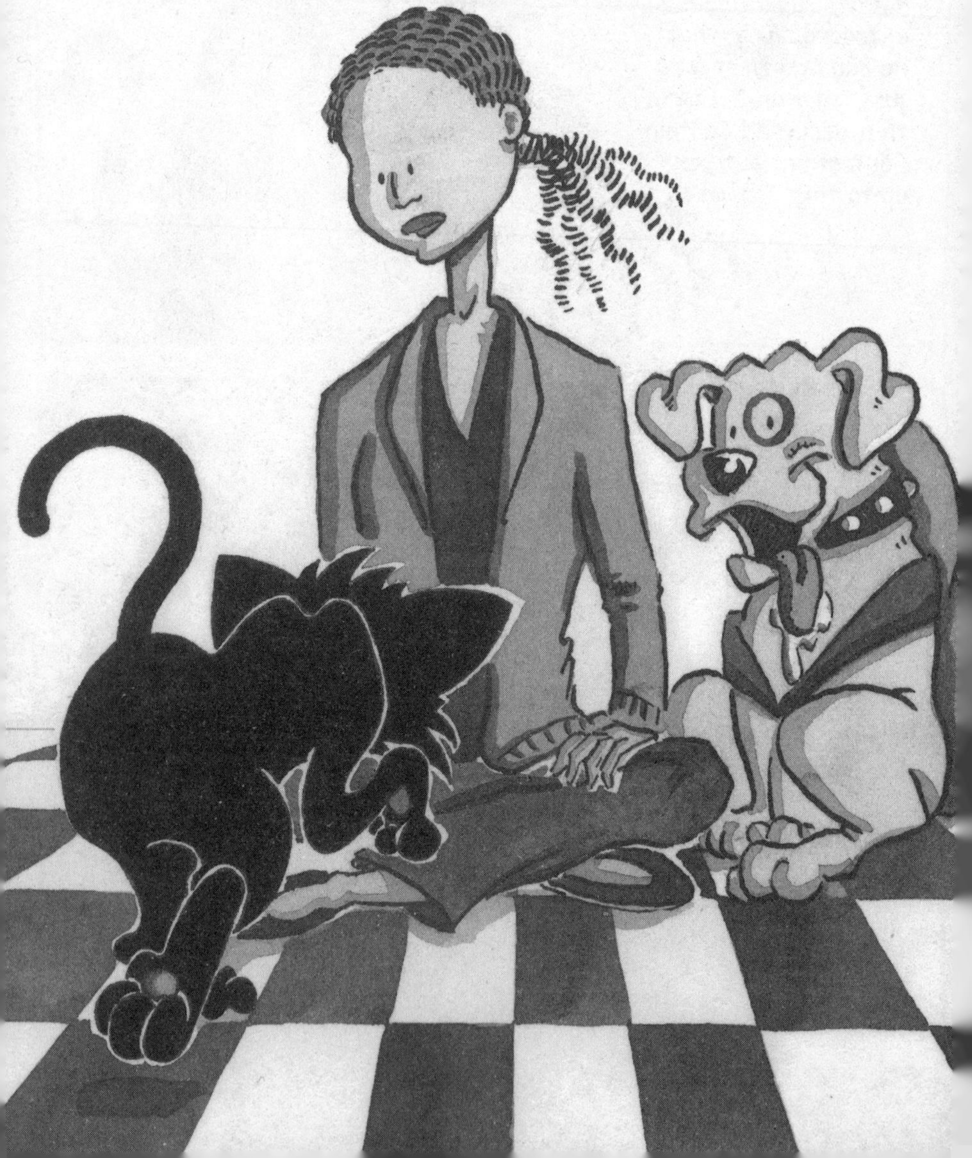

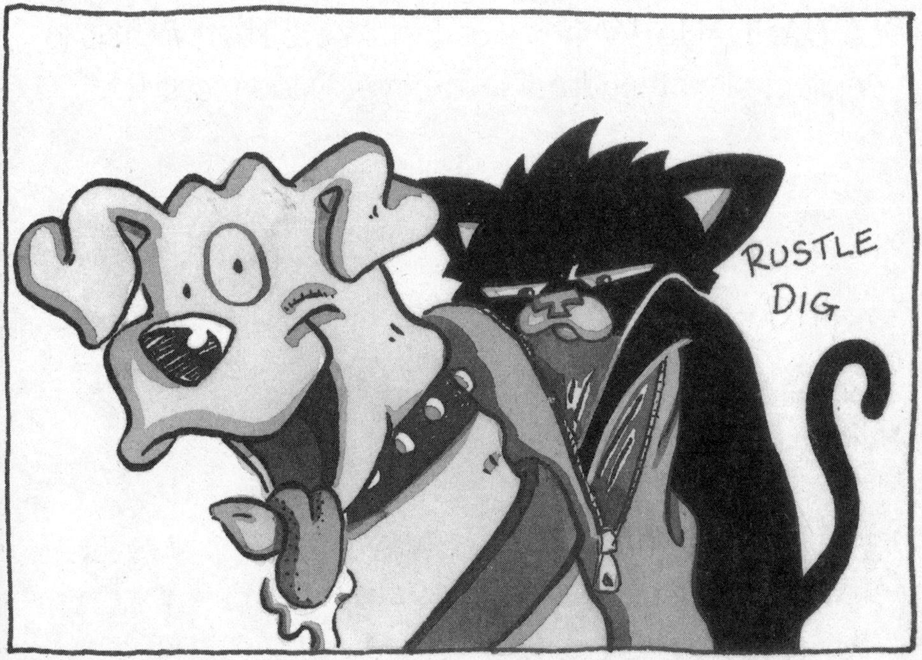
RUSTLE
DIG

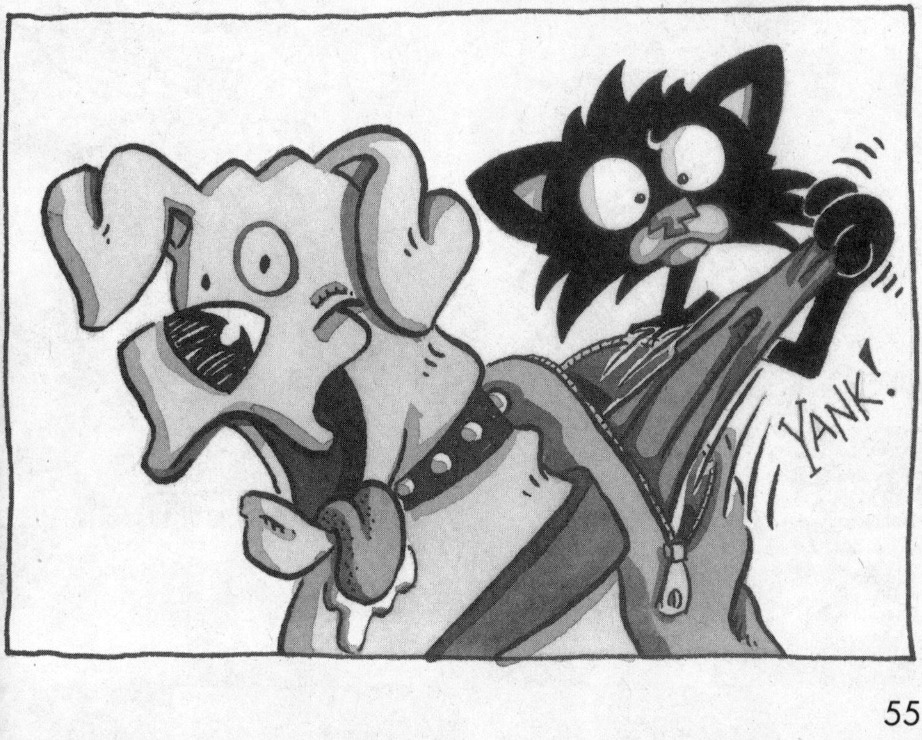
YANK!

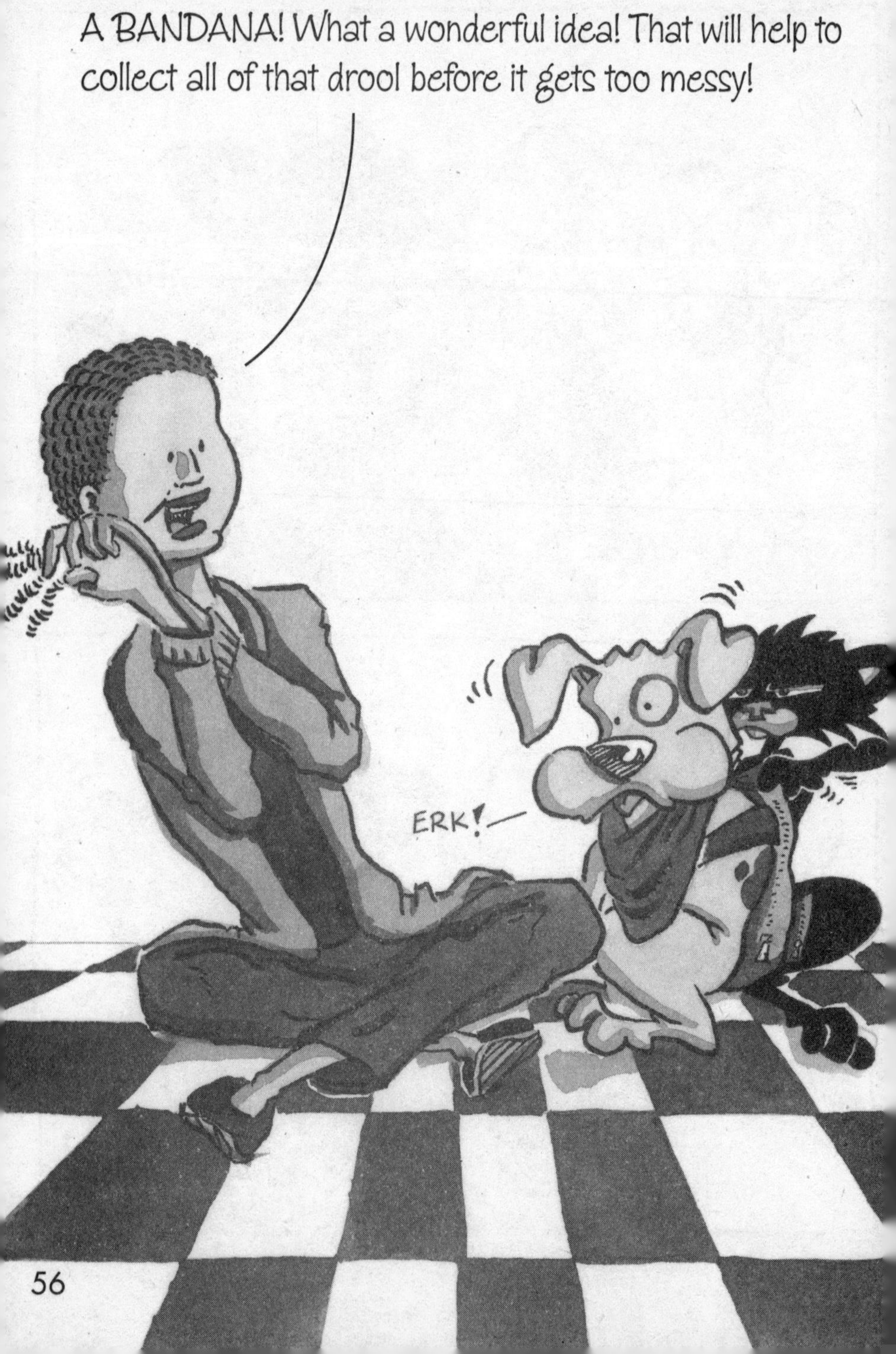
A BANDANA! What a wonderful idea! That will help to collect all of that drool before it gets too messy!
ERK!

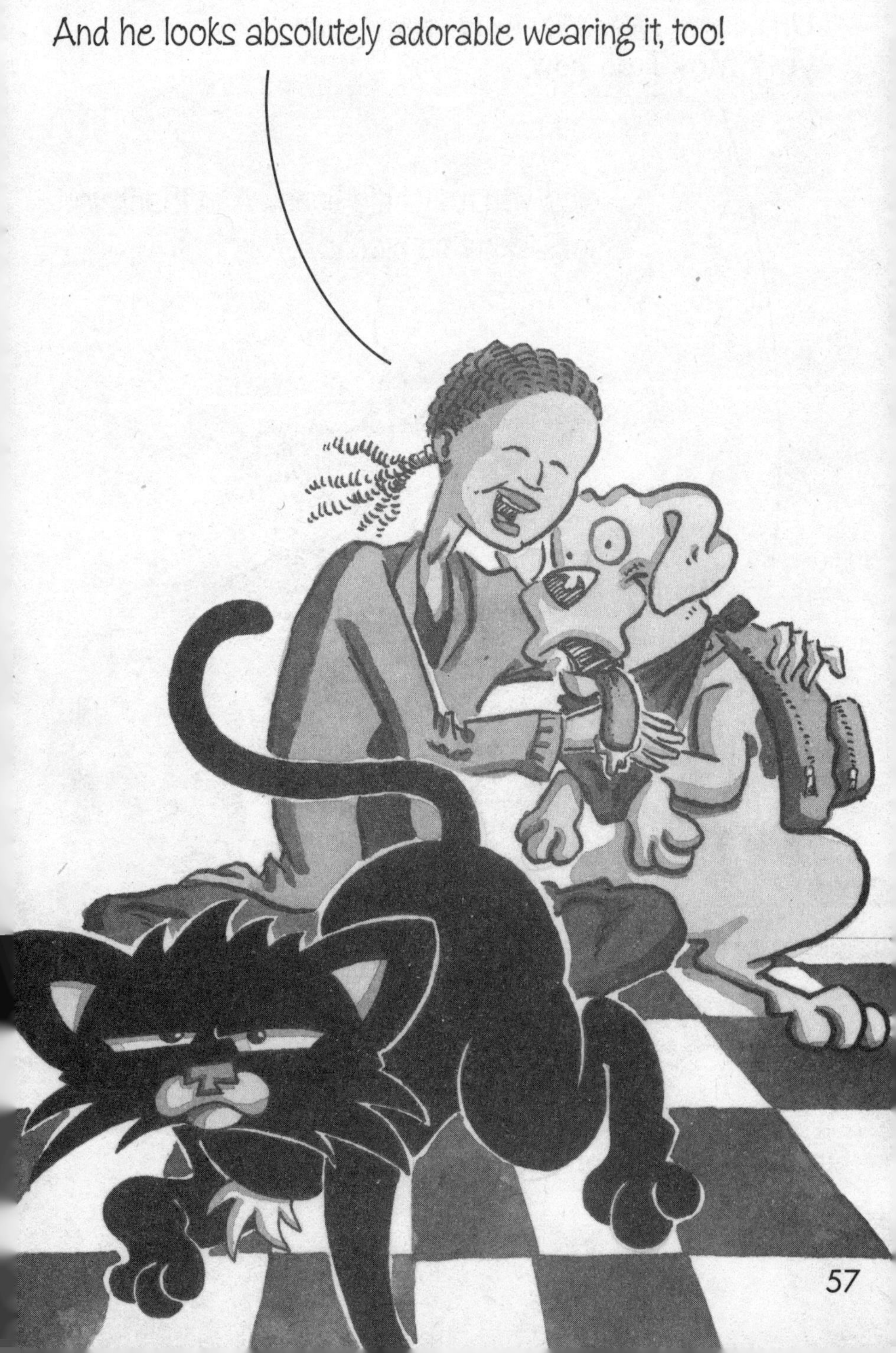
And he looks absolutely adorable wearing it, too!

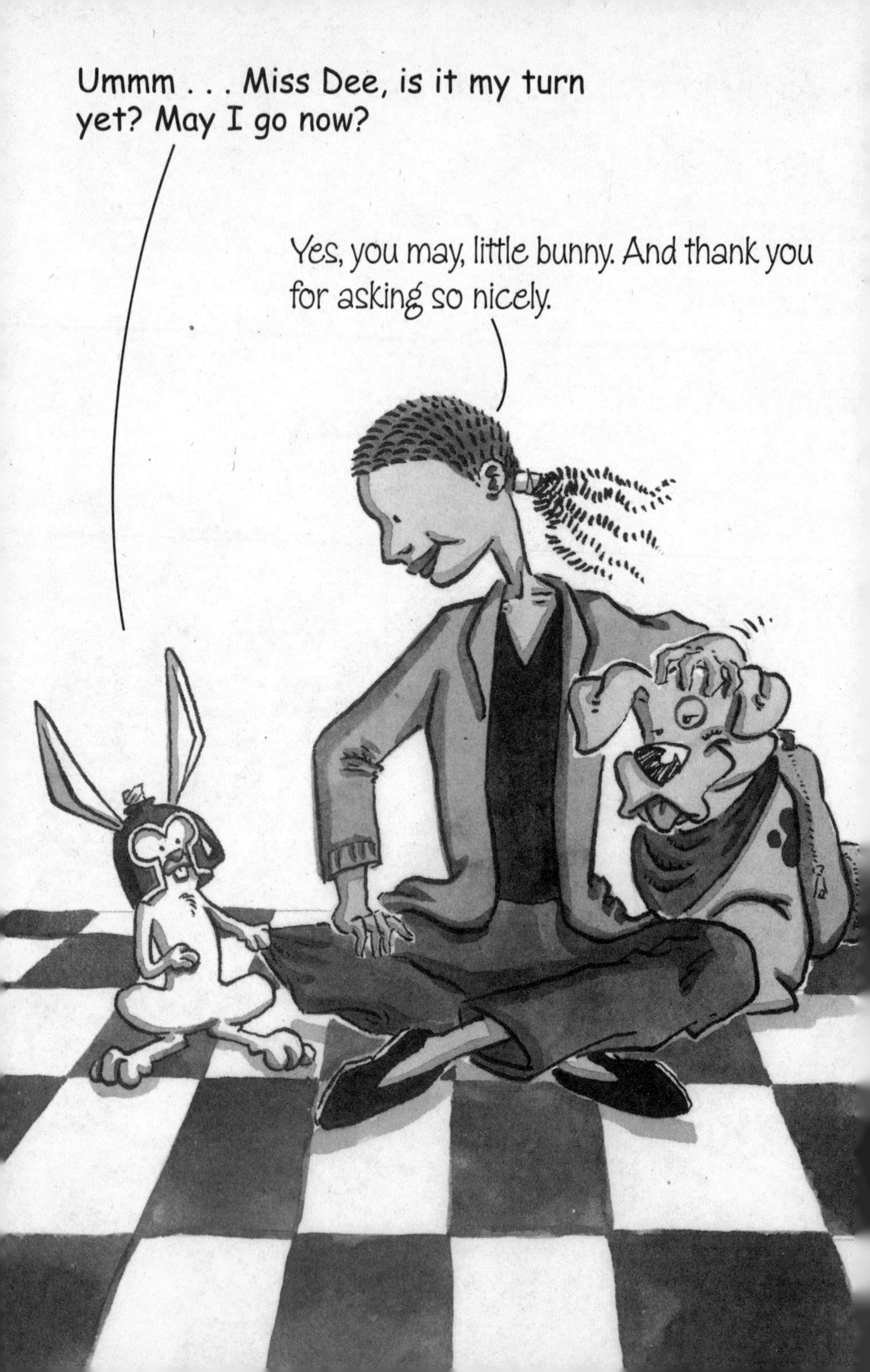
Ummm . . . Miss Dee, is it my turn yet? May I go now?
Yes, you may, little bunny. And thank you for asking so nicely.

NOW IS THE TIME FOR DR. LAGOMORPH! BEHOLD THE MIGHTY POWER OF THE WORLD'S MOST AWESOME MUTANT SUPER-VILLAIN! TREMBLE BEFORE MY DREADFUL AUTHORITY! COWER BEFORE MY FIERCE SUPREMACY! CRINGE BEFORE MY FORMIDABLE EFFICACY! FOR I AM **DR. LAGO-MORPH!**

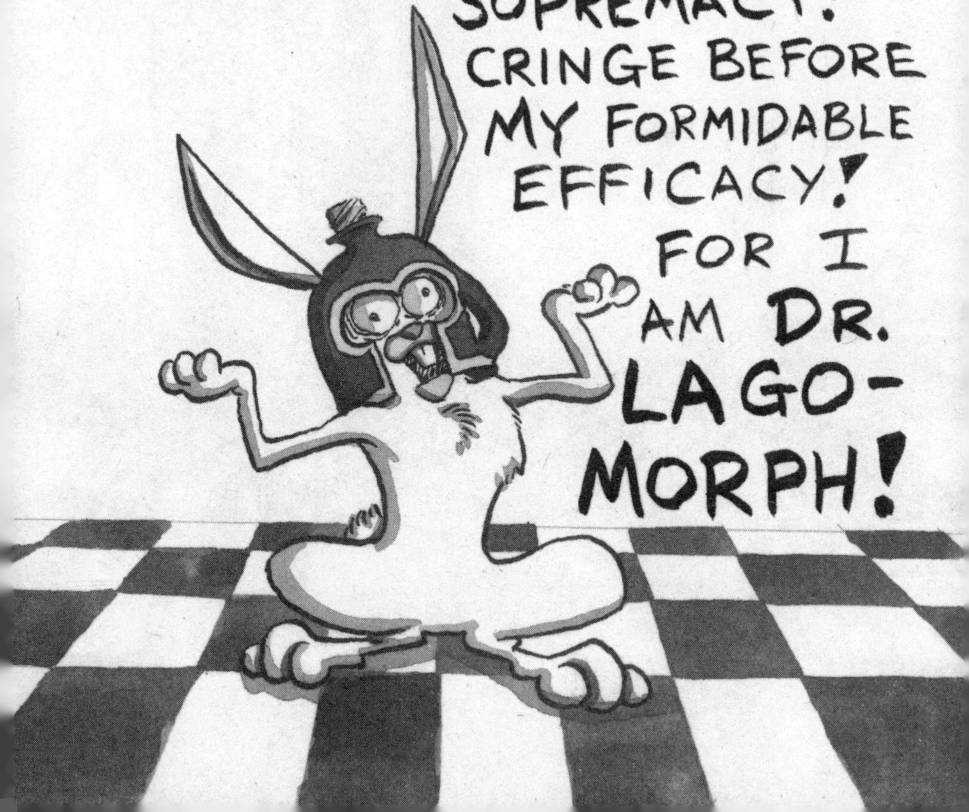

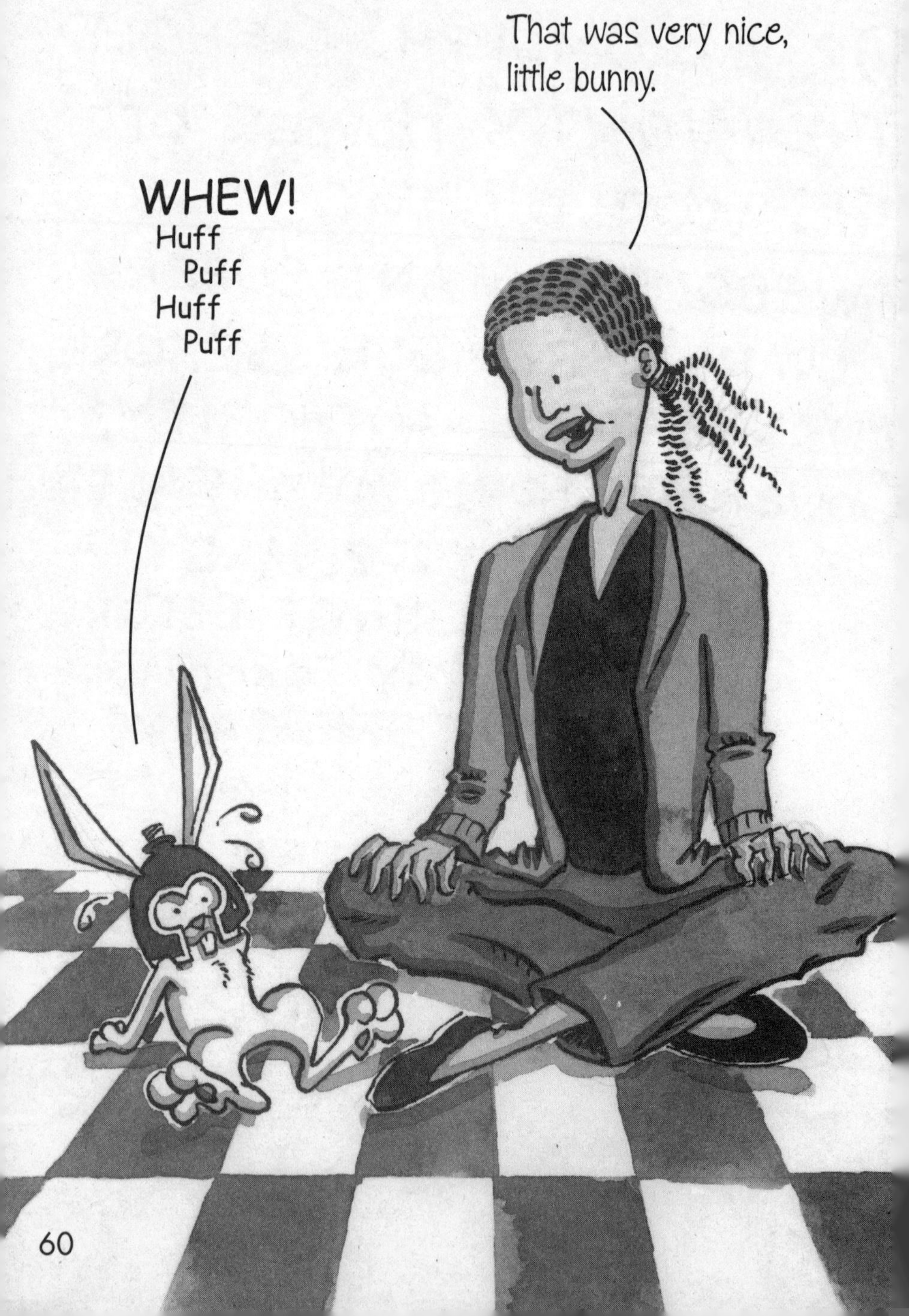
That was very nice, little bunny.
WHEW! Huff Puff Huff Puff

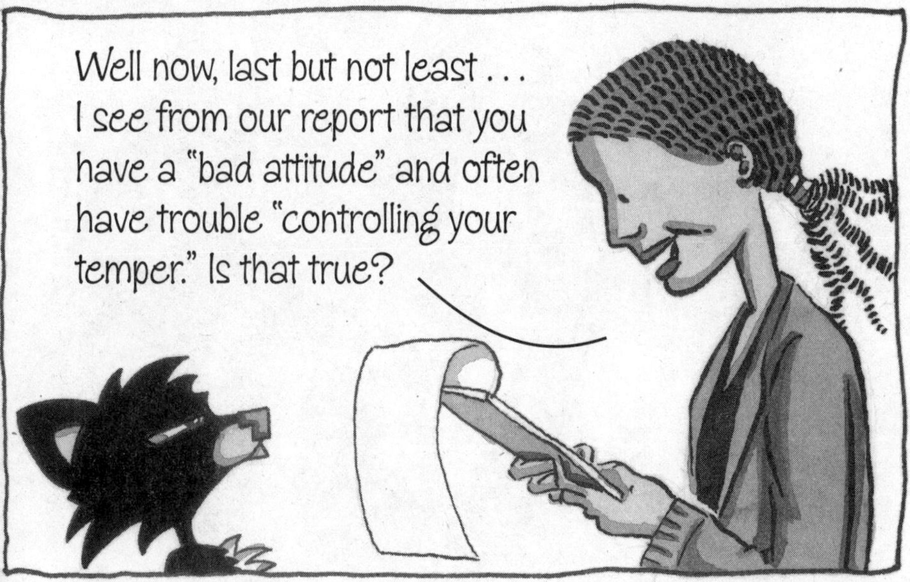
Well now, last but not least . . . I see from our report that you have a "bad attitude" and often have trouble "controlling your temper." Is that true?

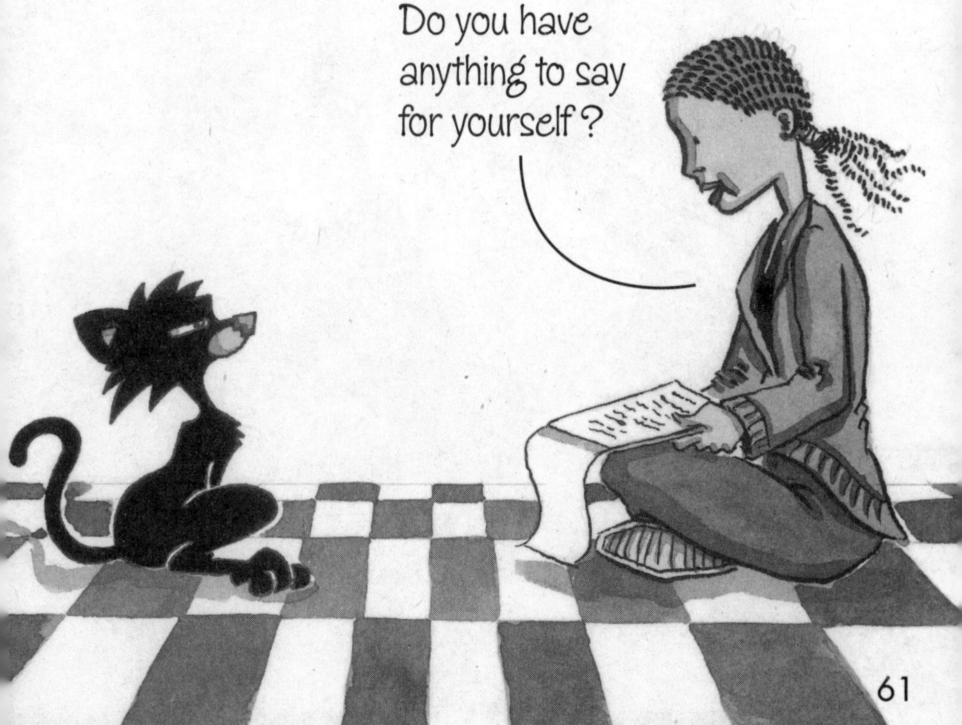
Do you have anything to say for yourself ?

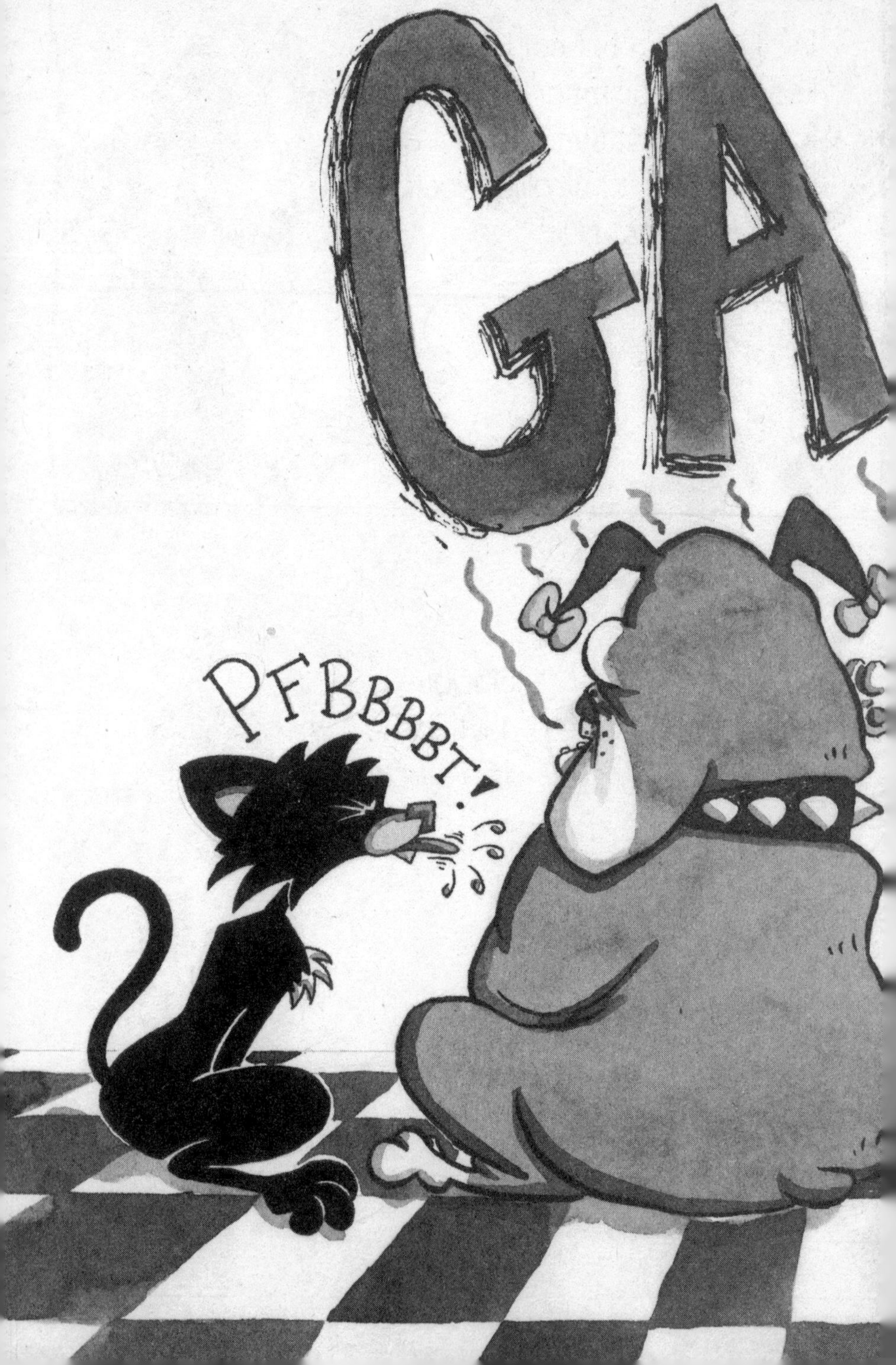
GA
PFBBBBT!

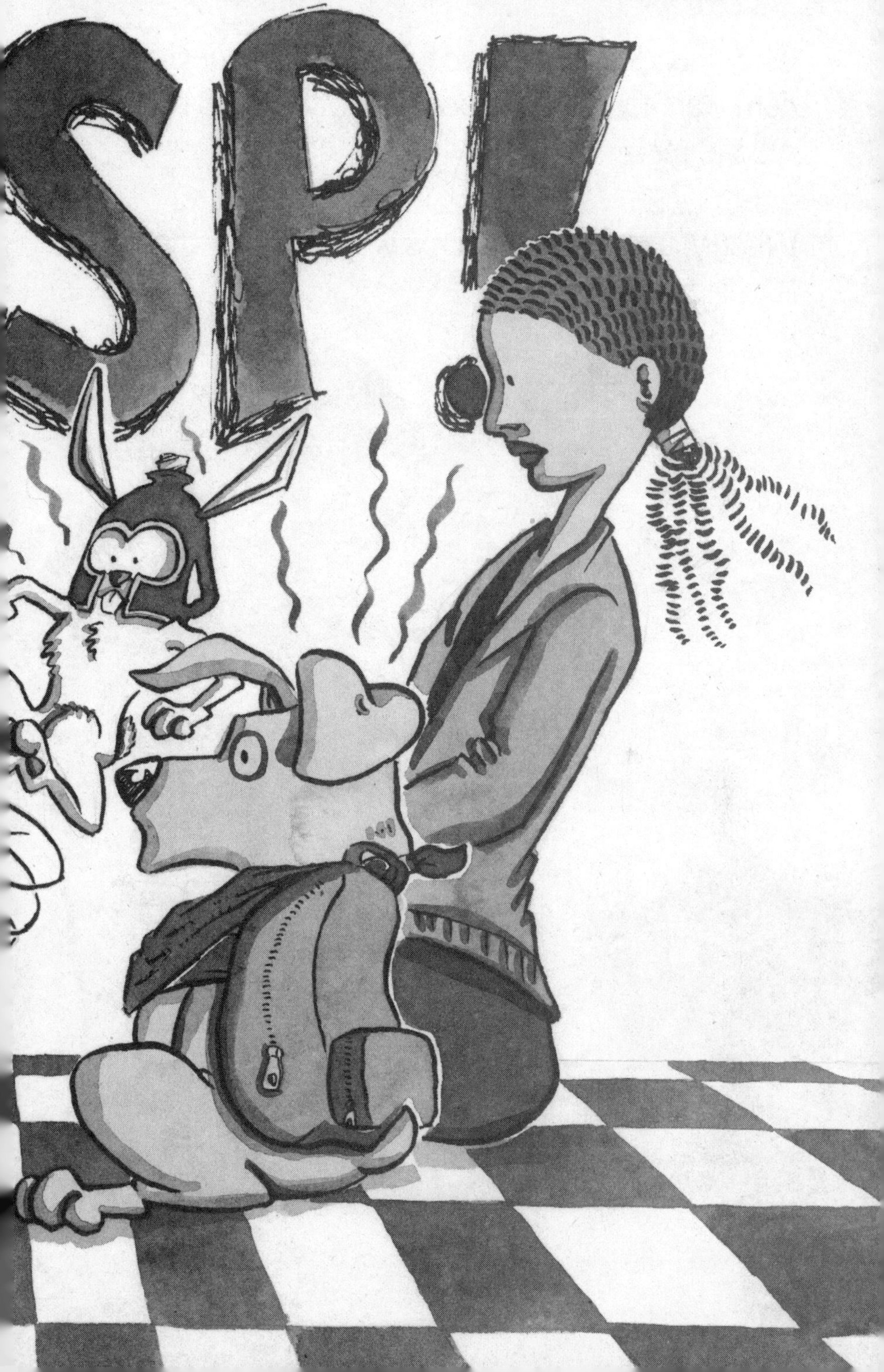
SP

Okay, then. You don't have to answer the question if you don't want to, but that does not give you the right to be rude to me.

When you're ready to tell me why you're so angry, I'll be listening.

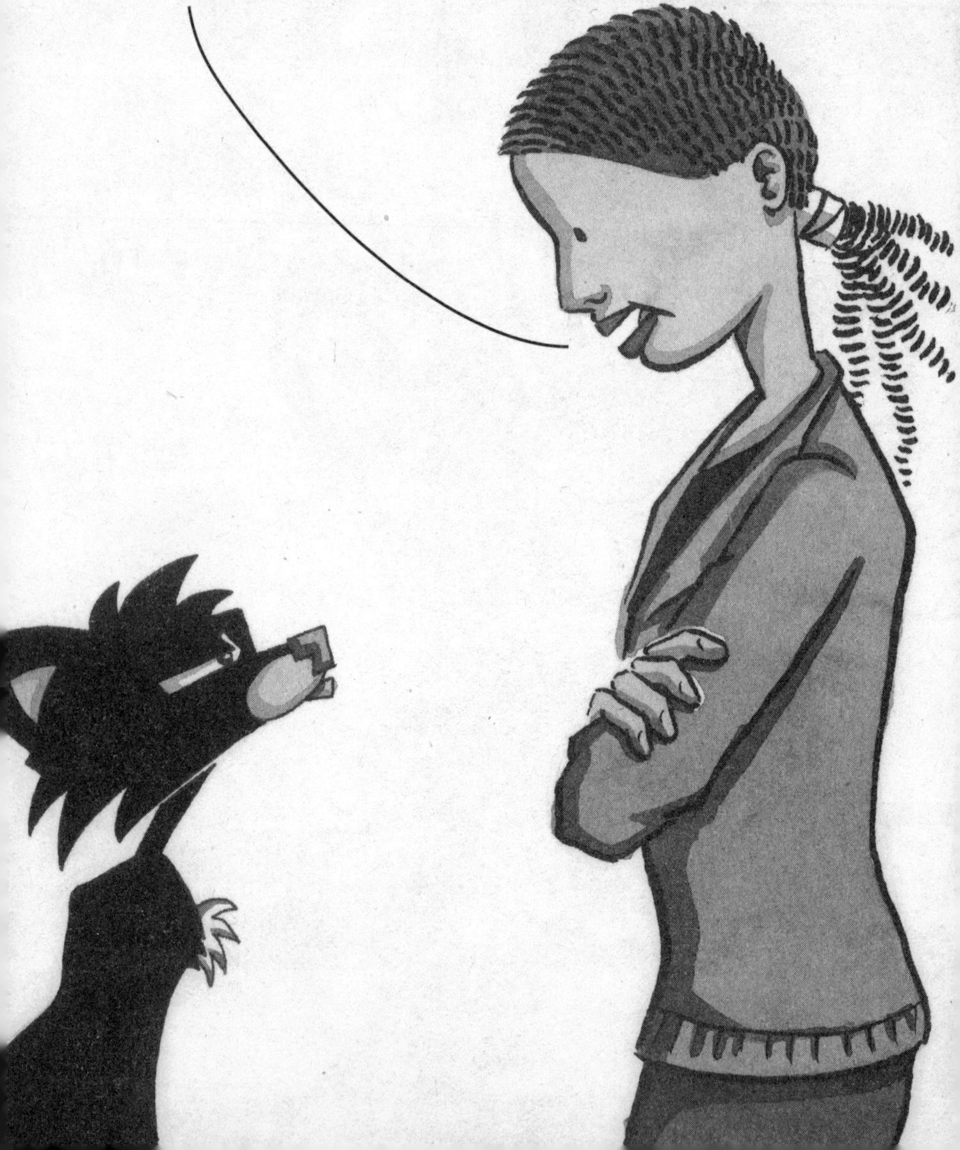

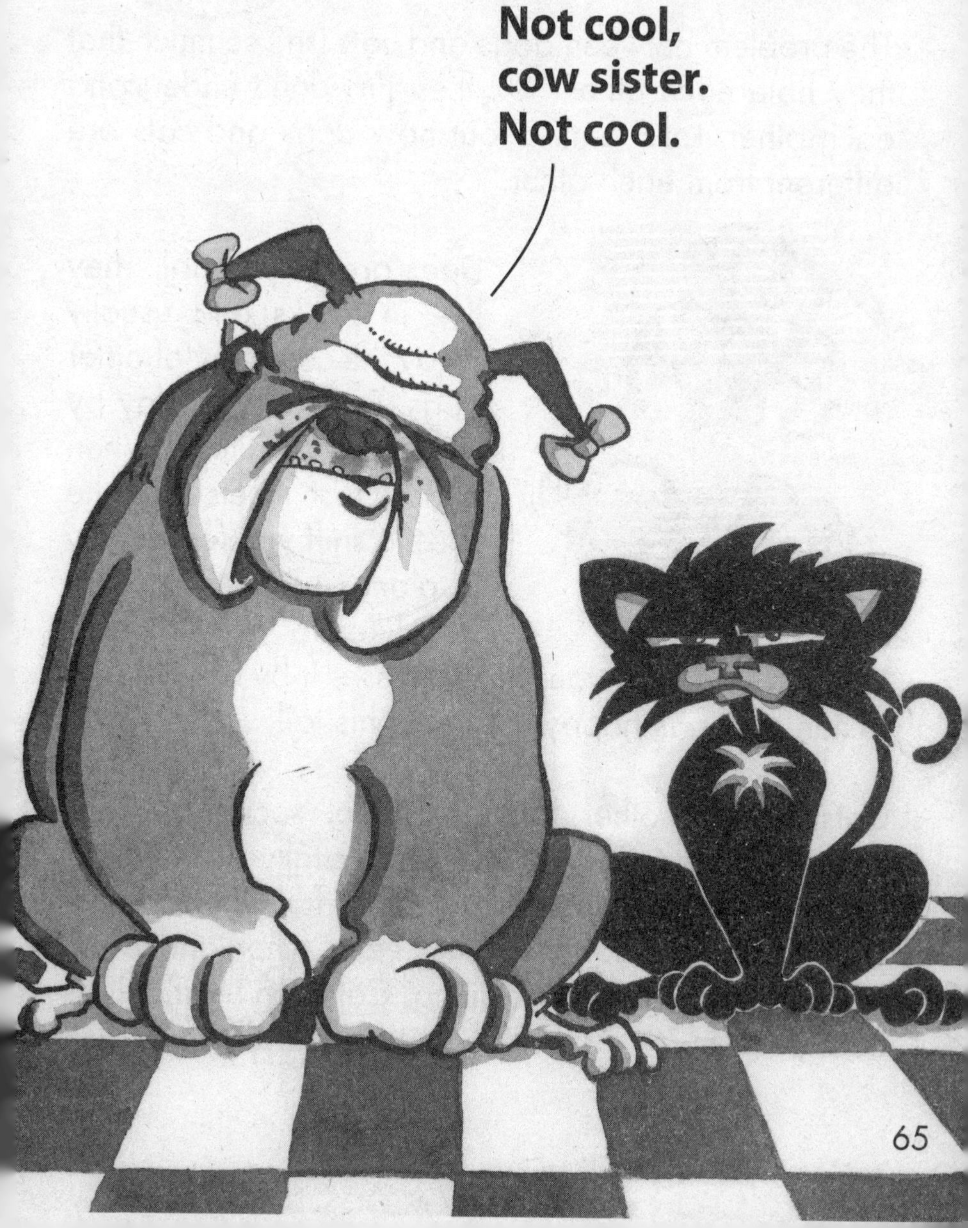
Not cool,
cow sister.
Not cool.

UNCLE MURRAY'S FUN FACTS

WHY DO DOGS AND CATS HATE EACH OTHER?

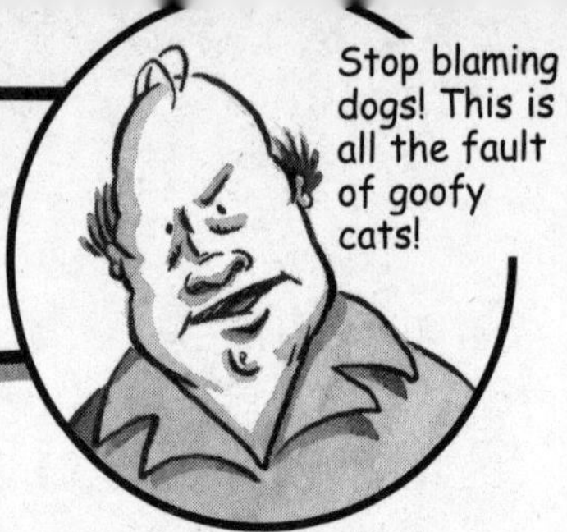
Stop blaming dogs! This is all the fault of goofy cats!

The problem between dogs and cats isn't so much that they hate each other . . . they just don't understand each other. Let's think about how dogs and cats are different from each other.

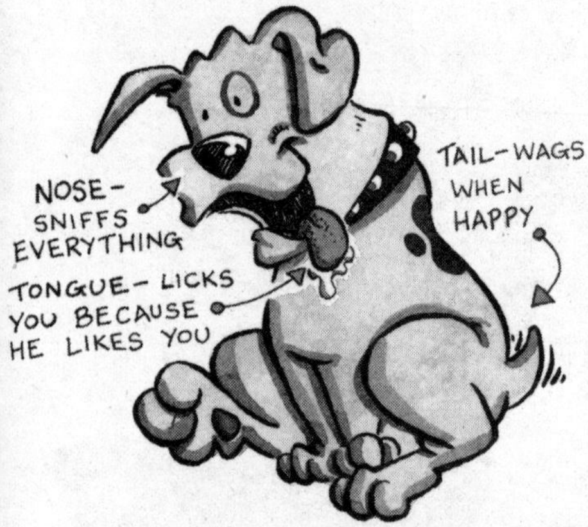
NOSE- SNIFFS EVERYTHING
TONGUE- LICKS YOU BECAUSE HE LIKES YOU
TAIL-WAGS WHEN HAPPY

Dogs are very social. They live in packs and usually enjoy the company of other dogs. Dogs like to play by wrestling and biting. When a dog first meets you, he likes to sniff you (especially in places where you may not like to be sniffed). When a dog likes you, he expresses it by licking you. When a dog is happy, he wags his tail.

Cats, on the other hand, are not social animals. They lead independent lives and usually do not seek the company of other cats. Except for when they're young, cats do not play with each other and especially not by wrestling or biting. Cats don't sniff things nearly as much as dogs. Cats generally only lick themselves, and then only to clean themselves. And cats only shake their tails when they're feeling nervous or angry.

TAIL— SHAKES WHEN NERVOUS

NOSE—USUALLY ONLY SNIFFS TO SENSE DANGER OR SAFETY

TONGUE— ONLY LICKS HERSELF

Now imagine what happens when a strange dog and cat meet for the first time. The dog runs up to the cat with its tail wagging, expecting to sniff her, lick her, and play with her. But the cat meanwhile sees the dog's running as an attack. She sees the wagging tail as a sign of anger. And the last thing the cat wants is to be sniffed (especially in a place where she doesn't want to be sniffed), licked, and played with. So the cat either runs away or attacks, neither of which the dog expected.

Okay, so maybe the dogs are just kinda sorta partly to blame.

So now the dog has a perception that cats just *aren't* friendly. This isn't going to encourage the dog to be friendly with any cats in the future. And so begins a cycle of misunderstanding that can sometimes lead to a real mess.

•CHAPTER FIVE•

ARTS + CRAFTS

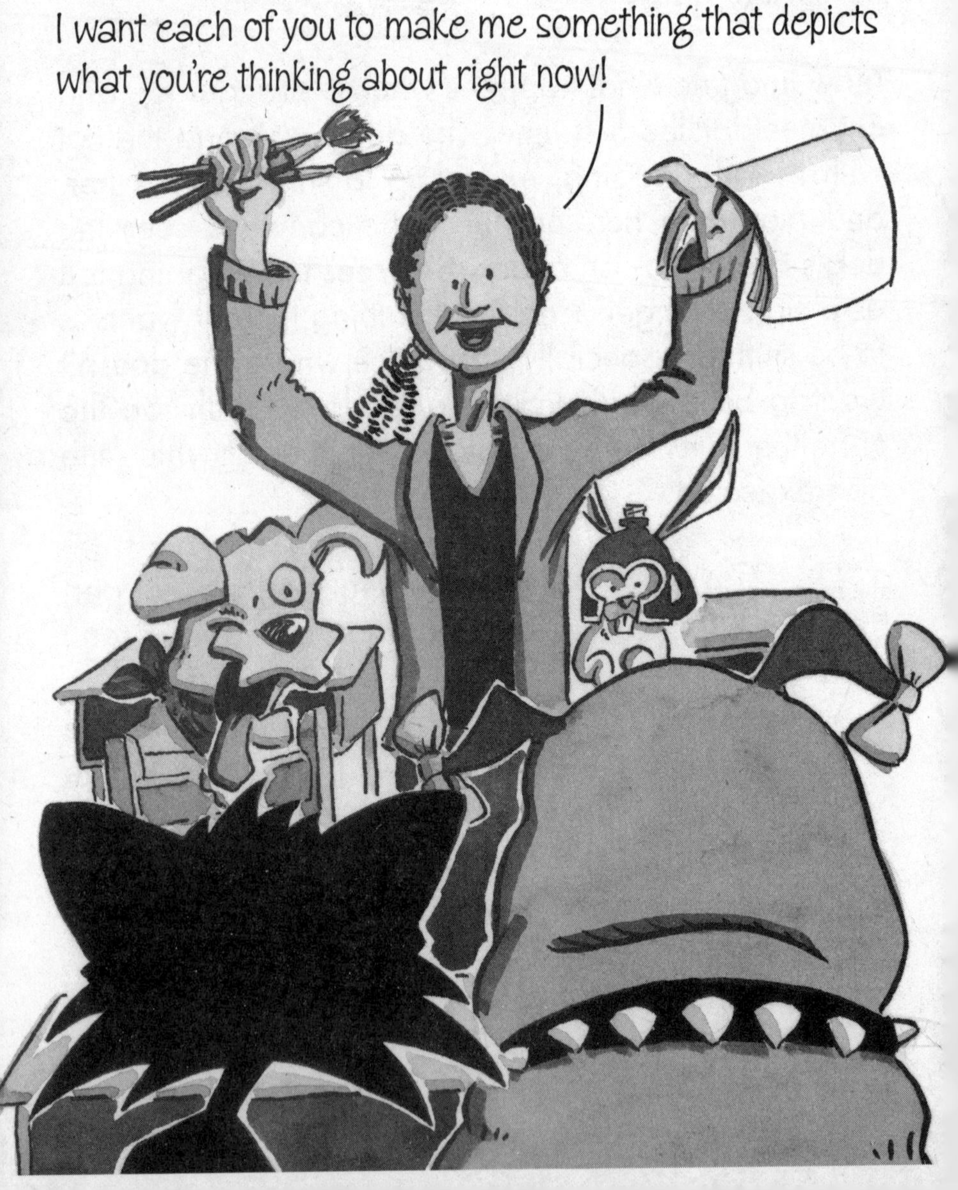
I want each of you to make me something that depicts what you're thinking about right now!

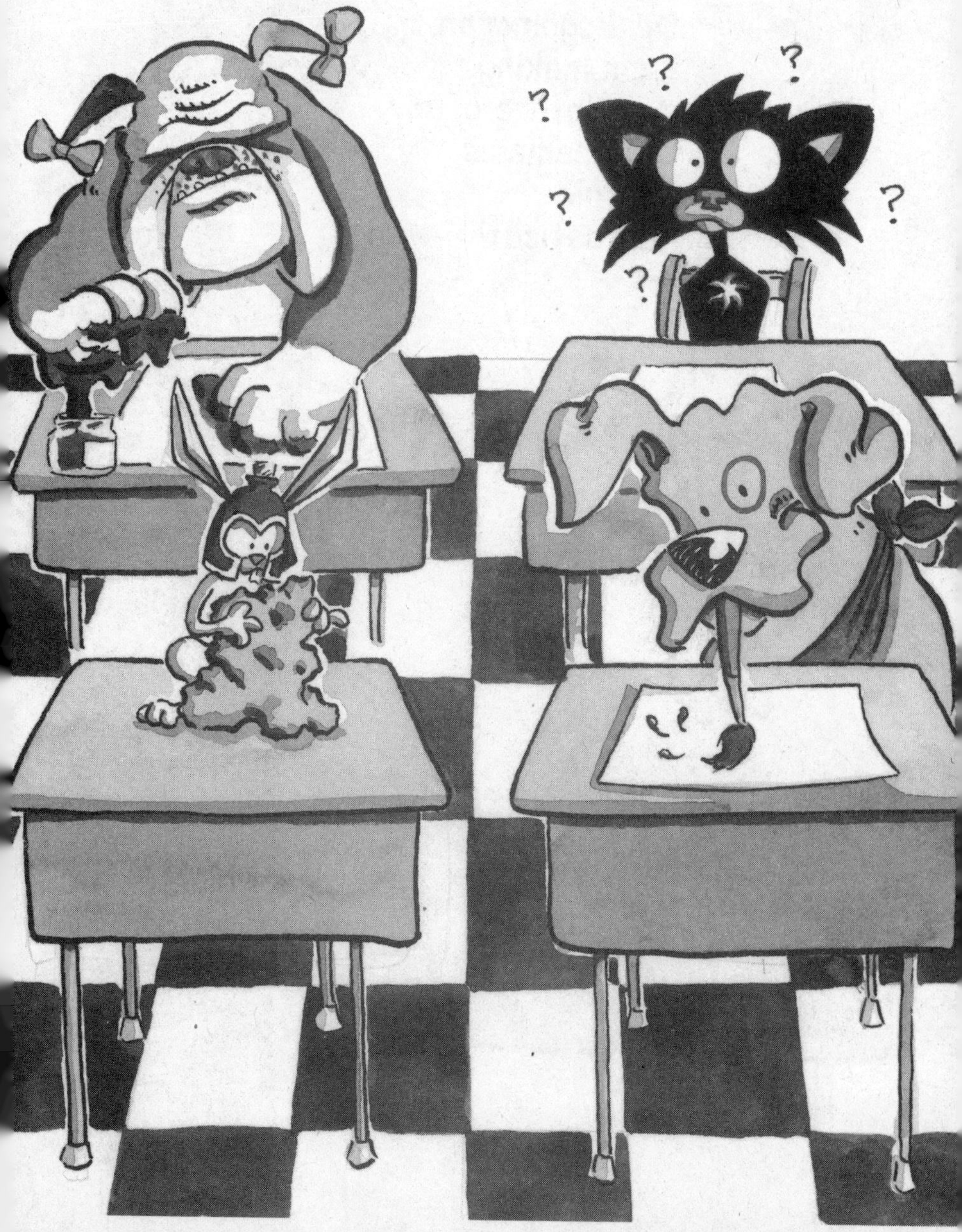

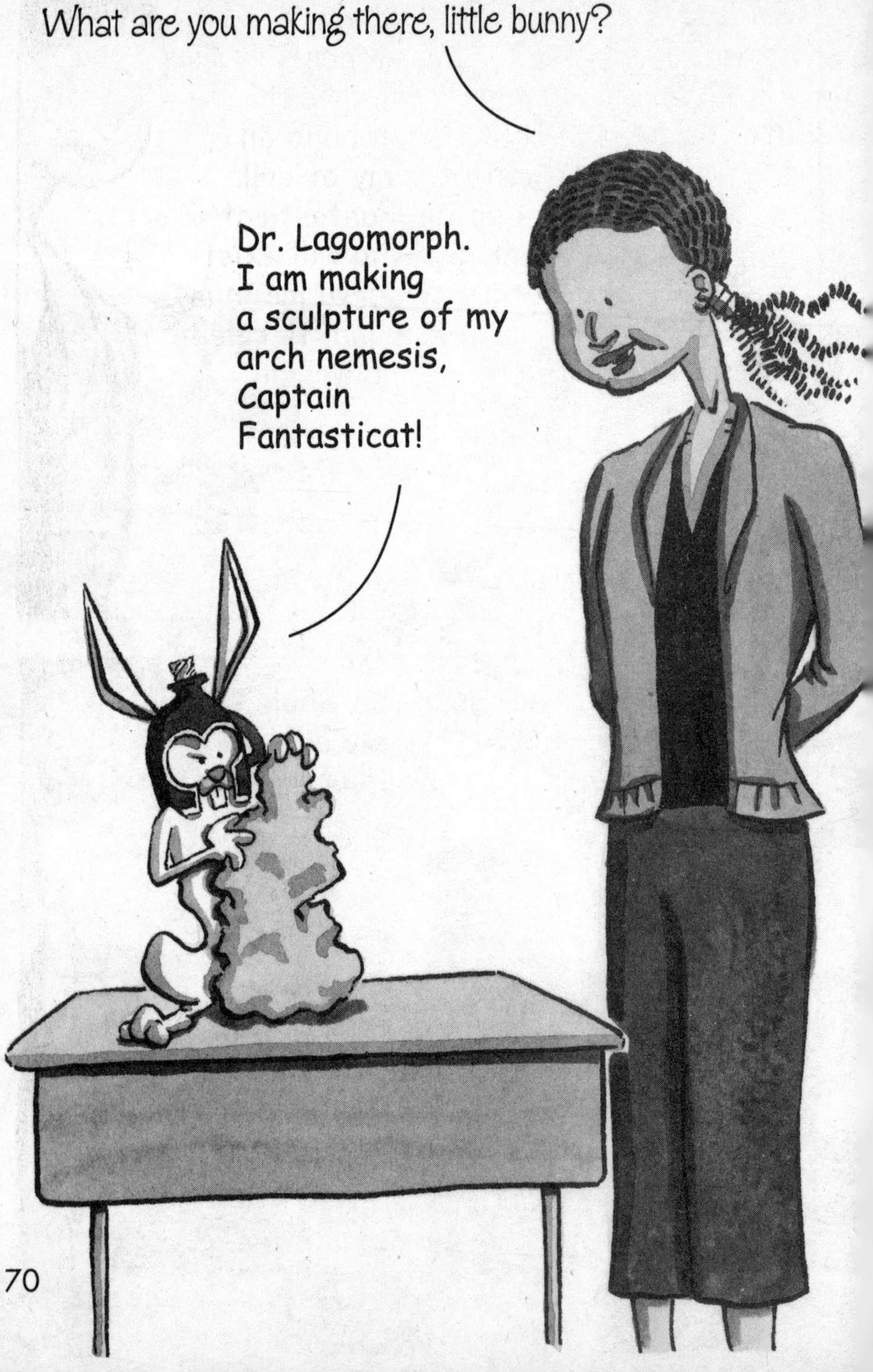
What are you making there, little bunny?
Dr. Lagomorph. I am making a sculpture of my arch nemesis, Captain Fantasticat!

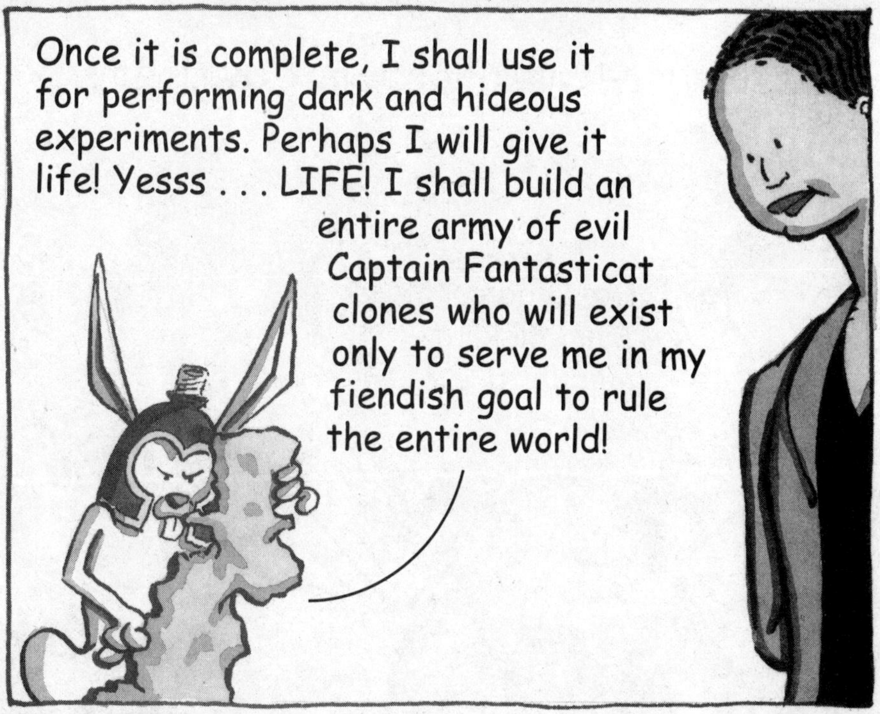
Once it is complete, I shall use it for performing dark and hideous experiments. Perhaps I will give it life! Yesss . . . LIFE! I shall build an entire army of evil Captain Fantasticat clones who will exist only to serve me in my fiendish goal to rule the entire world!

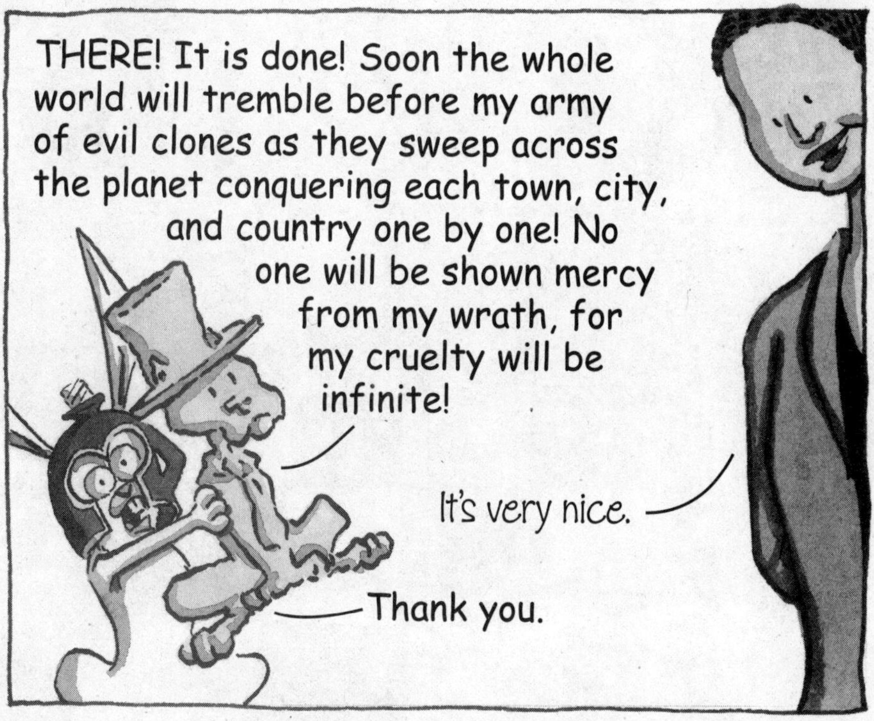
THERE! It is done! Soon the whole world will tremble before my army of evil clones as they sweep across the planet conquering each town, city, and country one by one! No one will be shown mercy from my wrath, for my cruelty will be infinite!
It's very nice.
Thank you.

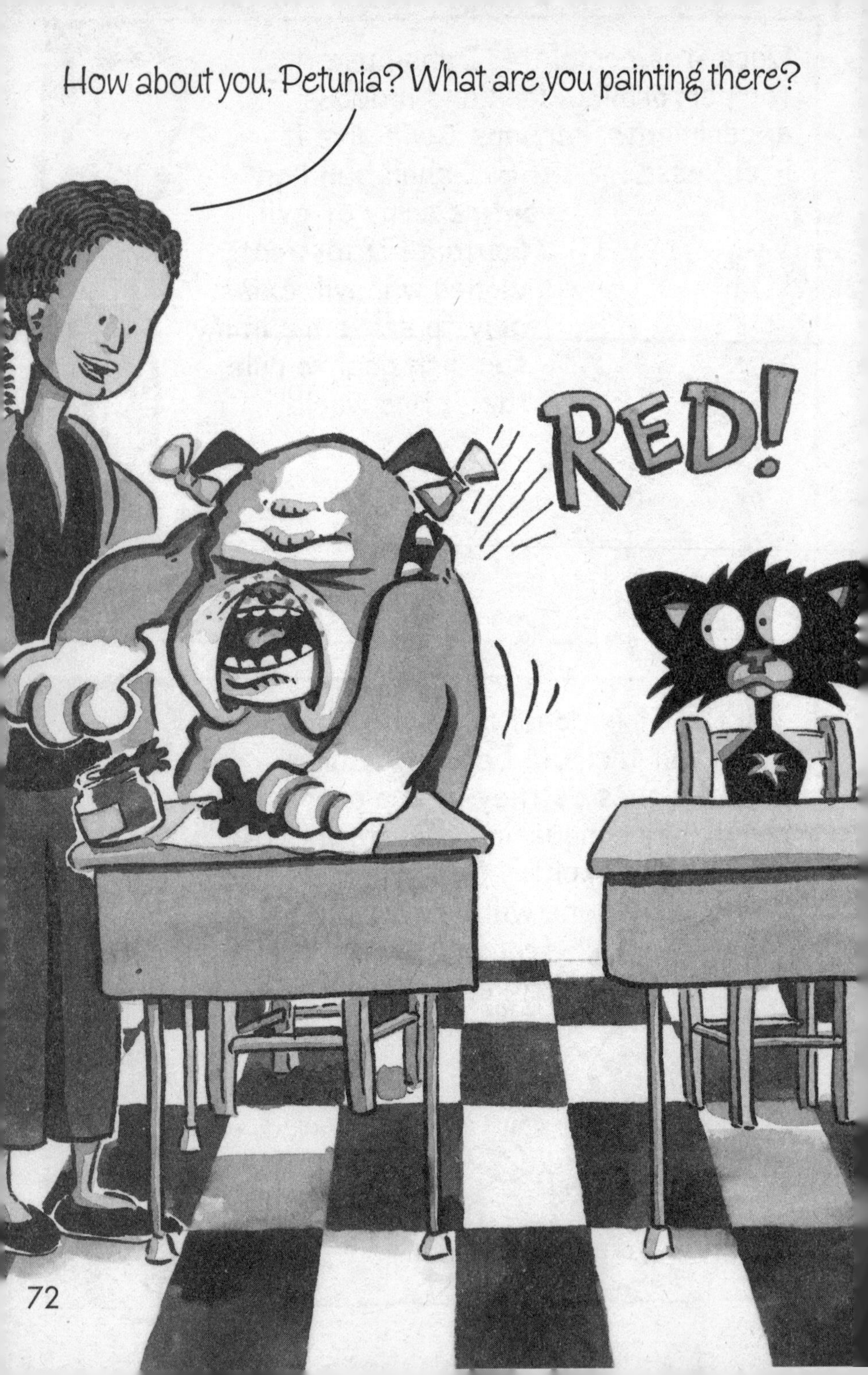
How about you, Petunia? What are you painting there?
RED!

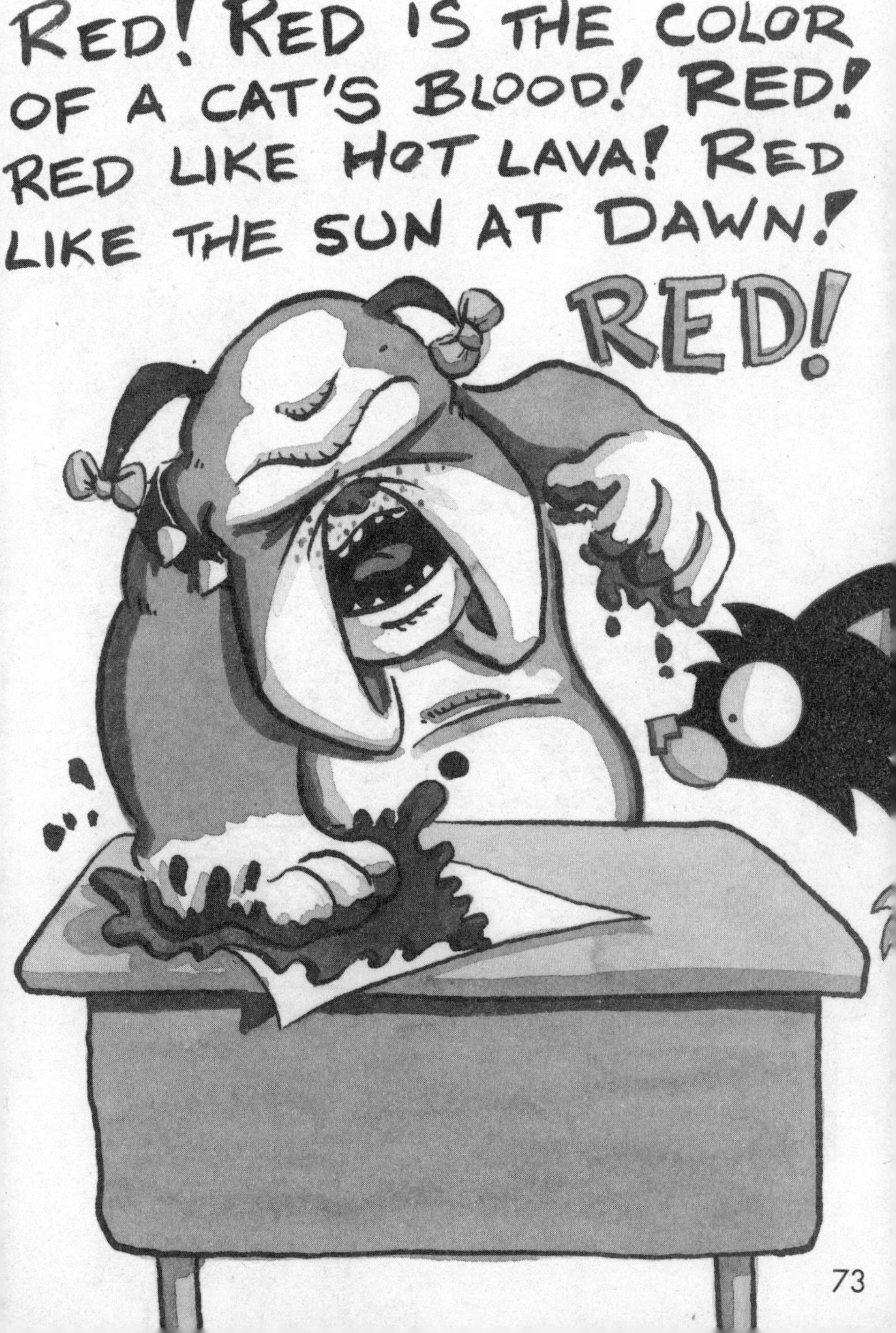
RED! RED IS THE COLOR OF A CAT'S BLOOD! RED! RED LIKE HOT LAVA! RED LIKE THE SUN AT DAWN!
RED!

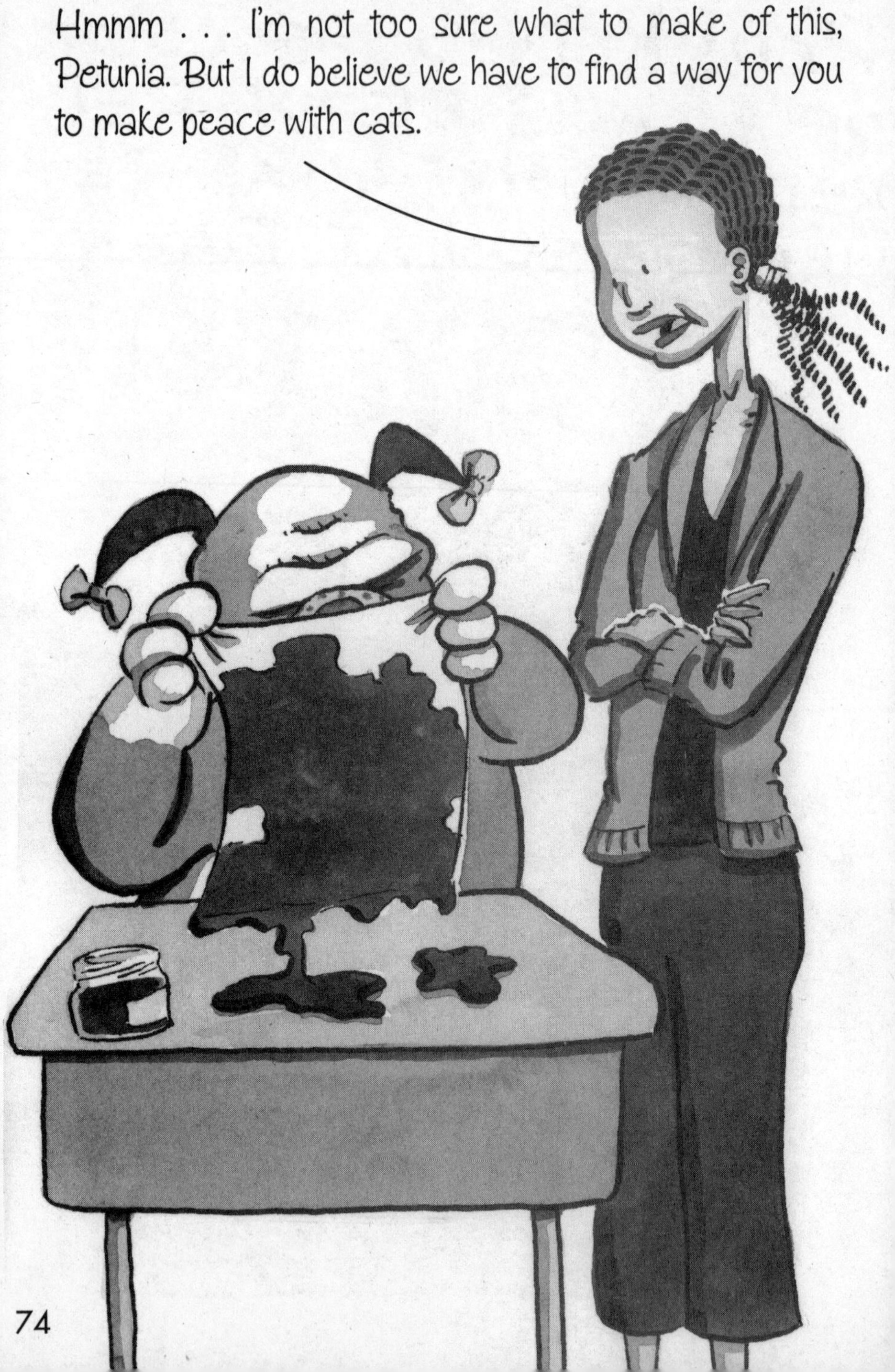
Hmmm . . . I'm not too sure what to make of this, Petunia. But I do believe we have to find a way for you to make peace with cats.

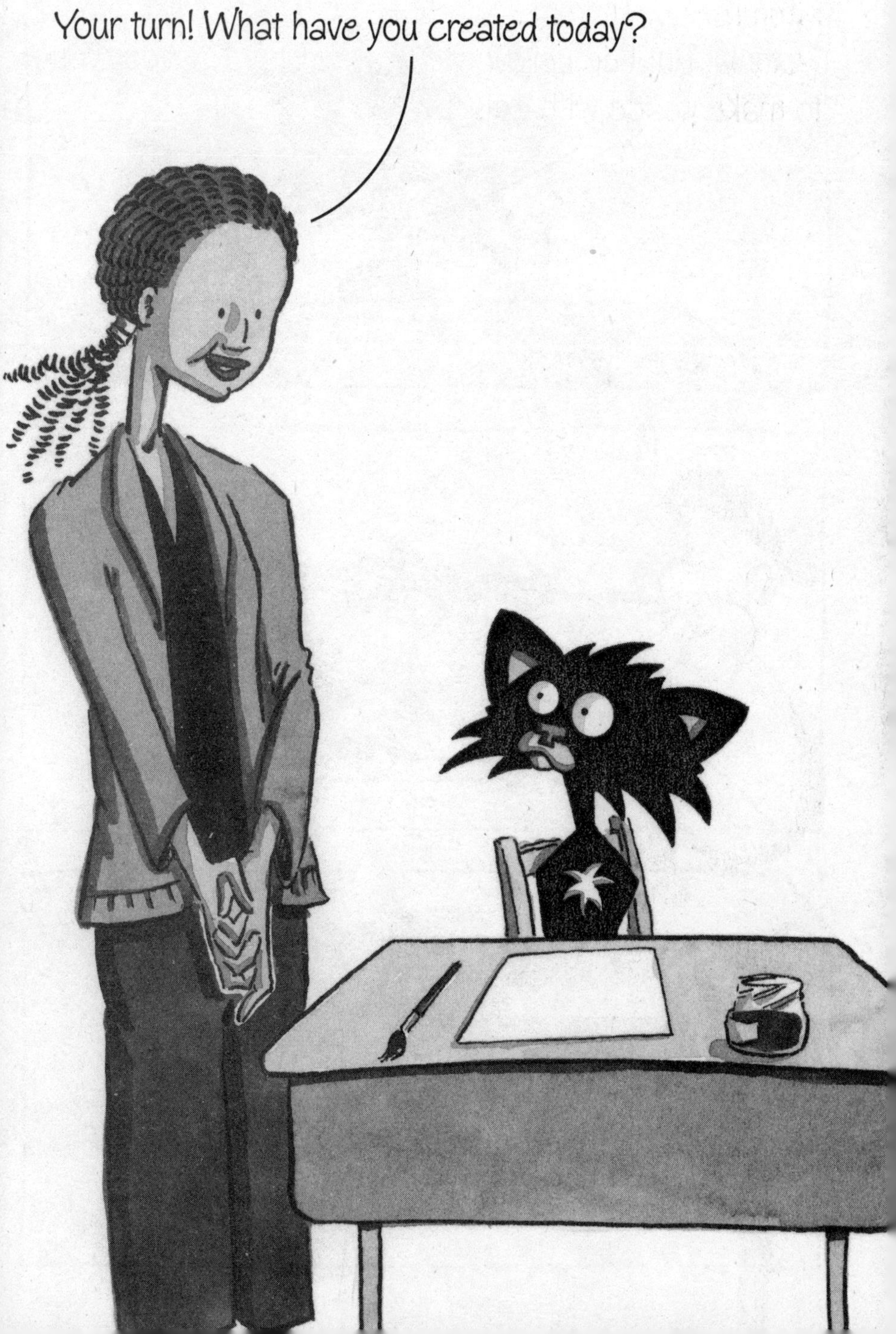
Your turn! What have you created today?

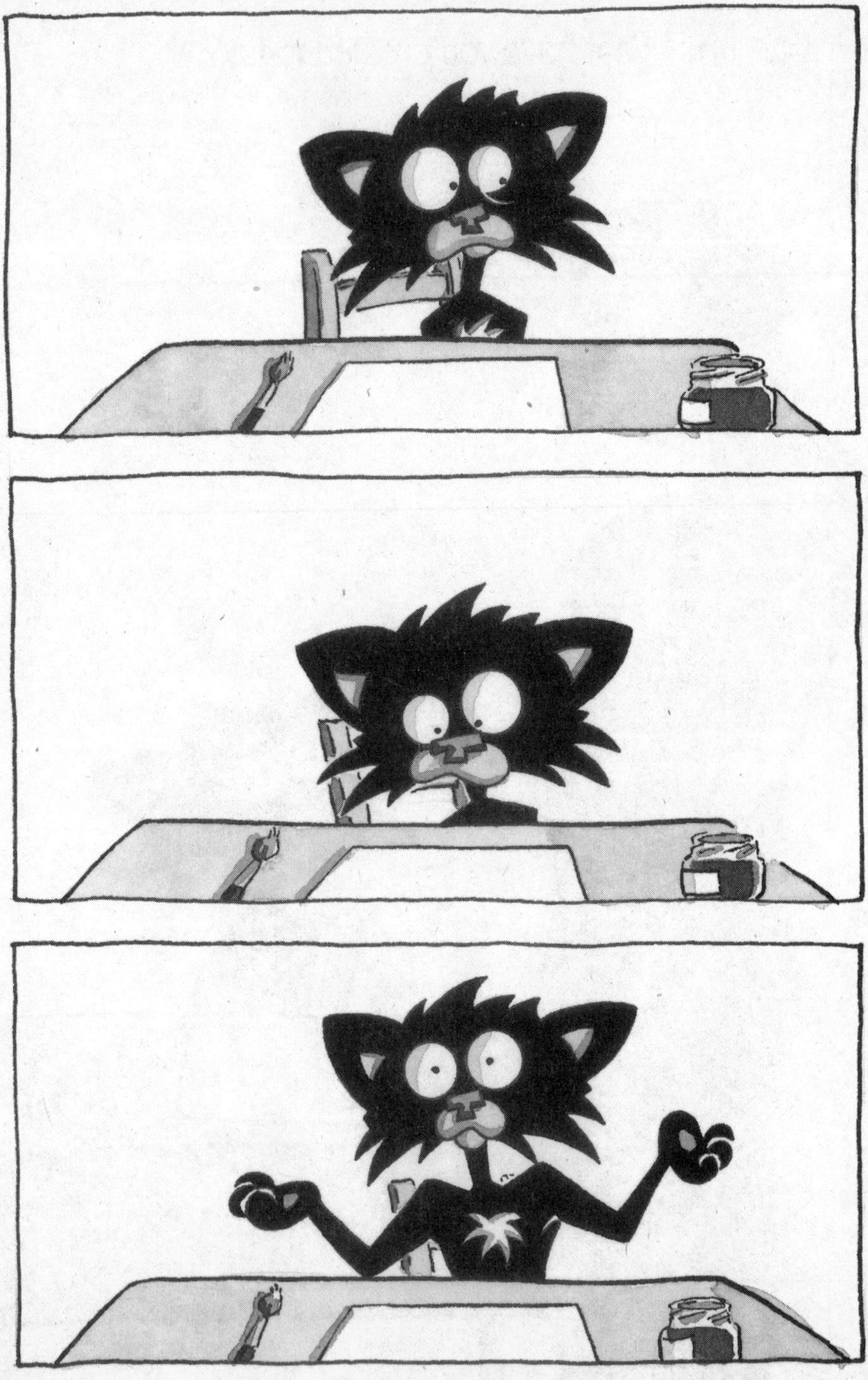

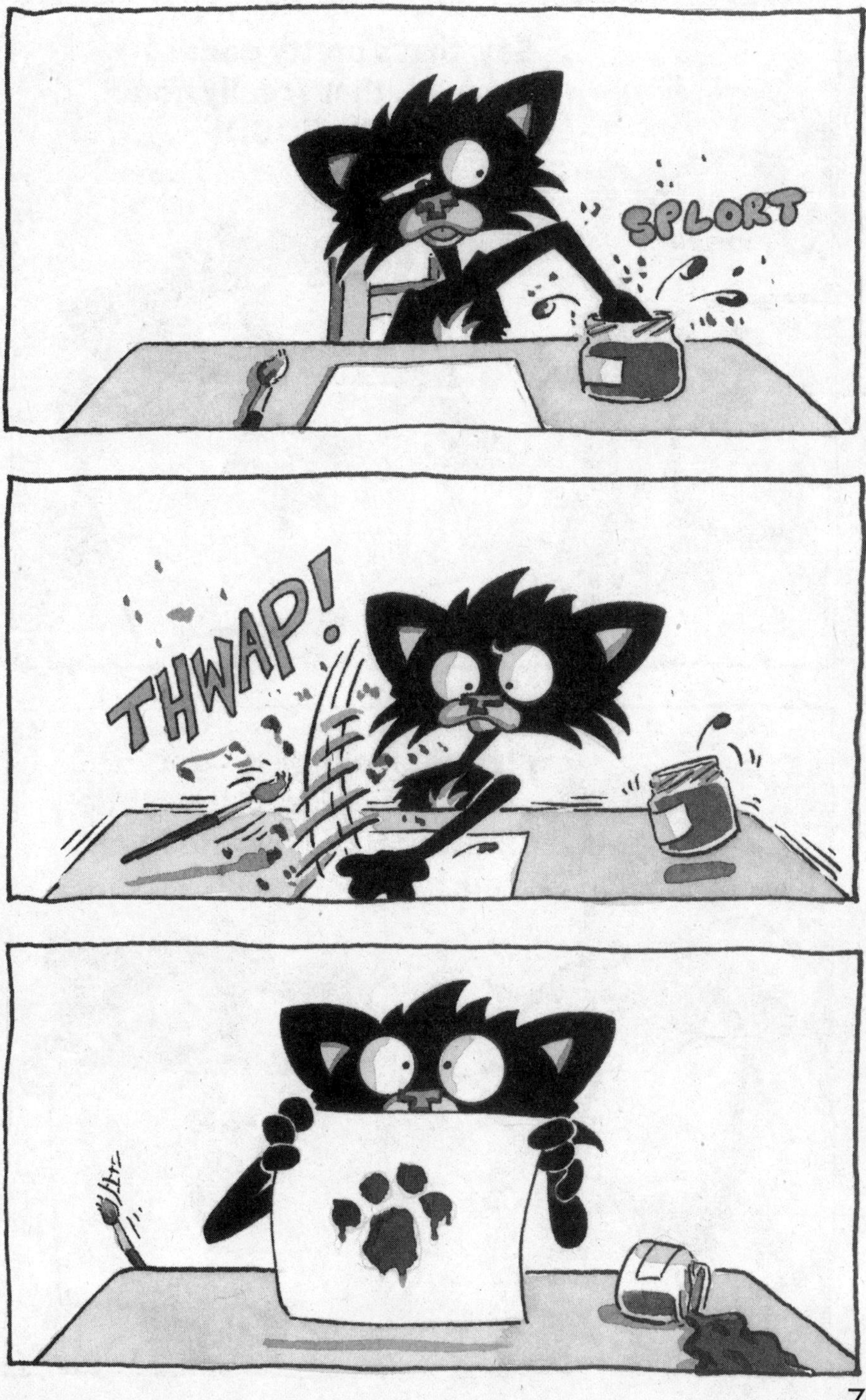
SPLORT
THWAP!

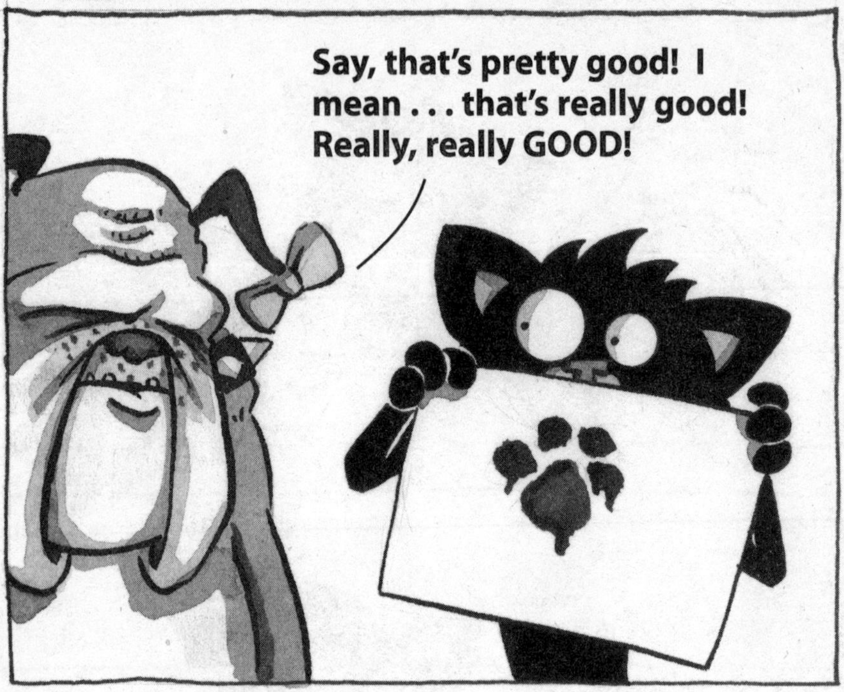
Say, that's pretty good! I mean . . . that's really good! Really, really GOOD!

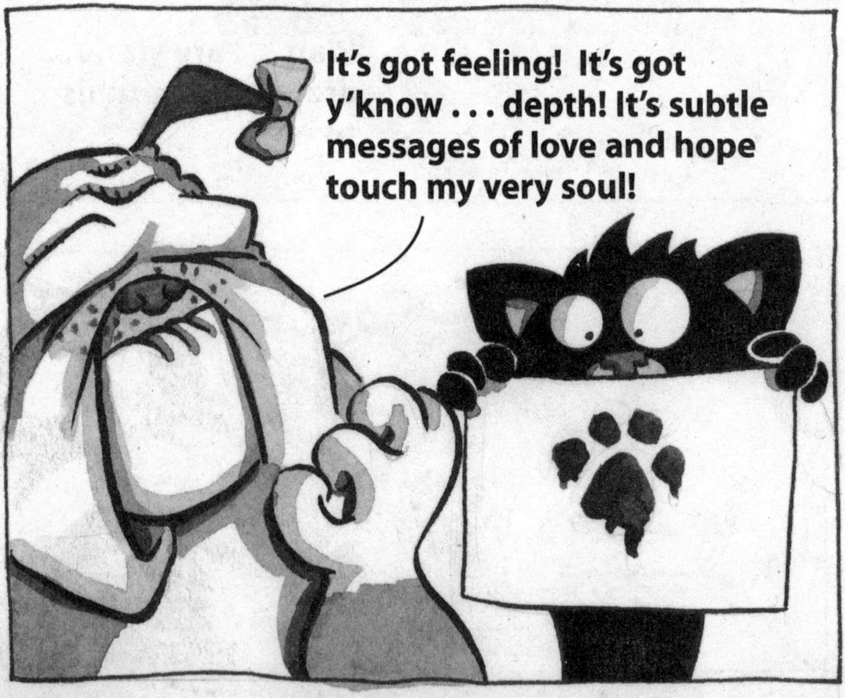
It's got feeling! It's got y'know . . . depth! It's subtle messages of love and hope touch my very soul!

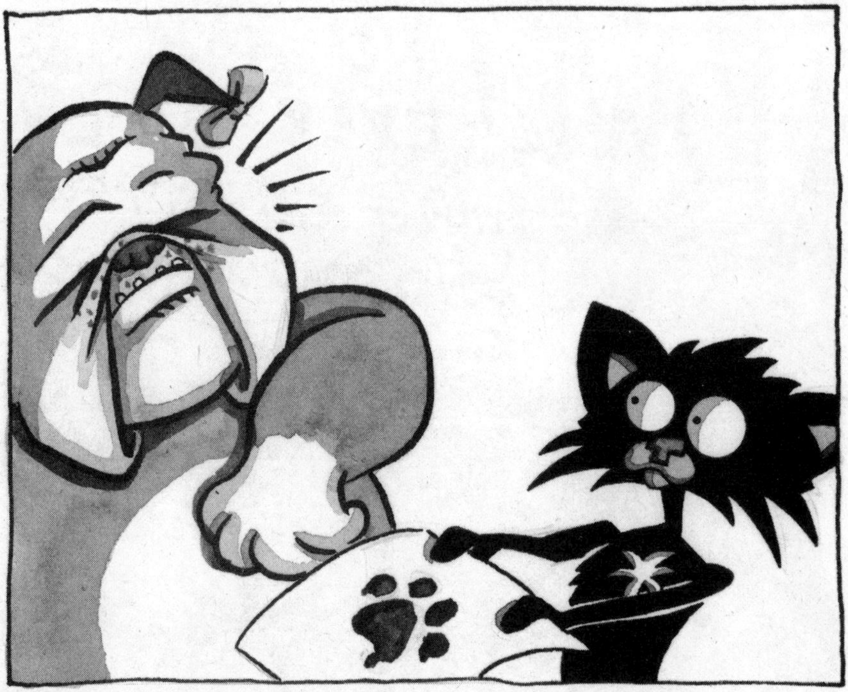

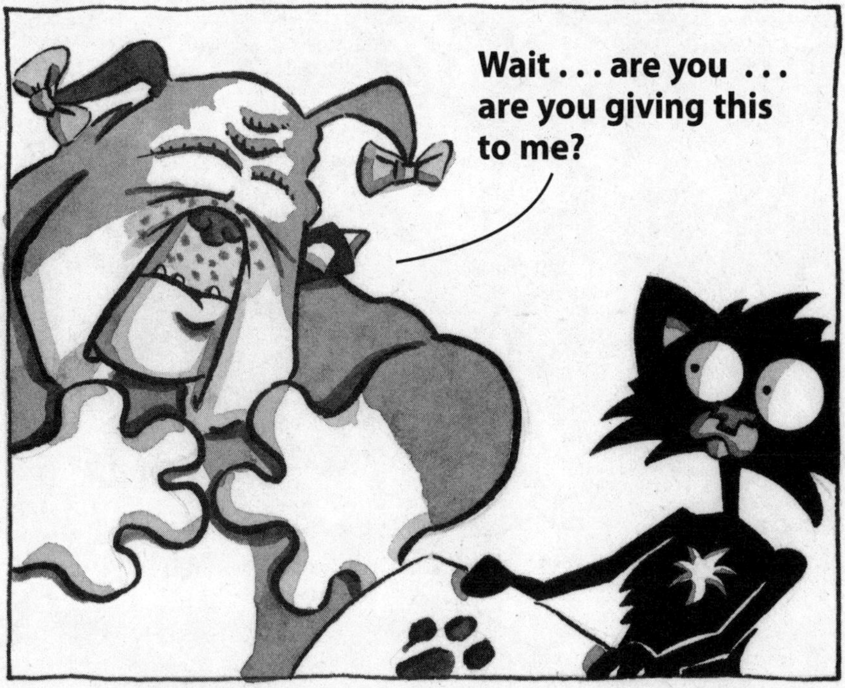
Wait . . . are you . . .
are you giving this
to me?

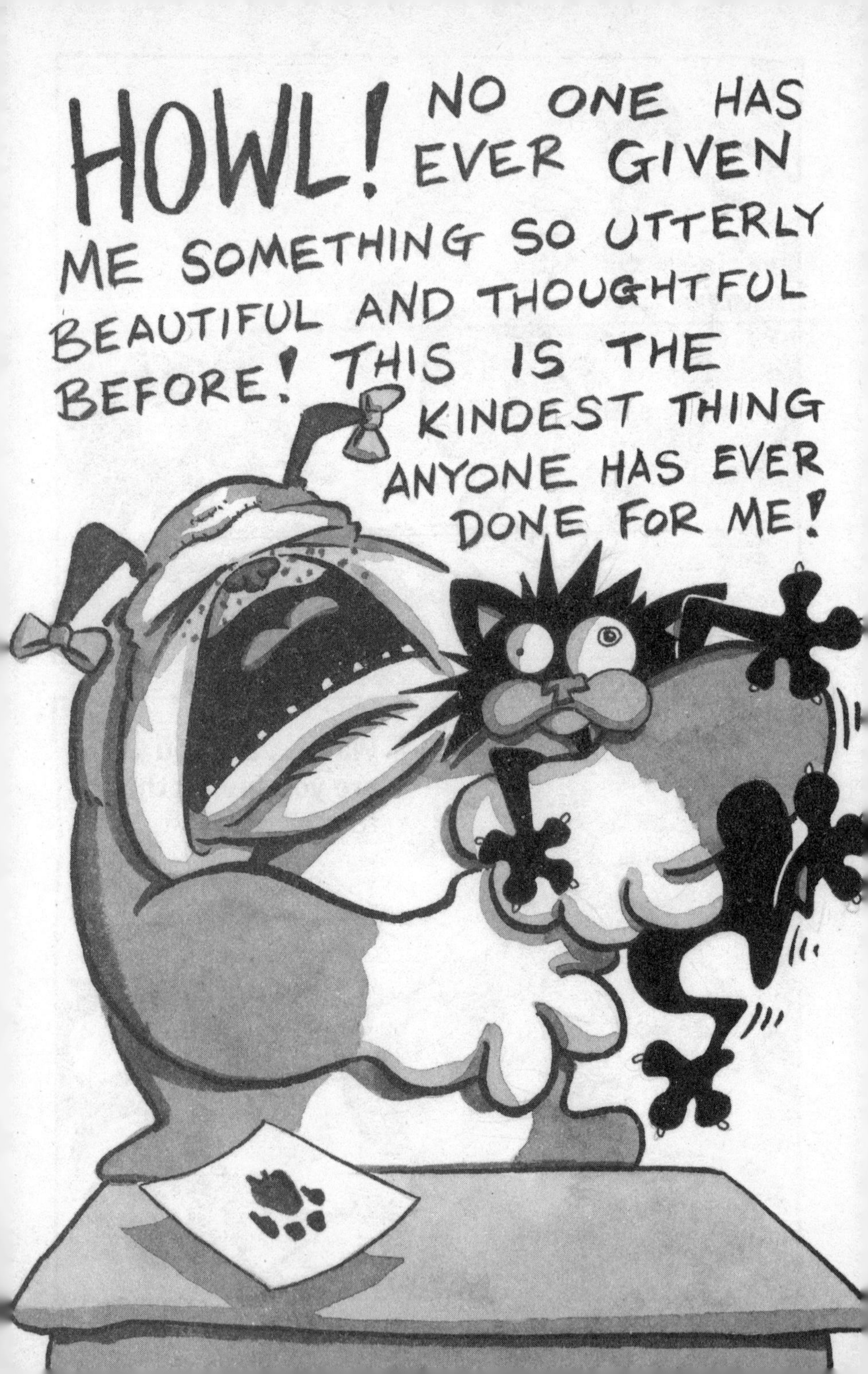
HOWL! NO ONE HAS EVER GIVEN ME SOMETHING SO UTTERLY BEAUTIFUL AND THOUGHTFUL BEFORE! THIS IS THE KINDEST THING ANYONE HAS EVER DONE FOR ME!

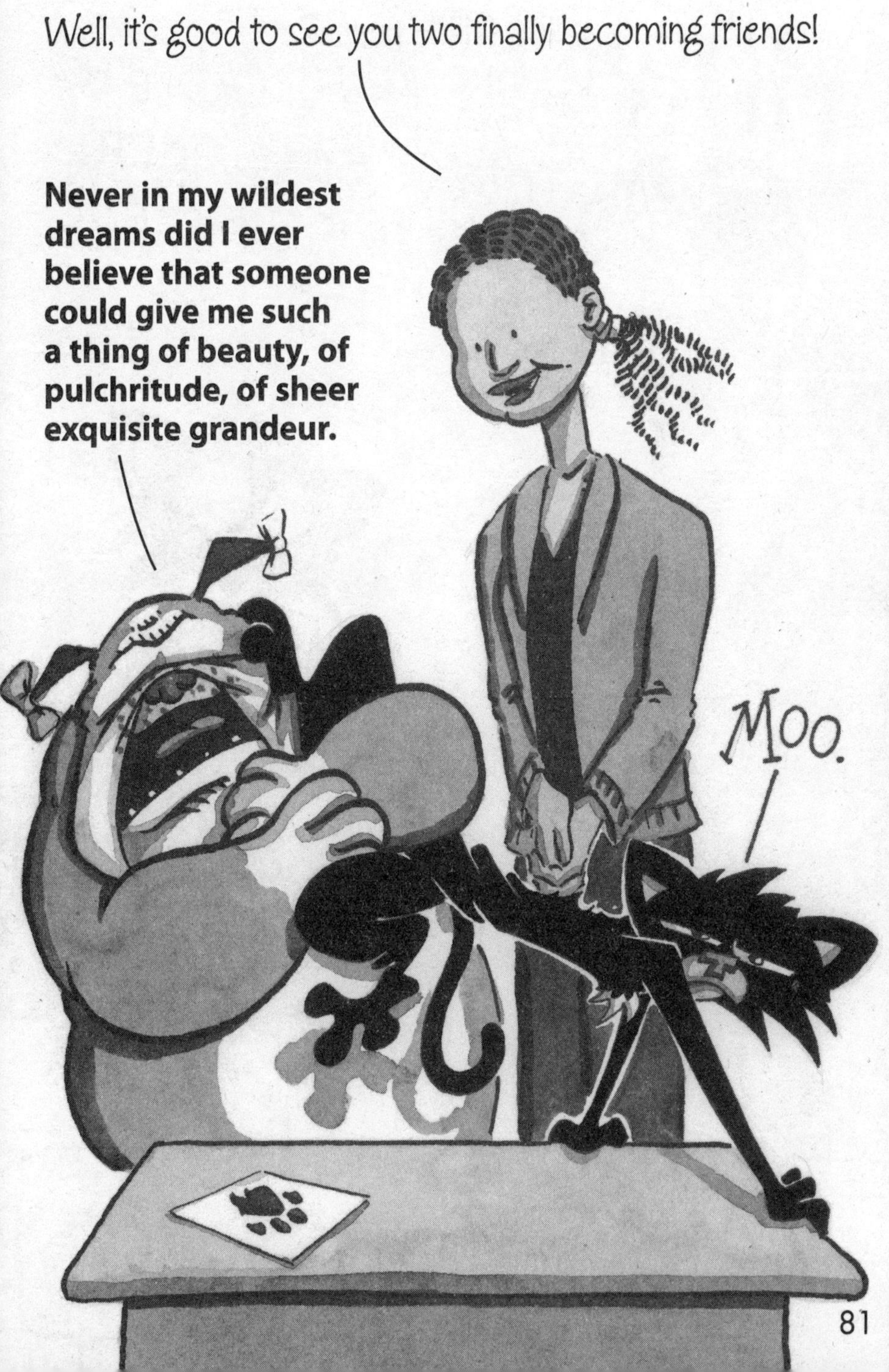
Well, it's good to see you two finally becoming friends!
Never in my wildest dreams did I ever believe that someone could give me such a thing of beauty, of pulchritude, of sheer exquisite grandeur.
Moo.

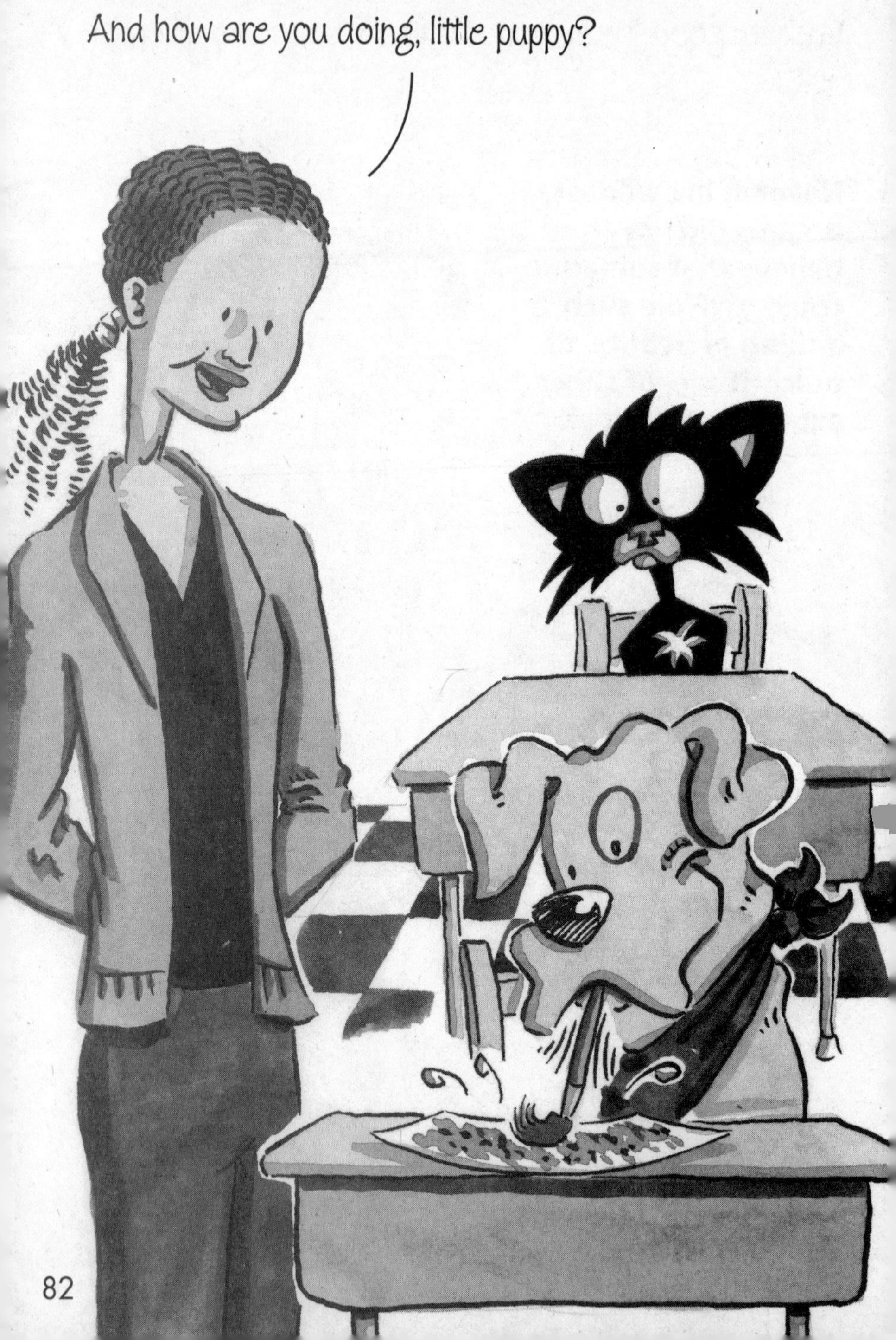
And how are you doing, little puppy?

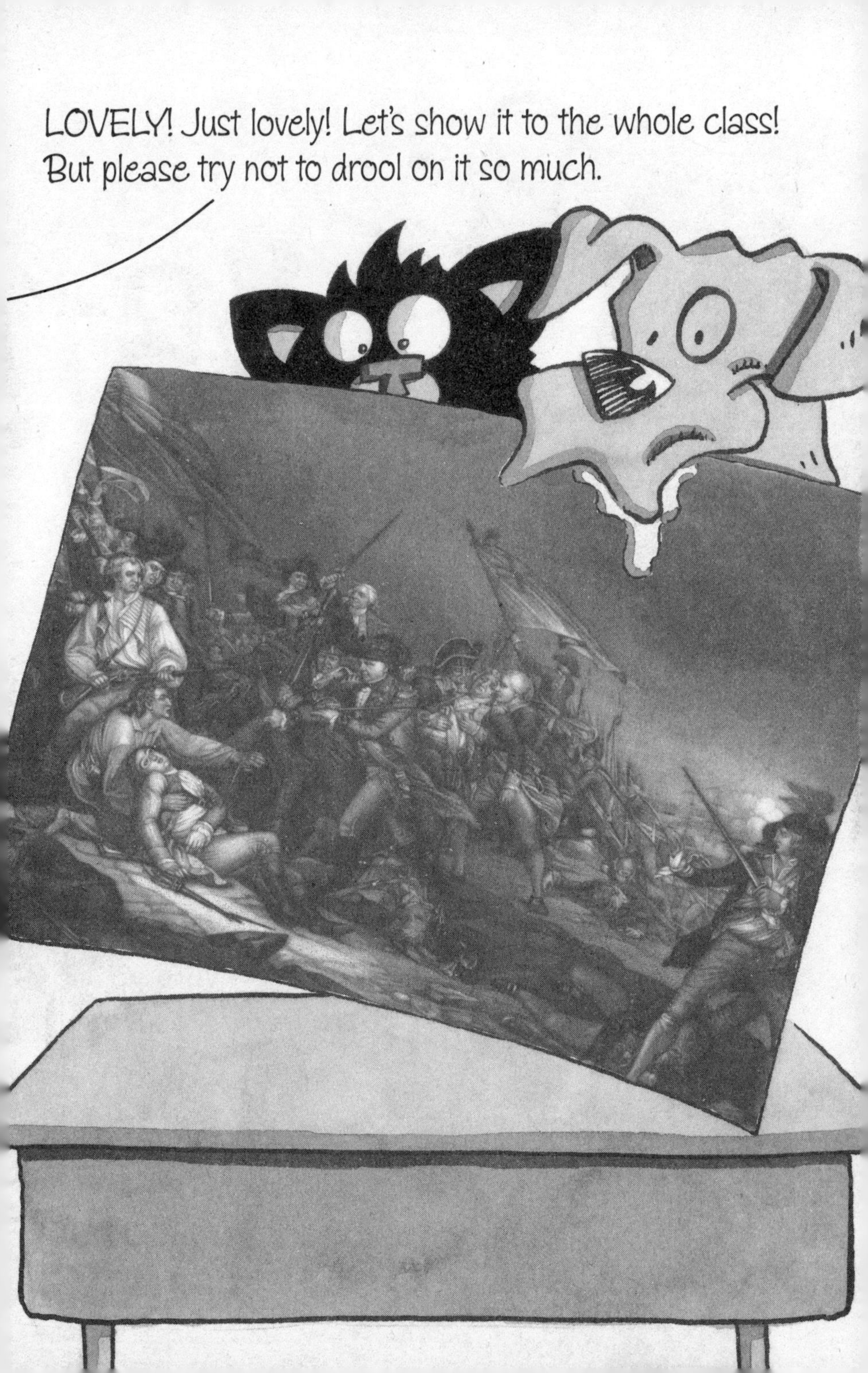
LOVELY! Just lovely! Let's show it to the whole class! But please try not to drool on it so much.

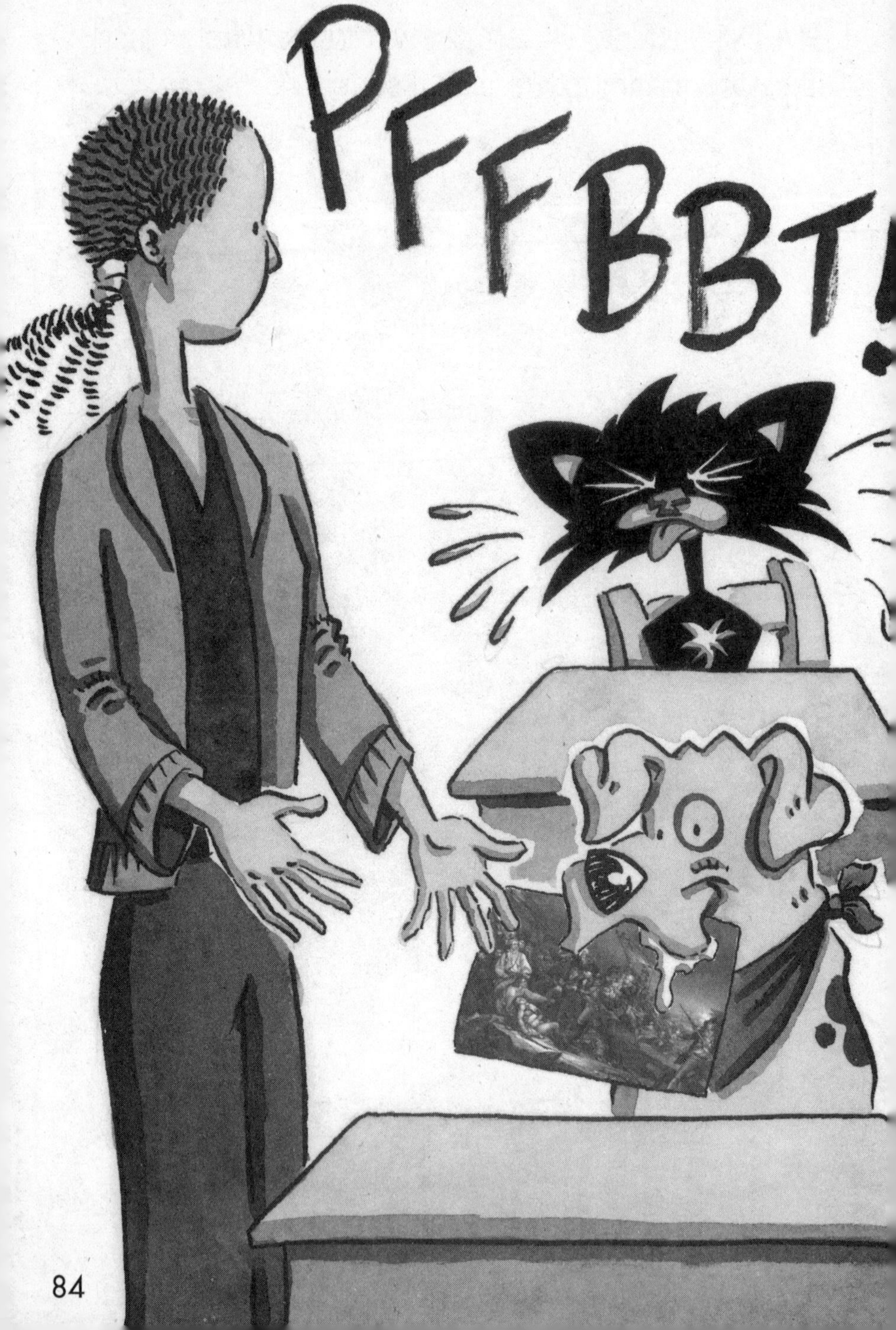
PFFBBT!

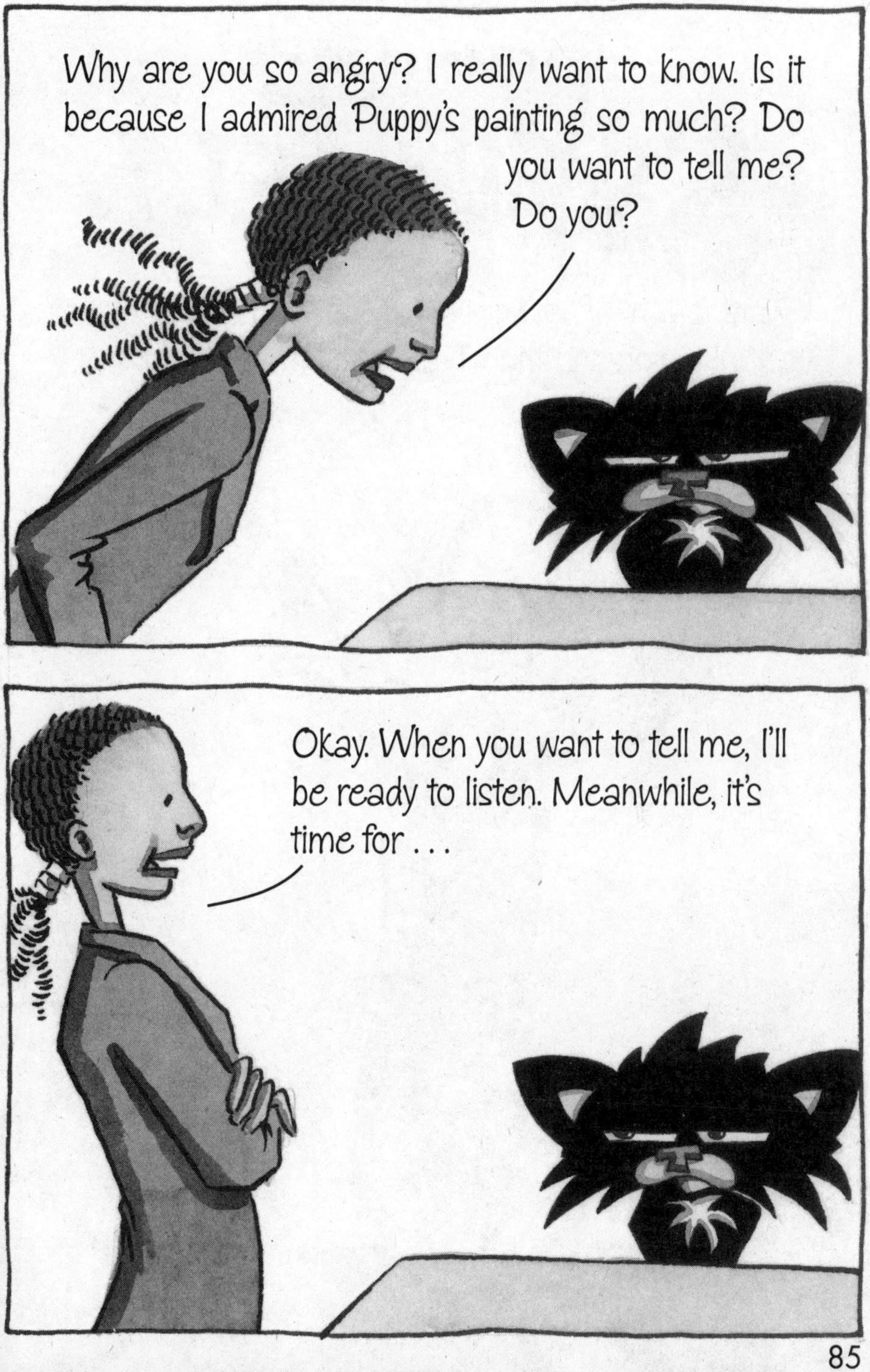
Why are you so angry? I really want to know. Is it because I admired Puppy's painting so much? Do you want to tell me? Do you?
Okay. When you want to tell me, I'll be ready to listen. Meanwhile, it's time for . . .

•CHAPTER SIX•

SHOW + TELL

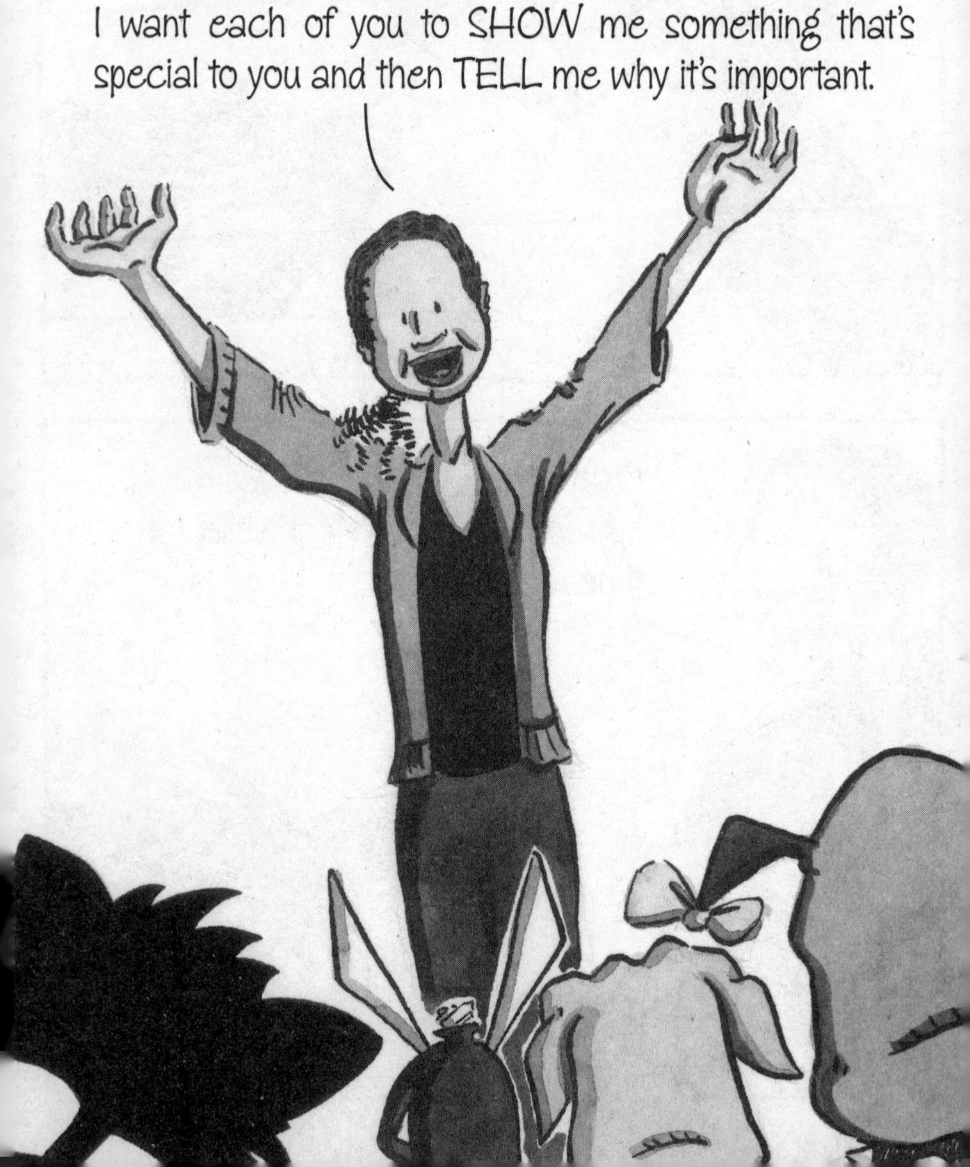
I want each of you to SHOW me something that's special to you and then TELL me why it's important.

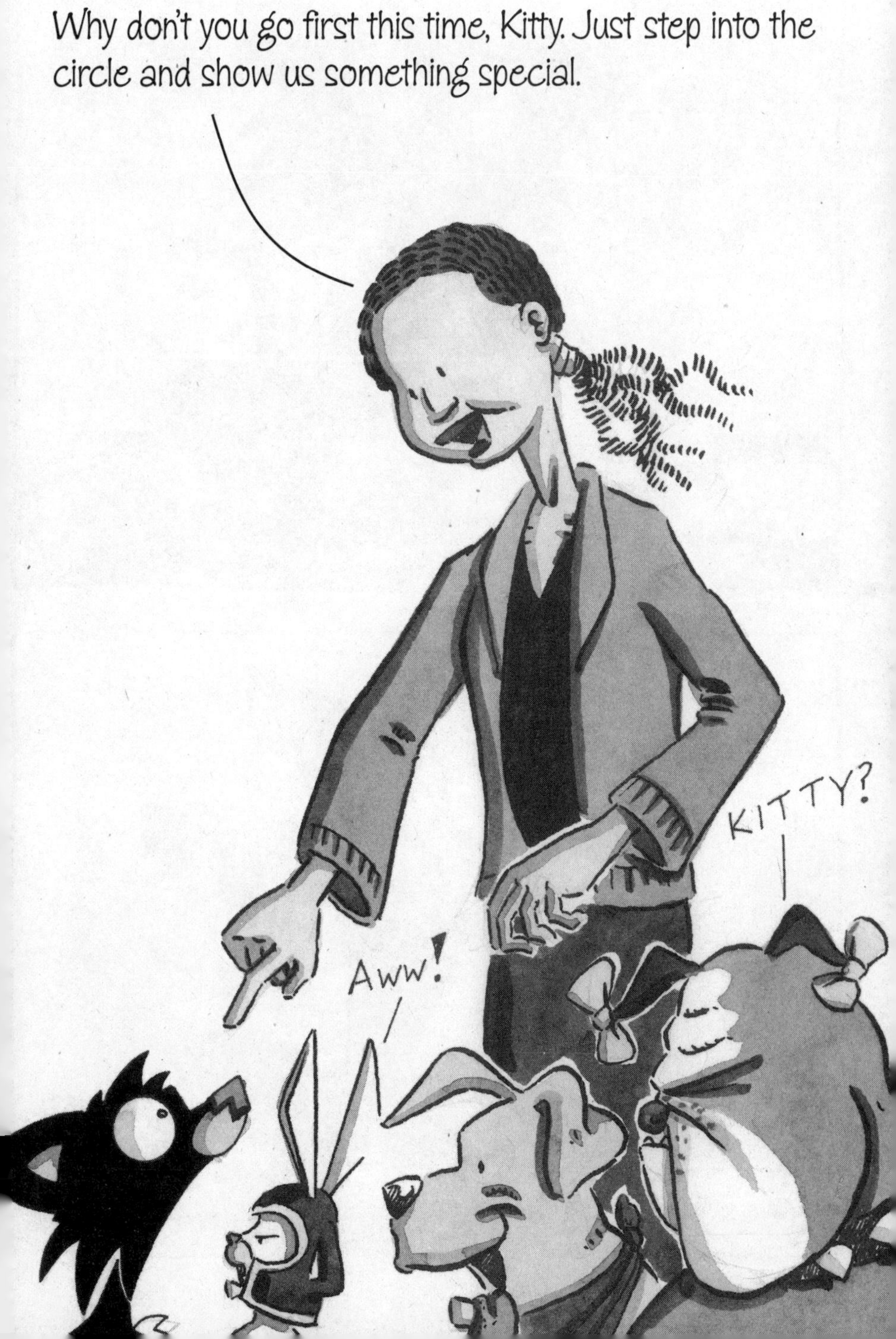
Why don't you go first this time, Kitty. Just step into the circle and show us something special.
KITTY?
AWW!

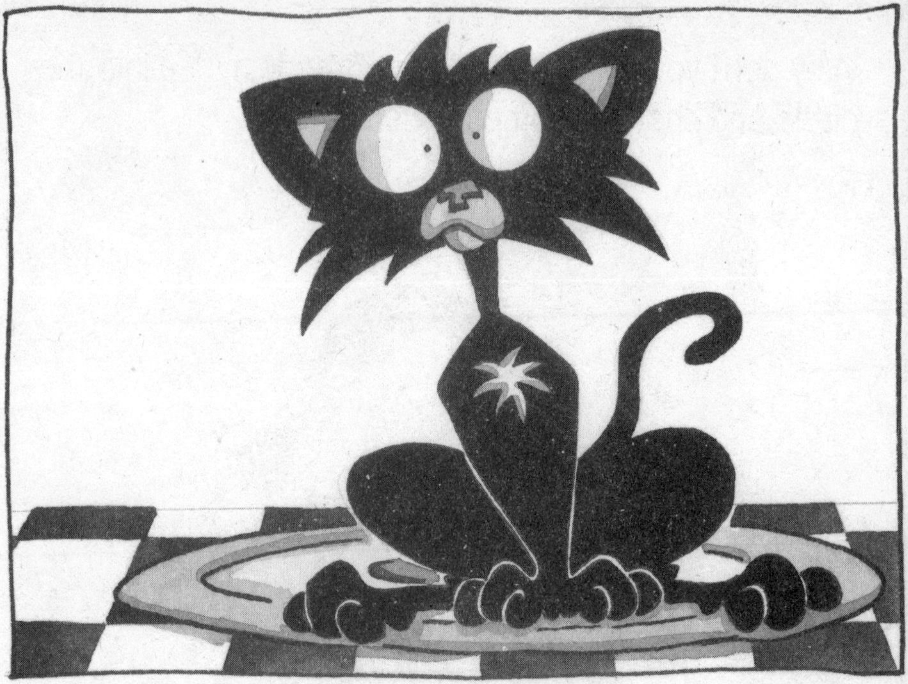

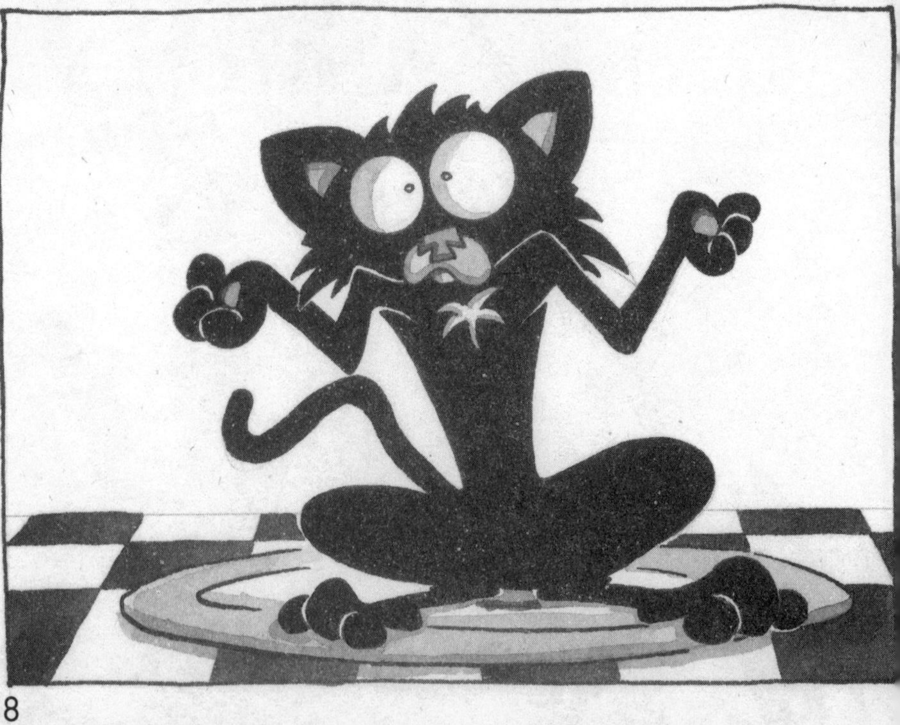

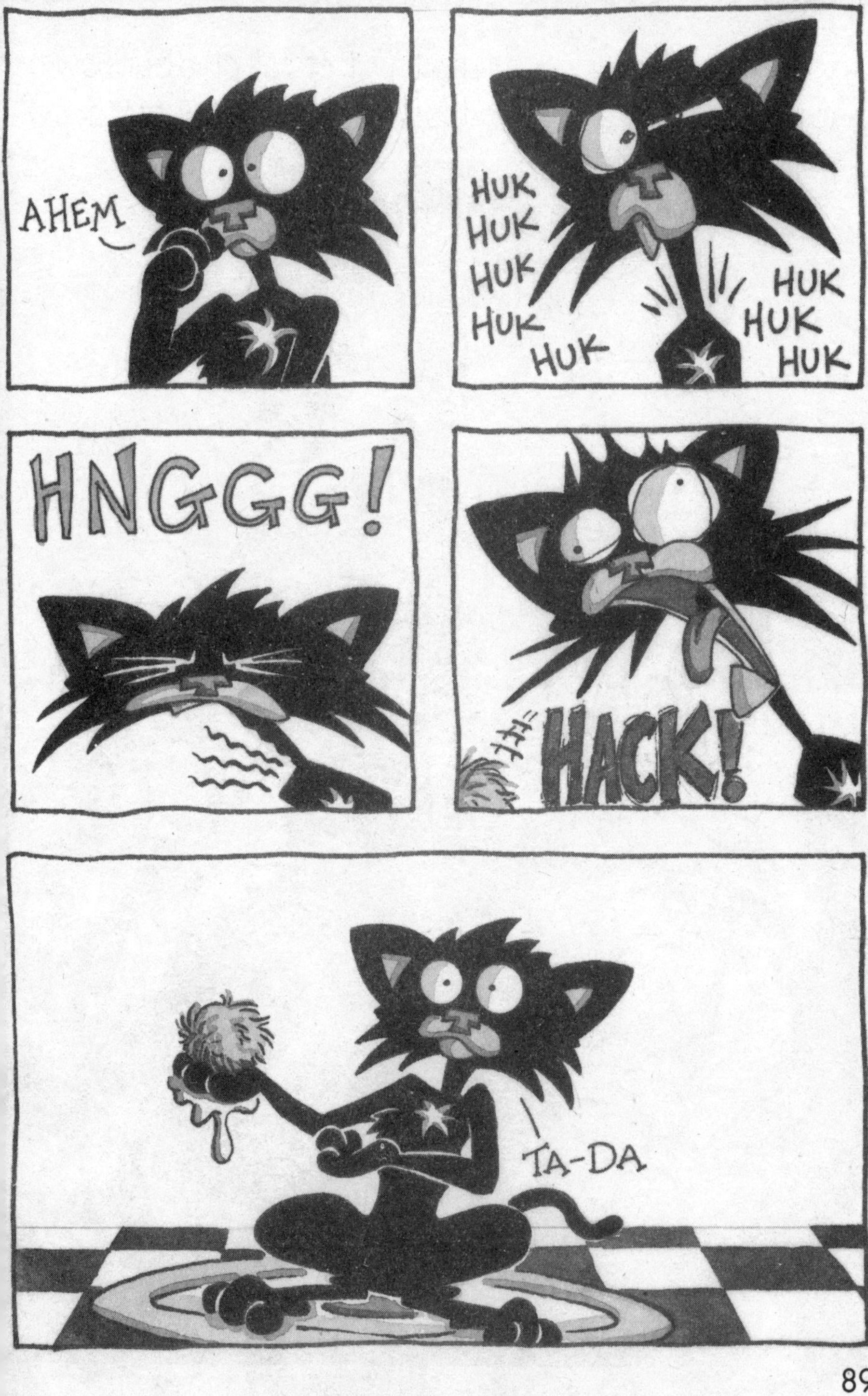
AHEM
HUK
HUK
HUK
HUK
HUK
HUK
HUK
HUK
HNGGG!
HACK!
TA-DA

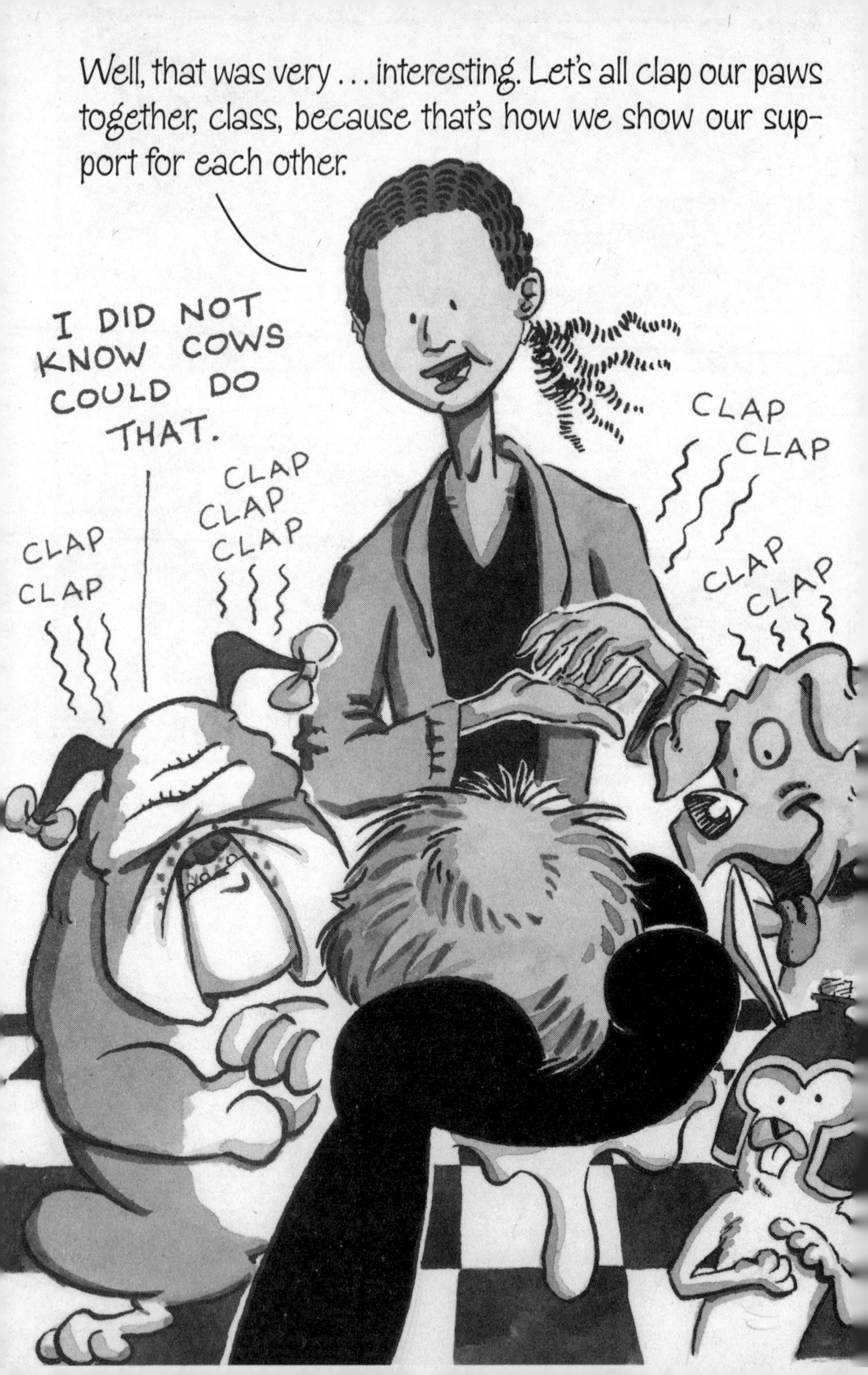
Well, that was very . . . interesting. Let's all clap our paws together, class, because that's how we show our support for each other.
I DID NOT KNOW COWS COULD DO THAT.
CLAP CLAP
CLAP CLAP CLAP
CLAP CLAP
CLAP CLAP

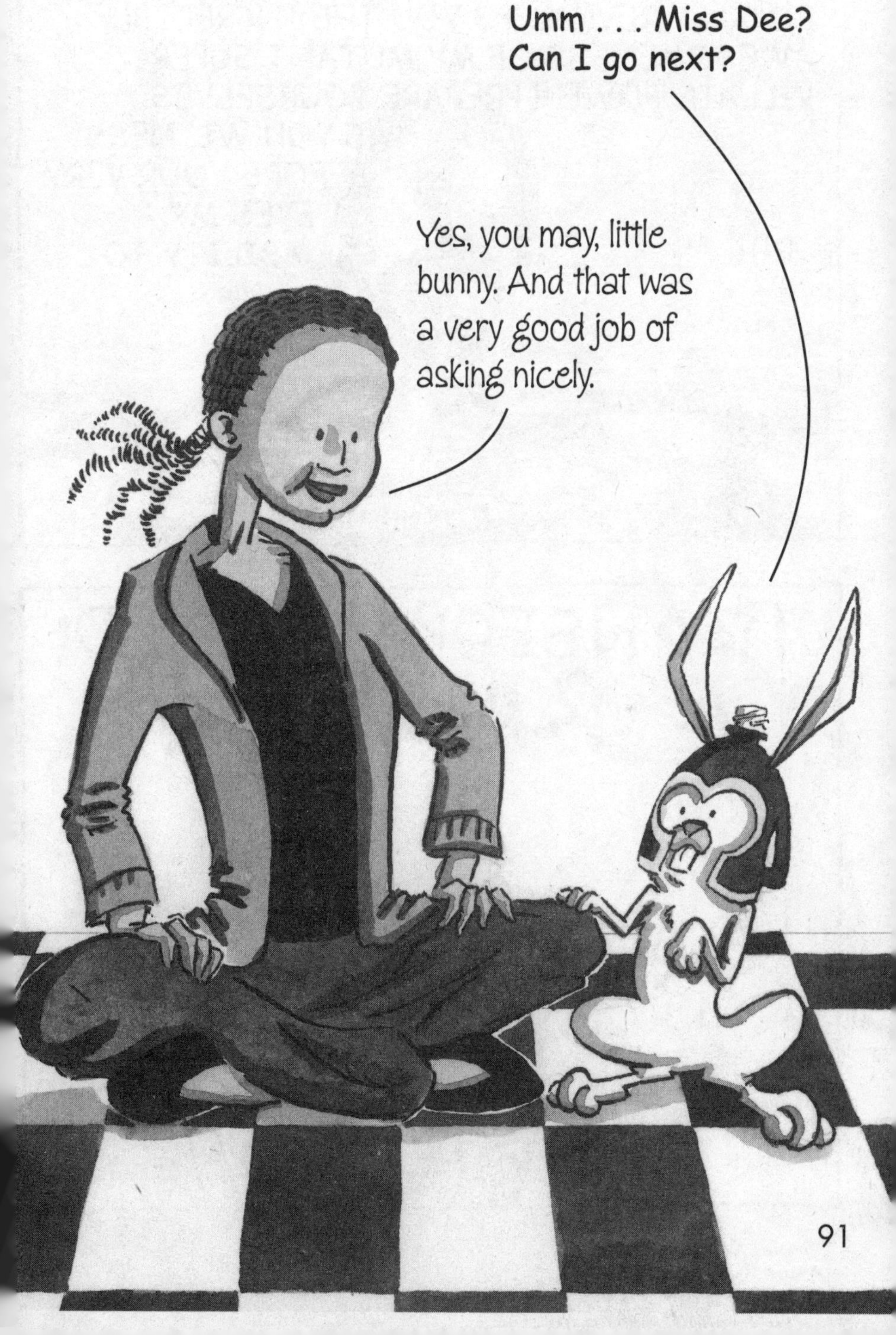
Umm . . . Miss Dee? Can I go next?
Yes, you may, little bunny. And that was a very good job of asking nicely.

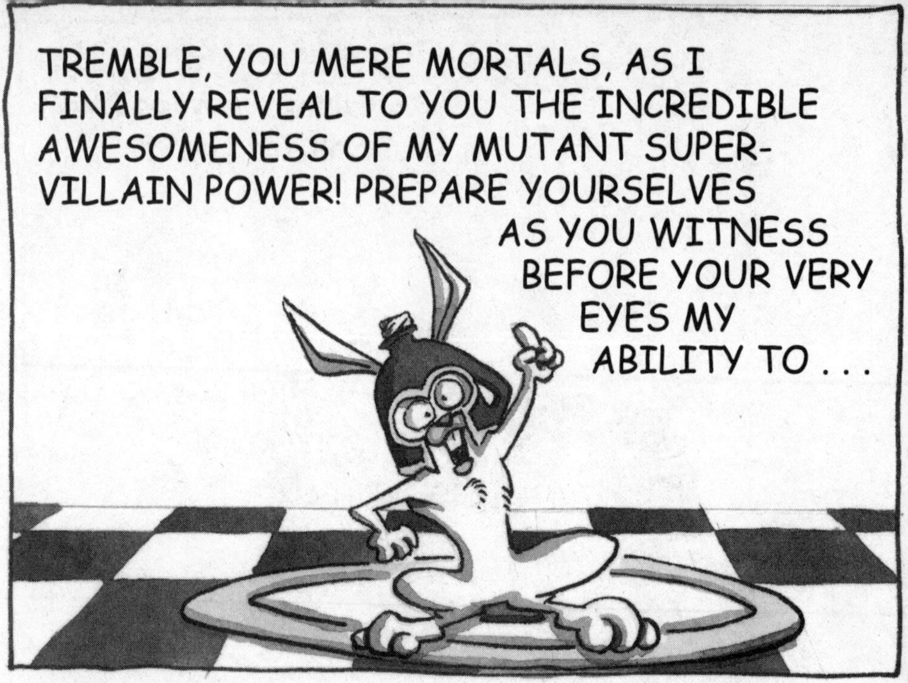
TREMBLE, YOU MERE MORTALS, AS I FINALLY REVEAL TO YOU THE INCREDIBLE AWESOMENESS OF MY MUTANT SUPER-VILLAIN POWER! PREPARE YOURSELVES AS YOU WITNESS BEFORE YOUR VERY EYES MY ABILITY TO . . .

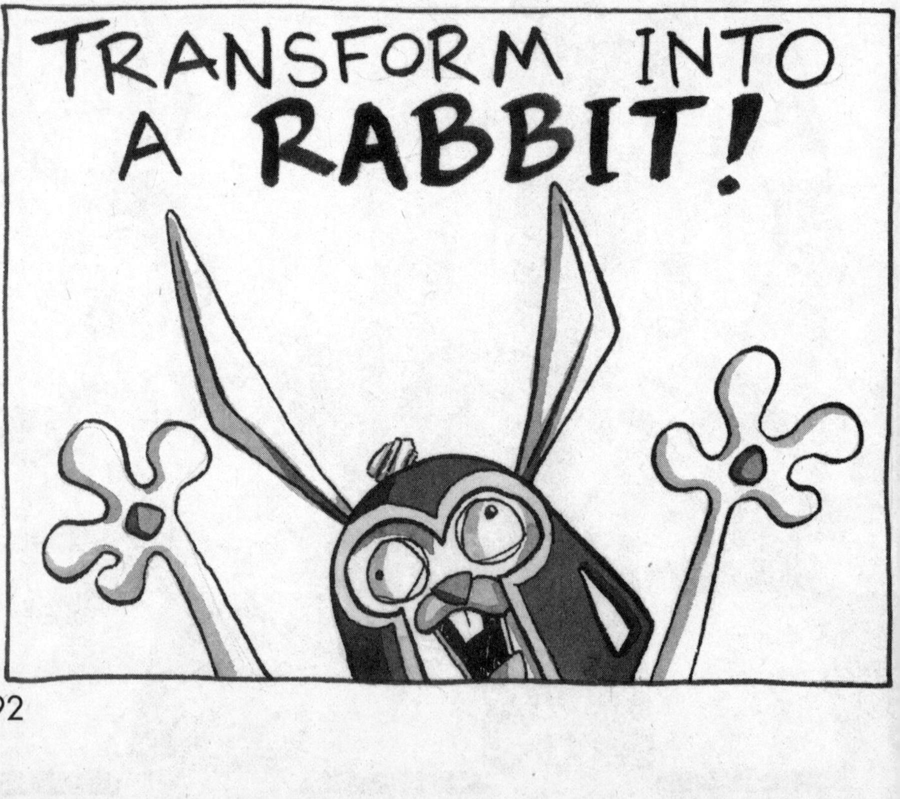
TRANSFORM INTO A RABBIT!

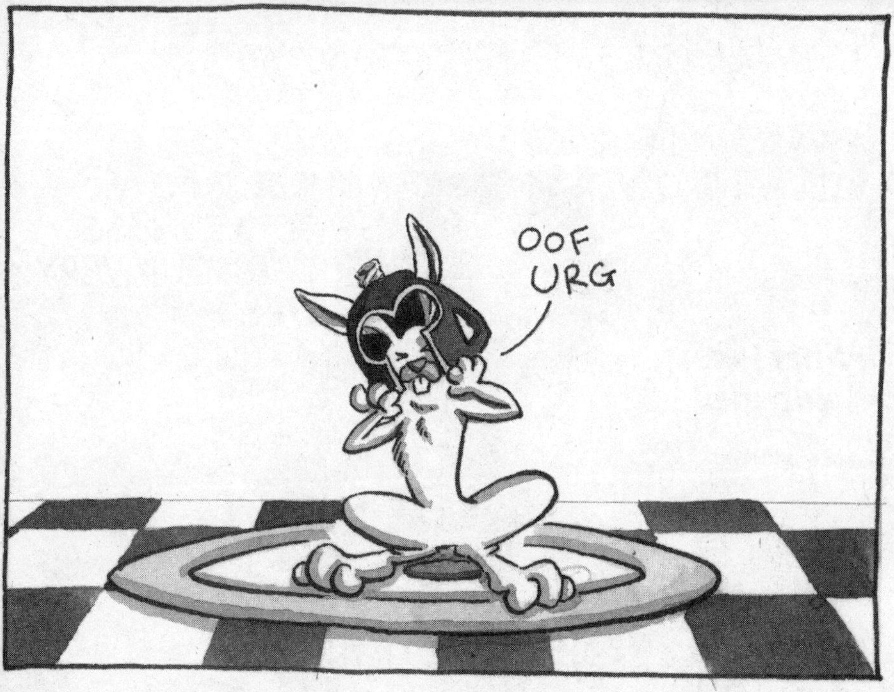
OOF
URG

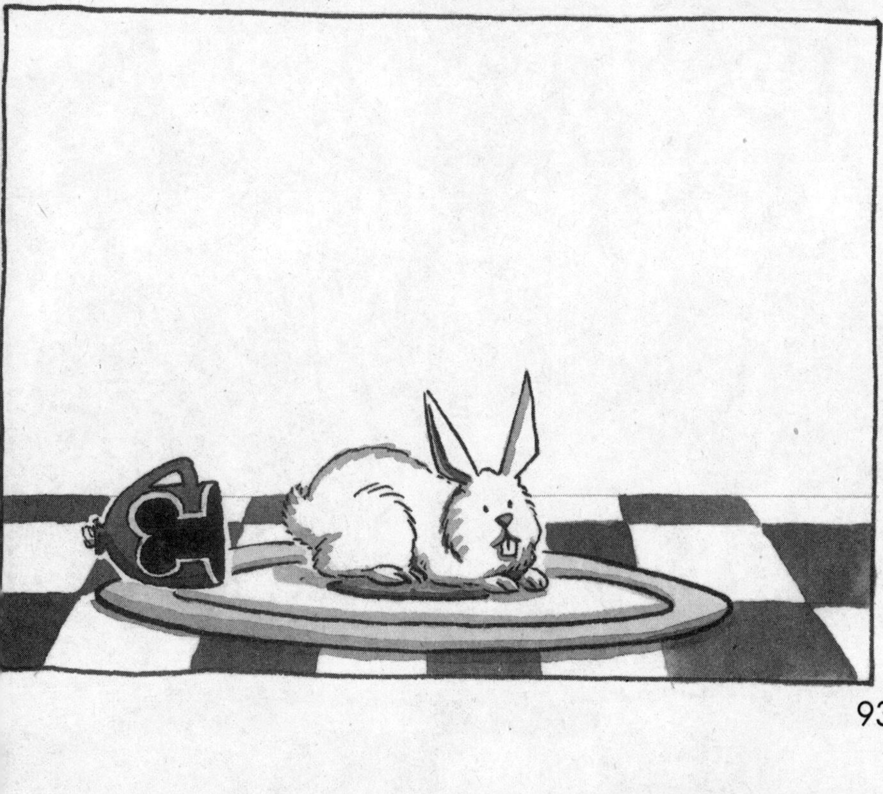

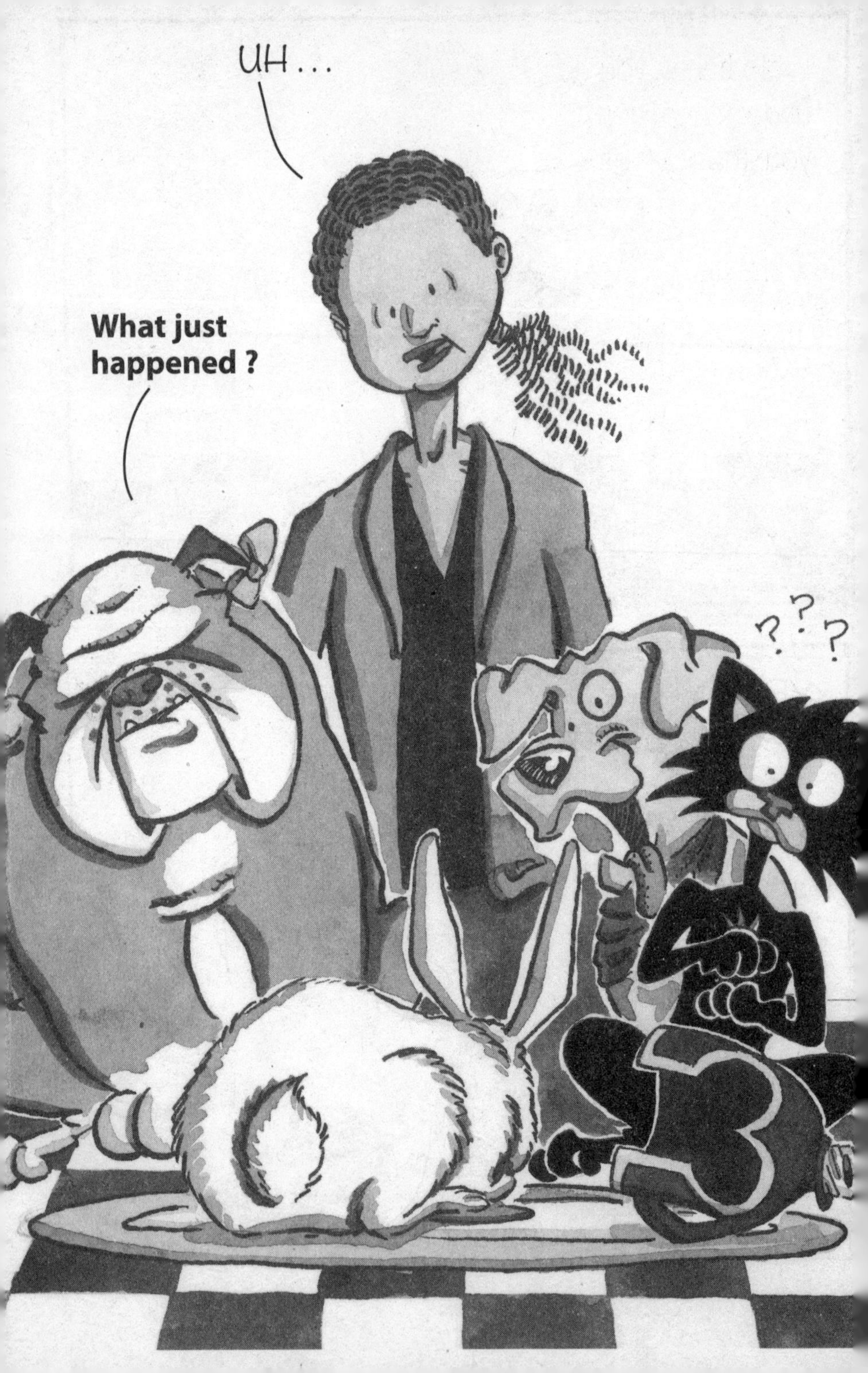
UH...
What just happened ?
???

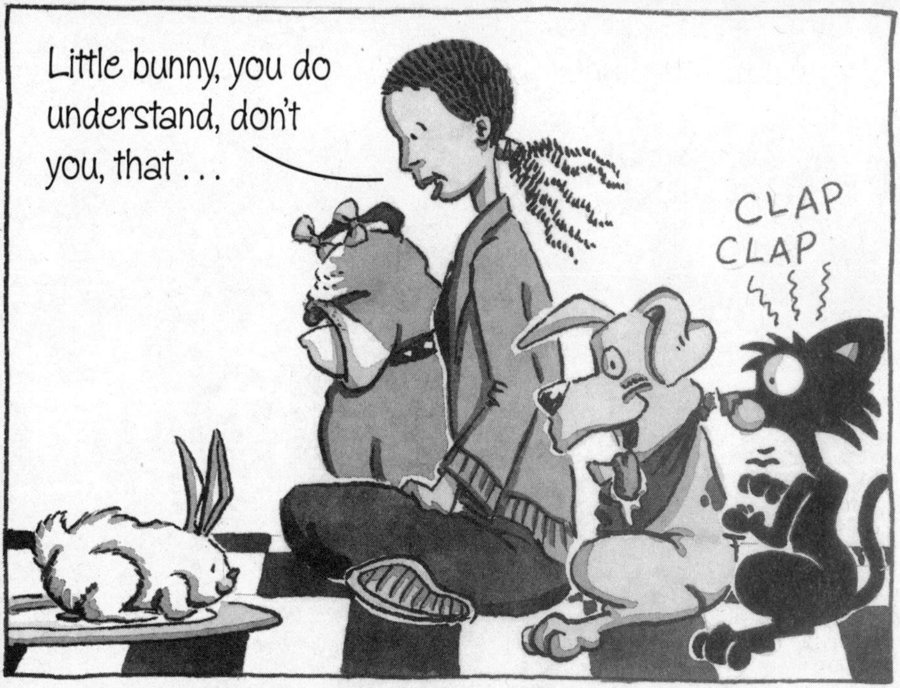
Little bunny, you do understand, don't you, that . . .
CLAP
CLAP

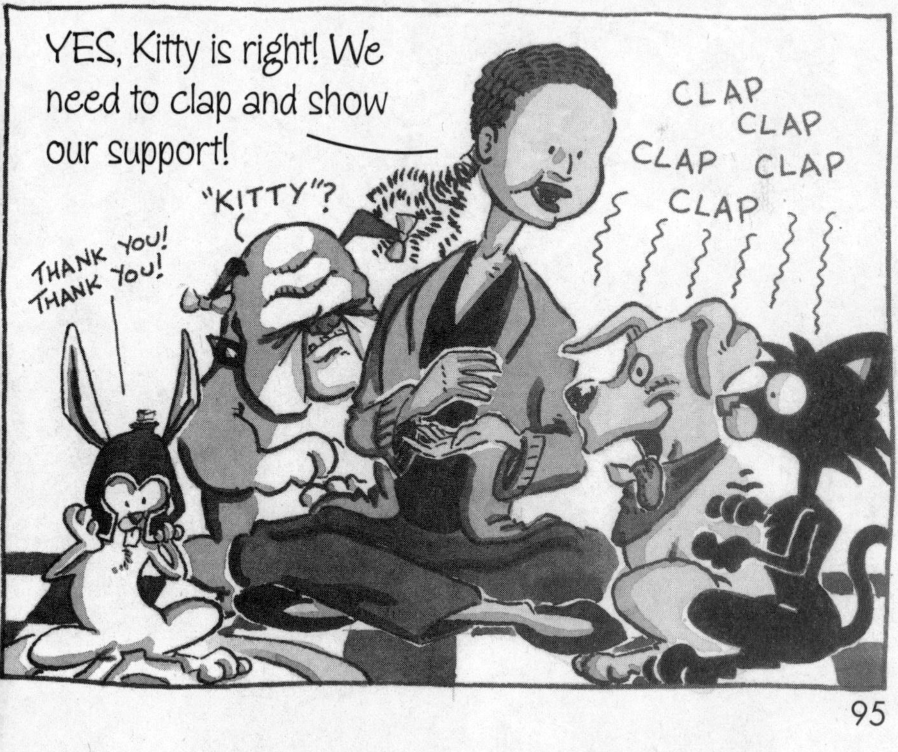
YES, Kitty is right! We need to clap and show our support!
"KITTY"?
THANK YOU!
THANK YOU!
CLAP
CLAP
CLAP
CLAP
CLAP

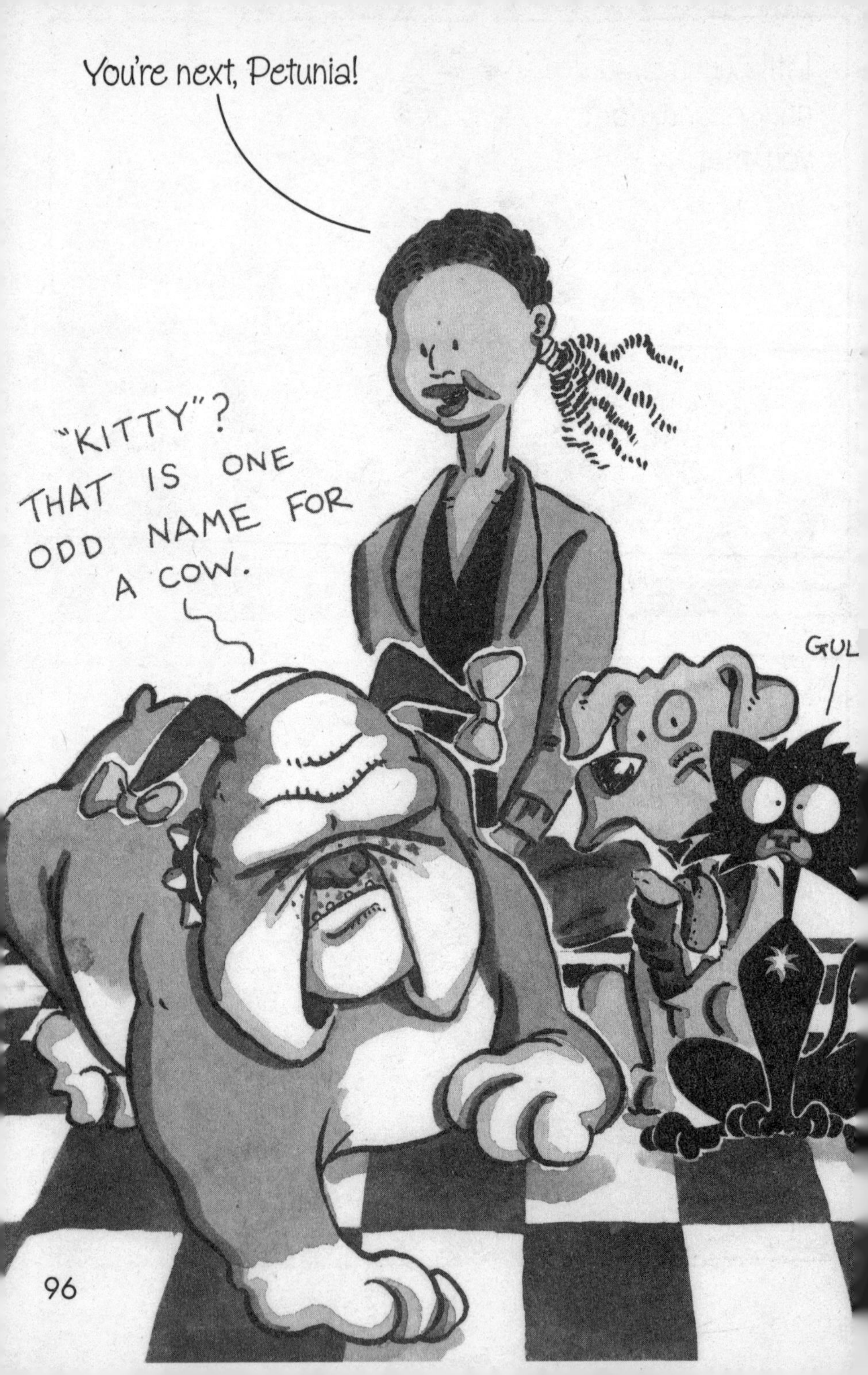
You're next, Petunia!
"KITTY"? THAT IS ONE ODD NAME FOR A COW.
GUL

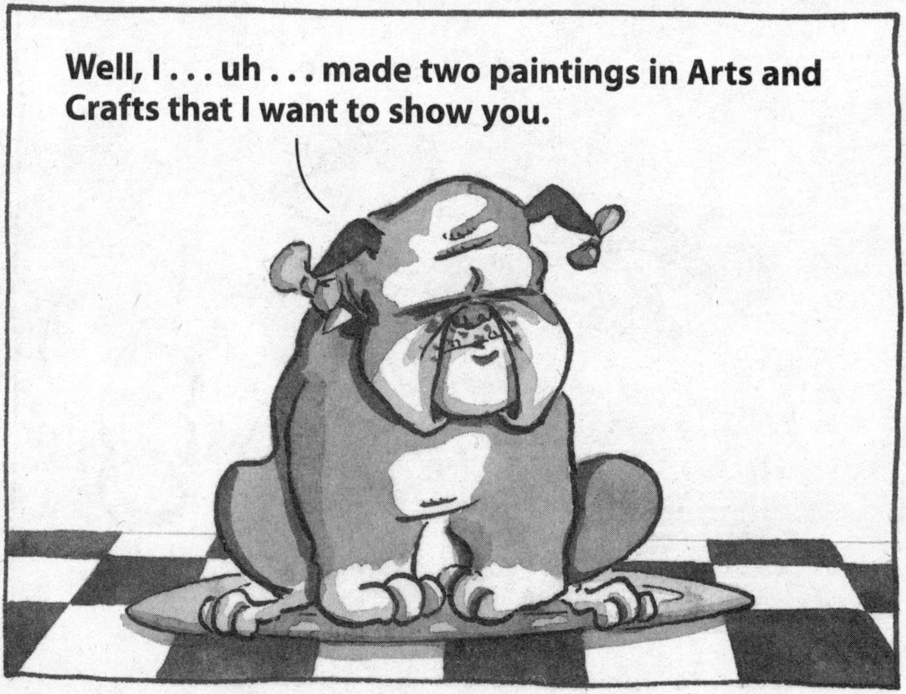
Well, I . . . uh . . . made two paintings in Arts and Crafts that I want to show you.

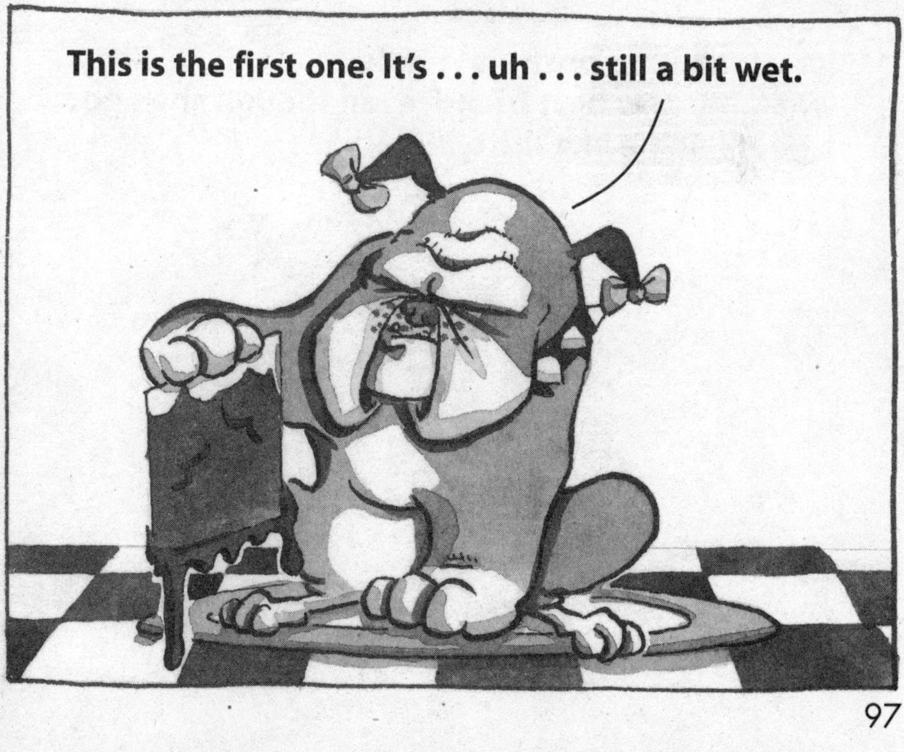
This is the first one. It's . . . uh . . . still a bit wet.

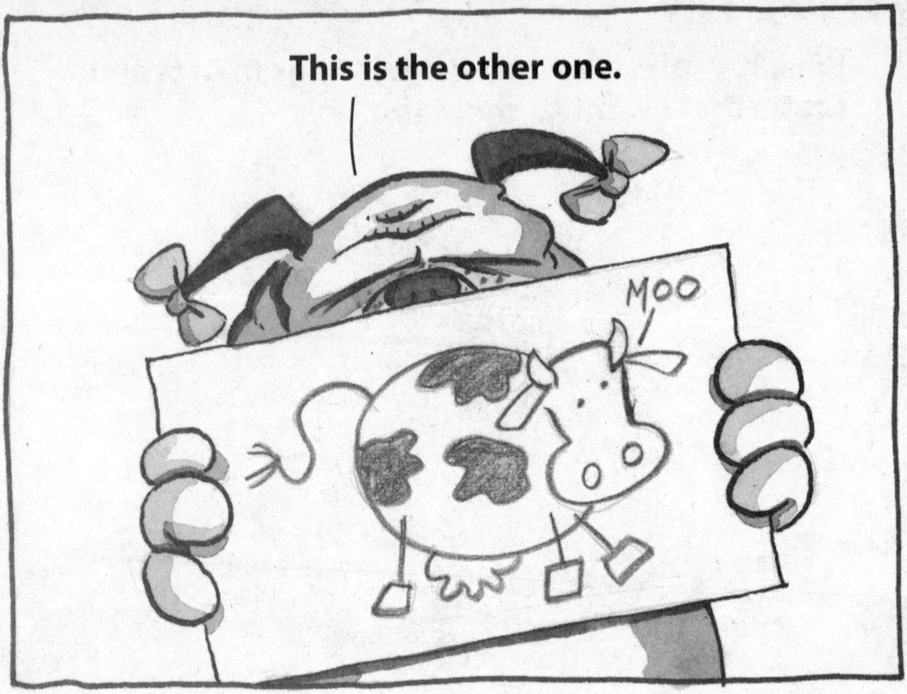
This is the other one.
MOO

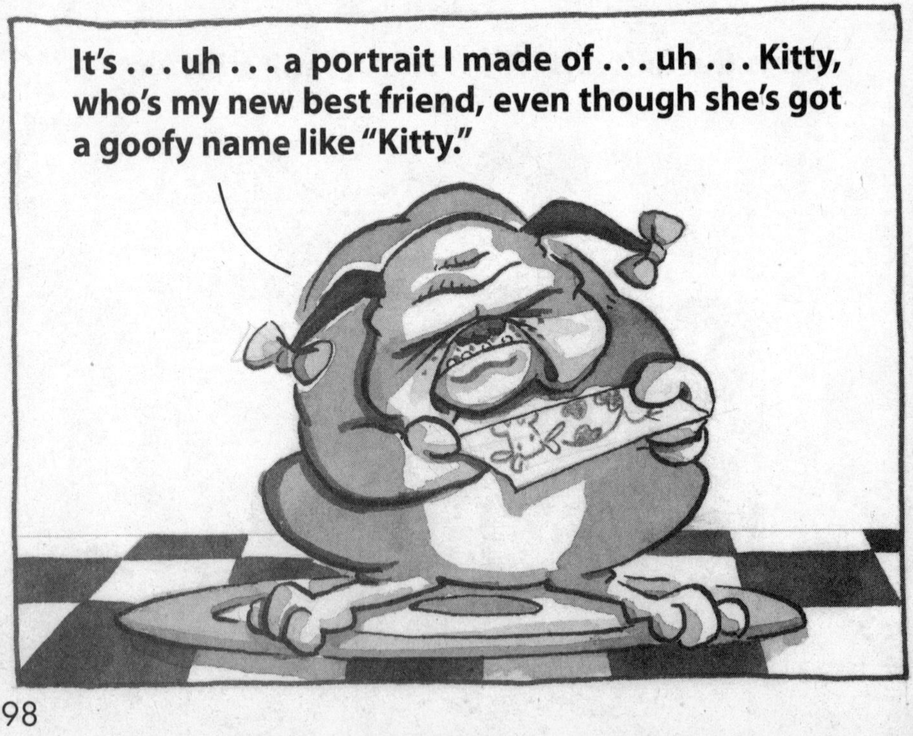
It's . . . uh . . . a portrait I made of . . . uh . . . Kitty, who's my new best friend, even though she's got a goofy name like "Kitty."

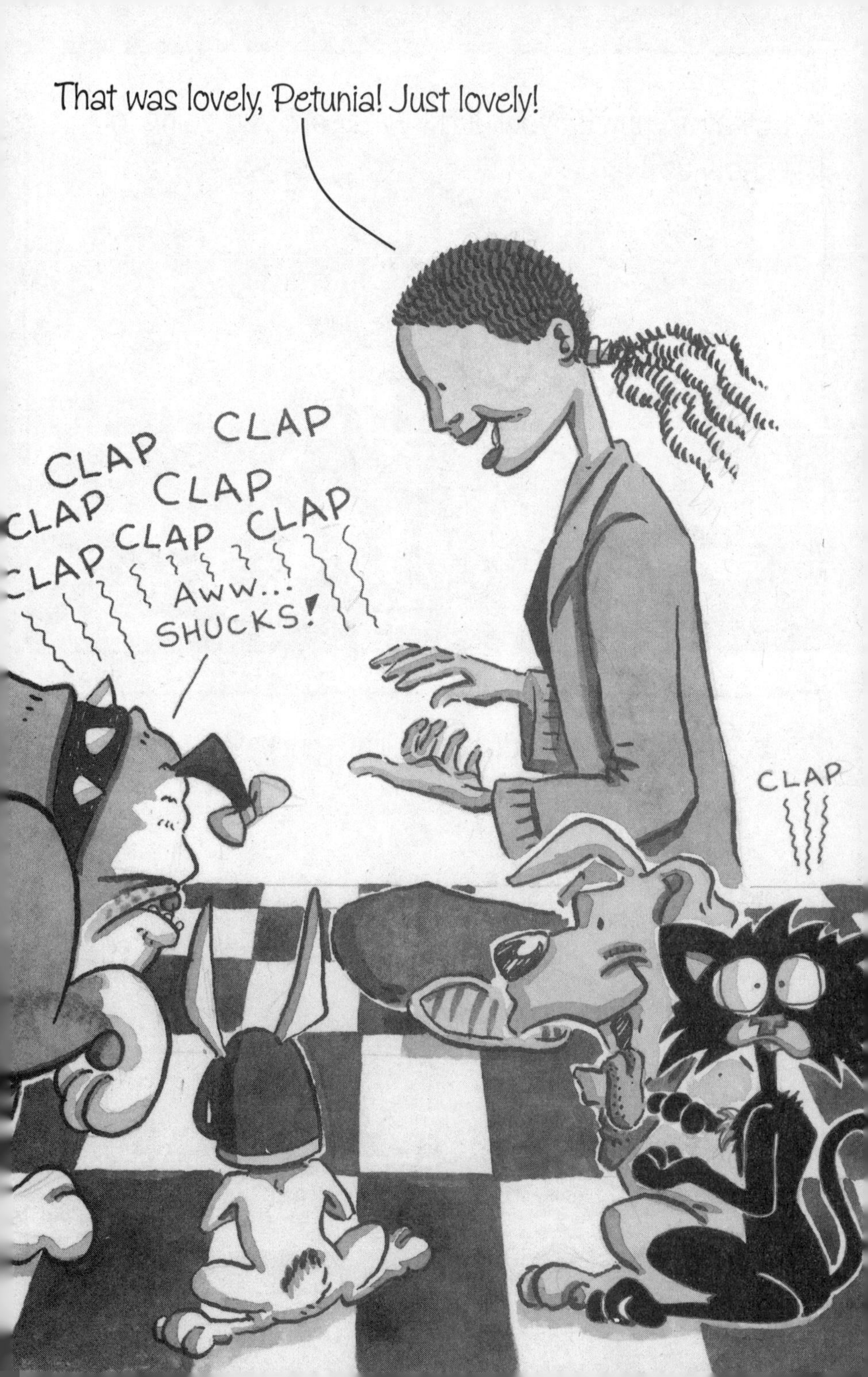
That was lovely, Petunia! Just lovely!
CLAP CLAP
CLAP CLAP
CLAP CLAP CLAP
CLAP
AWW... SHUCKS!
CLAP

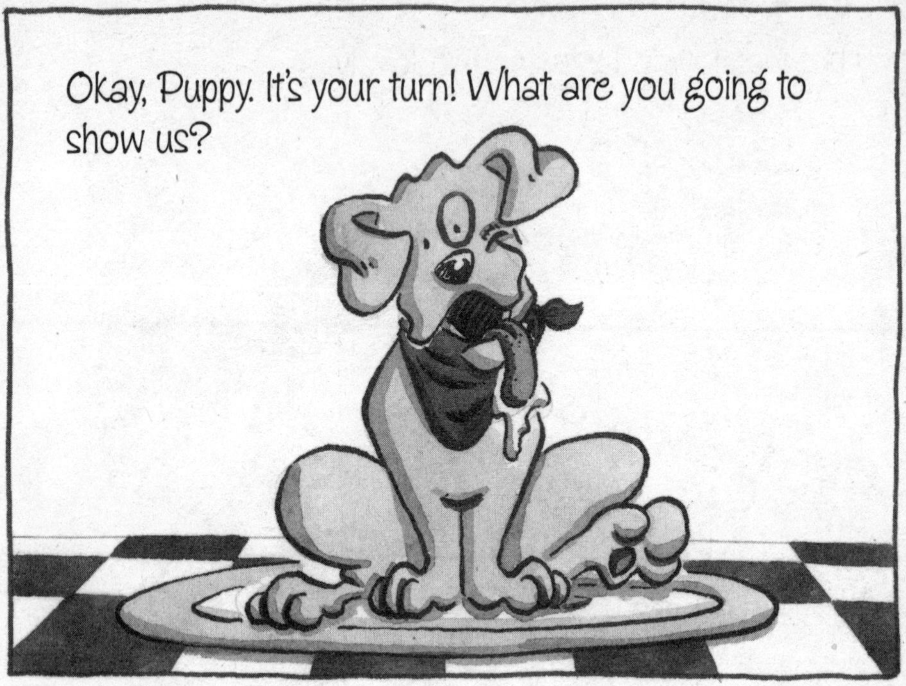
Okay, Puppy. It's your turn! What are you going to show us?

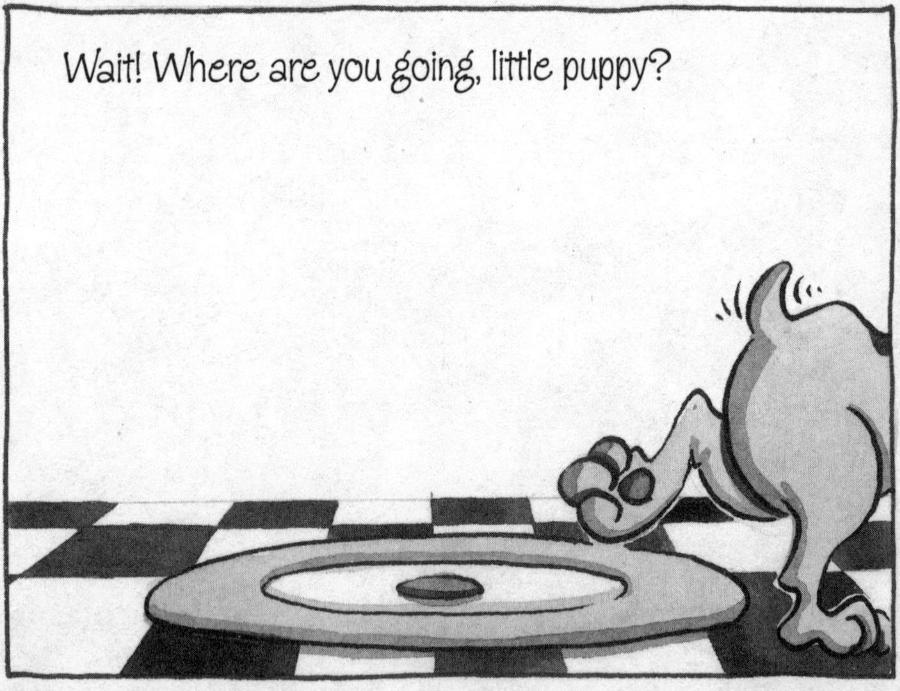
Wait! Where are you going, little puppy?

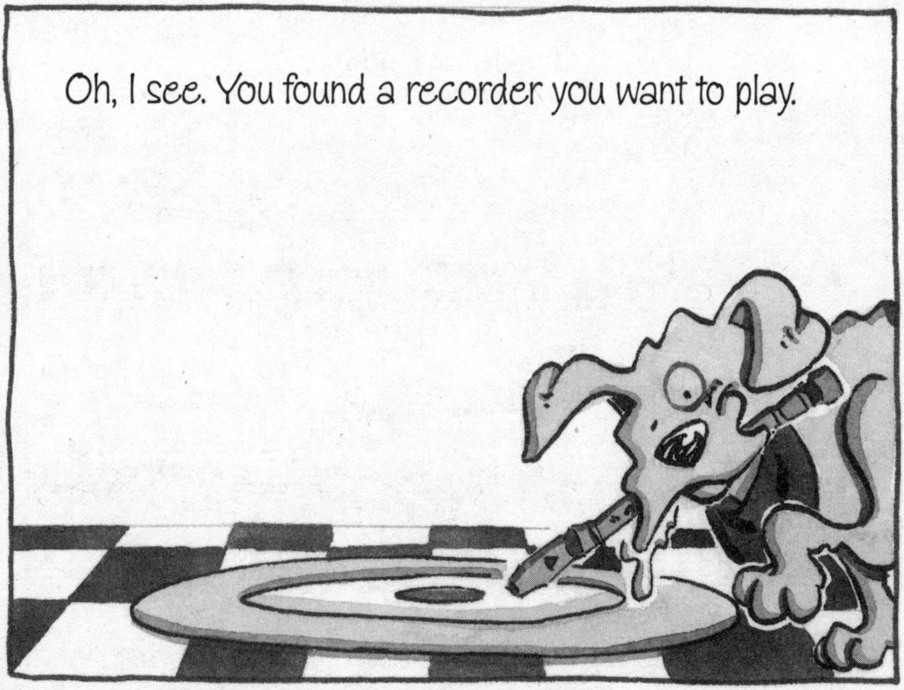
Oh, I see. You found a recorder you want to play.

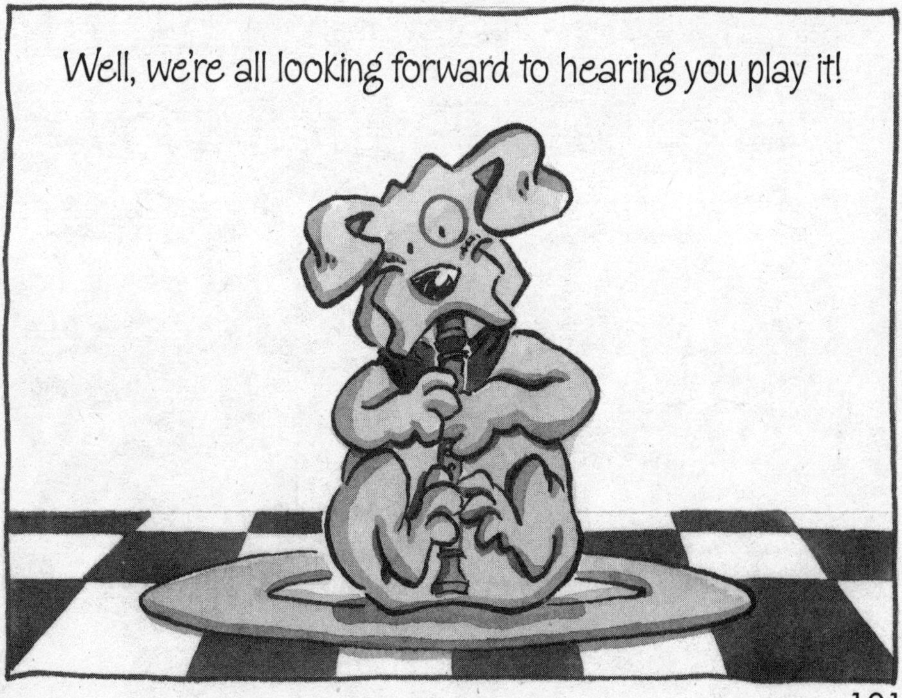
Well, we're all looking forward to hearing you play it!

Partita in a minor

for Solo Flute

Allemande

J. S. Bach
BWV 1013

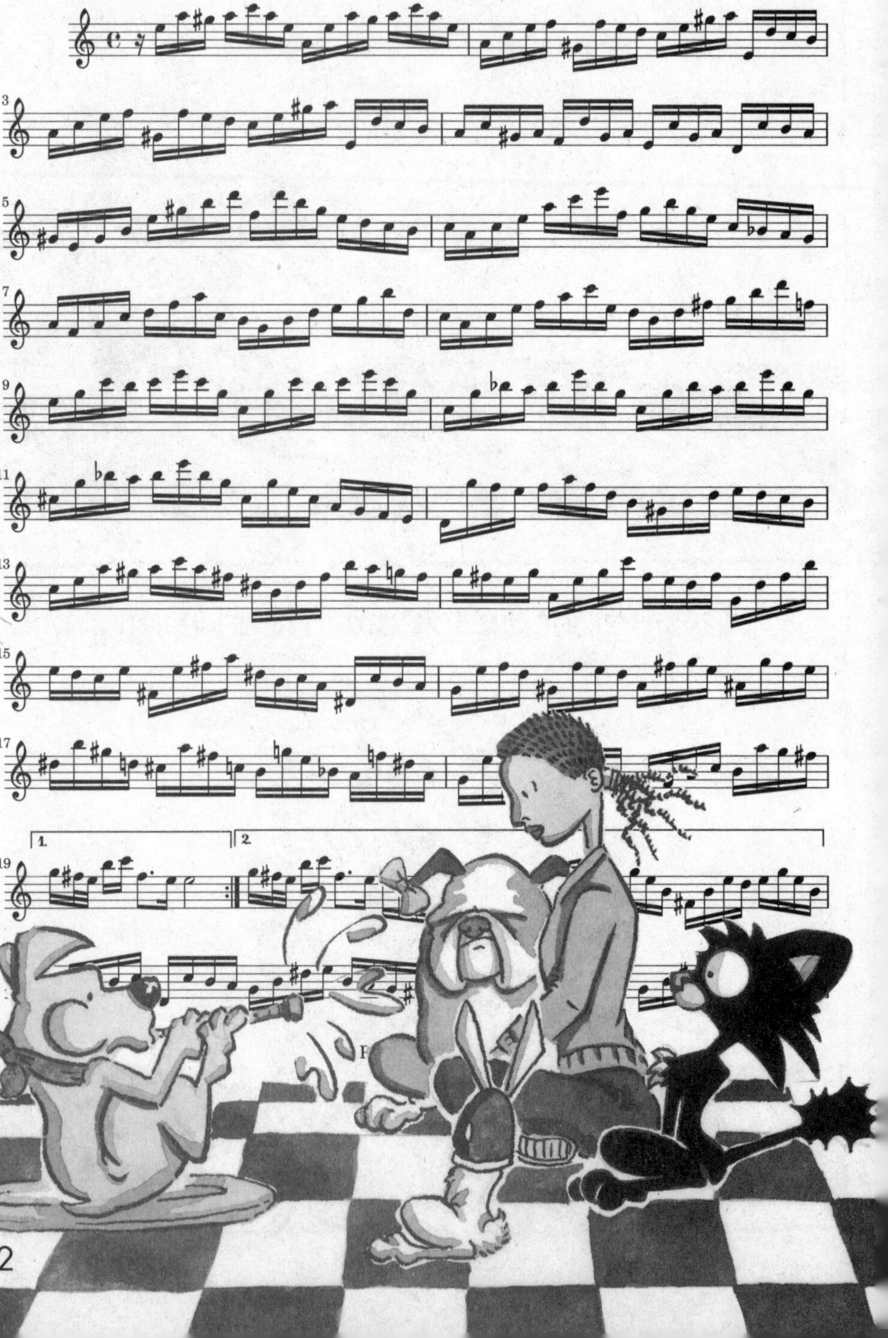

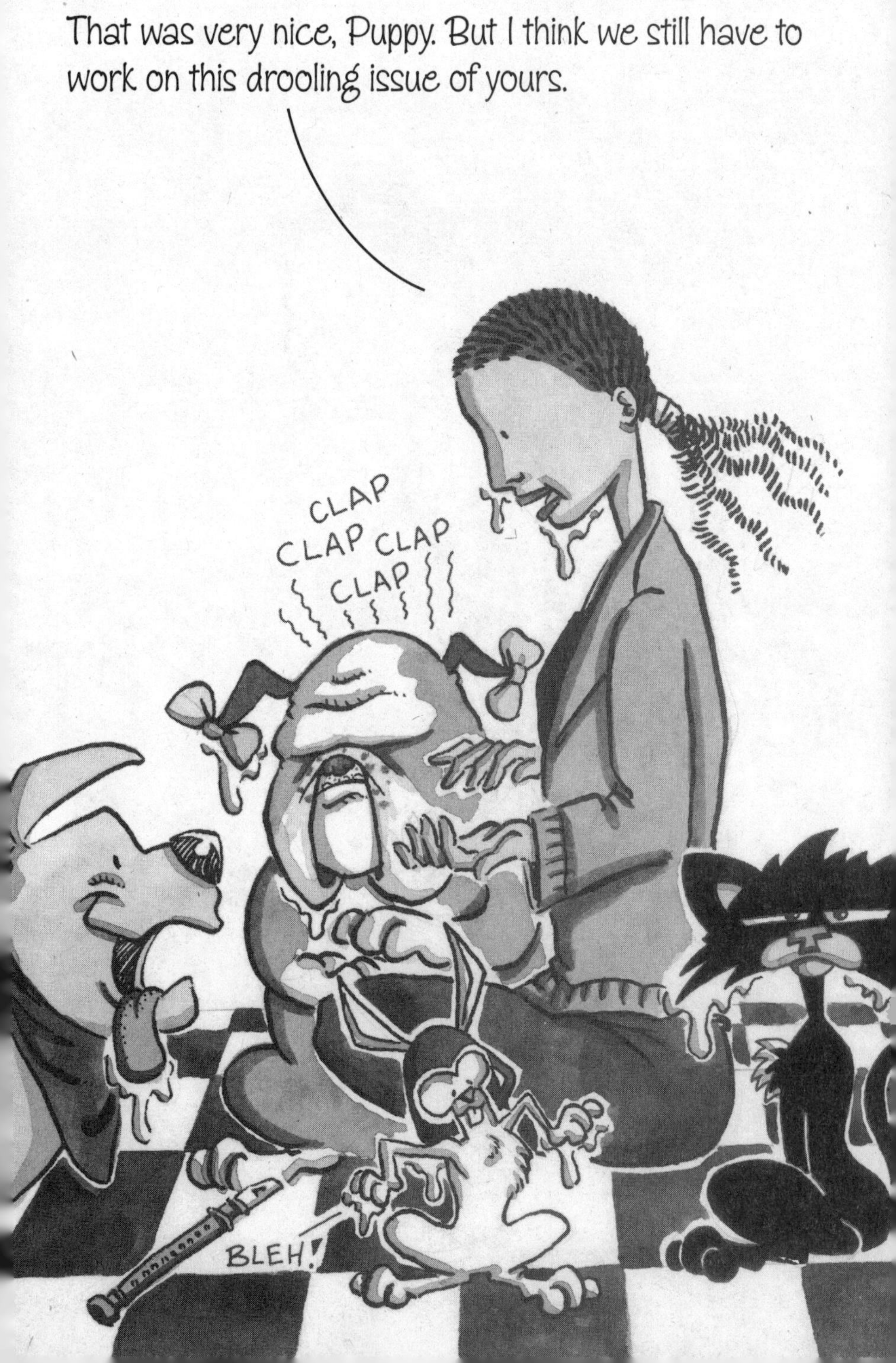
That was very nice, Puppy. But I think we still have to work on this drooling issue of yours.
CLAP
CLAP CLAP
CLAP
BLEH!

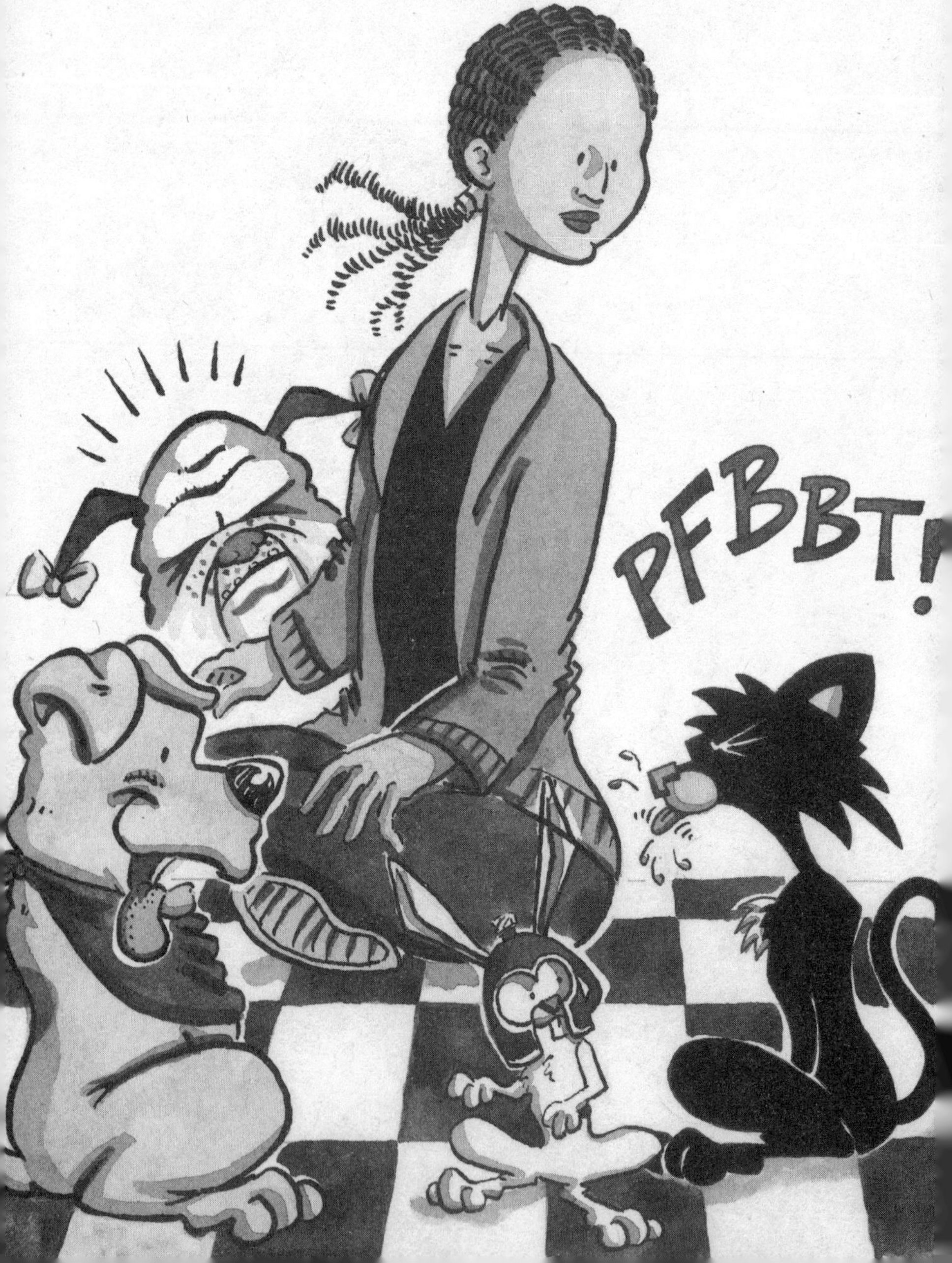
PFBBT!

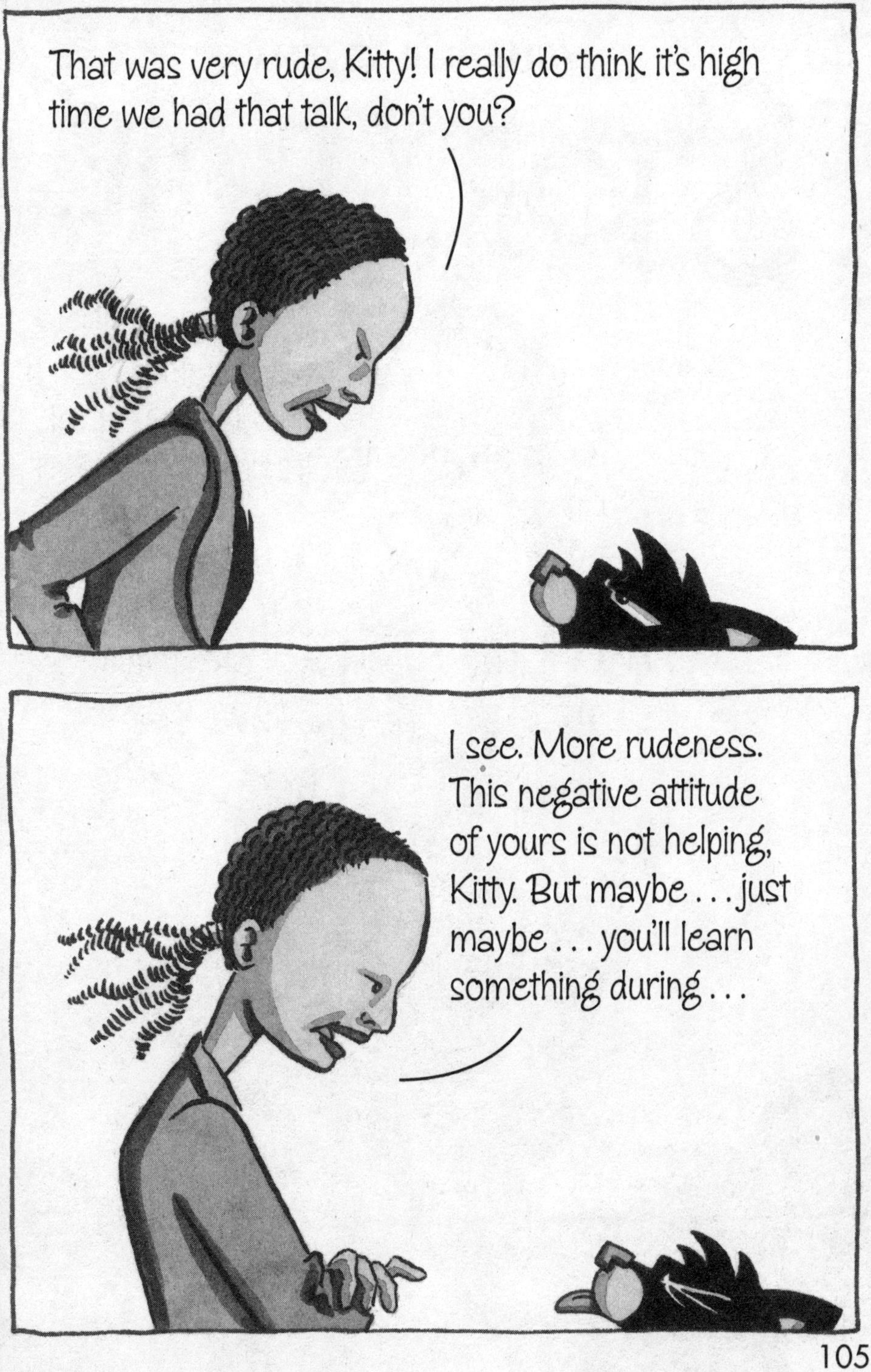
That was very rude, Kitty! I really do think it's high time we had that talk, don't you?
I see. More rudeness. This negative attitude of yours is not helping, Kitty. But maybe . . . just maybe . . . you'll learn something during . . .

•CHAPTER SEVEN•

STORYTIME

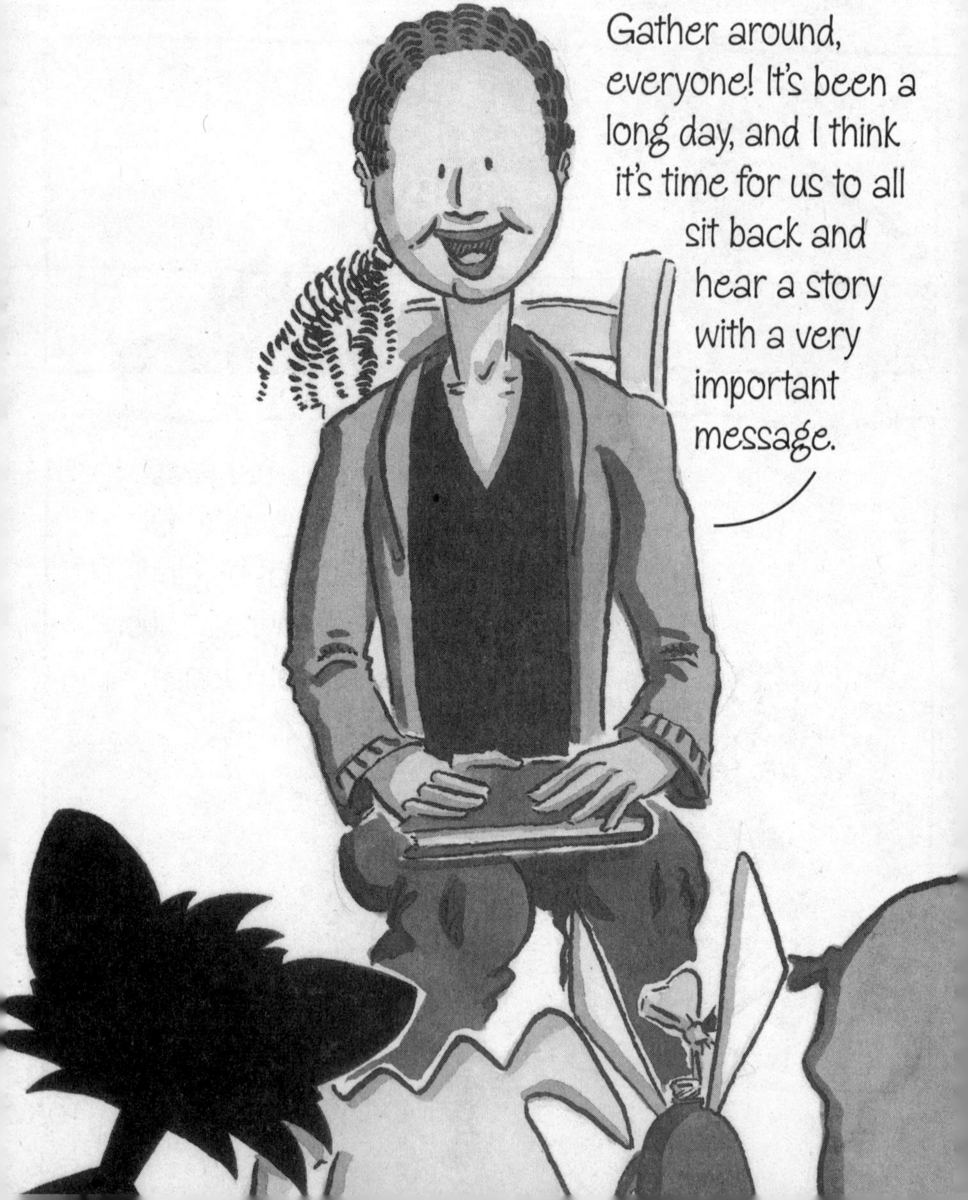
Gather around, everyone! It's been a long day, and I think it's time for us to all sit back and hear a story with a very important message.

Today's story is "Love Love Angel Kitten and Her Friends on the Farm."

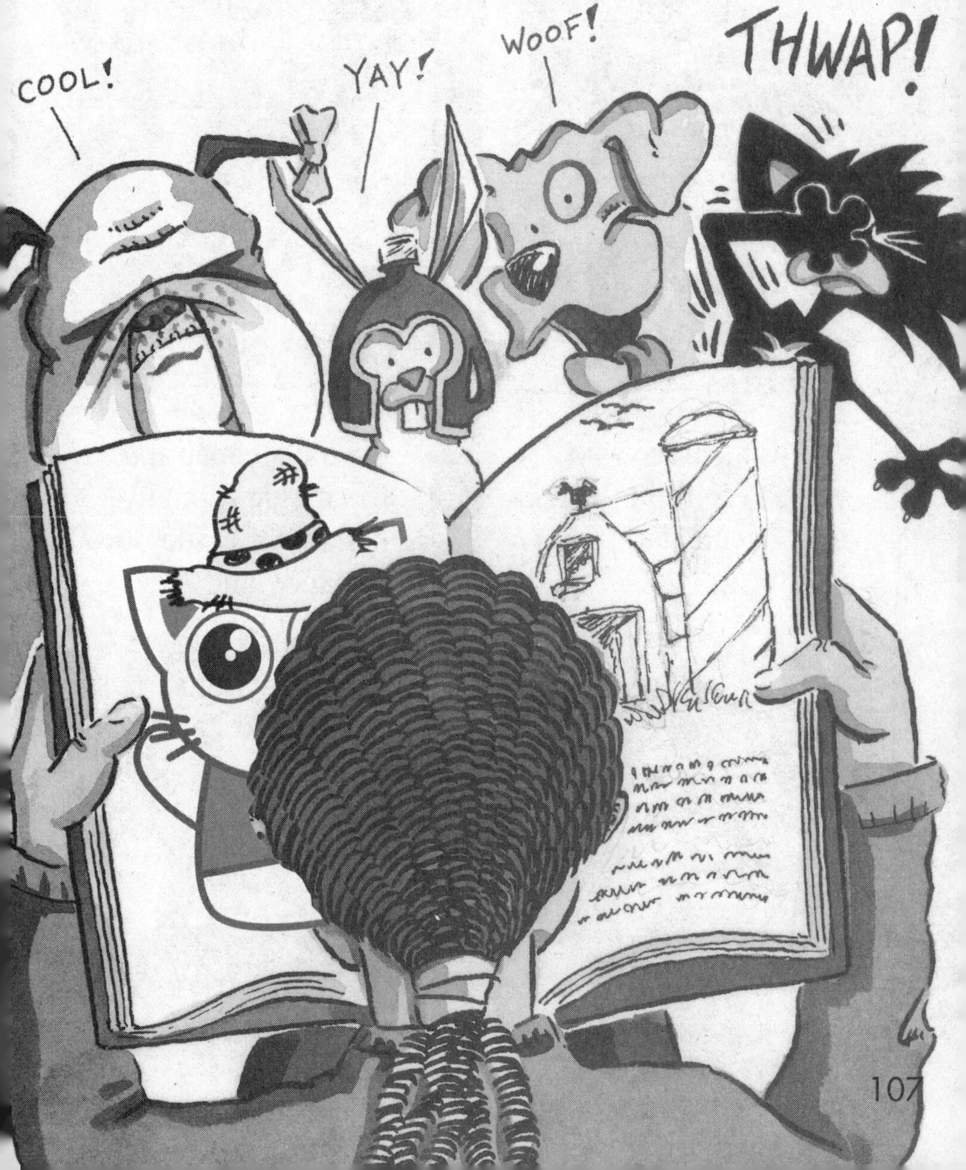
COOL!
YAY!
WOOF!
THWAP!

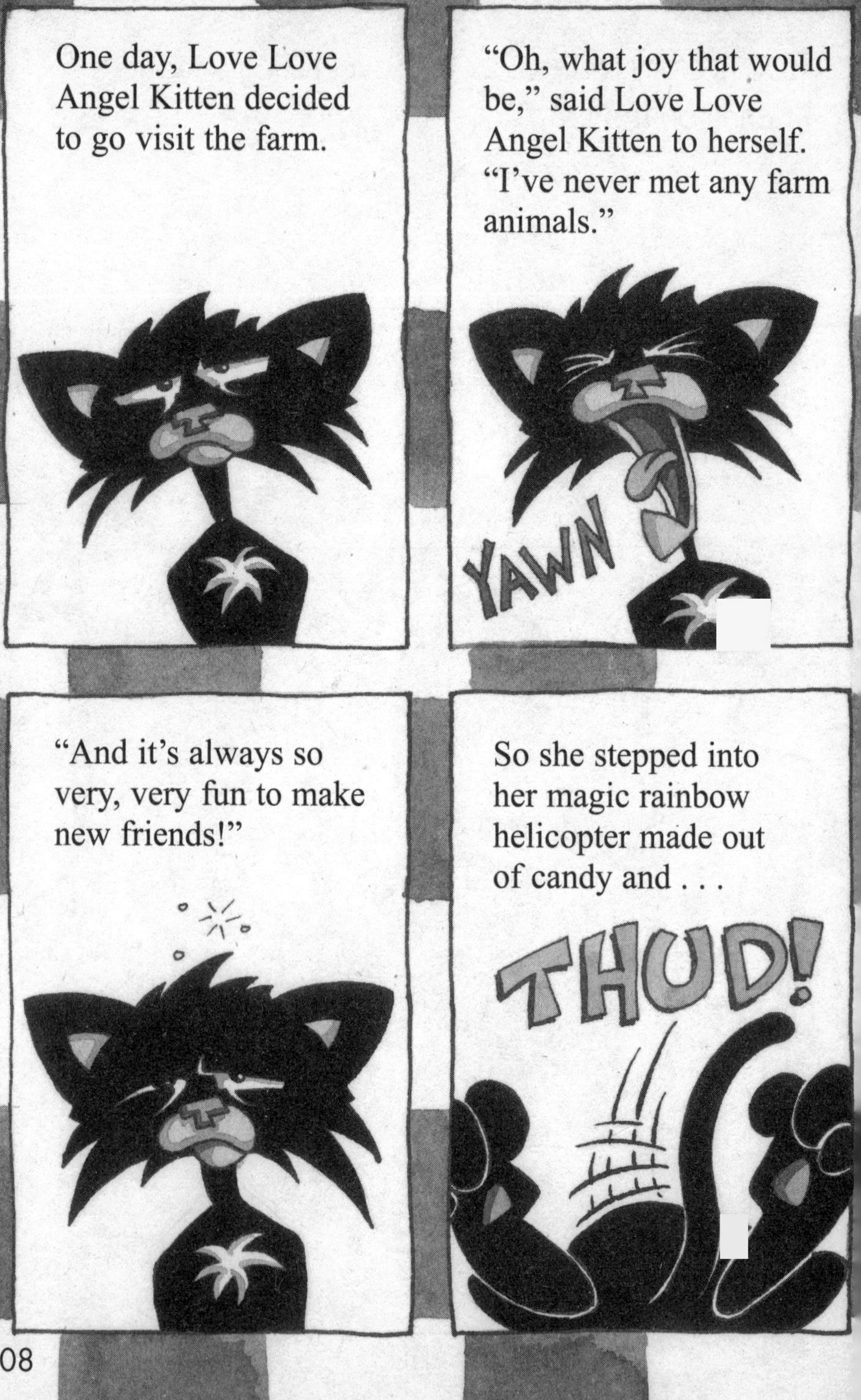
One day, Love Love Angel Kitten decided to go visit the farm.
"Oh, what joy that would be," said Love Love Angel Kitten to herself. "I've never met any farm animals."
YAWN
"And it's always so very, very fun to make new friends!"
So she stepped into her magic rainbow helicopter made out of candy and . . .
THUD!

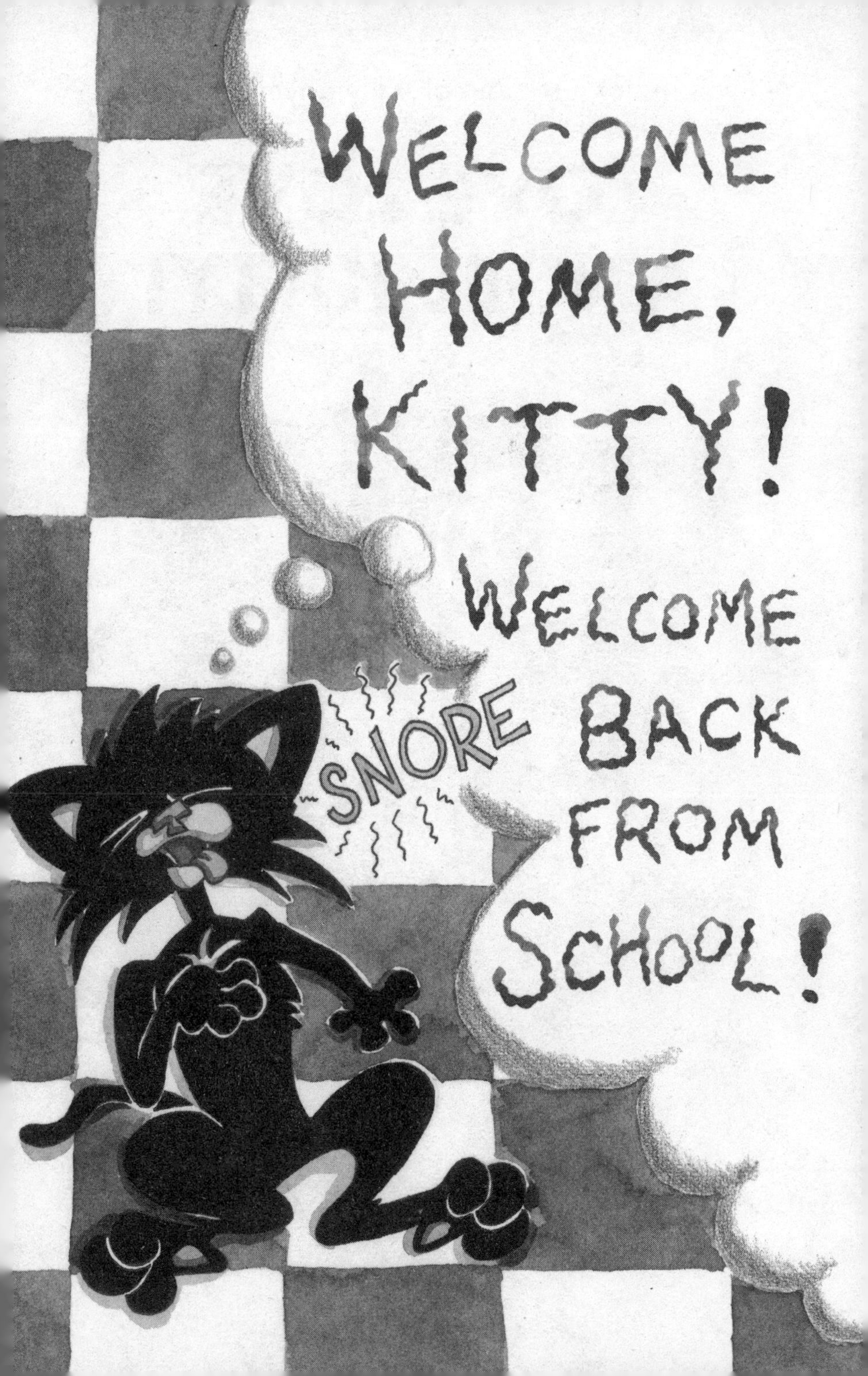
WELCOME HOME, KITTY!
WELCOME BACK FROM SCHOOL!
SNORE

But you're not just plain ol' Kitty anymore, are you? No, now you're . . .

LOVE LOVE ANGEL KITTY!

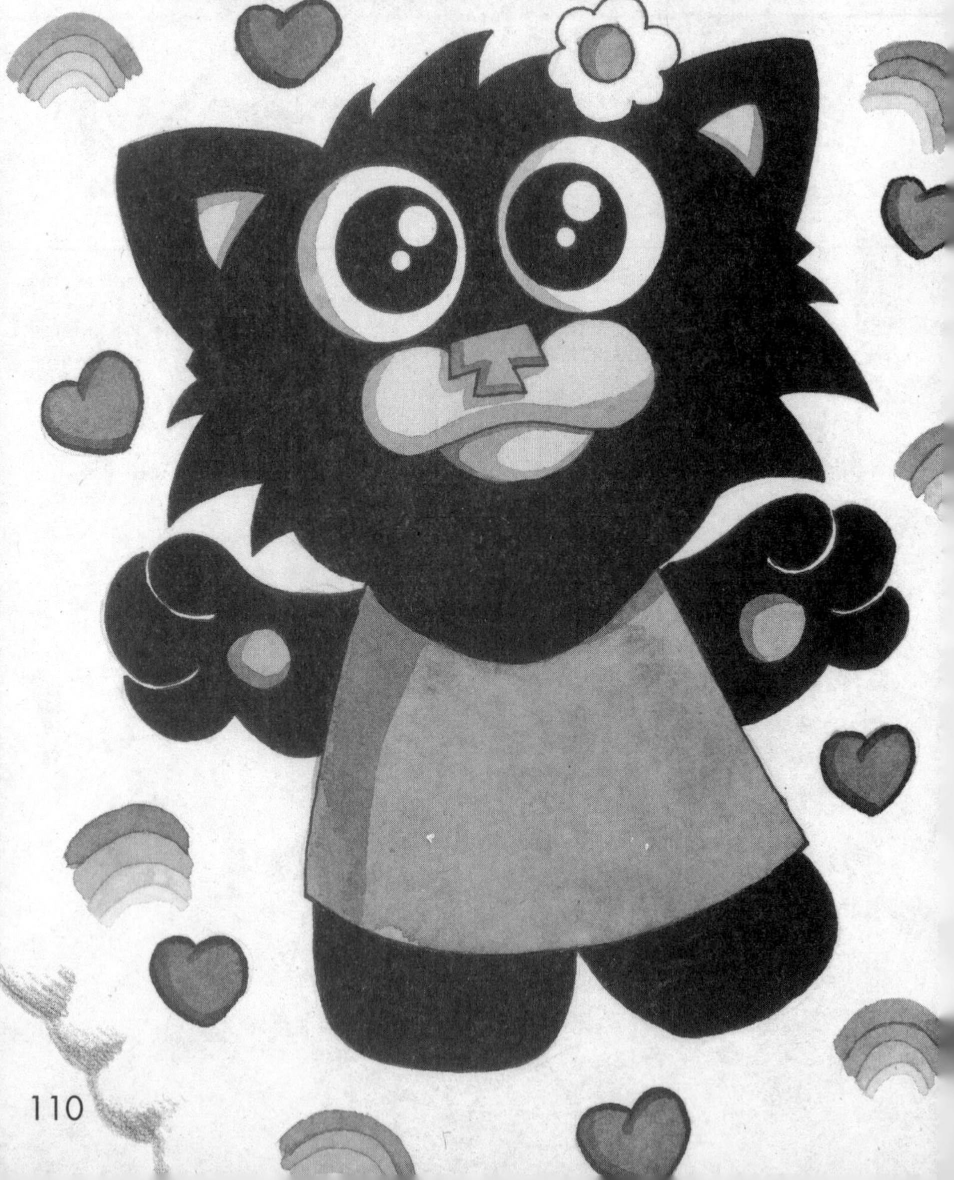

HEY, EVERYBODY! Look at Love Love Angel Kitty!

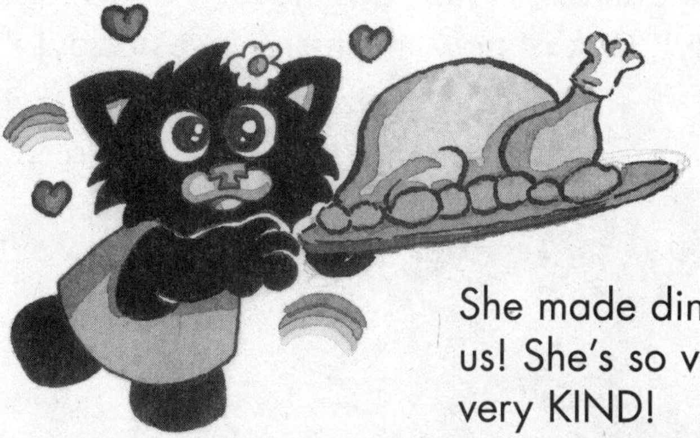

She made dinner for us! She's so very, very KIND!

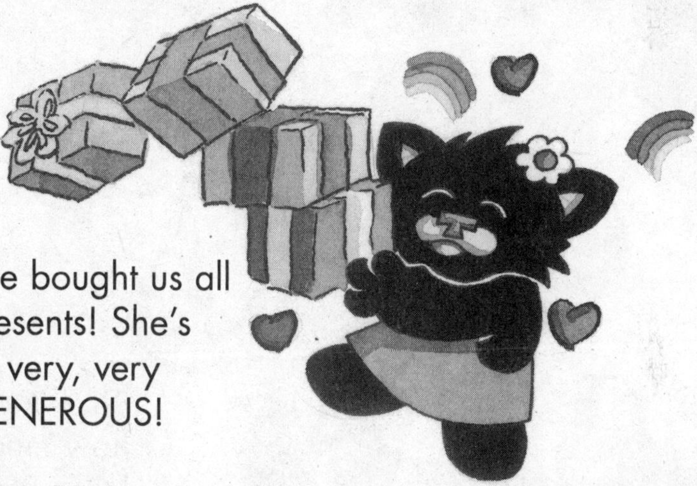

She bought us all presents! She's so very, very GENEROUS!

She cleaned her own litterbox! She's so very, very HELPFUL!

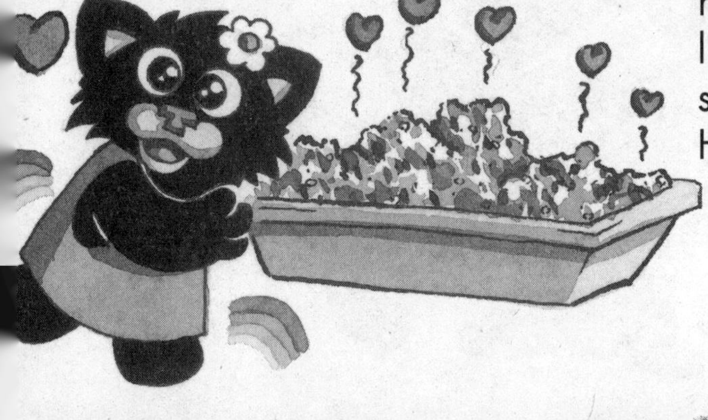

Love Love Angel Kitty is such a very, very, good, good, GOOD Kitty! Look at how much she loves Baby!

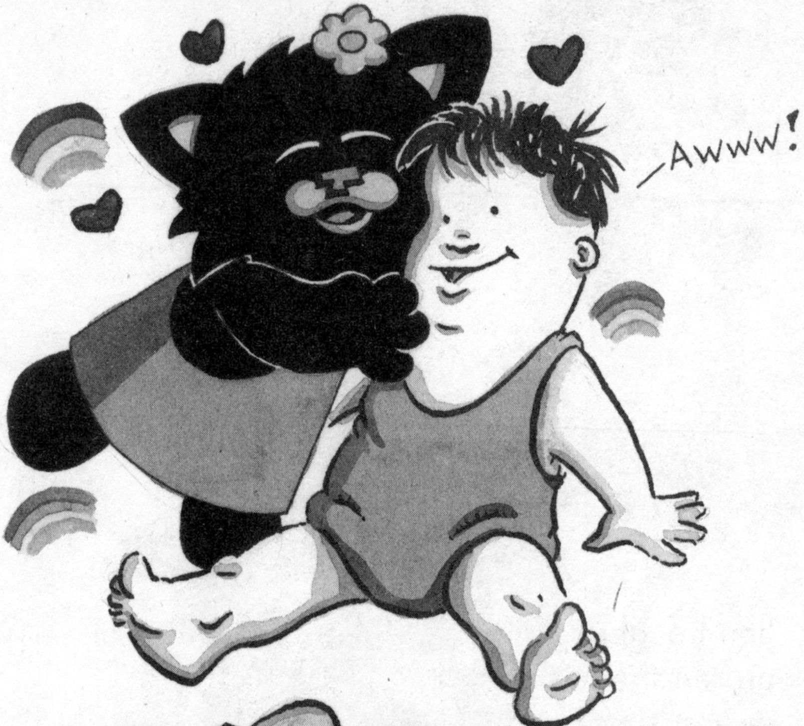
—Awww!

Now look at how much she loves Puppy!

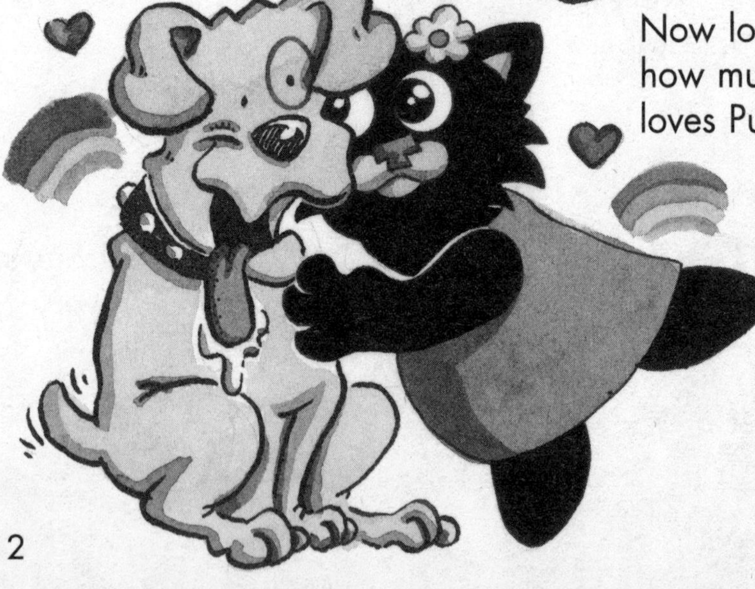

Finally, there is peace in our home. Where once there were screaming temper tantrums, now there are only kisses. Where once there were fights and shrieks and howls, now there are only hugs. Where once there was only mayhem, now there is only love. Sweet, wonderful LOVE.

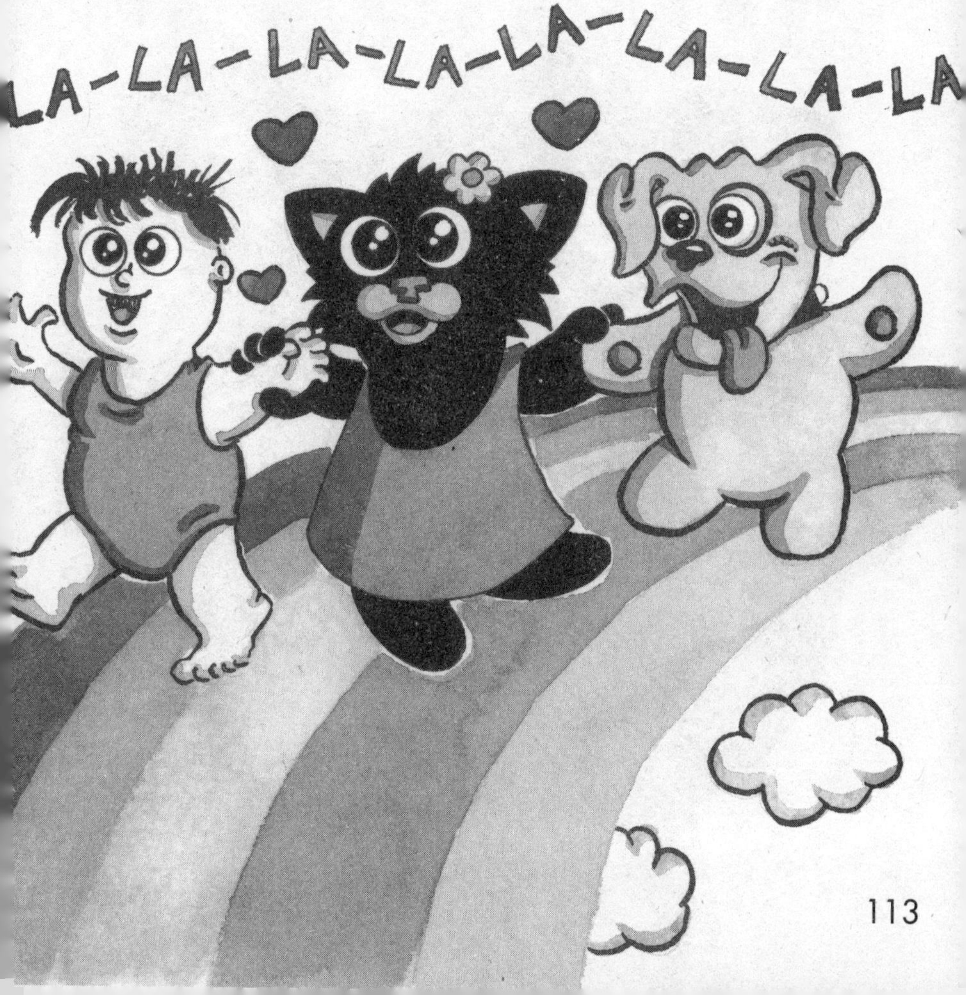
LA-LA-LA-LA-LA-LA-LA-LA

And it's all thanks to

SCHOOL
SCHOOL
SCHOOL
SCHOOL
SCHOOL
SCHOOL

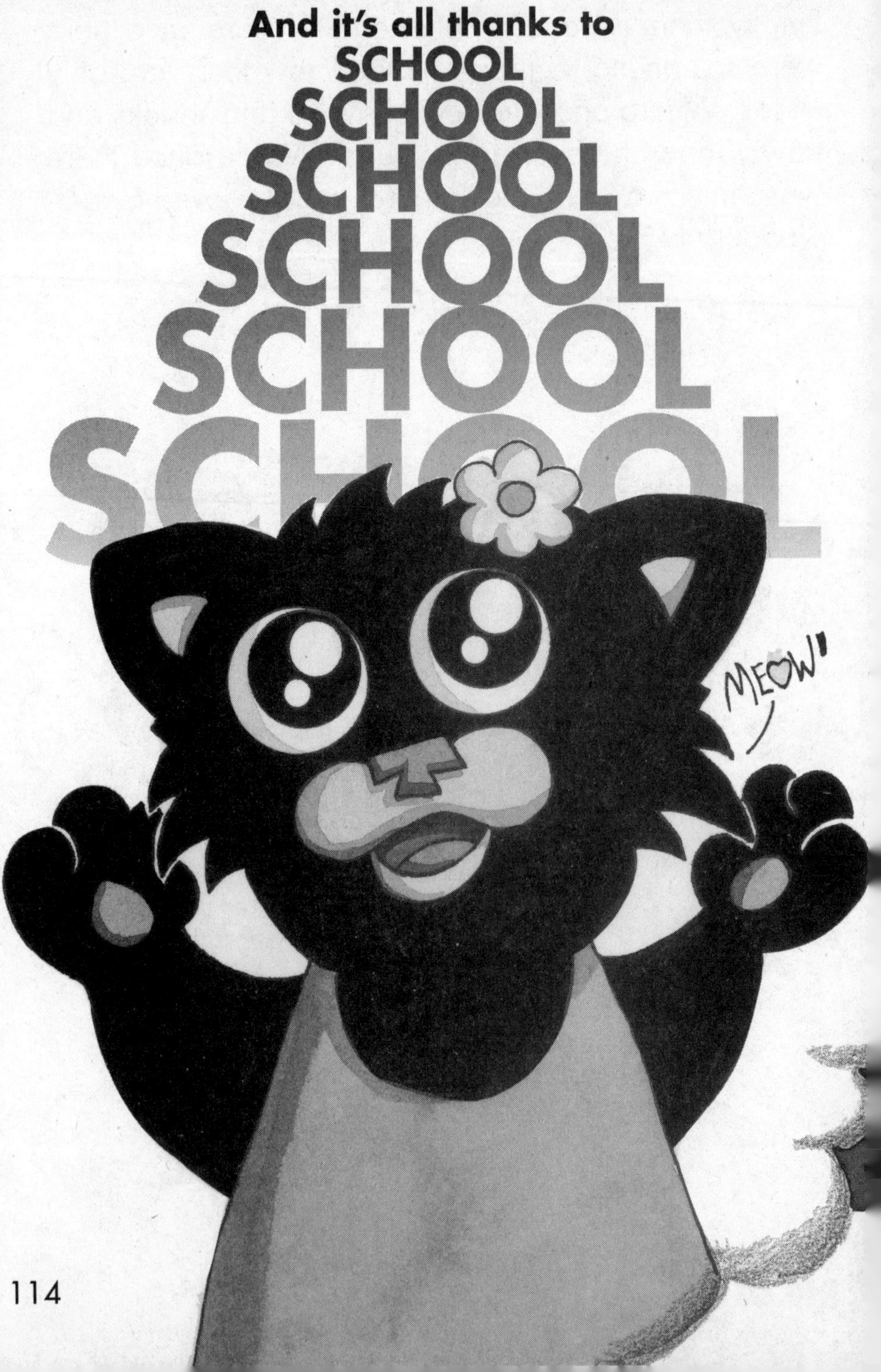
MEOW!

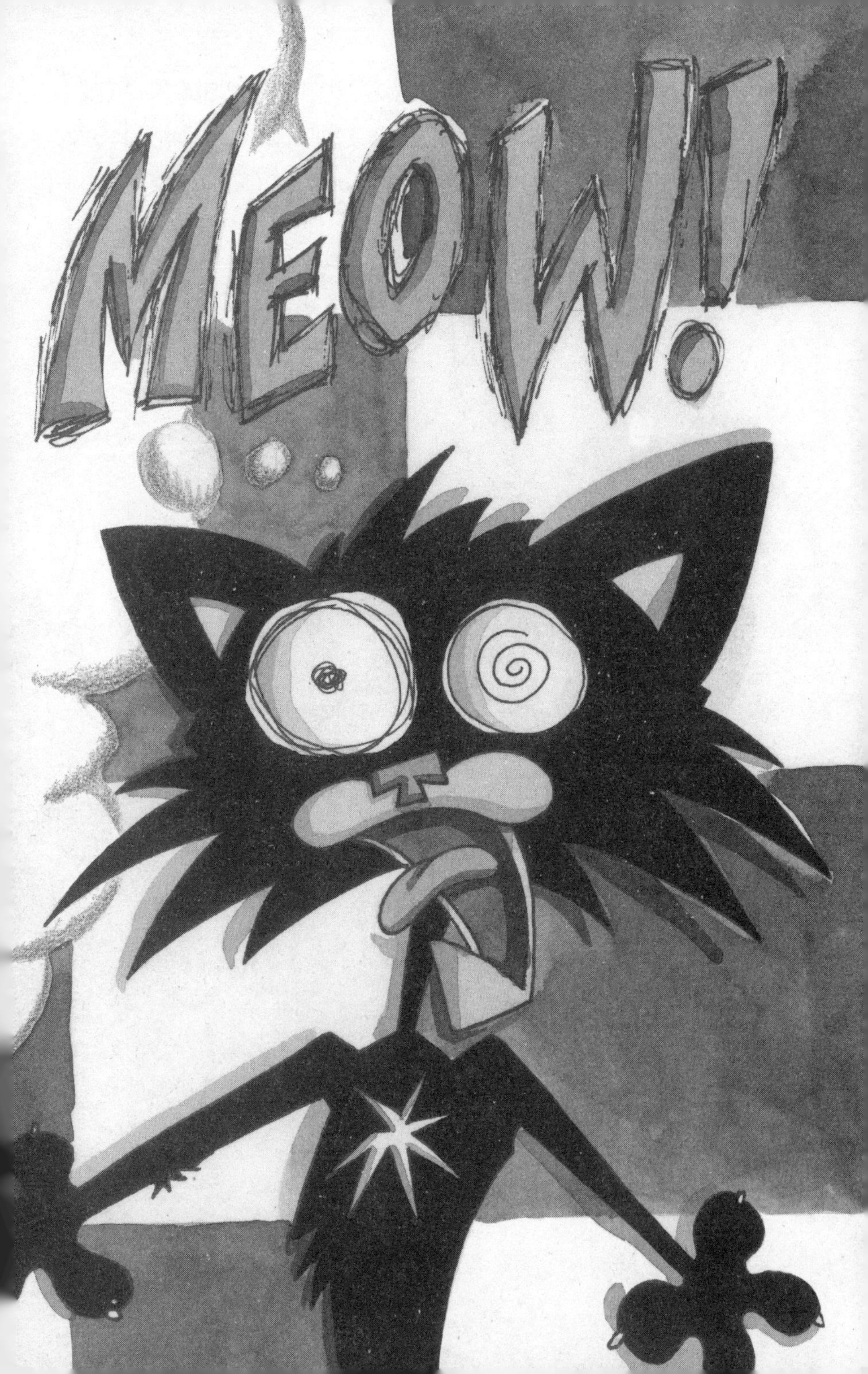
MEOW!

Are you all right, Kitty? Did something upset you? Were you frightened by the part where Love Love Angel Kitten tried to hug the disobedient chicken?

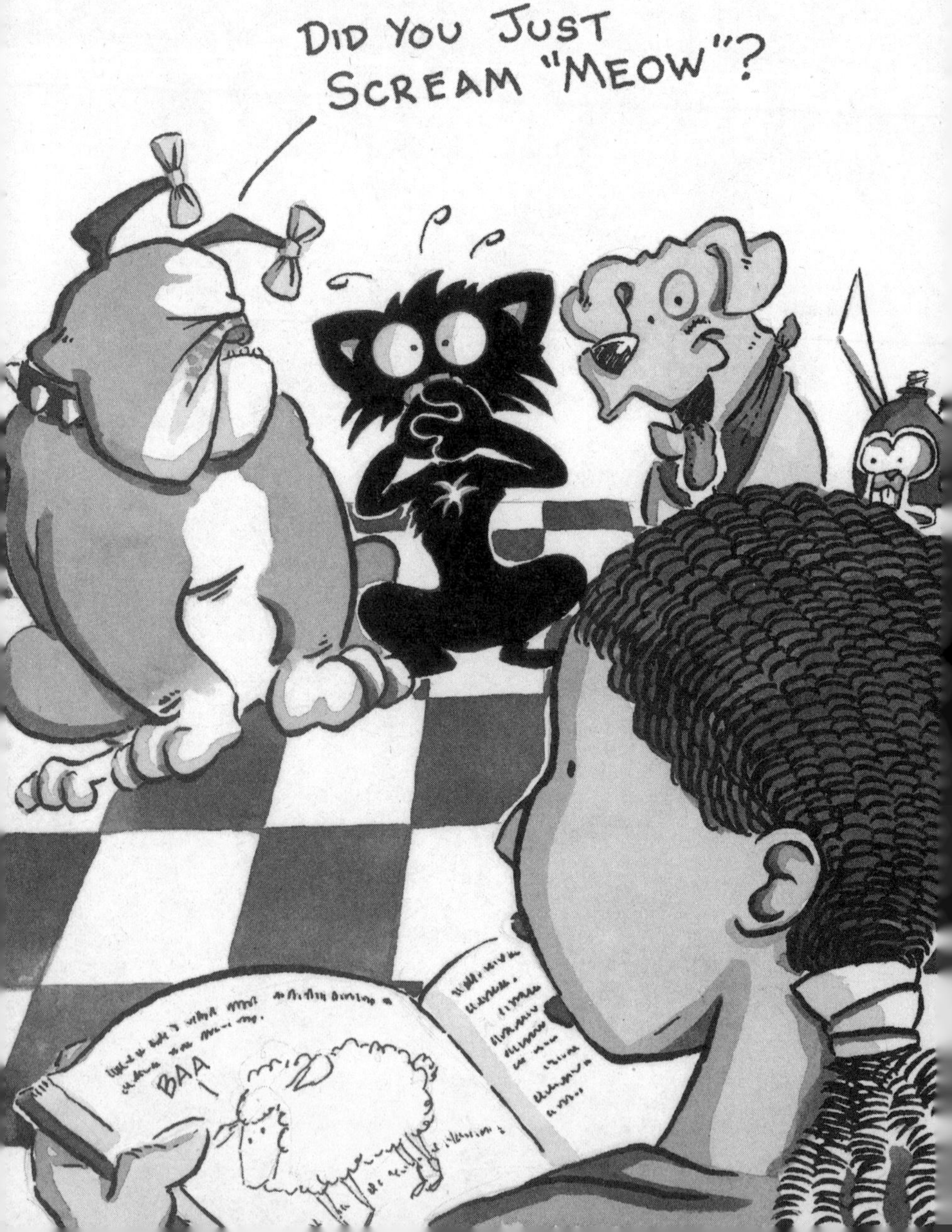
DID YOU JUST SCREAM "MEOW"?
BAA

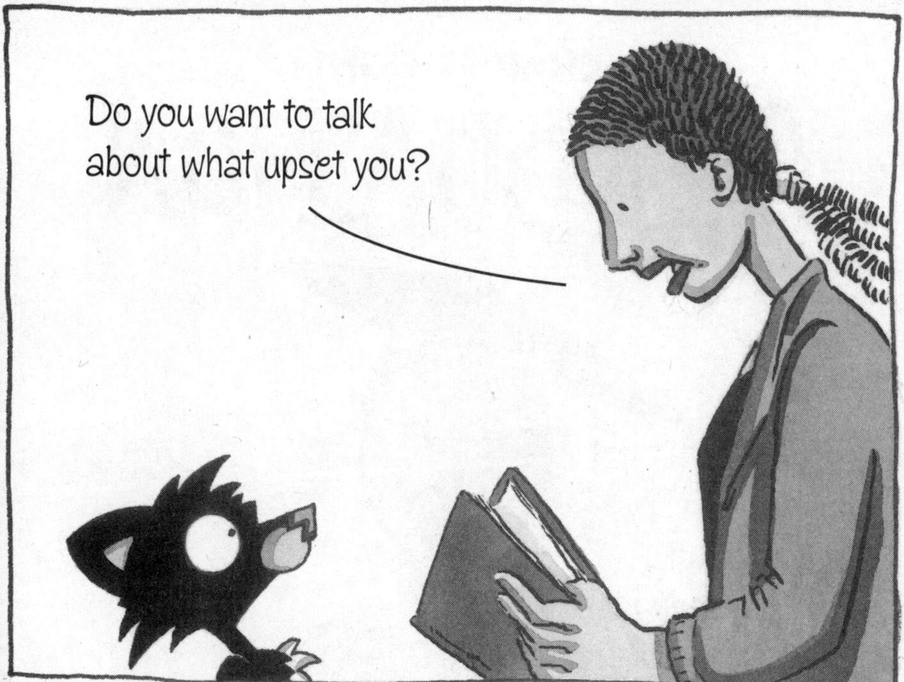
Do you want to talk about what upset you?

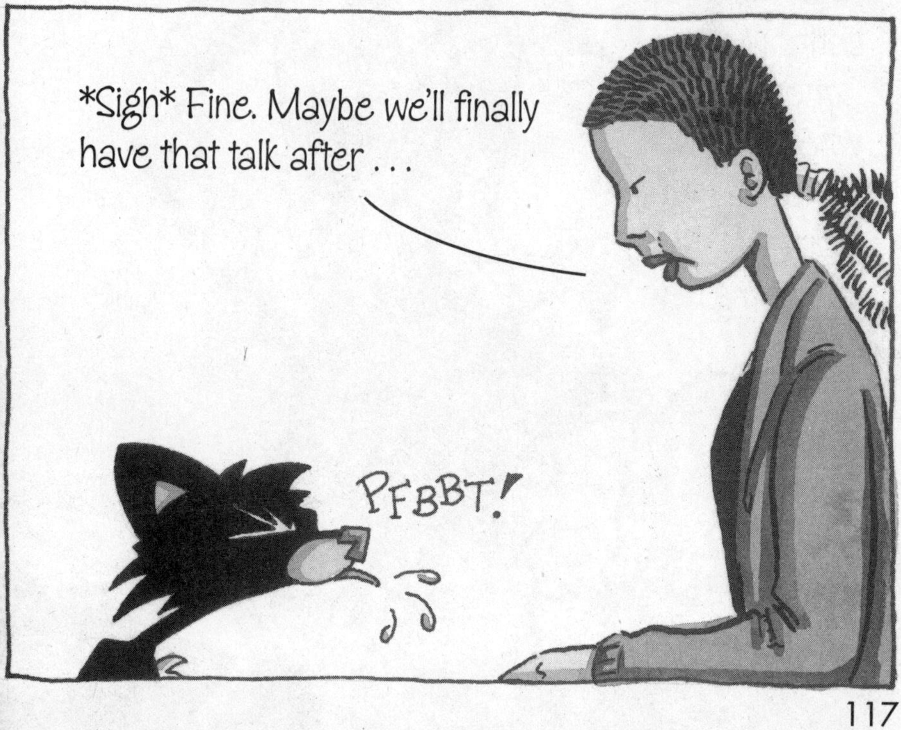
Sigh Fine. Maybe we'll finally have that talk after . . .
PFBBT!

•CHAPTER EIGHT•

GRADUATION

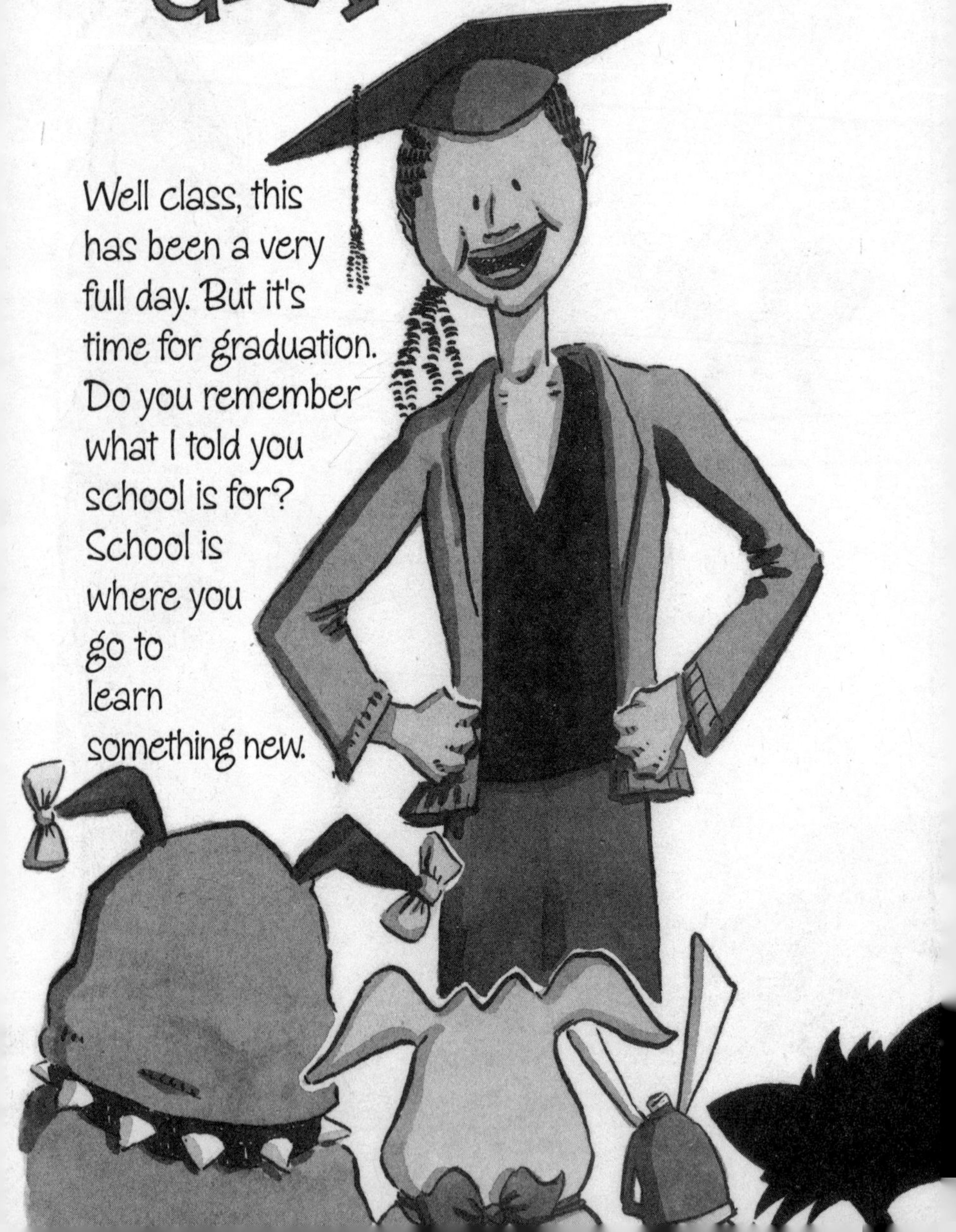

Well class, this has been a very full day. But it's time for graduation. Do you remember what I told you school is for? School is where you go to learn something new.

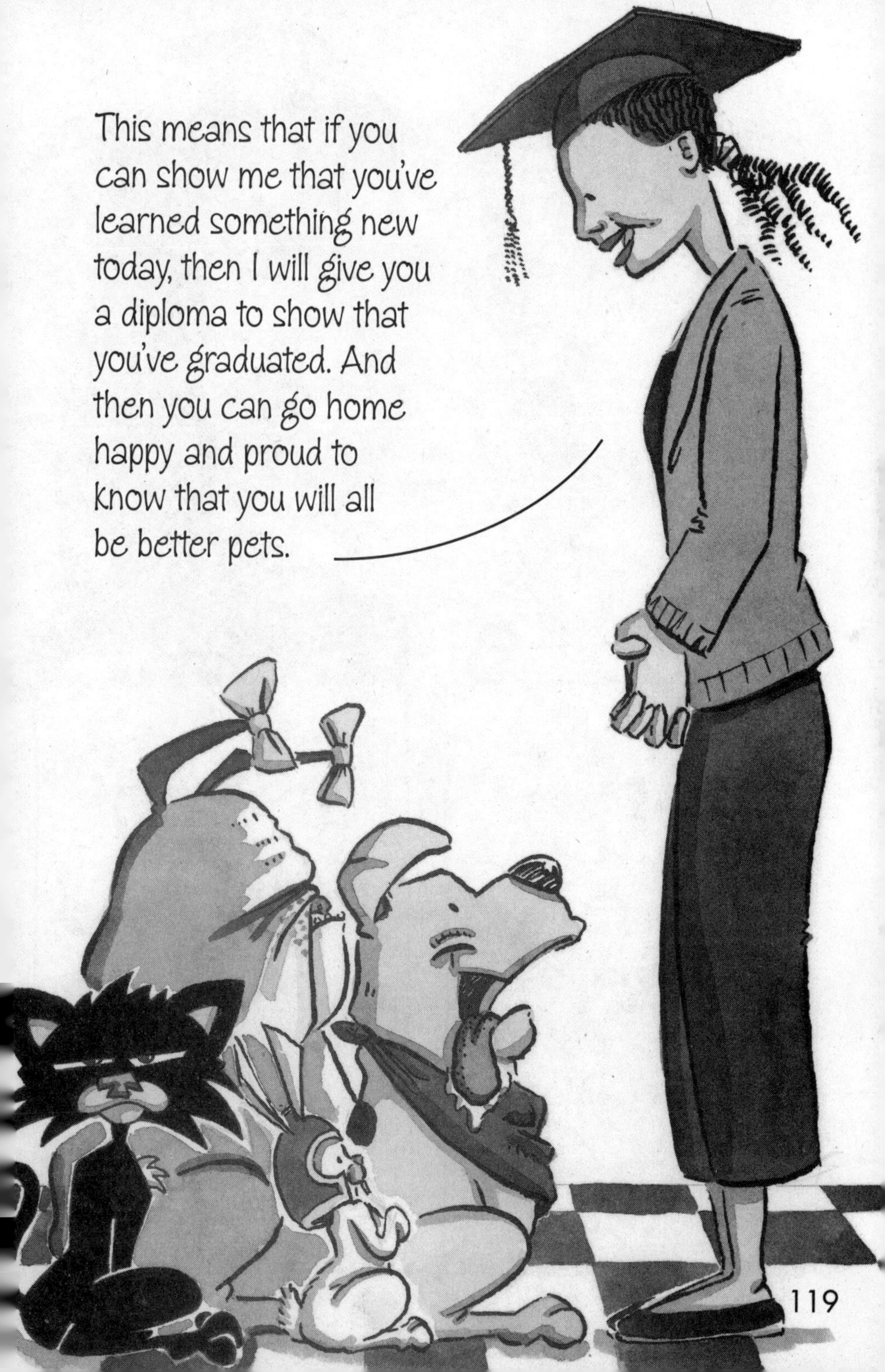
This means that if you can show me that you've learned something new today, then I will give you a diploma to show that you've graduated. And then you can go home happy and proud to know that you will all be better pets.

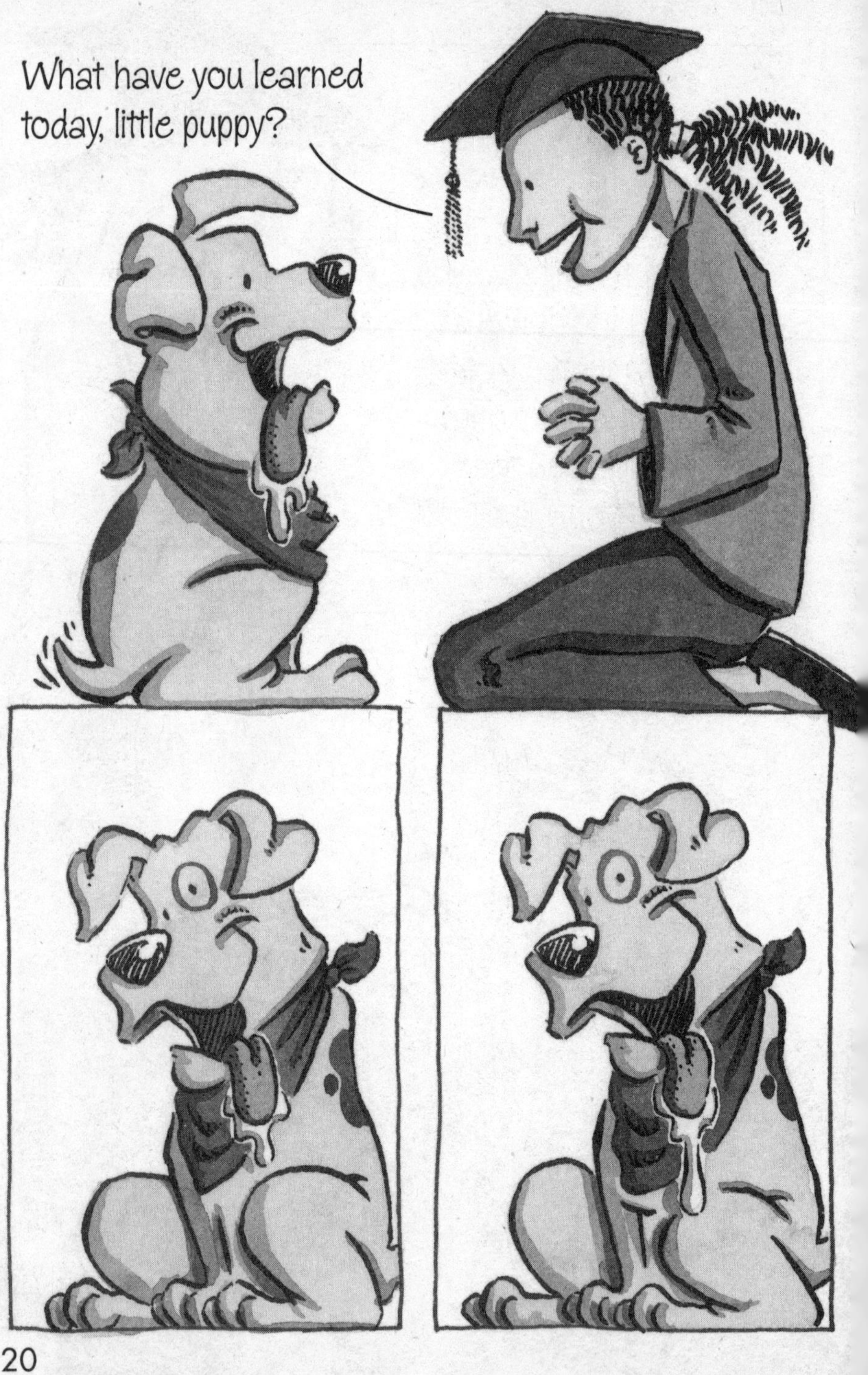
What have you learned today, little puppy?

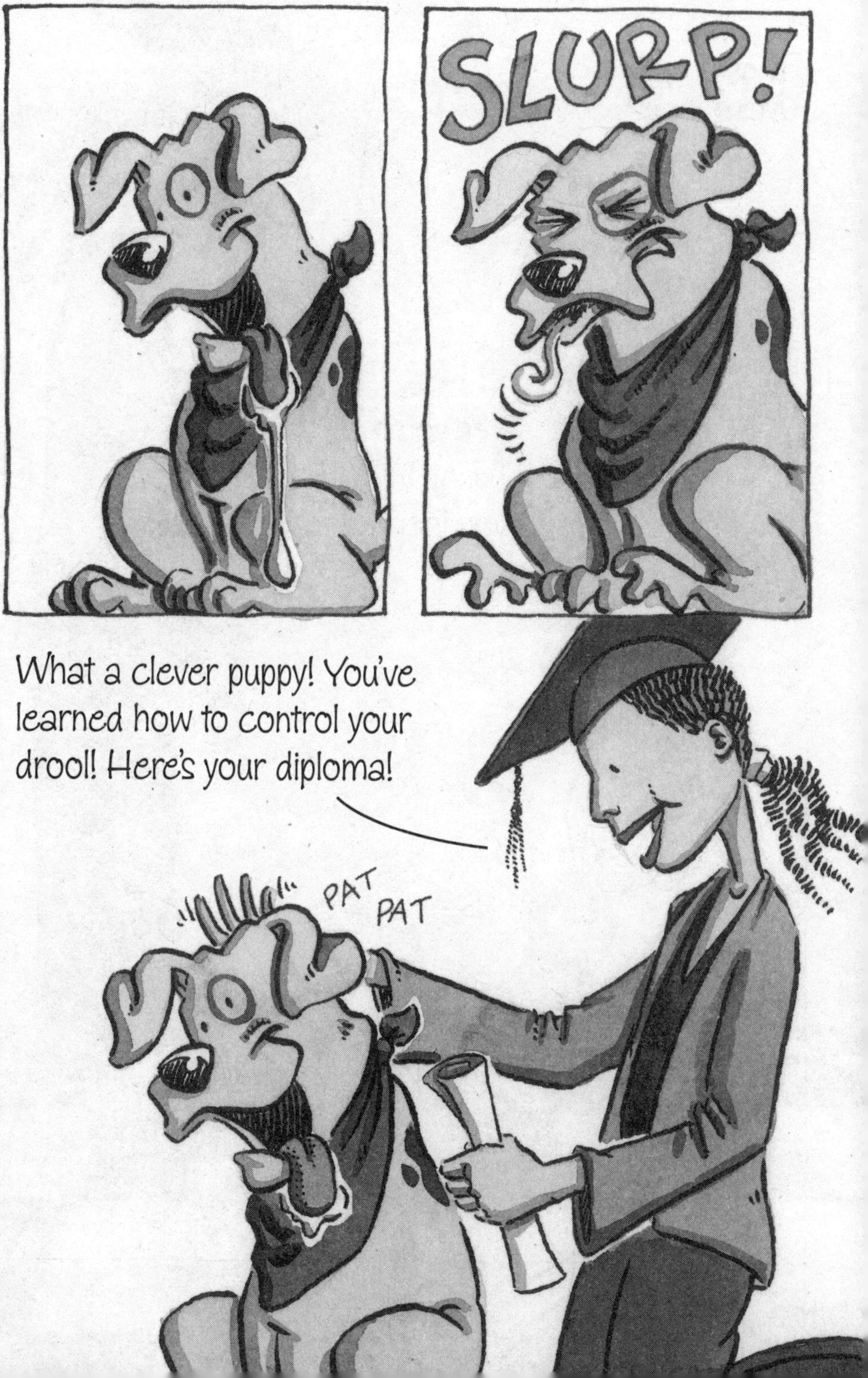
SLURP!
What a clever puppy! You've learned how to control your drool! Here's your diploma!
PAT
PAT

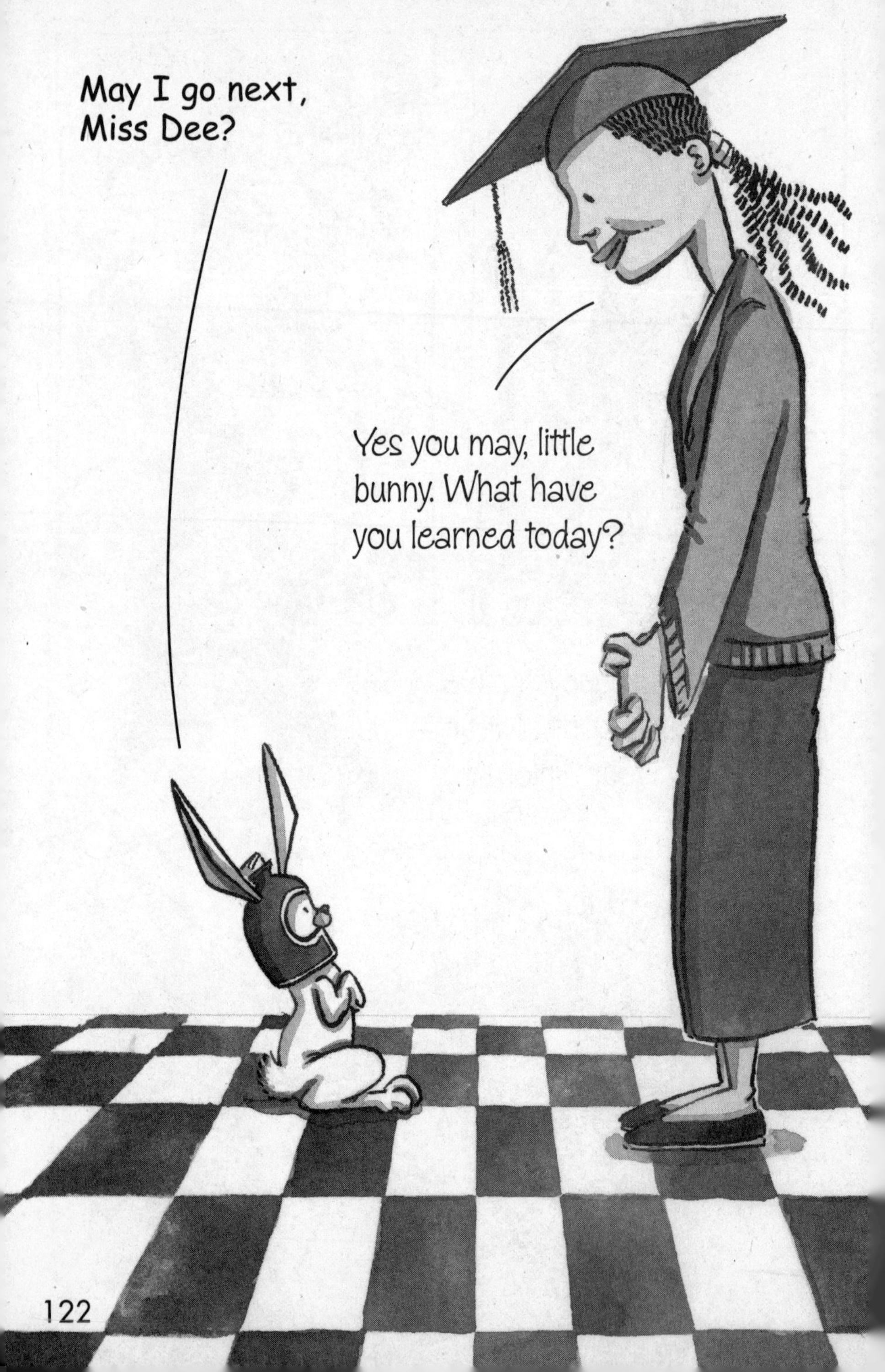
May I go next, Miss Dee?
Yes you may, little bunny. What have you learned today?

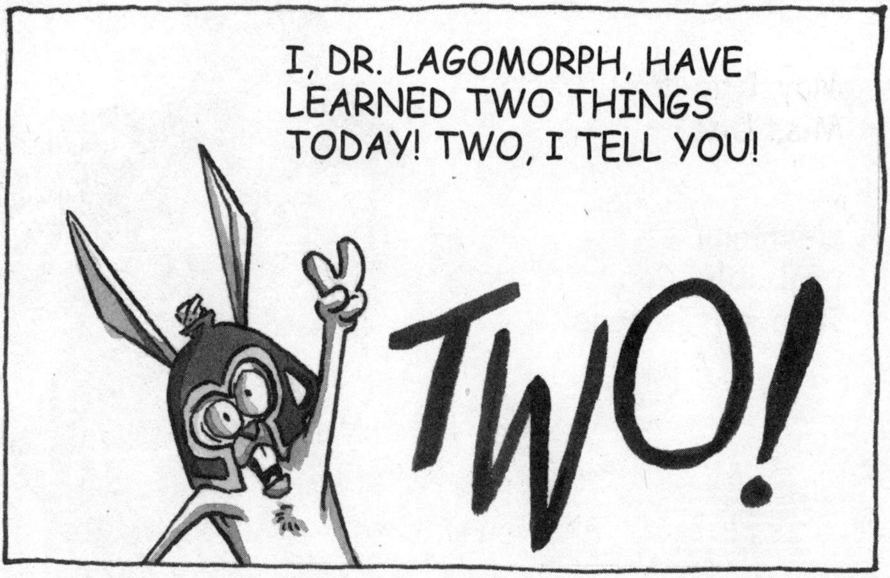
I, DR. LAGOMORPH, HAVE LEARNED TWO THINGS TODAY! TWO, I TELL YOU!
TWO!

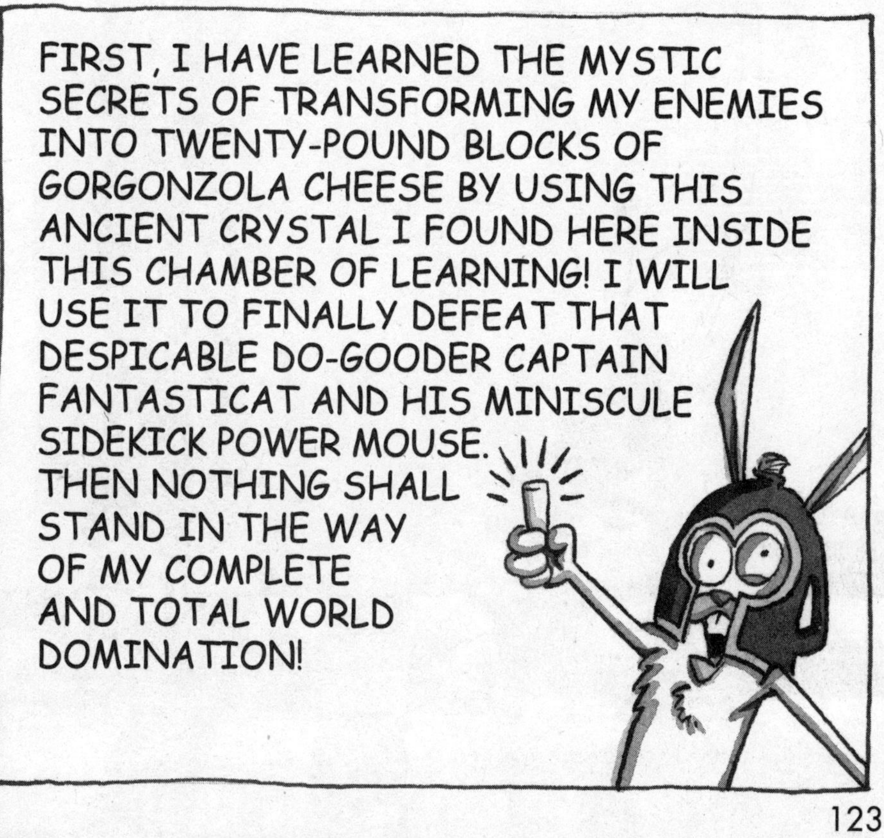
FIRST, I HAVE LEARNED THE MYSTIC SECRETS OF TRANSFORMING MY ENEMIES INTO TWENTY-POUND BLOCKS OF GORGONZOLA CHEESE BY USING THIS ANCIENT CRYSTAL I FOUND HERE INSIDE THIS CHAMBER OF LEARNING! I WILL USE IT TO FINALLY DEFEAT THAT DESPICABLE DO-GOODER CAPTAIN FANTASTICAT AND HIS MINISCULE SIDEKICK POWER MOUSE. THEN NOTHING SHALL STAND IN THE WAY OF MY COMPLETE AND TOTAL WORLD DOMINATION!

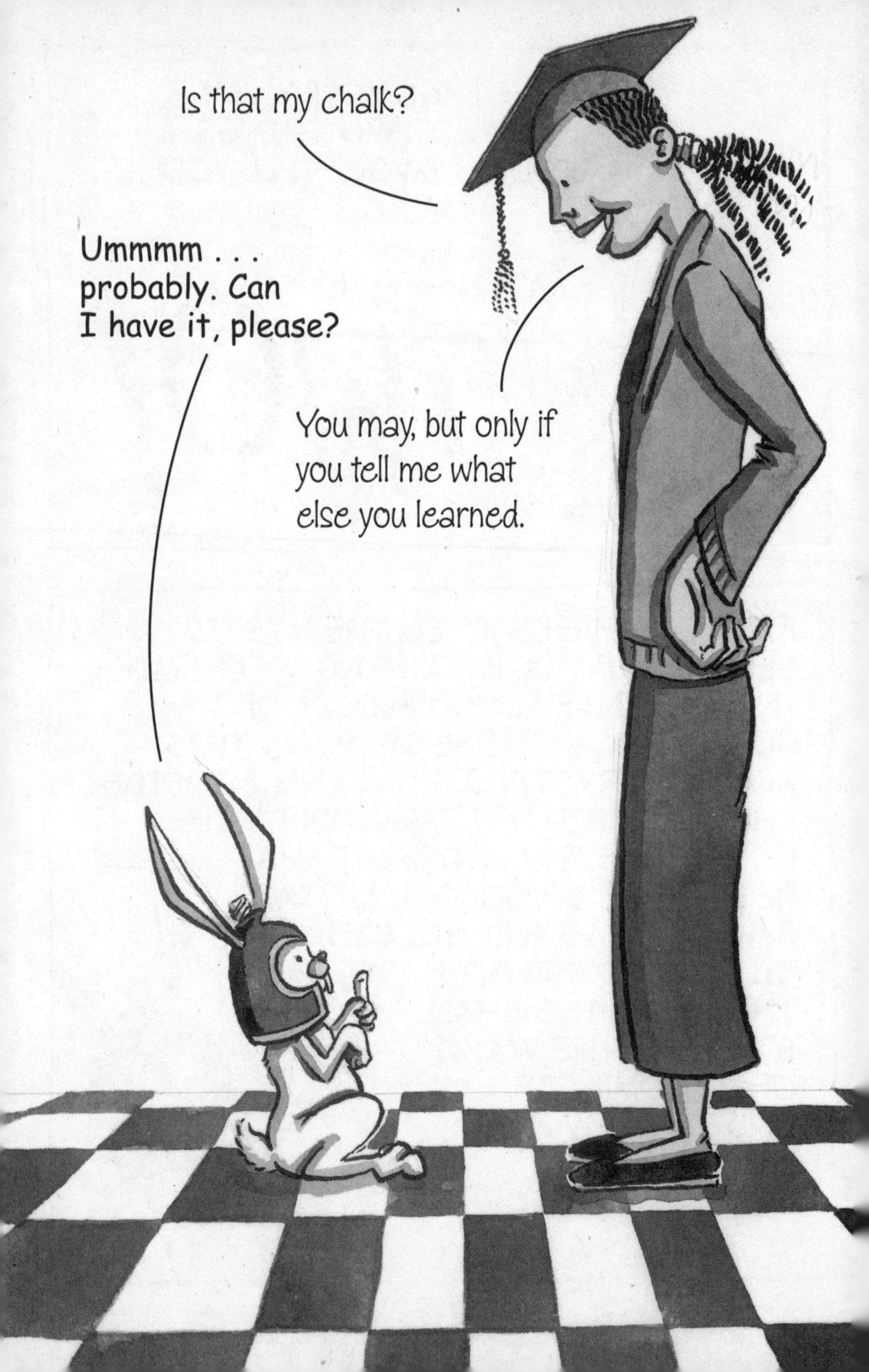
Is that my chalk?
Ummmm . . . probably. Can I have it, please?
You may, but only if you tell me what else you learned.

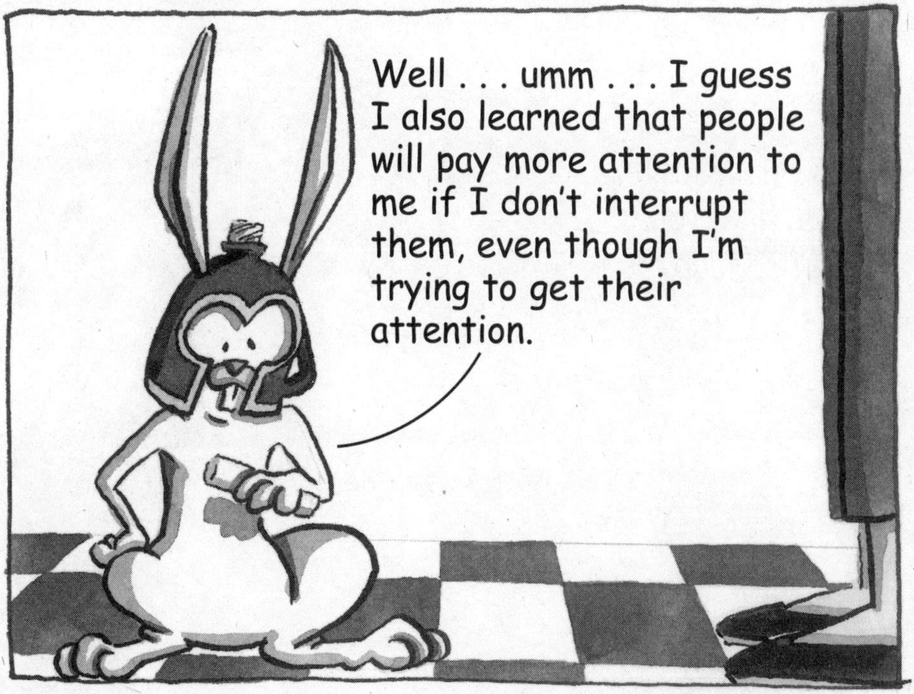
Well . . . umm . . . I guess I also learned that people will pay more attention to me if I don't interrupt them, even though I'm trying to get their attention.

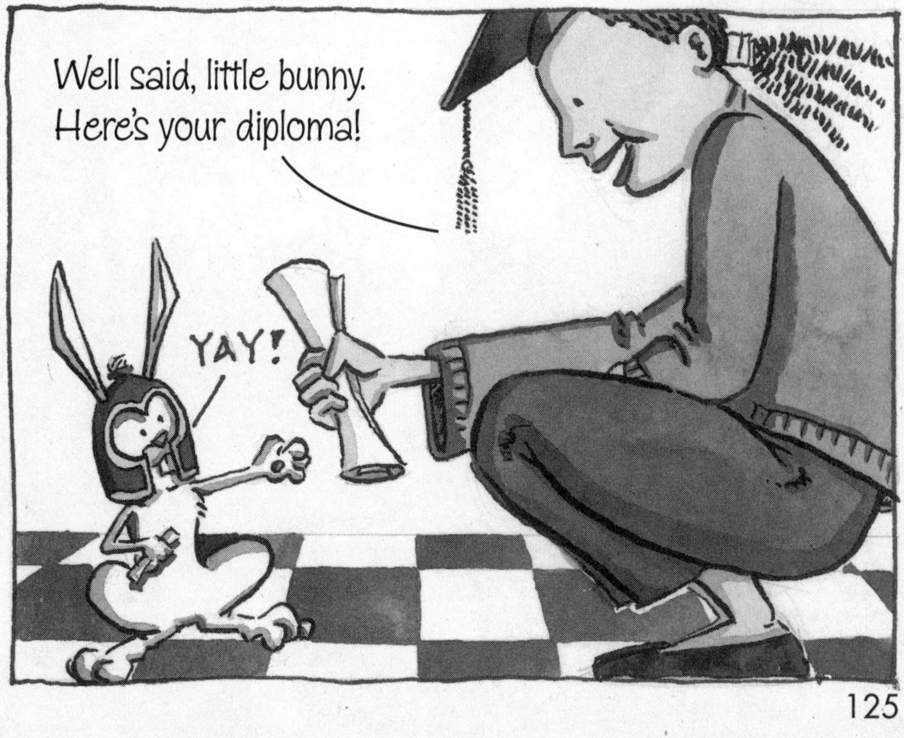
Well said, little bunny. Here's your diploma!
YAY!

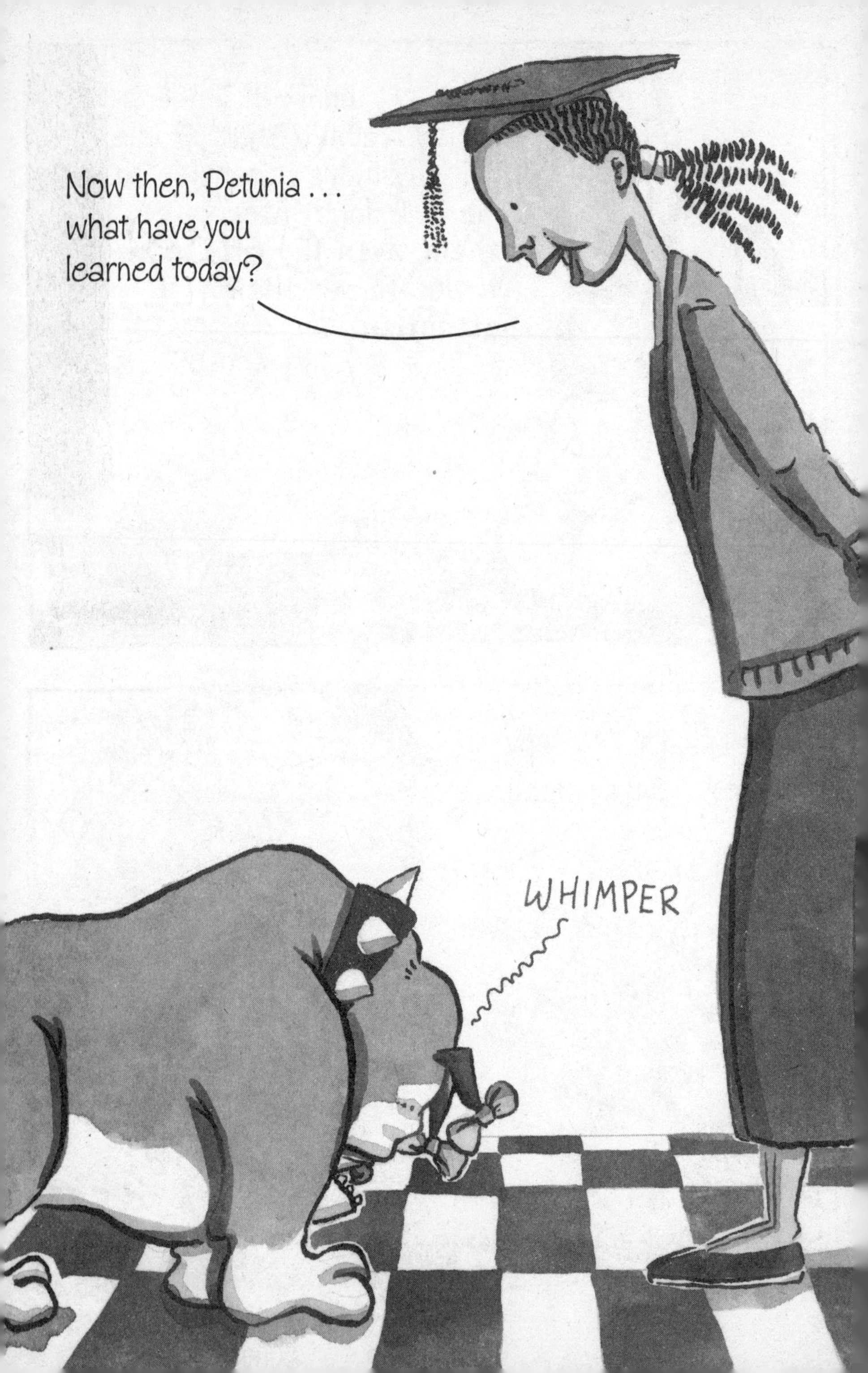
Now then, Petunia . . . what have you learned today?
WHIMPER

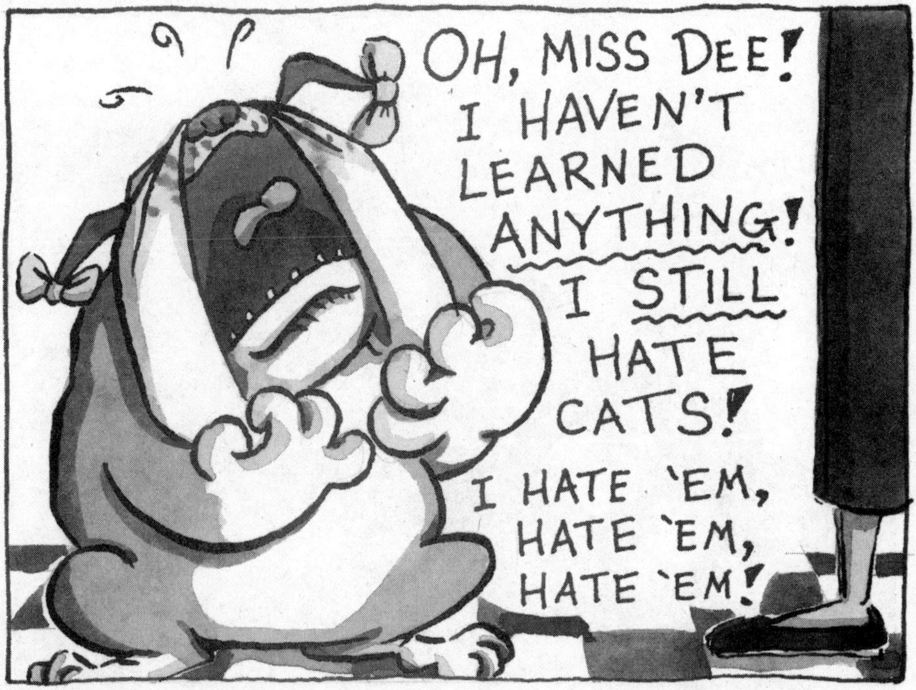
OH, MISS DEE! I HAVEN'T LEARNED ANYTHING! I STILL HATE CATS!
I HATE 'EM, HATE 'EM, HATE 'EM!

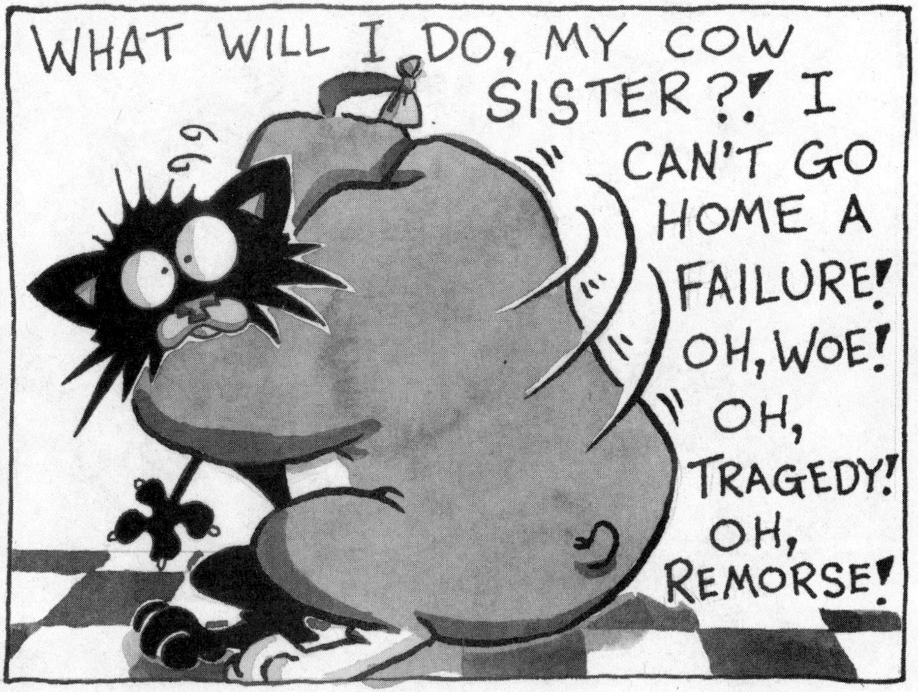
WHAT WILL I DO, MY COW SISTER?! I CAN'T GO HOME A FAILURE! OH, WOE! OH, TRAGEDY! OH, REMORSE!

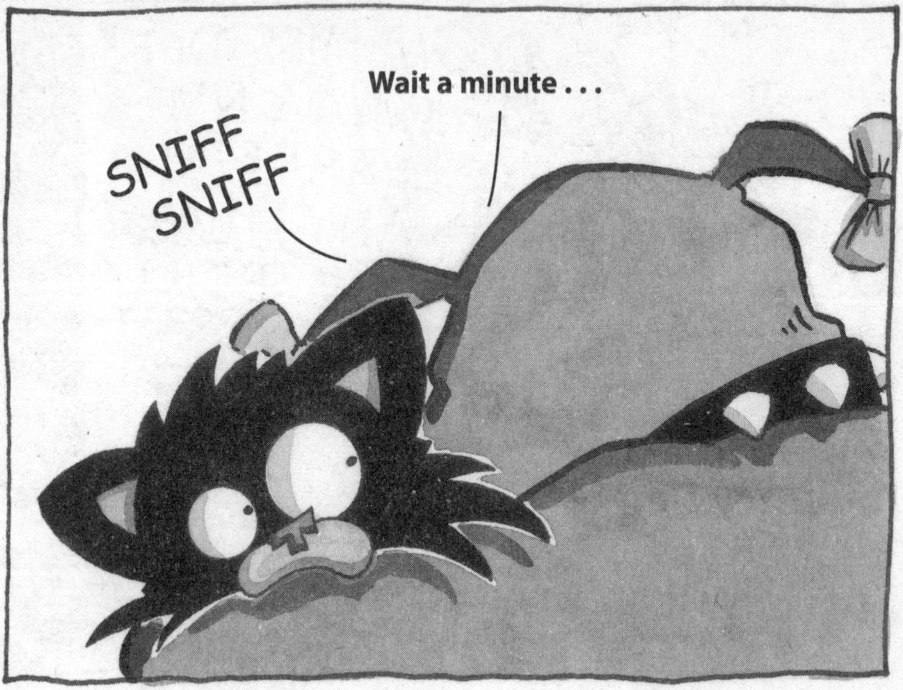
Wait a minute . . .
SNIFF
SNIFF

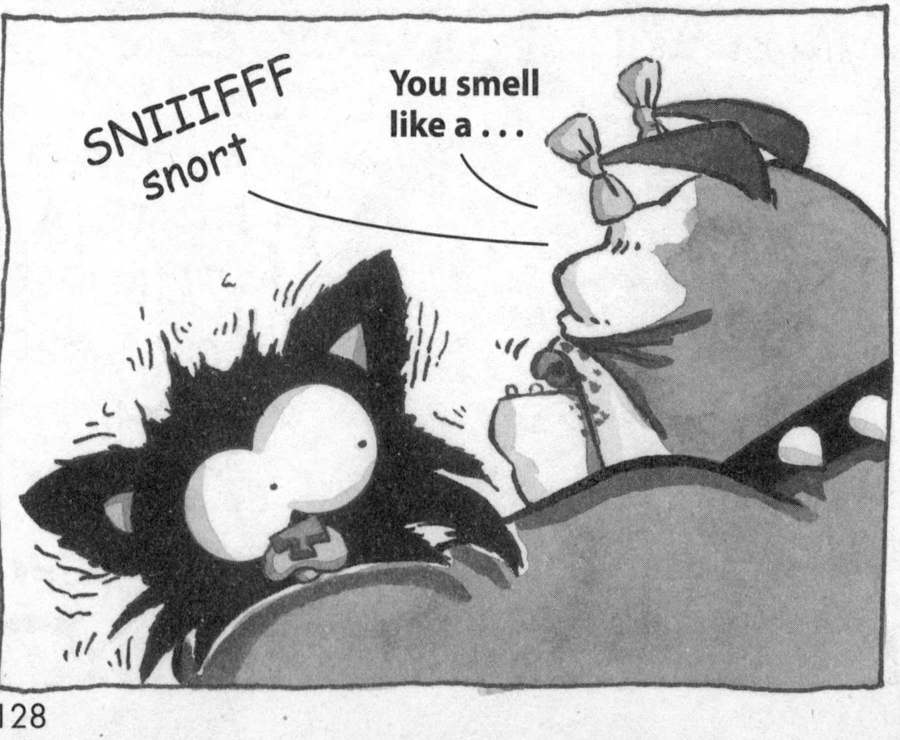
SNIIIFFF
snort
You smell
like a . . .

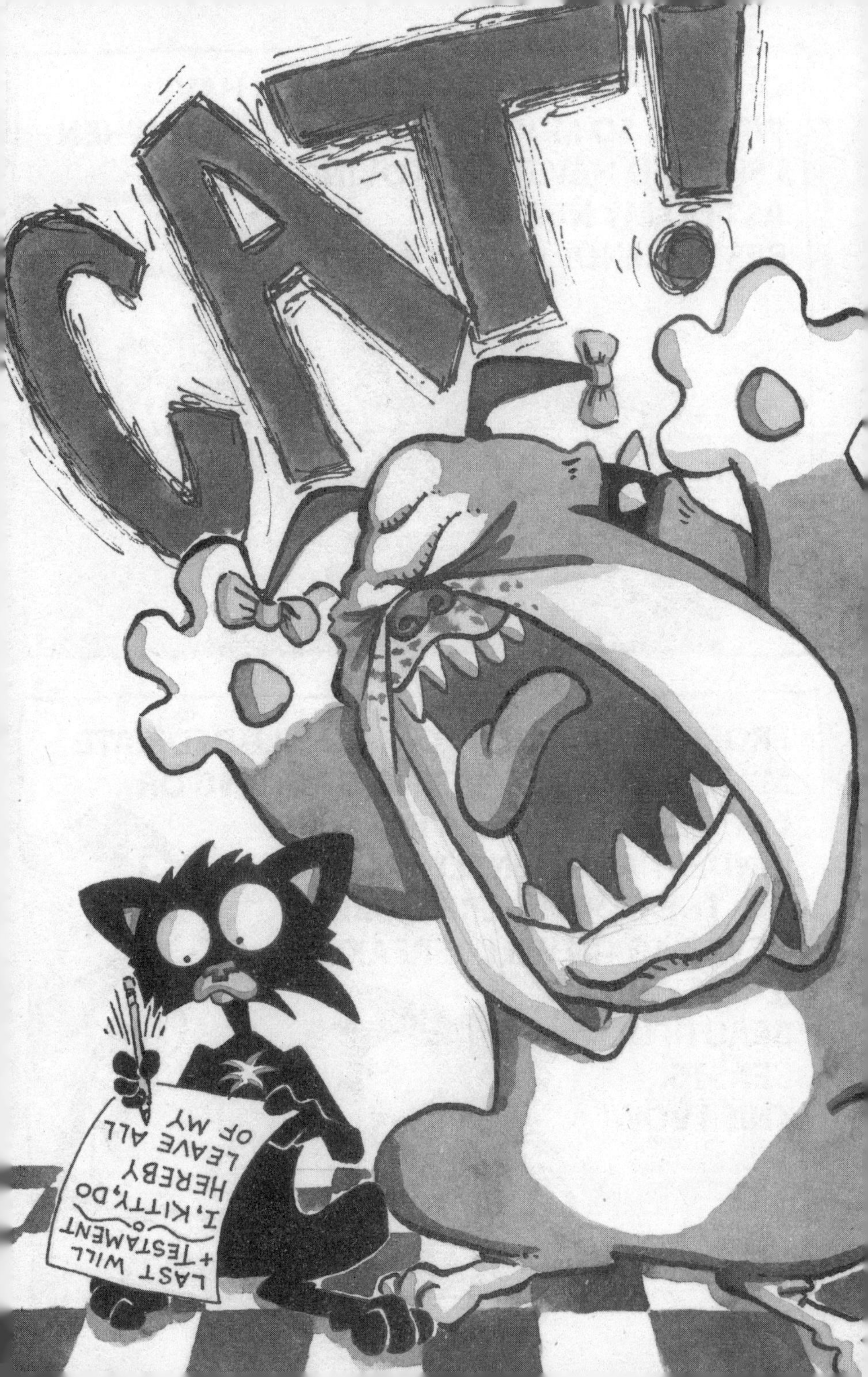
CAT!
LAST WILL + TESTAMENT
I, KITTY, DO HEREBY LEAVE ALL OF MY

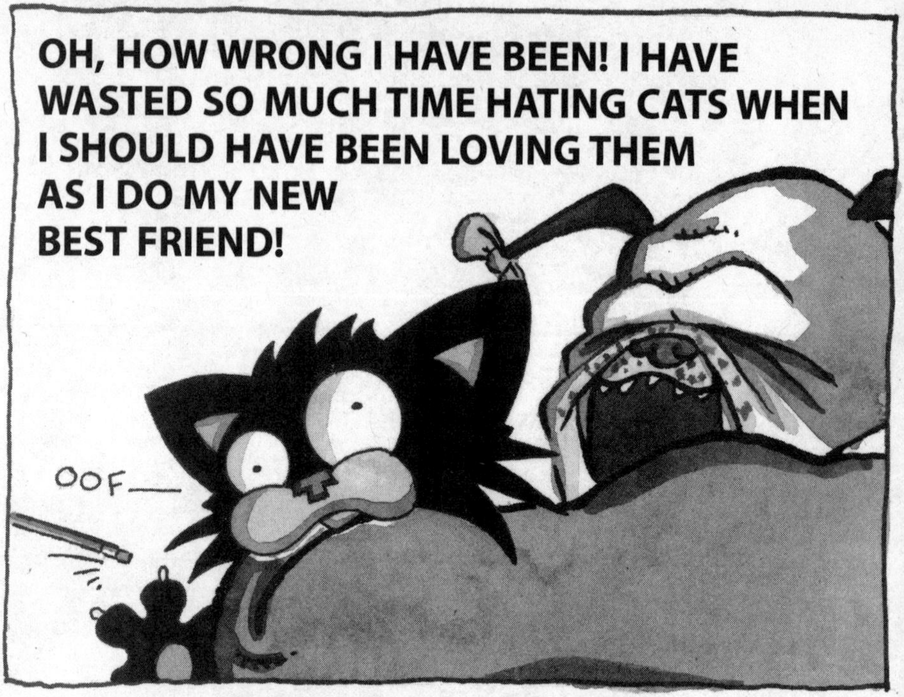
OH, HOW WRONG I HAVE BEEN! I HAVE WASTED SO MUCH TIME HATING CATS WHEN I SHOULD HAVE BEEN LOVING THEM AS I DO MY NEW BEST FRIEND!
OOF

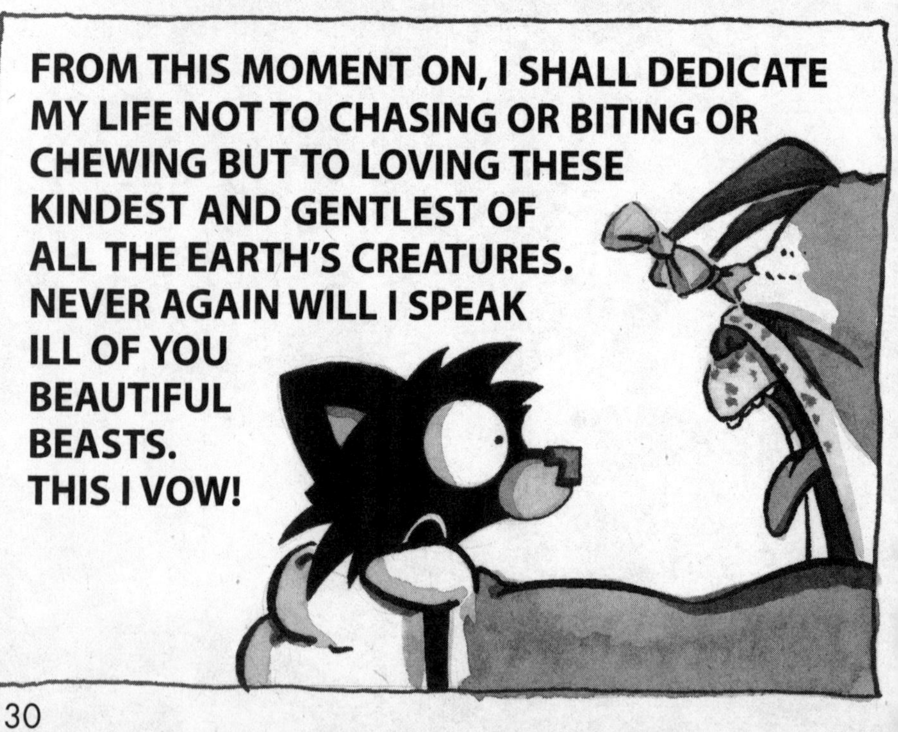
FROM THIS MOMENT ON, I SHALL DEDICATE MY LIFE NOT TO CHASING OR BITING OR CHEWING BUT TO LOVING THESE KINDEST AND GENTLEST OF ALL THE EARTH'S CREATURES. NEVER AGAIN WILL I SPEAK ILL OF YOU BEAUTIFUL BEASTS. THIS I VOW!

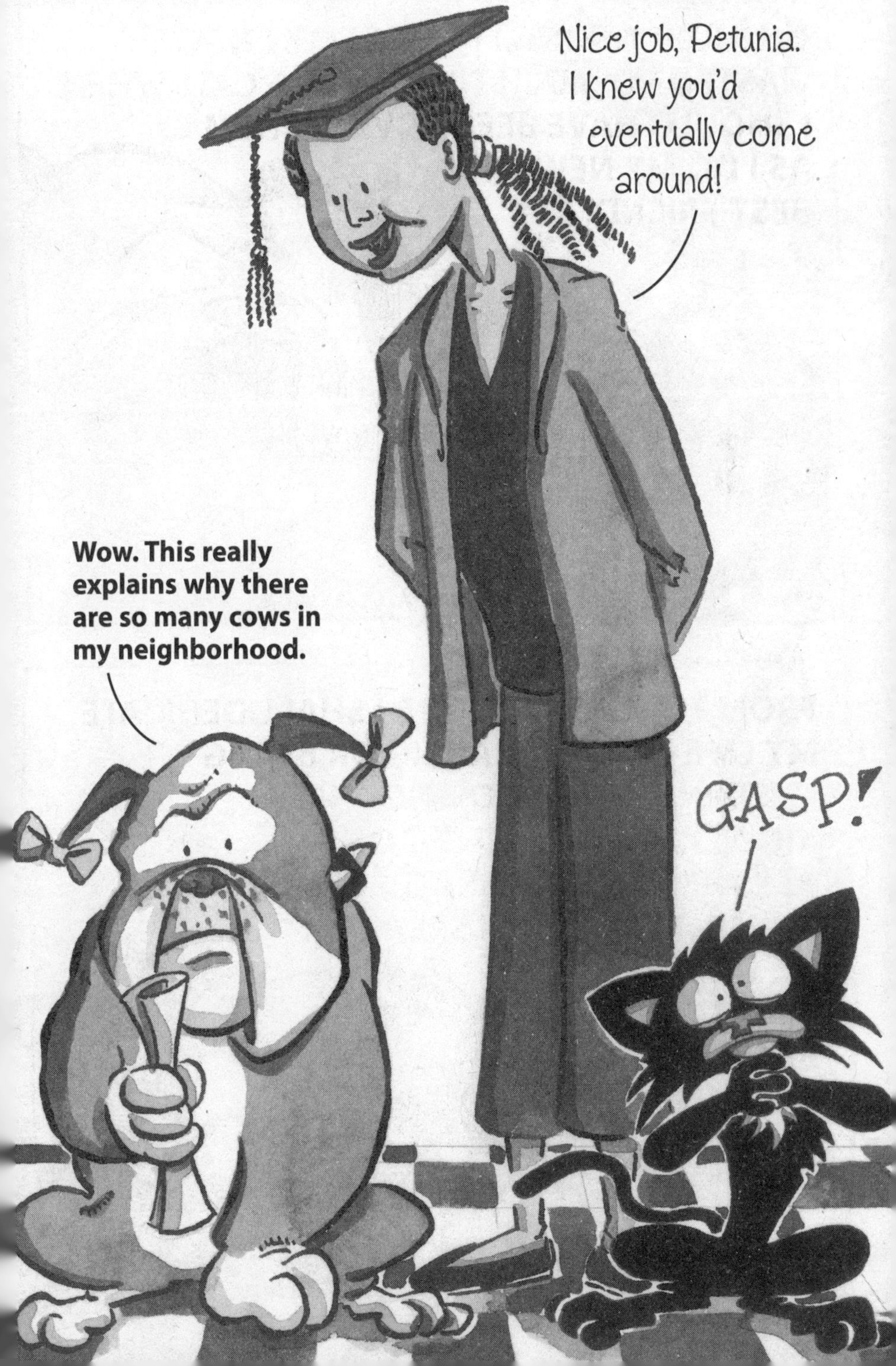
Nice job, Petunia. I knew you'd eventually come around!
Wow. This really explains why there are so many cows in my neighborhood.
GASP!

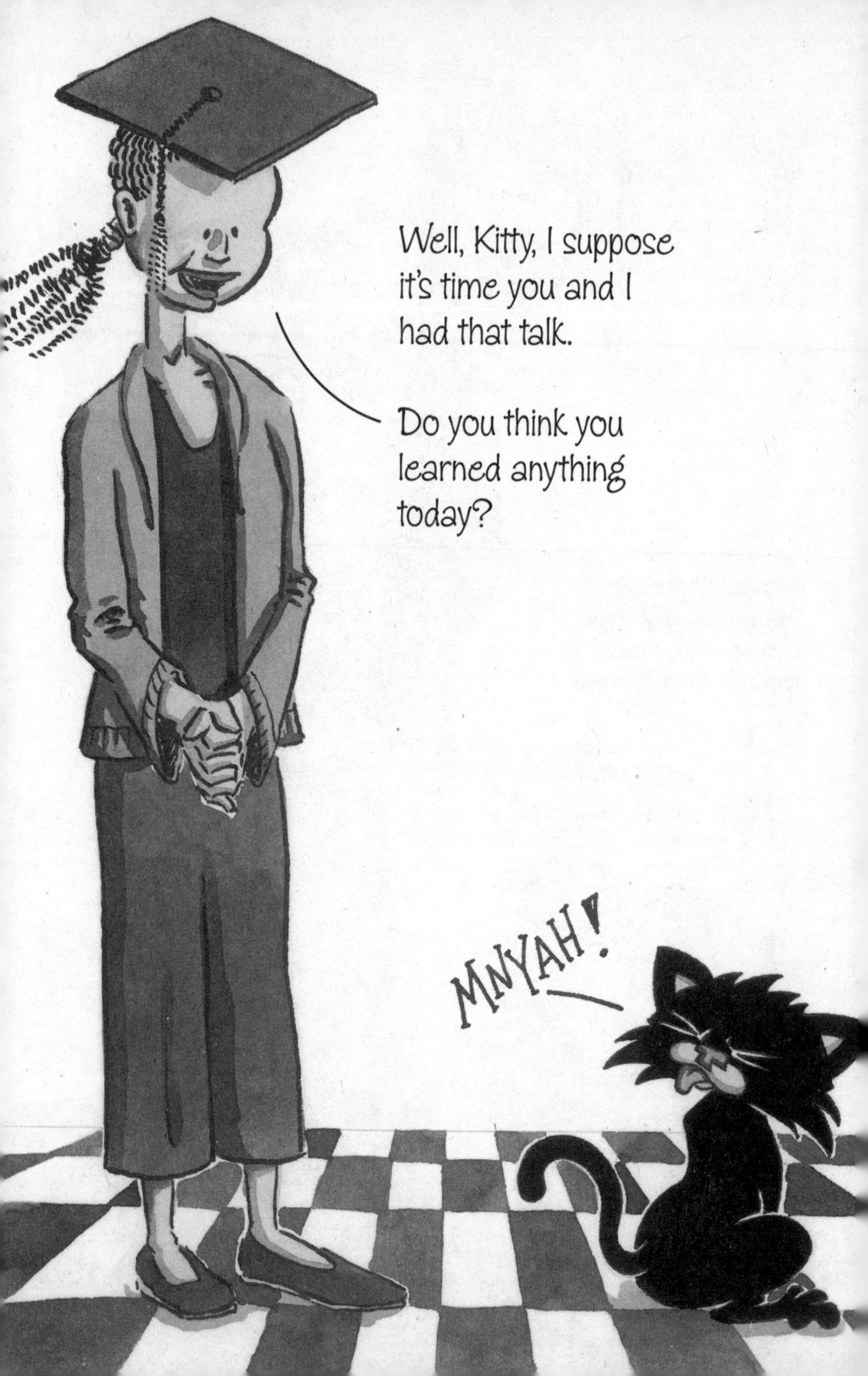
Well, Kitty, I suppose it's time you and I had that talk.
Do you think you learned anything today?
MNYAH!

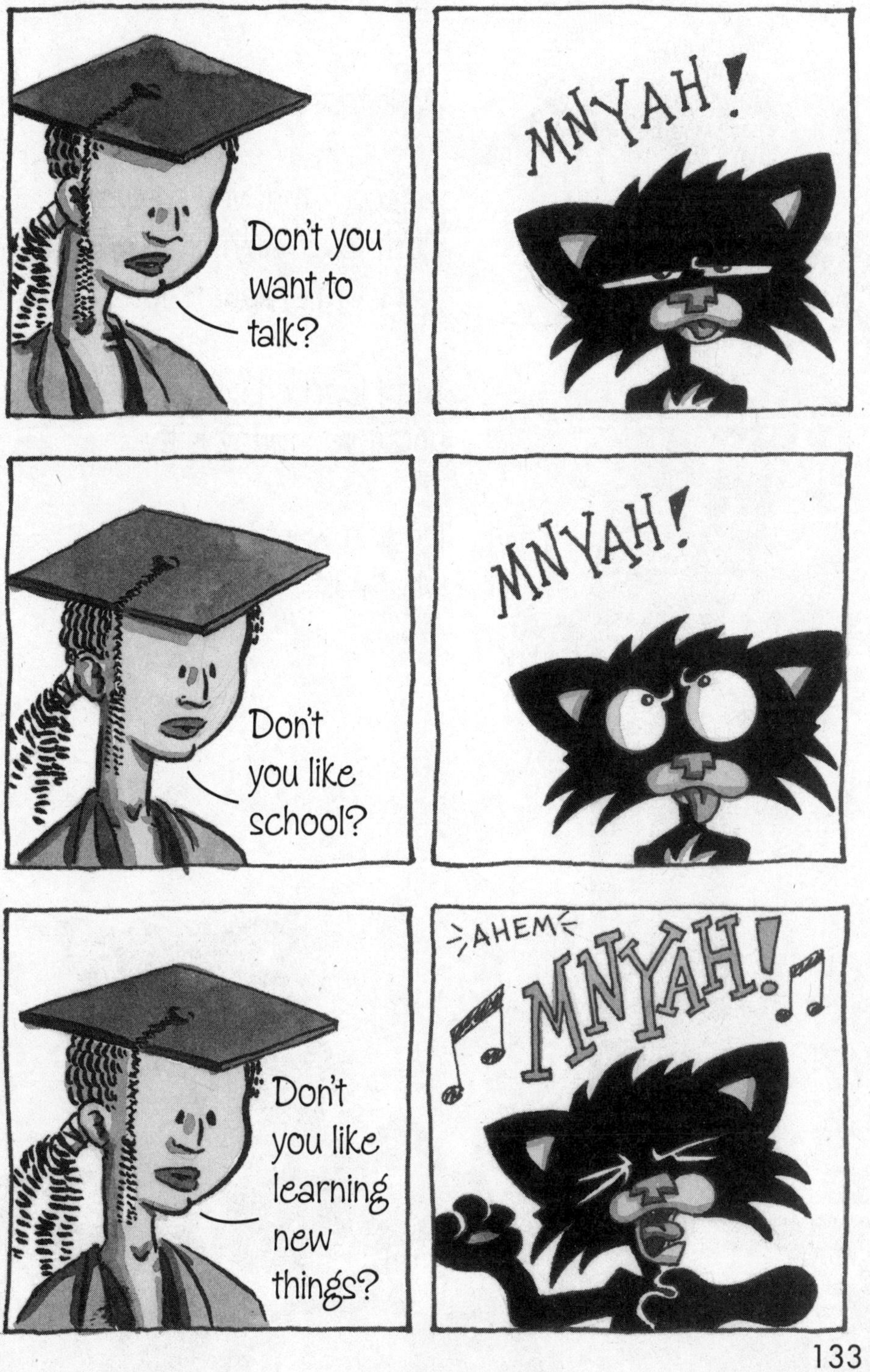
Don't you want to talk?
MNYAH!
Don't you like school?
MNYAH!
Don't you like learning new things?
AHEM
MNYAH!

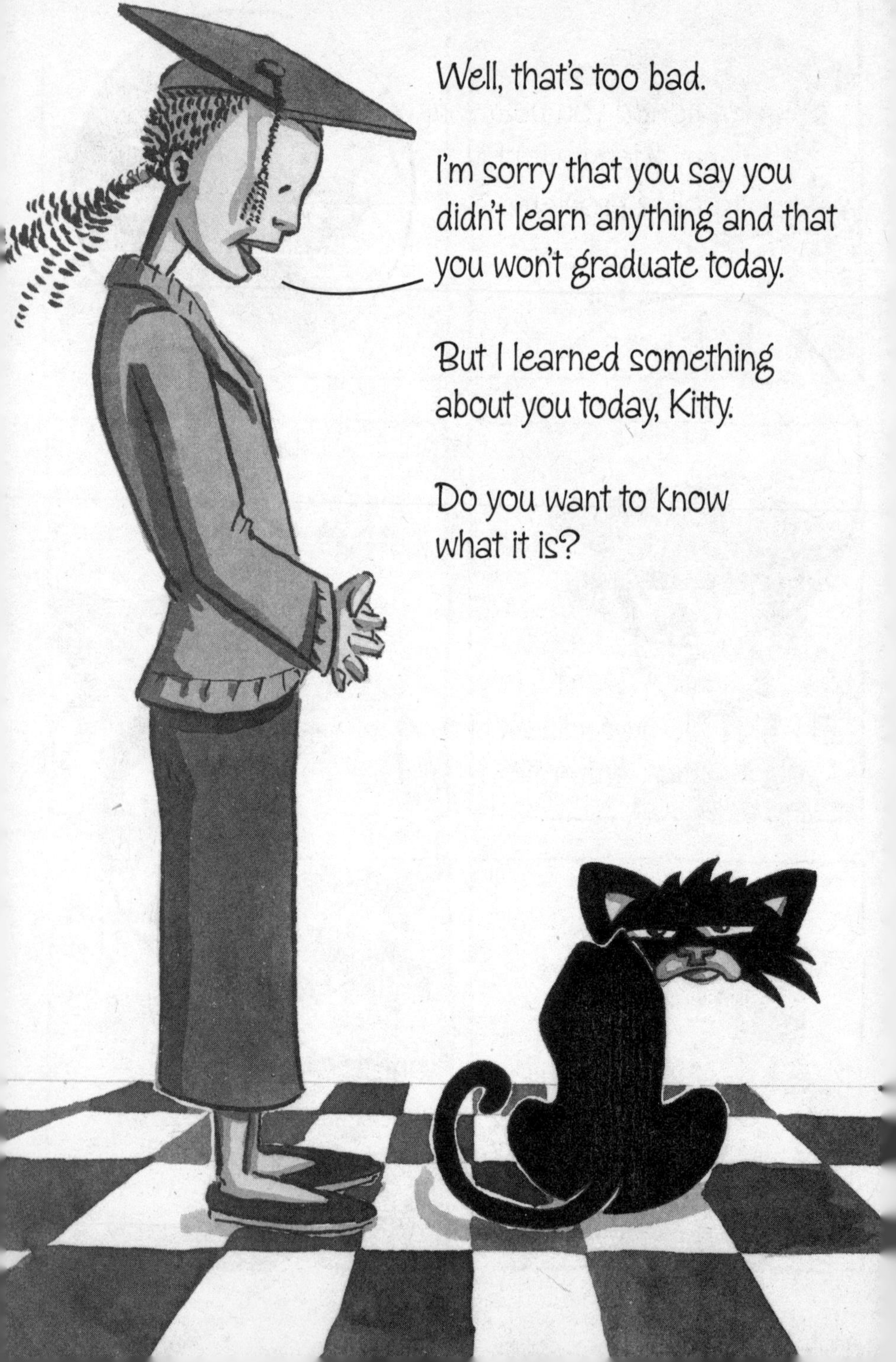
Well, that's too bad.
I'm sorry that you say you didn't learn anything and that you won't graduate today.
But I learned something about you today, Kitty.
Do you want to know what it is?

I watched you help your puppy friend with his drooling problem.

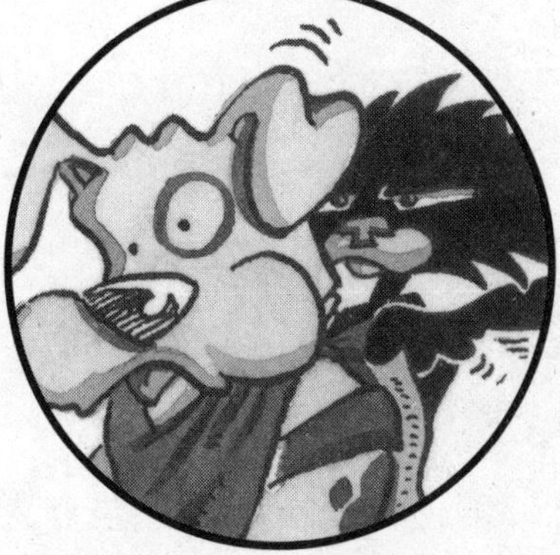

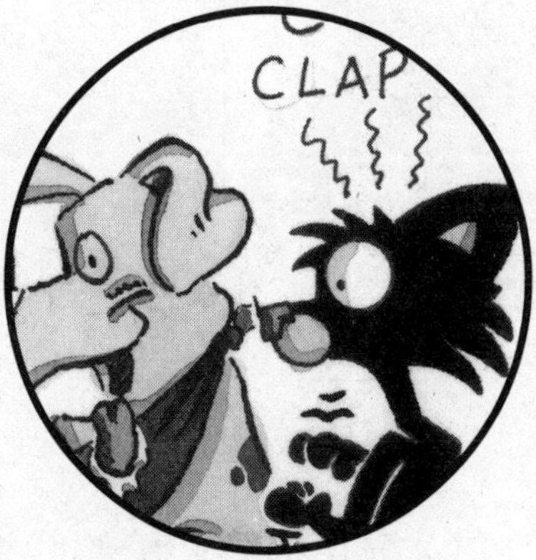
CLAP

I watched you be the first to support the little bunny with your applause.

I watched you give Petunia your painting and make a new friend.

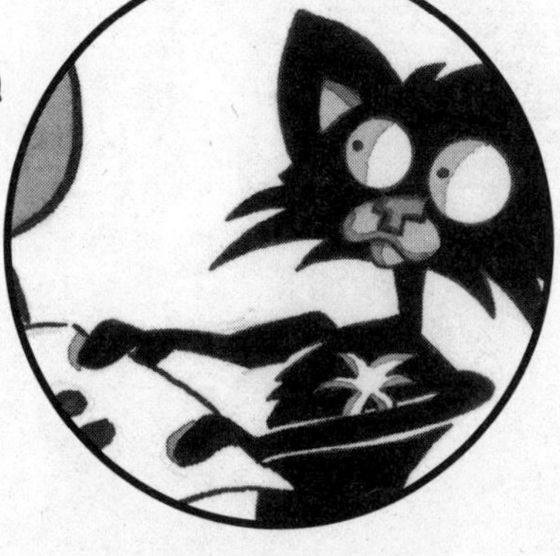

Do you want to know what I learned about you today, Kitty?

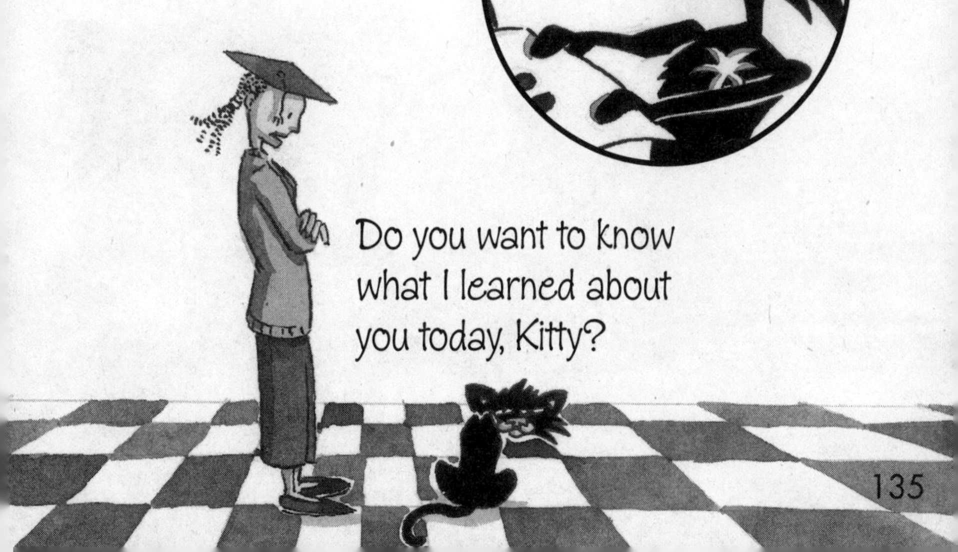

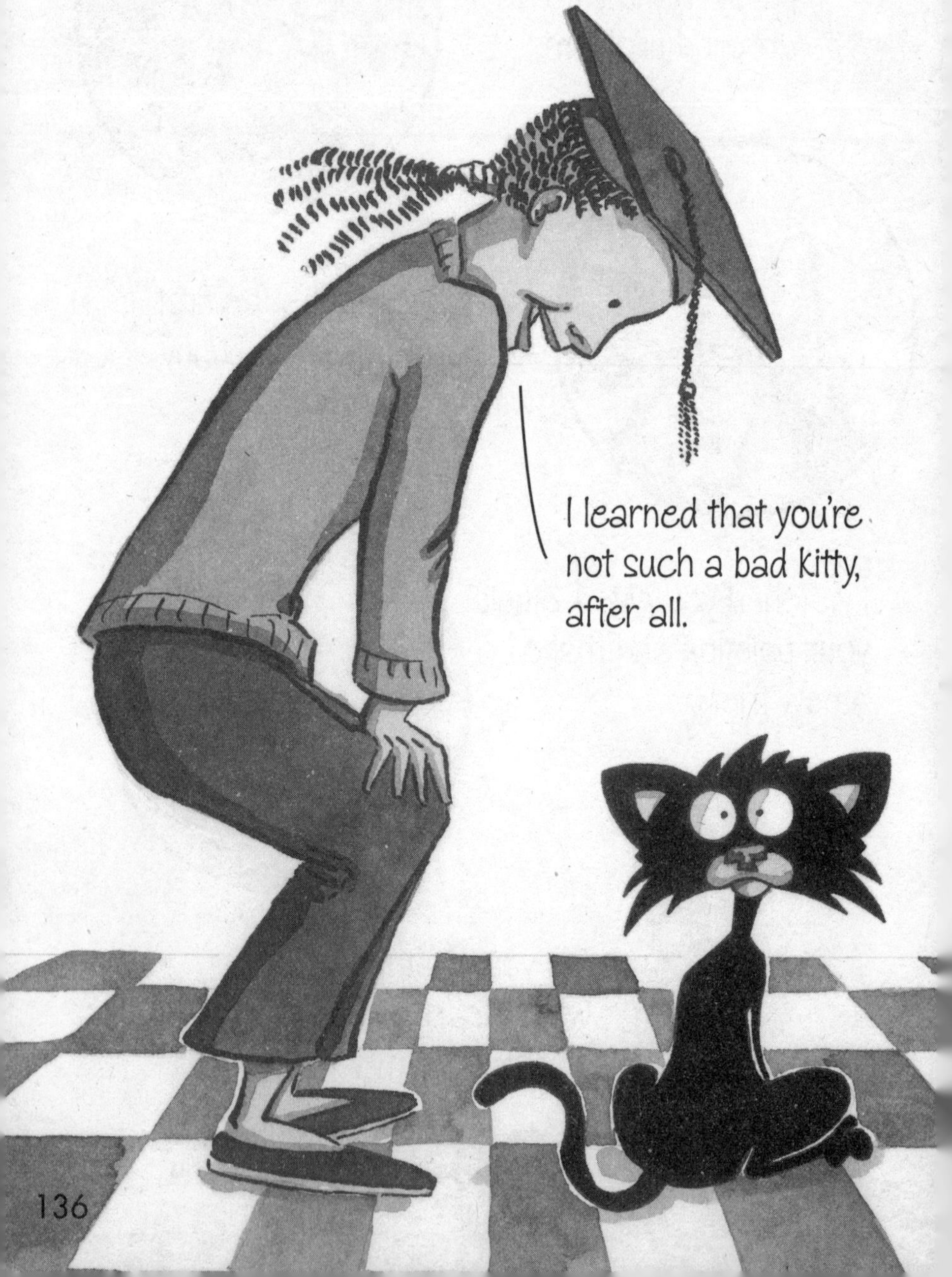
I learned that you're not such a bad kitty, after all.

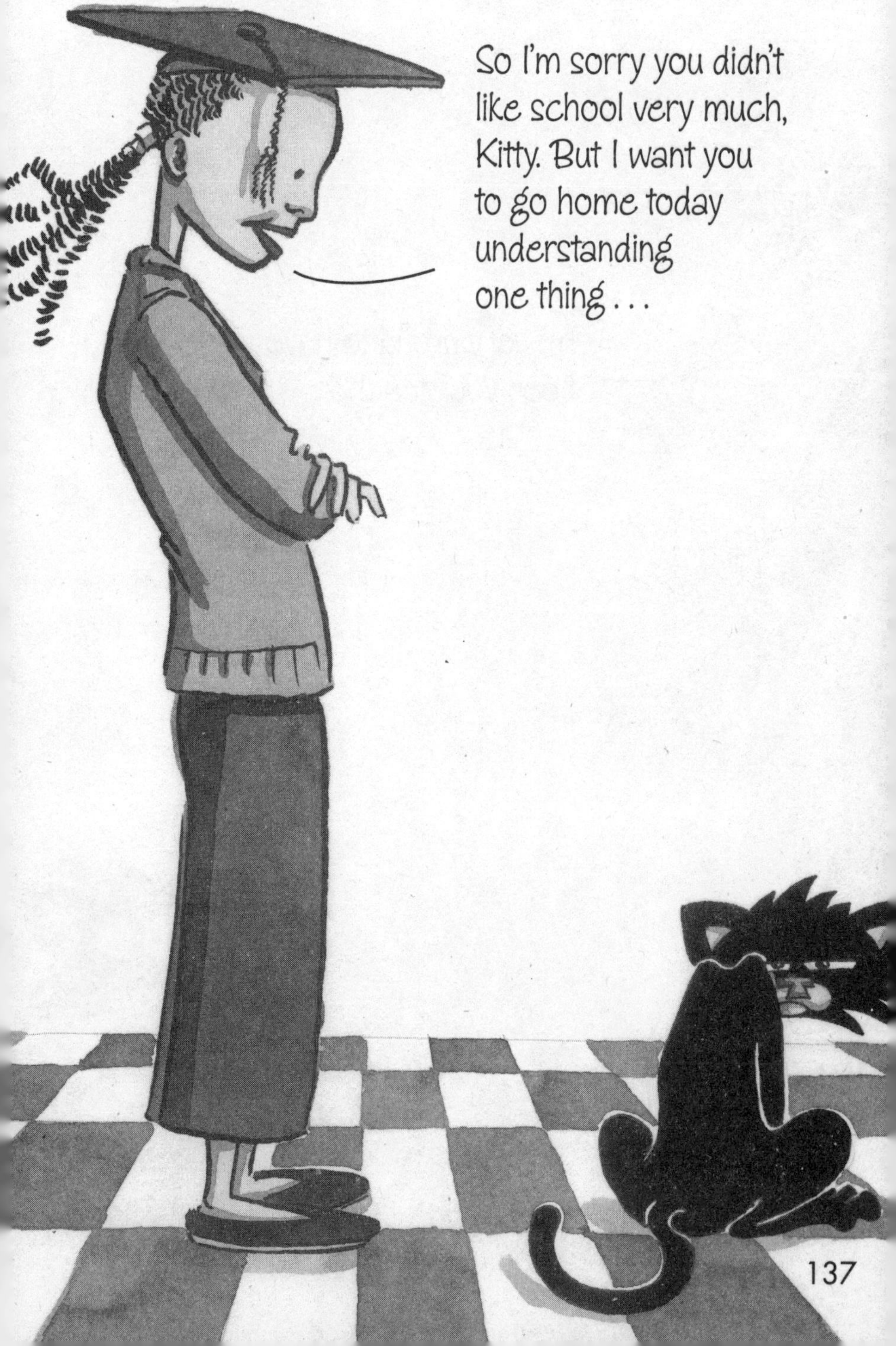
So I'm sorry you didn't like school very much, Kitty. But I want you to go home today understanding one thing . . .

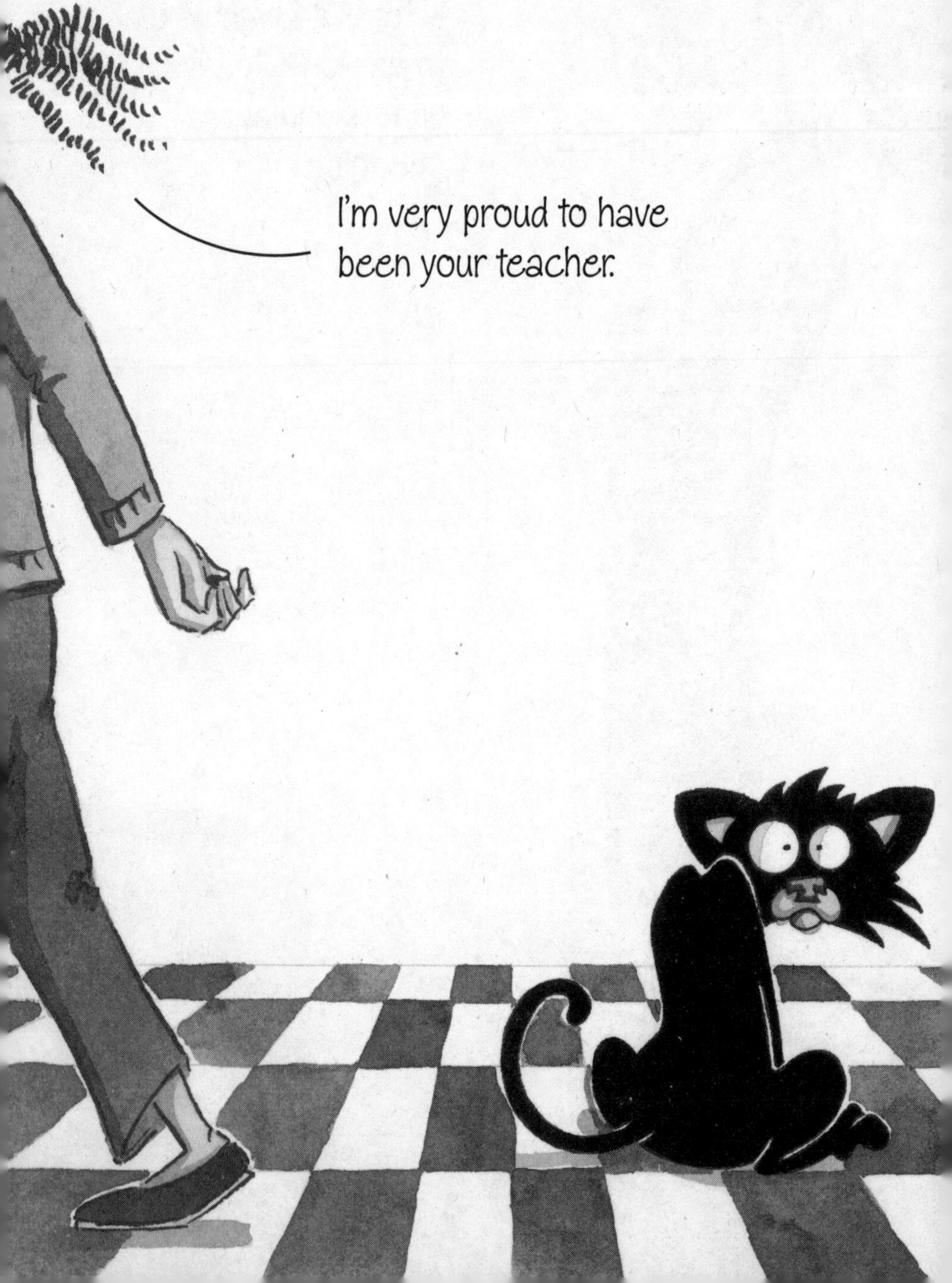
I'm very proud to have been your teacher.

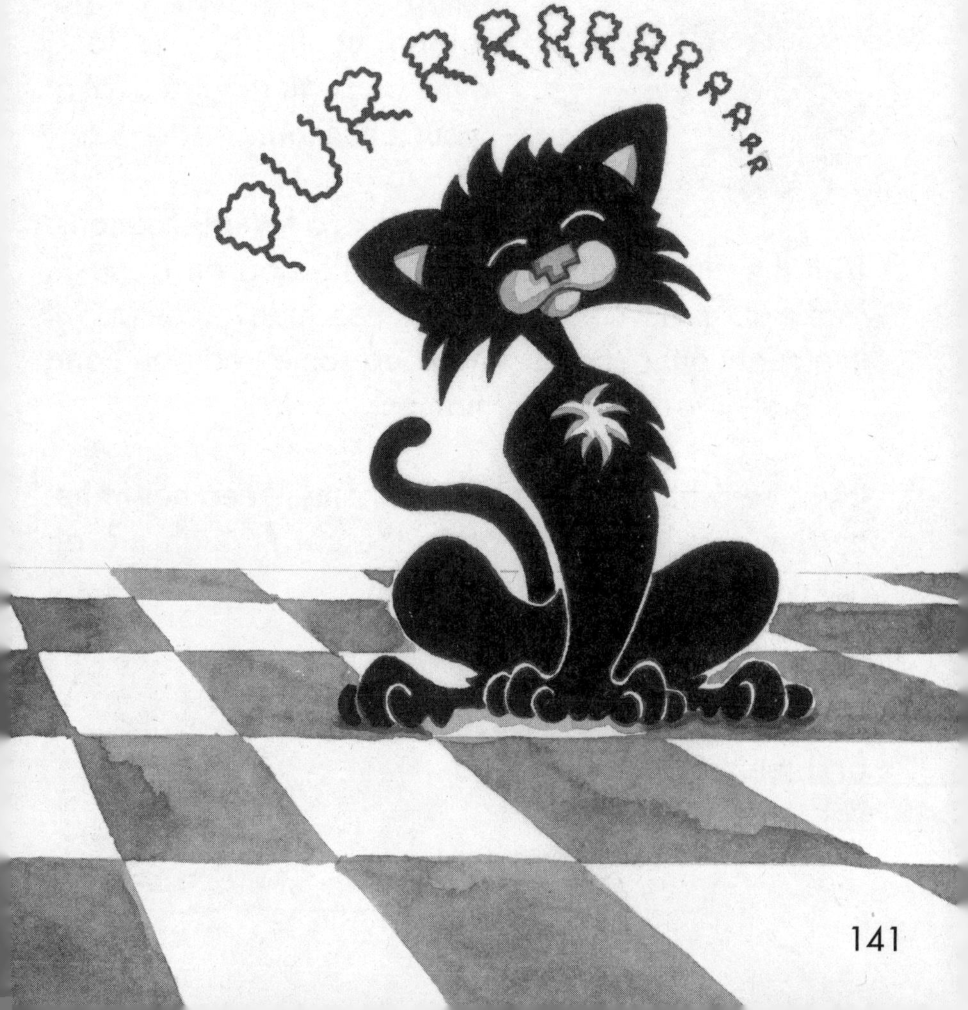
QURRRRRRRRRRR

UNCLE MURRAY'S FUN FACTS

Never!

CAN DOGS AND CATS EVER BECOME FRIENDS?

Dogs and cats can and will become friends, but they can't do this by themselves. They'll need your help. The key is PATIENCE. Helping your pets to get along could take a long time and will require a lot of your attention.

MEOW?

First, take a few precautions. Trim the claws on your cat. Put the dog on a leash. Make sure the cat has a place to hide or escape if things get out of hand. And keep some treats on hand . . . you'll see why in a moment.

If you're bringing a cat into the home, keep her in her carrier and let the dog sniff the cat through the air holes. If the dog is calm, give him some treats as a reward. If he barks or is excitable, pull on the leash and tell him "NO" until he calms down.

ARF?

If you're bringing a dog into the home, also keep the dog in a cage if you can, at first. Bring the cat into the room by carrying her and petting her to let her know it's okay. If your cat gets wiggly or runs, don't punish her for being understandably anxious. Just pet her and console her.

Another tactic you might try is to keep both animals inside their respective carriers and place them both in the same room with their doors facing each other. You should stay in the room, too, if only to give them both treats when they are calm. If either of your pets continues to be anxious about the situation, you should be prepared to keep them separate from each other the best you can and repeat this process each day for as long as it takes.

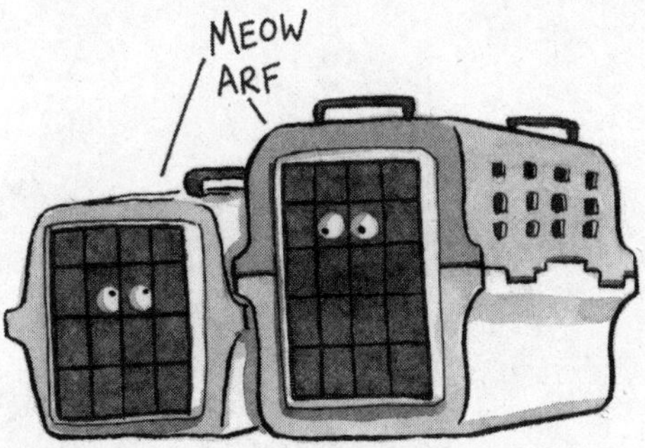
MEOW
ARF

In time, you should be able to train each pet to think of the other as another member of the family . . . an annoying member, perhaps, but part of the family nonetheless.

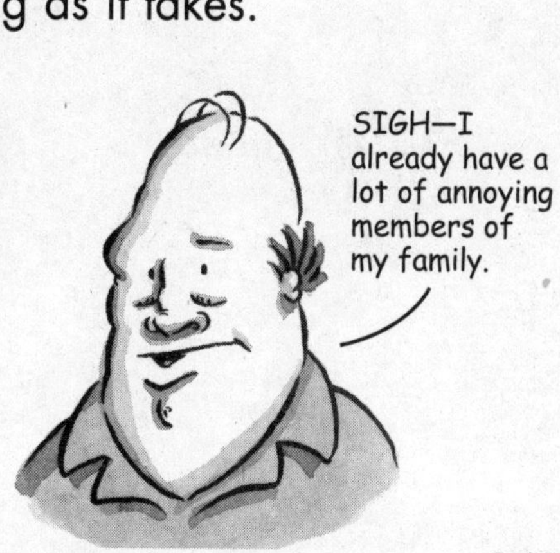
SIGH—I already have a lot of annoying members of my family.

•EPILOGUE•

Well, Kitty, I'm pretty disappointed with you that you didn't graduate. I can't help but think that maybe you just didn't try hard enough.

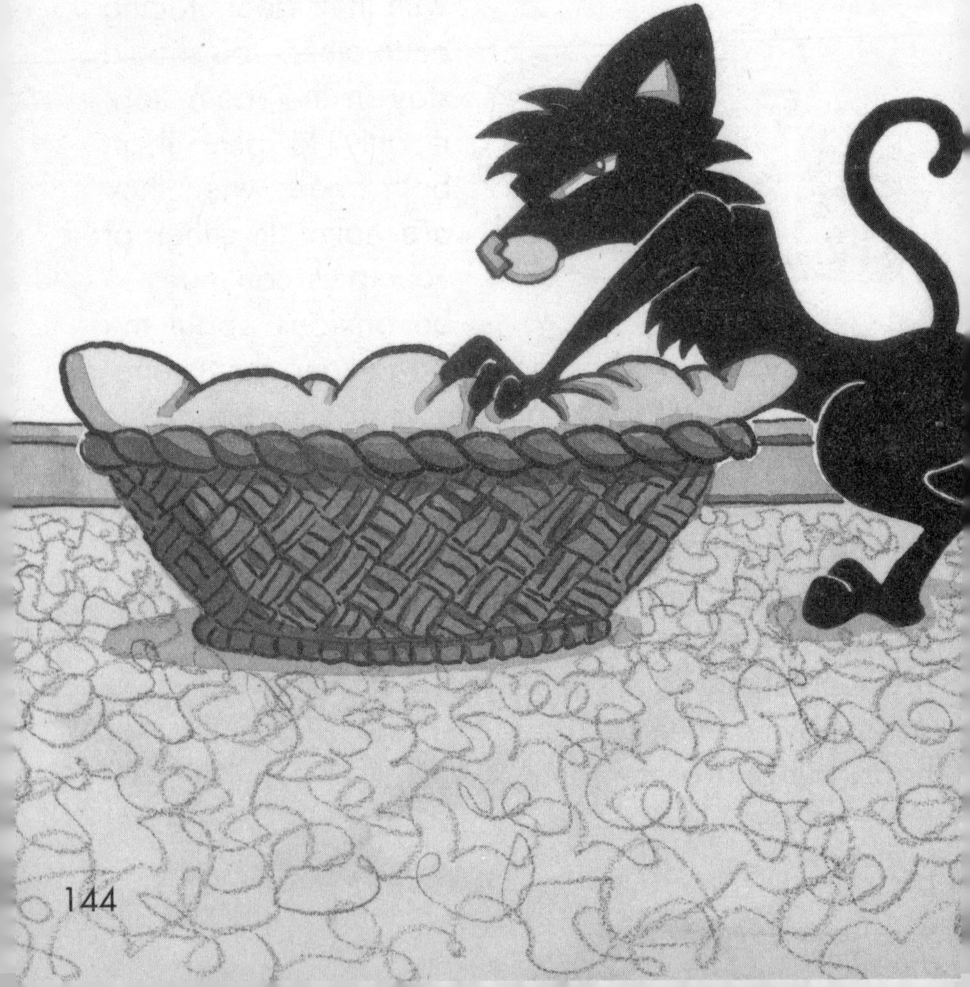

SIGH And I guess this means that you're the same old, cranky, ornery, disagreeable Kitty you've always been.

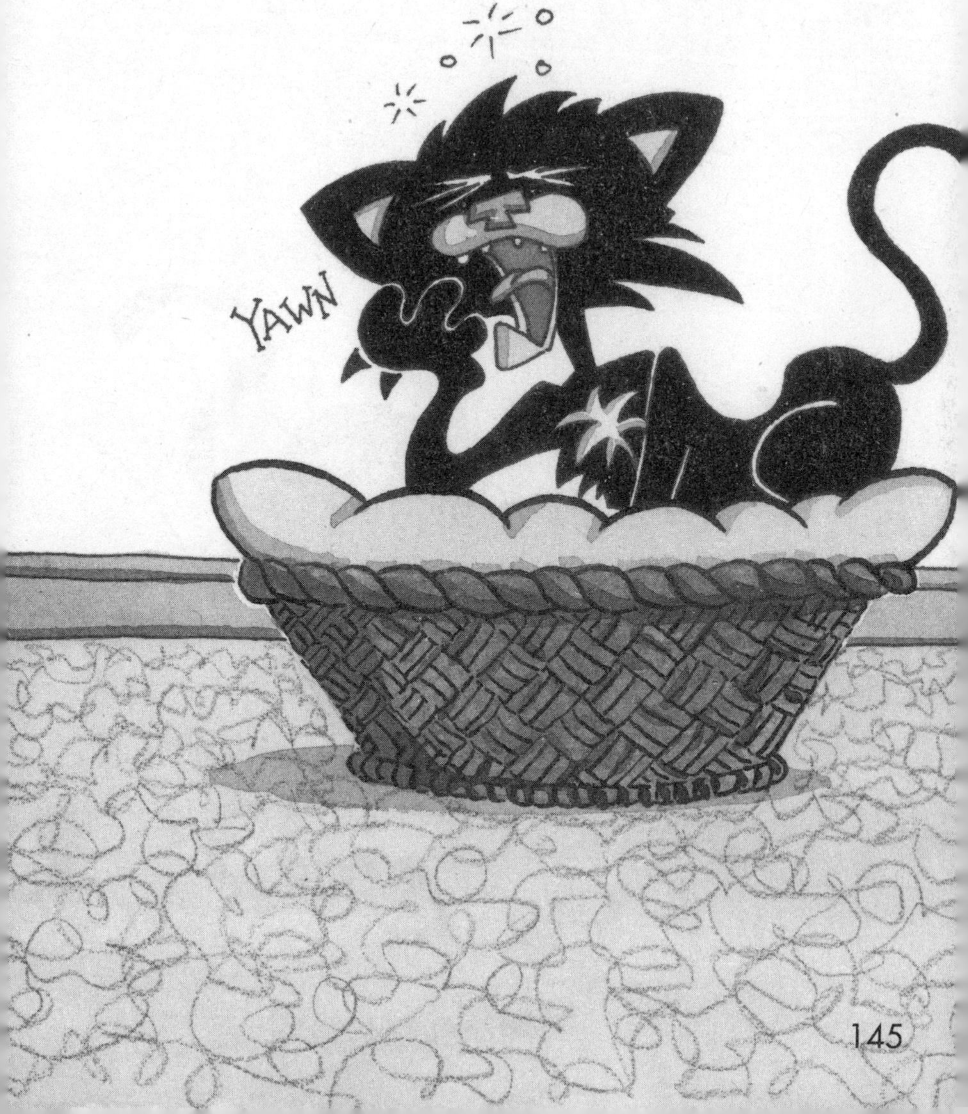
YAWN

Your teacher Miss Dee kept telling me how much she likes you and how much she hopes that you'll be able to go back to school for another chance. She seemed to really like you, Kitty. But I don't know. I just don't see any reason to send you back to that school . . .

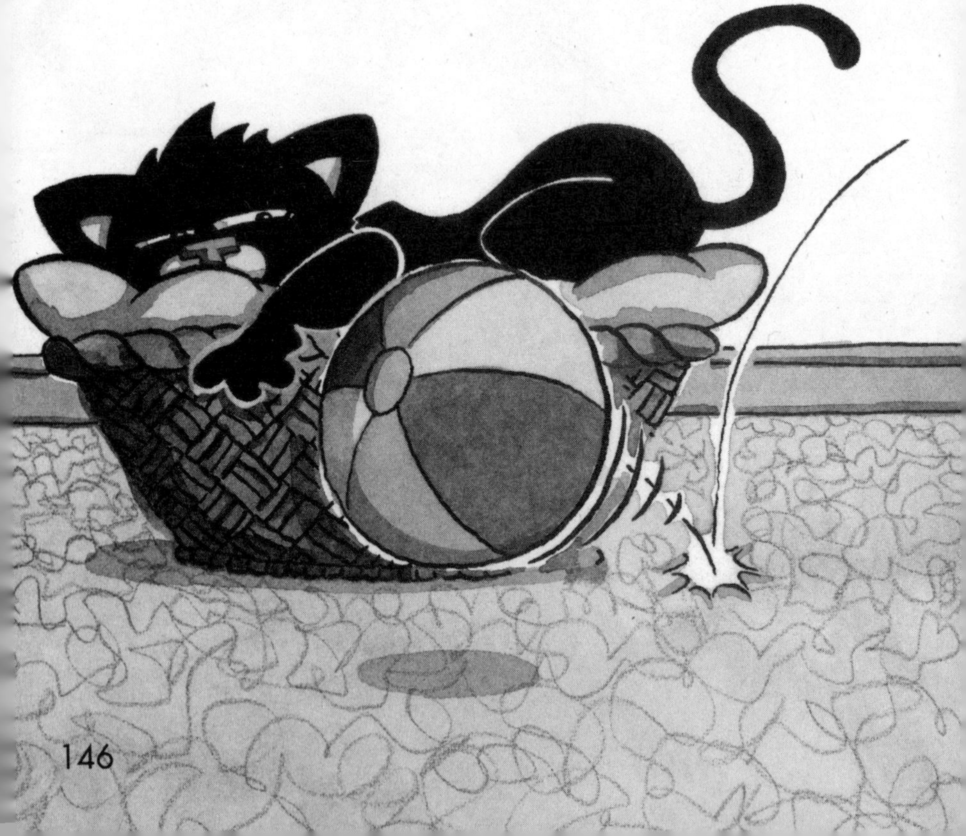

unless we really, really, REALLY have to.

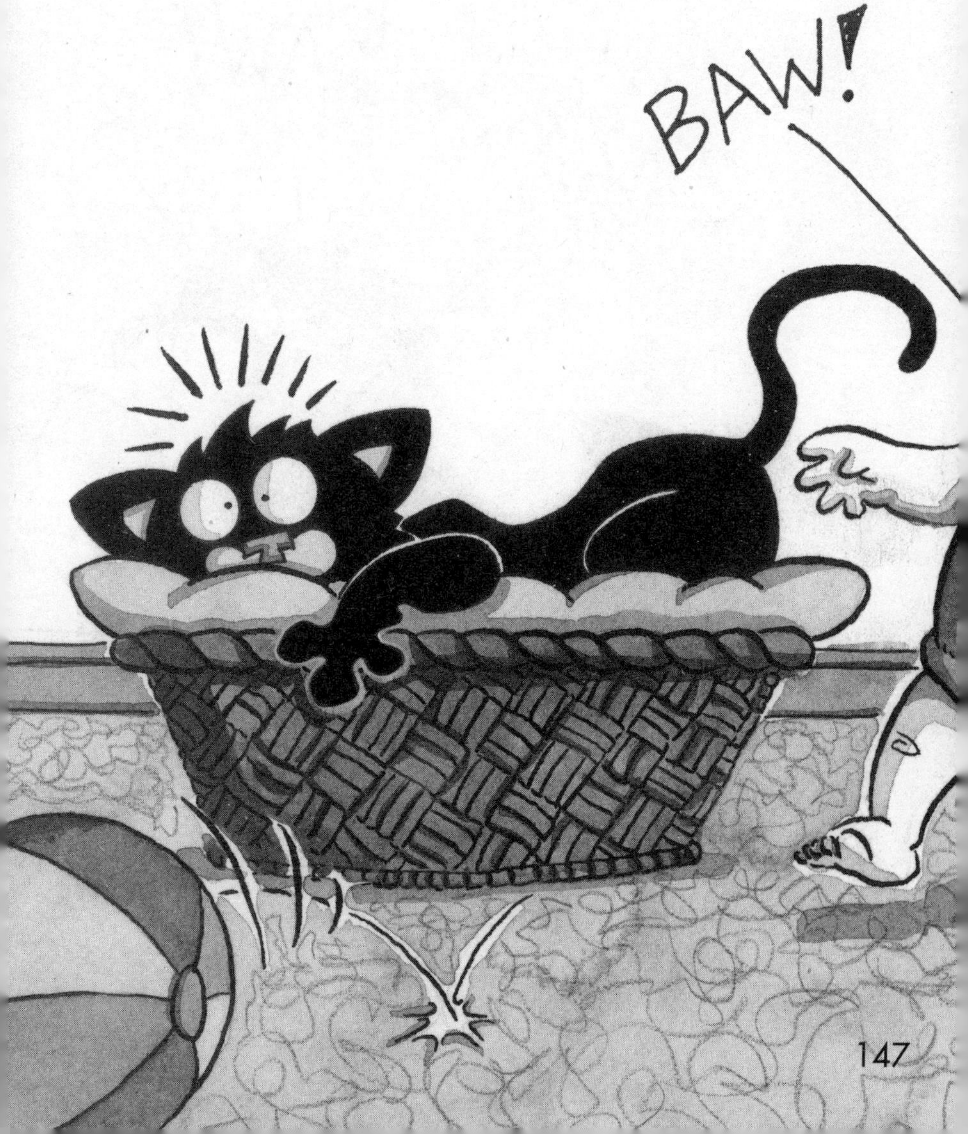
BAW!

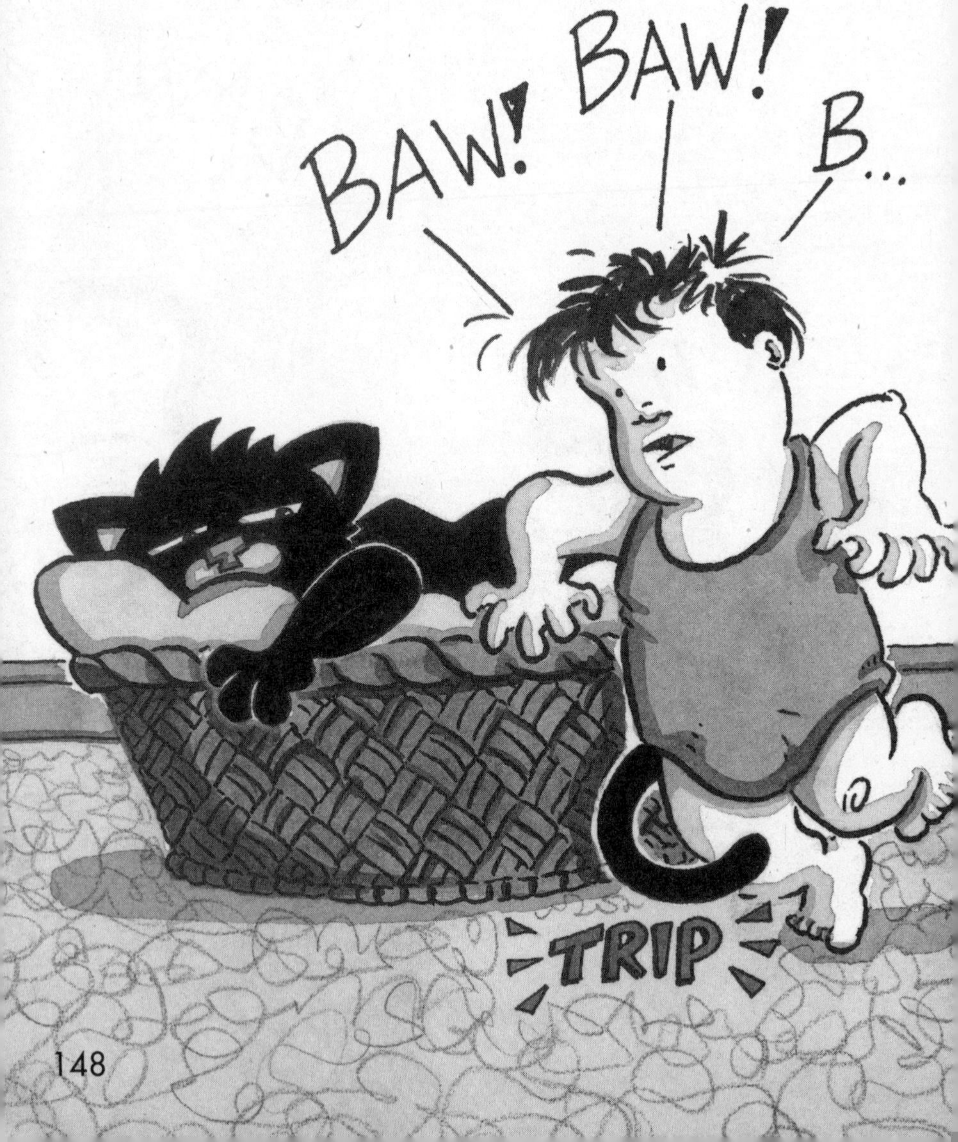
BAW! BAW! B...
TRIP

KITTY!

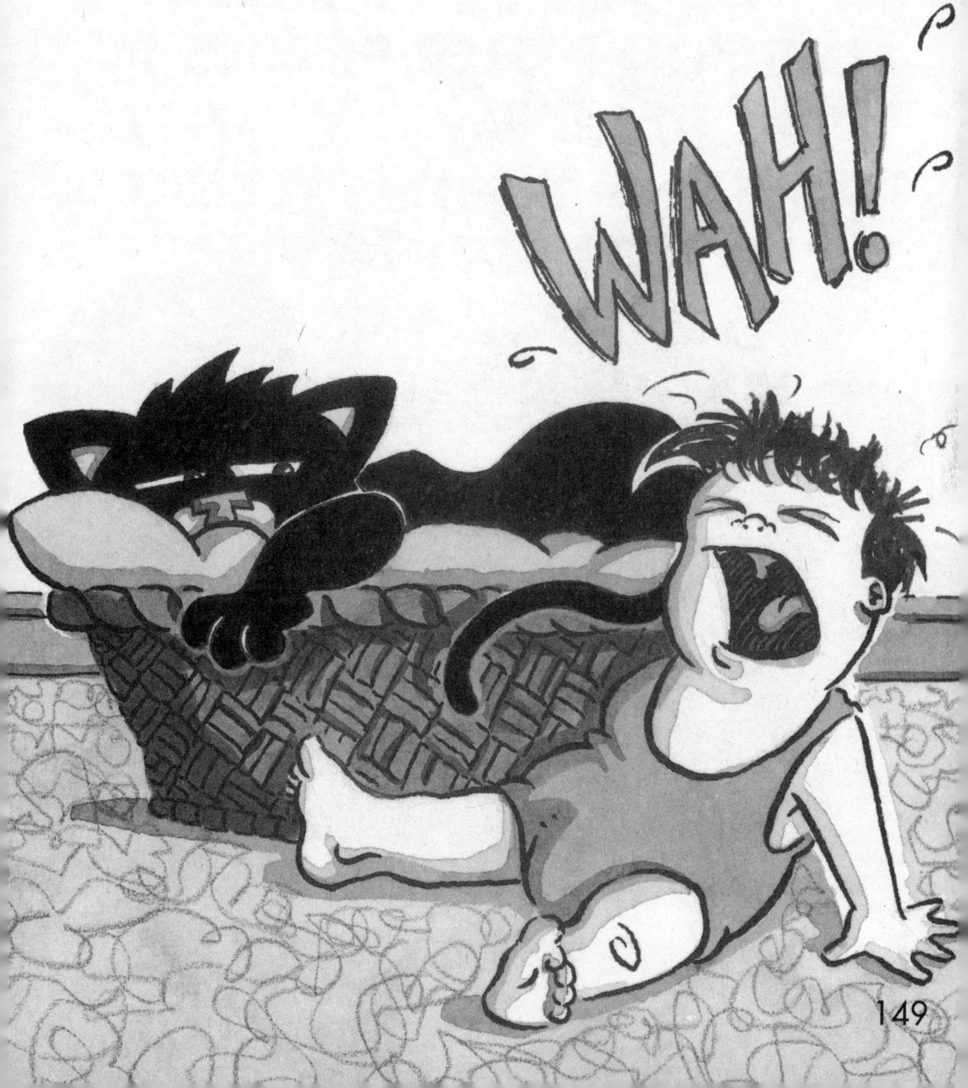
WAH!

THAT DOES IT! THAT'S THE LAST STRAW! I'M SENDING YOU BACK TO THAT SCHOOL AND I DON'T WANT TO HEAR ONE SINGLE COMPLAINT OUT OF YOU ABOUT IT! AND THIS TIME YOU BETTER BE NICE TO THAT TEACHER! I MEAN IT, KITTY. SHE SEEMS TO LIKE YOU, B… I DON'T KNOW WHY… THIING

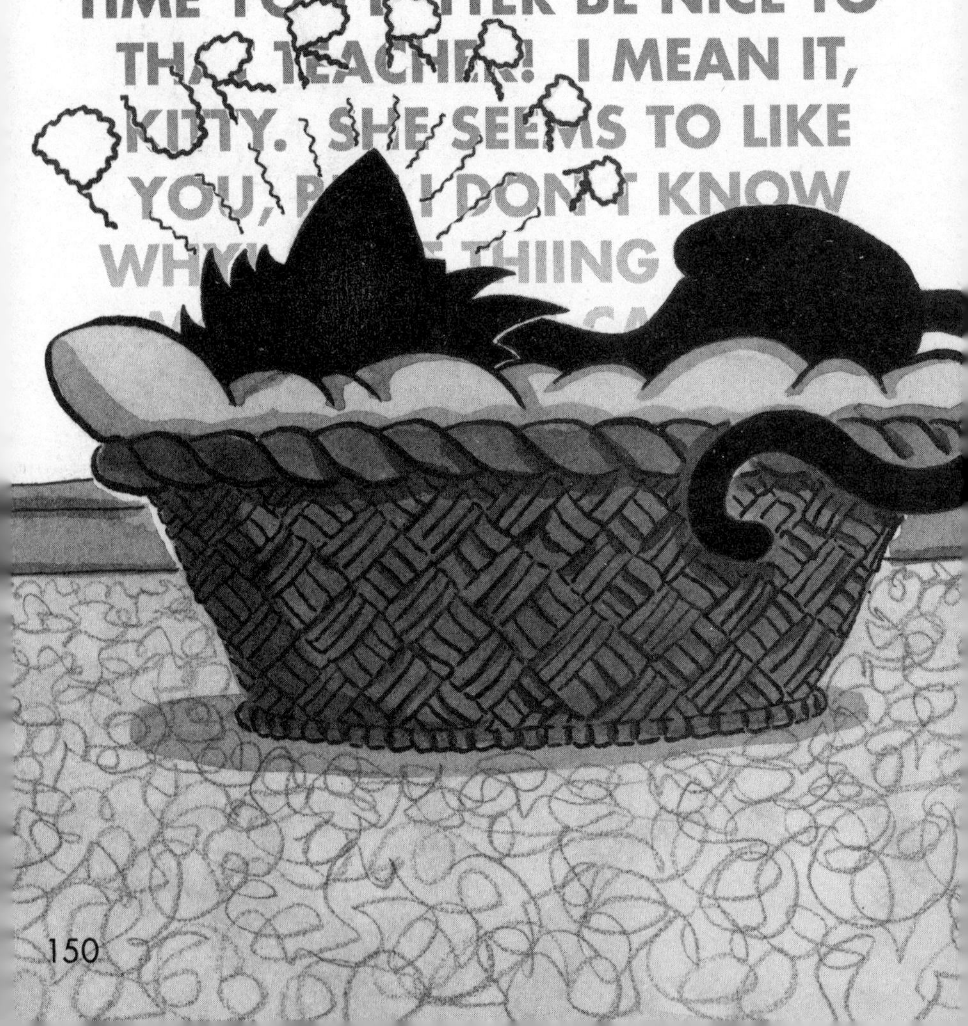

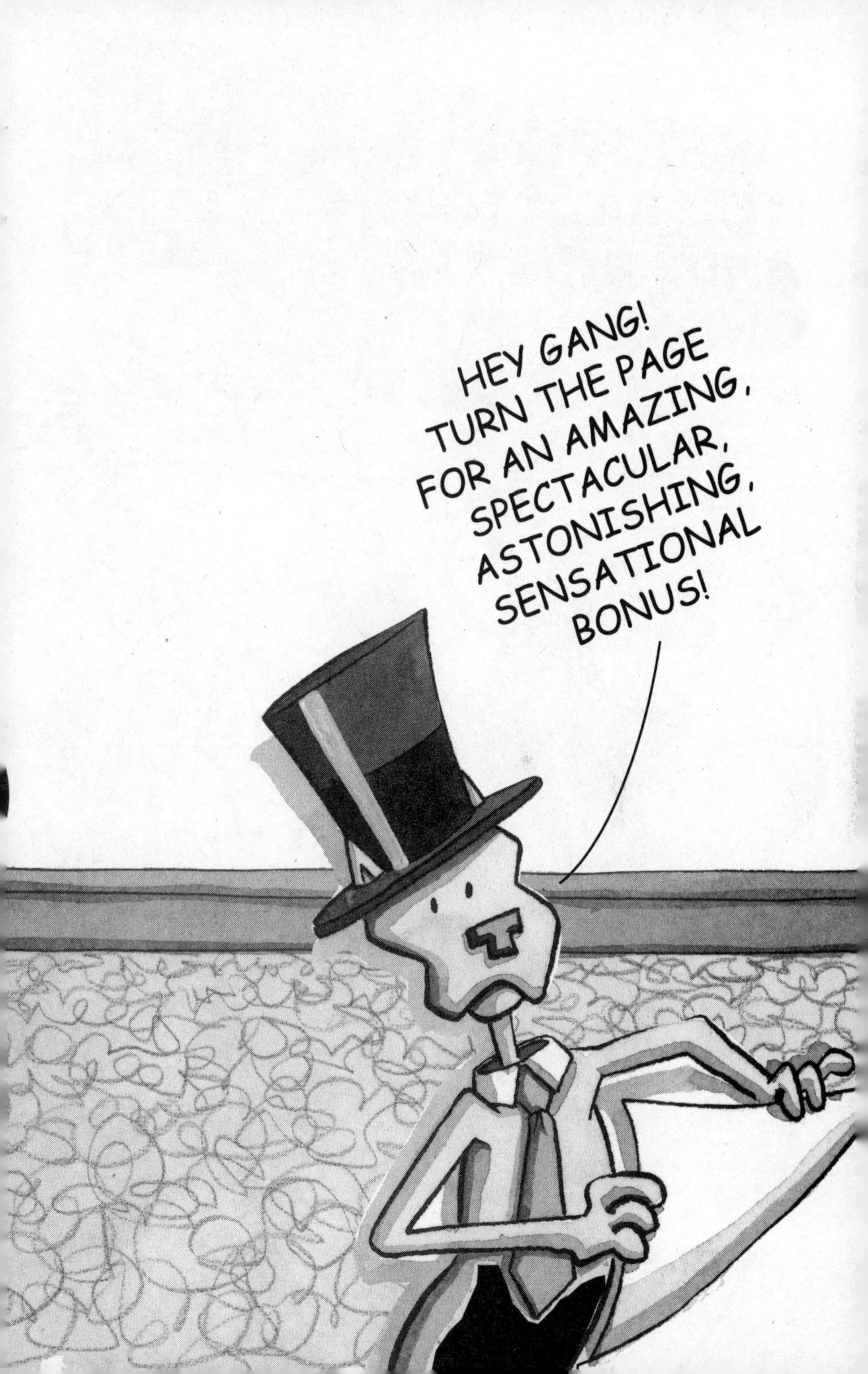
HEY GANG! TURN THE PAGE FOR AN AMAZING, SPECTACULAR, ASTONISHING, SENSATIONAL BONUS!

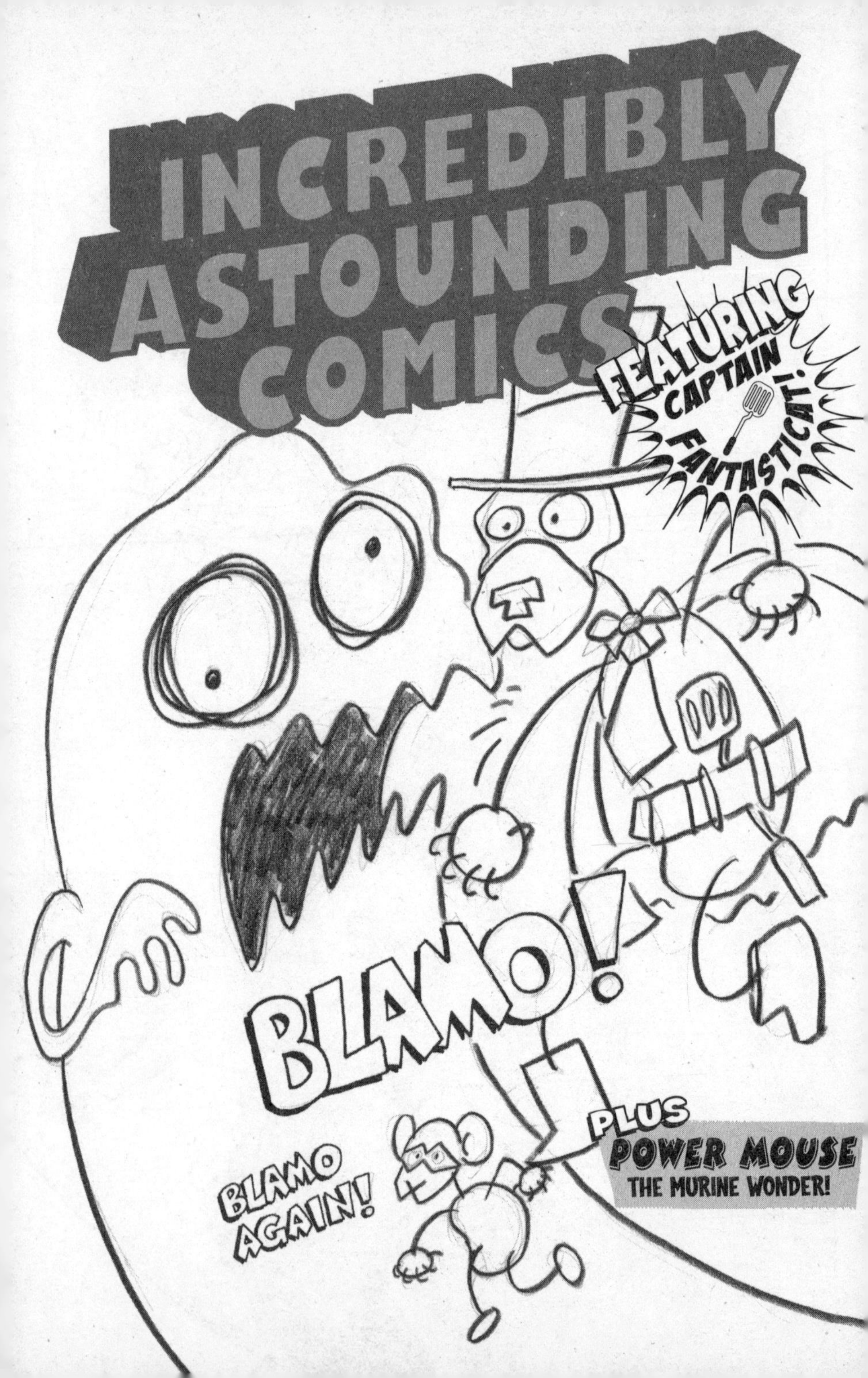
INCREDIBLY ASTOUNDING COMICS
FEATURING CAPTAIN FANTASTICAT!
BLAMO!
PLUS
POWER MOUSE
THE MURINE WONDER!
BLAMO AGAIN!

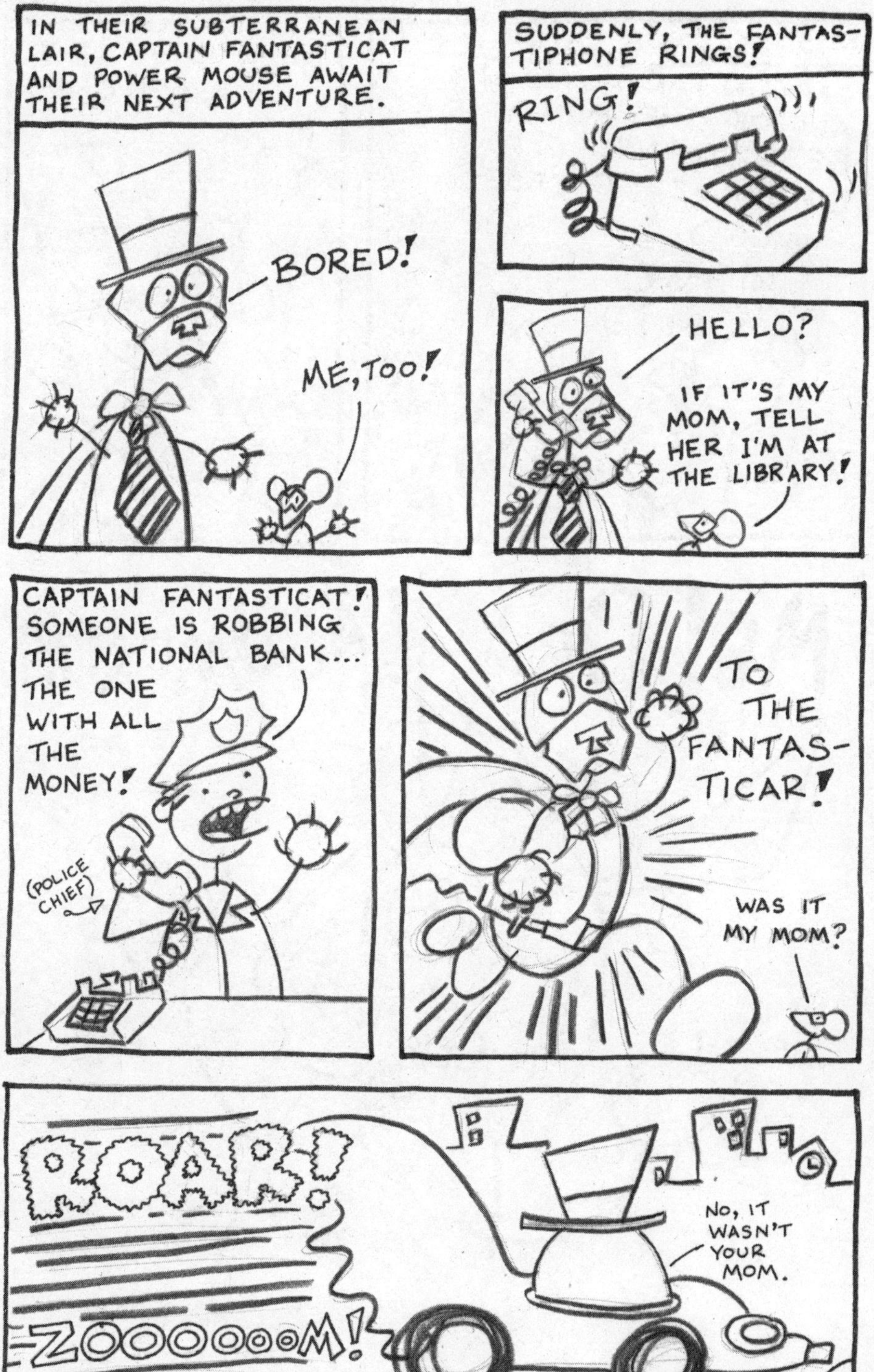
IN THEIR SUBTERRANEAN LAIR, CAPTAIN FANTASTICAT AND POWER MOUSE AWAIT THEIR NEXT ADVENTURE.
BORED!
ME, TOO!
SUDDENLY, THE FANTASTIPHONE RINGS!
RING!
HELLO?
IF IT'S MY MOM, TELL HER I'M AT THE LIBRARY!
CAPTAIN FANTASTICAT! SOMEONE IS ROBBING THE NATIONAL BANK... THE ONE WITH ALL THE MONEY!
(POLICE CHIEF)
TO THE FANTASTICAR!
WAS IT MY MOM?
ROAR!
ZOOOOOOOM!
NO, IT WASN'T YOUR MOM.
1

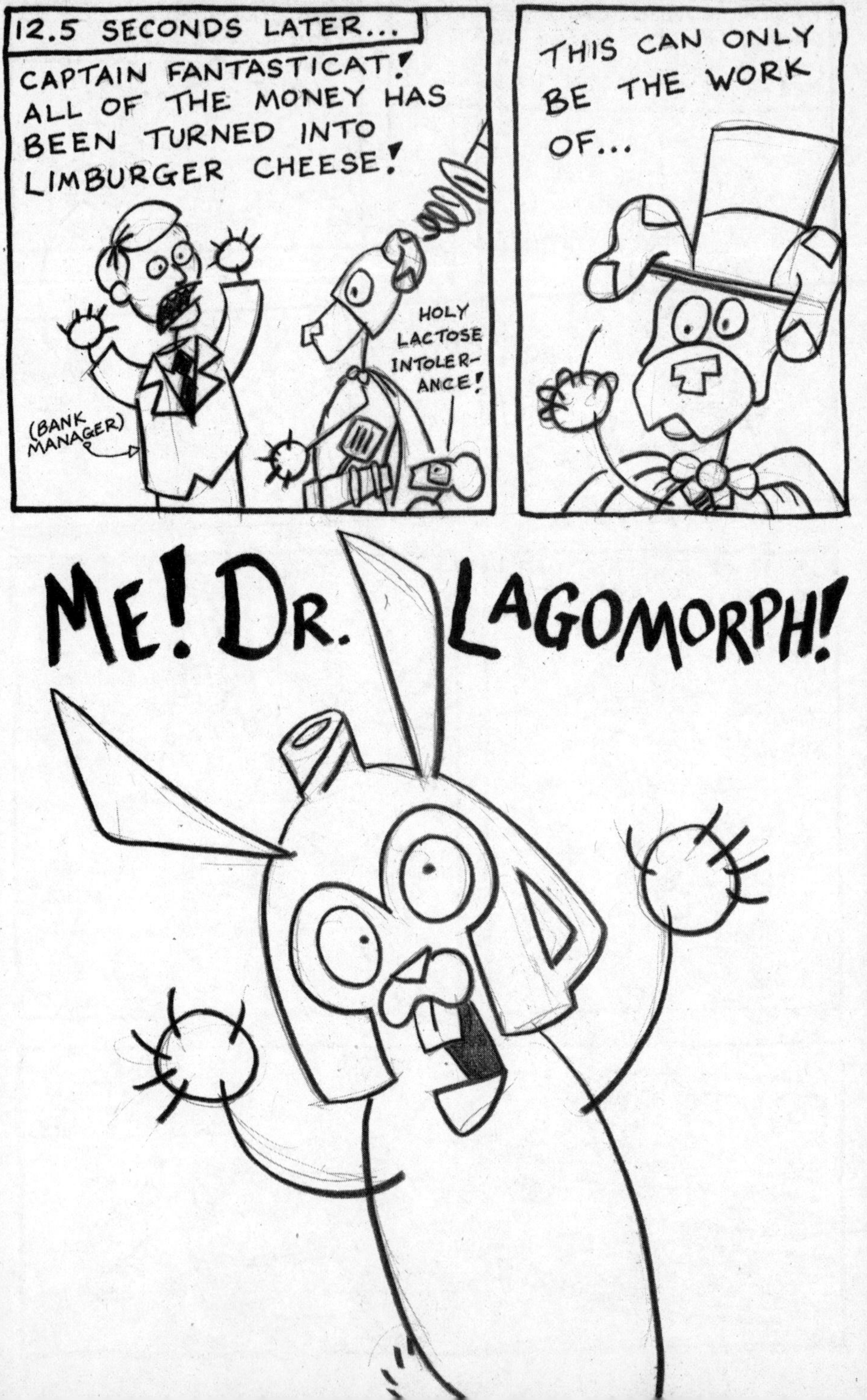
12.5 SECONDS LATER...
CAPTAIN FANTASTICAT! ALL OF THE MONEY HAS BEEN TURNED INTO LIMBURGER CHEESE!
(BANK MANAGER)
HOLY LACTOSE INTOLER-ANCE!
THIS CAN ONLY BE THE WORK OF...
ME! DR. LAGOMORPH!

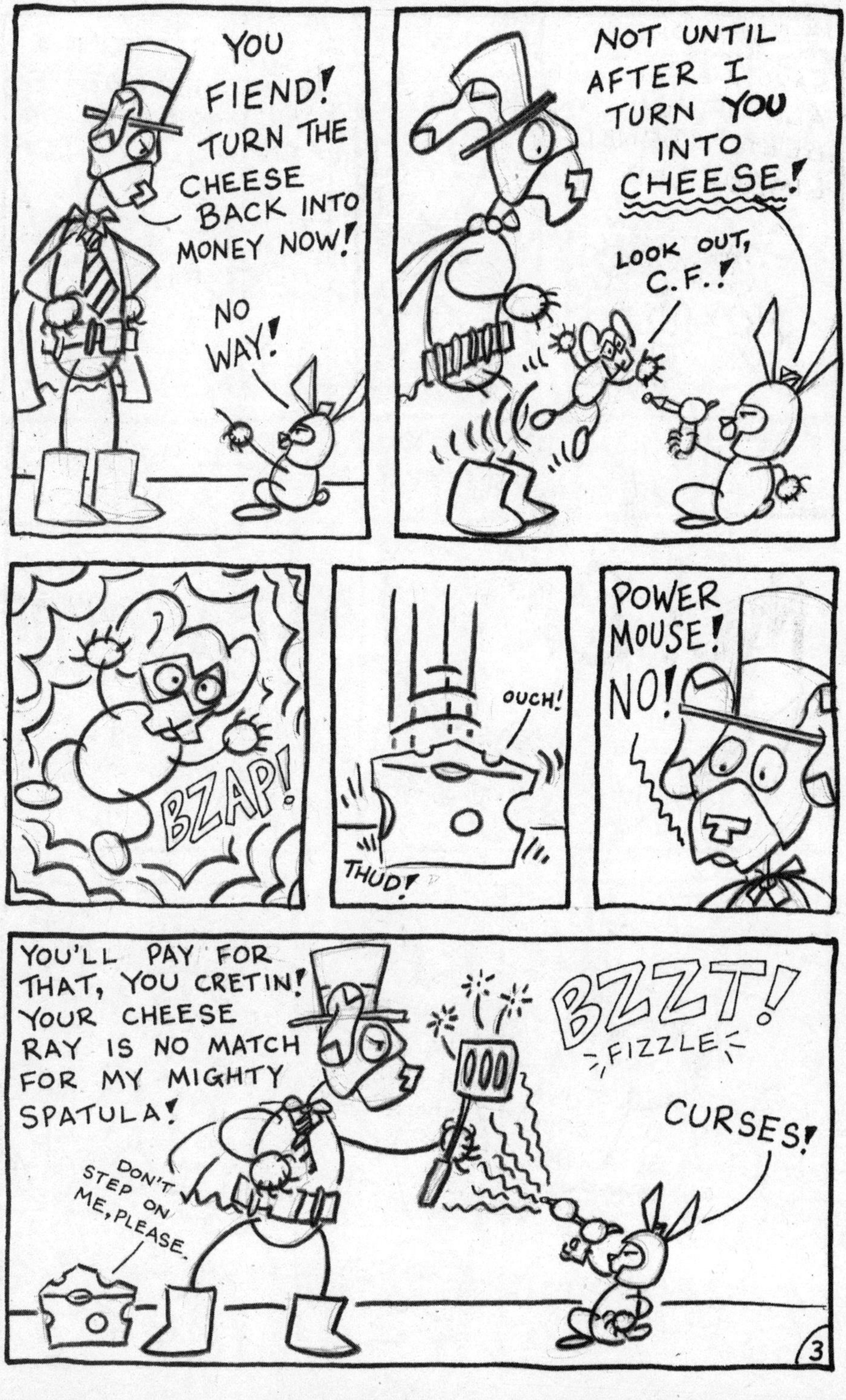
YOU FIEND! TURN THE CHEESE BACK INTO MONEY NOW!
NO WAY!
NOT UNTIL AFTER I TURN YOU INTO CHEESE!
LOOK OUT, C.F.!
BZAP!
OUCH!
THUD!
POWER MOUSE! NO!
YOU'LL PAY FOR THAT, YOU CRETIN! YOUR CHEESE RAY IS NO MATCH FOR MY MIGHTY SPATULA!
BZZZT!
FIZZLE
CURSES!
DON'T STEP ON ME, PLEASE.

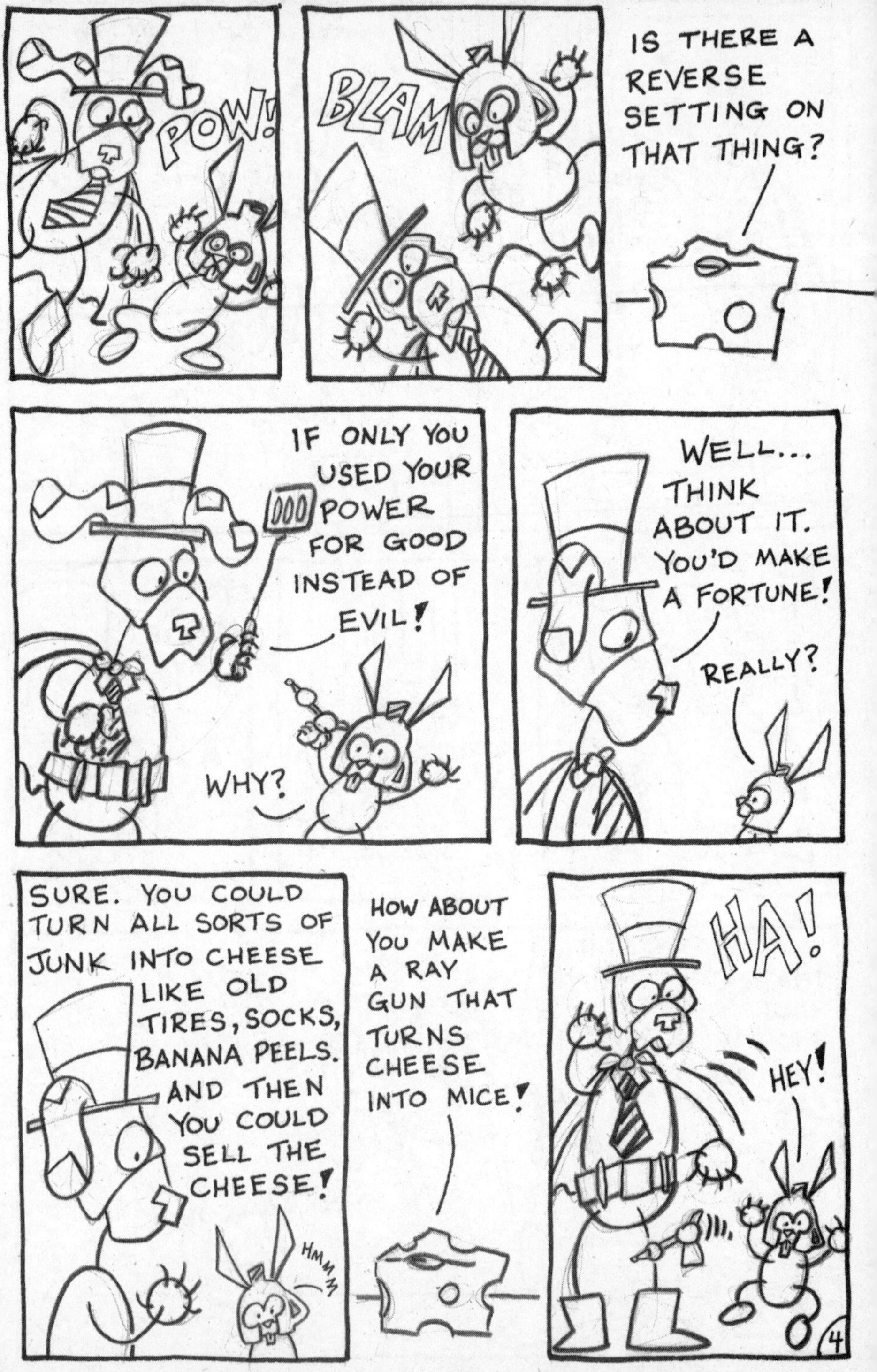
POW!
BLAM
IS THERE A REVERSE SETTING ON THAT THING?
IF ONLY YOU USED YOUR POWER FOR GOOD INSTEAD OF EVIL!
WHY?
WELL... THINK ABOUT IT. YOU'D MAKE A FORTUNE!
REALLY?
SURE. YOU COULD TURN ALL SORTS OF JUNK INTO CHEESE LIKE OLD TIRES, SOCKS, BANANA PEELS. AND THEN YOU COULD SELL THE CHEESE!
HMMM
HOW ABOUT YOU MAKE A RAY GUN THAT TURNS CHEESE INTO MICE!
HA!
HEY!
4

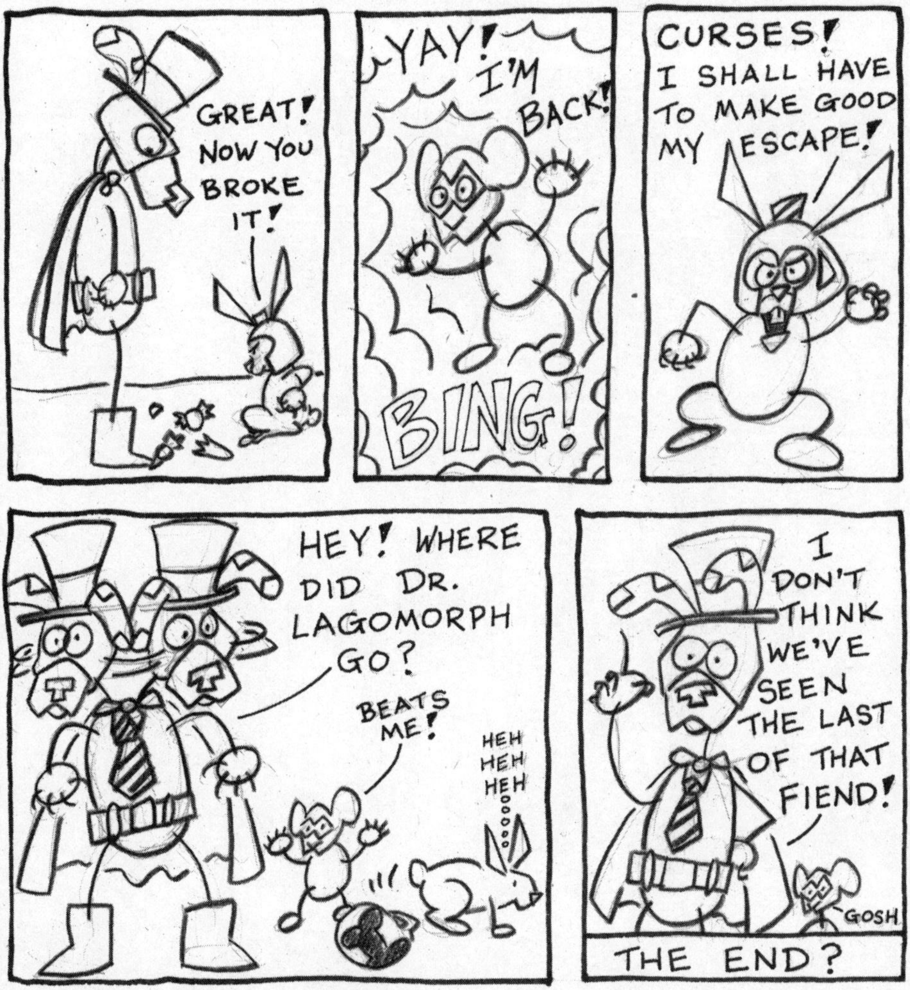
GREAT! NOW YOU BROKE IT!
YAY! I'M BACK!
BING!
CURSES! I SHALL HAVE TO MAKE GOOD MY ESCAPE!
HEY! WHERE DID DR. LAGOMORPH GO?
BEATS ME!
HEH HEH HEH
I DON'T THINK WE'VE SEEN THE LAST OF THAT FIEND!
GOSH
THE END?

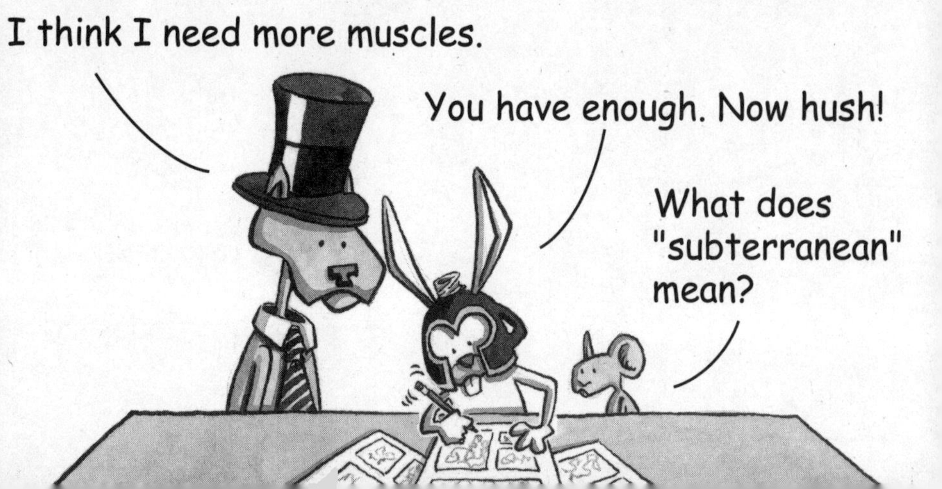
I think I need more muscles.
You have enough. Now hush!
What does "subterranean" mean?

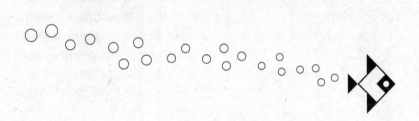

Go Fish!

GOFISH

questions for the author

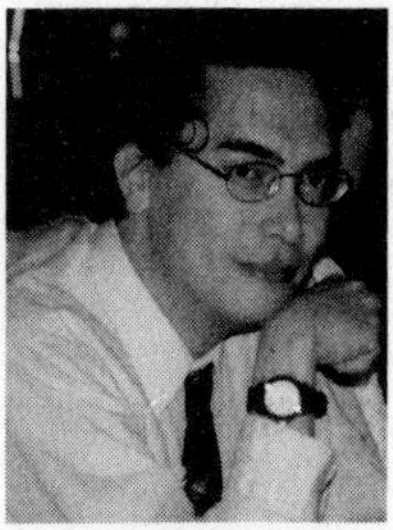

NICK BRUEL

What did you want to be when you grew up?
I tell this story all the time when I visit schools. When I was in first grade, there was nothing I liked to do more than to write stories and make little drawings to go with them. I thought the best job in the world was the one held by those people who had the comic strips in the newspapers. What better job is there than to wake up each morning and spend the day writing little stories and making little drawings to go along with them? So that's what I did. I wrote stories and I drew pictures to go along with them. And I still do that to this day.

When did you realize you wanted to be a writer?
I always liked to write stories. But it wasn't until high school when I spent a lot of time during summer vacations writing plays for my own amusement that I began to think this was something I could do as a career.

What's your first childhood memory?
Sitting in my high chair, feeling outraged that my parents were eating steak and green beans while all I had was a bowl of indescribable mush.

What's your most embarrassing childhood memory?
Crying my eyes out while curled up in my cubbyhole in first grade for reasons I can't remember. I didn't come back out until my mother came in to pick me up from school.

What's your favorite childhood memory?
Waking up early on Christmas morning to see what Santa brought me.

As a young person, who did you look up to most?
My father. He was a kind man with a great sense of humor.

What was your worst subject in school?
True story: In eighth grade, I was on the second string of the B-team of middle school baseball. I was up at bat only twice the entire season. I struck out and was beaned. It was generally recognized that I was the worst player on the team. And since our team lost every single game it played that year, it was decided that I was probably the worst baseball player in all of New York State in 1978.

What was your best subject in school?
Art, with English coming in a close second.

What was your first job?
I spent most of the summer after my junior year in college as an arts-and-crafts director at a camp for kids with visual disabilities in Central Florida. I won't say any more, because I'm likely to write a book about it someday.

How did you celebrate publishing your first book?
I honestly don't remember. A lot was happening at that time. When *Boing* came out, I was also preparing to get married. Plus, I was hard at work on *Bad Kitty*.

Where do you write your books?

As I write this, I'm the father of a one-year-old baby. Because of all the attention she needs, I've developed a recent habit, when the babysitter comes by to watch Isabel, of collecting all of my work together and bringing it to a nice little Chinese restaurant across the street called A Taste of China. They know me pretty well, and let me sit at one of their tables for hours while I nibble on a lunch special.

Where do you find inspiration for your writing?

Other books. The only true axiom to creative expression is that to be productive at what you do, you have to pay attention to what everyone else is doing. I think this is true for writing, for painting, for playing music, for anything that requires any sort of creative output. To put it more simply for my situation . . . if you want to write books, you have to read as many books as you can.

Which of your characters is most like you?

In *Happy Birthday, Bad Kitty*, I introduce a character named Strange Kitty. I can say without any hesitation that Strange Kitty is me as a child. I was definitely the cat who would go to a birthday party and spend the entire time sitting in the corner reading comic books rather than participating in all of the pussycat games.

When you finish a book, who reads it first?

My wife, Carina. Even if I'm on a tight deadline, she'll see it first before I send it to my editor, Neal Porter. Carina has a fine sense of taste for the work I do. I greatly respect her opinion even when she's a little more honest than I'd like her to be.

Are you a morning person or a night owl?
Both. I suspect that I need less sleep than most people. I'm usually the first one up to make breakfast. And I'm rarely in bed before 11:00 PM. Maybe this is why I'm exhausted all the time.

What's your idea of the best meal ever?
So long as it's Chinese food, I don't care. I just love eating it. If I had to pick a favorite dish, it would be Duck Chow Fun, which I can only find in a few seedy diners in Chinatown.

Which do you like better: cats or dogs?
Oh, I know everyone is going to expect me to say cats, but in all honesty, I love them both.

What do you value most in your friends?
Sense of humor and reliability.

Where do you go for peace and quiet?
I'm the father of a one-year-old. What is this "peez kwiet" thing you speak of?

What makes you laugh out loud?
The Marx Brothers. W. C. Fields. Buster Keaton. And my daughter.

What's your favorite song?
I don't think I have one favorite song, but "If You Want to Sing Out, Sing Out" by Cat Stevens comes to mind.

Who is your favorite fictional character?
The original Captain Marvel. He's the kind of superhero designed for kids who need superheroes. SHAZAM!

What are you most afraid of?
Scorpions. ACK! They're like the creepiest parts of spiders and crabs smashed together into one nasty-looking character. Whose idea was that?

What time of year do you like best?
Spring and summer.

What's your favorite TV show?
I have to give my propers to *The Simpsons,* of course. But I'm very partial to the British mystery series *Lovejoy.*

If you were stranded on a desert island, who would you want for company?
I'm going to defy the implications of that question and say no one. As much as I'm comfortable talking for hours with any number of people, I'm also one of those people who relishes solitude. I've never had any problem with being alone for long periods of time. . . . You get a lot more work done that way.

If you could travel in time, where would you go?
America in the 1920s. All of my favorite literature, movies, and music comes from that period. I would love to have witnessed or even participated in the artistic movements of that period in history.

What's the best advice you have ever received about writing?
I had a playwriting teacher in college named Bob Butman who gave me superb advice on the subject of writer's block—it's all about PRIDE. It's a complete myth to believe that you can't think about what you want to write next because your mind is a blank. In truth, when you feel

"blocked," it's because you DO have something in mind that you want to put to paper, but you don't feel it's good enough for what you're trying to accomplish. That's the pride part. The best thing, I find, is to put it down anyways and move on. Half the challenge of the writing process is the self-editing process.

What would you do if you ever stopped writing?
I would seriously consider becoming a teacher.

What do you like best about yourself?
I have nice hands. They've always served me well.

What is your worst habit?
Biting other people's toenails.

What do you consider to be your greatest accomplishment?
Adopting our spectacular daughter, Isabel. Actually managing to get my first book (*Boing*) published comes in second.

Where in the world do you feel most at home?
Home. I'm a homebody. I like to work at home. I like to cook at home. I like to grow my garden vegetables at home. I like being in new and different places, but I despise the process of getting there. So, because I'm not a big fan of traveling, I just like being at HOME. It's a quality about myself that runs closely with my love of solitude.

What do you wish you could do better?
I wish I was a better artist. I look at the fluidity of line and the luminous colors of paintings by such artists as Ted Lewin, Anik McGrory, Jerry Pinkney, and Arthur Rackham with complete awe.

Find out where Kitty comes from and how Kitty copes when she confronts her greatest foe yet—her creator,

Nick Bruel!

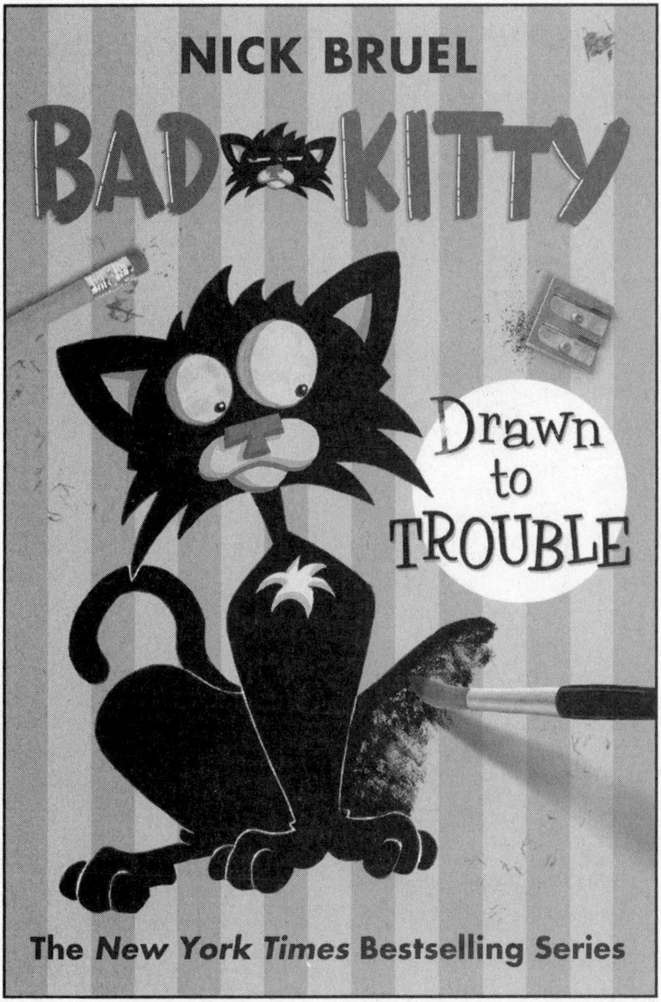
NICK BRUEL
BAD KITTY
Drawn to TROUBLE
The New York Times Bestselling Series

MEET THE CHARACTER

Okay. Let's get started!

We're lucky! We already have a character for our story. That's YOU, Kitty!

Yes, YOU! You are someone who has a personality, and as our story moves forward we're going to get to know you better.

In fact, Kitty, you're not just any character. You're going to be this story's PROTAGONIST, which is a fancy word that means you'll be the most important character in this story.

It's a bit like being the star in a movie.

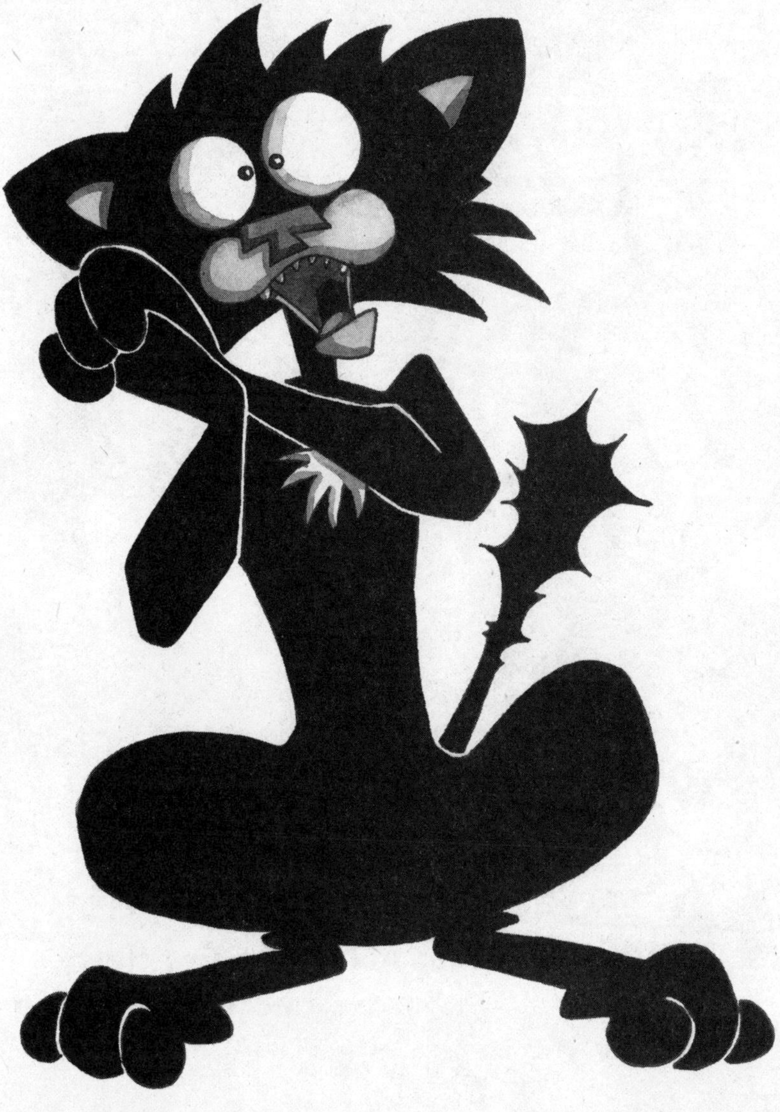

I thought you might like that, Kitty.

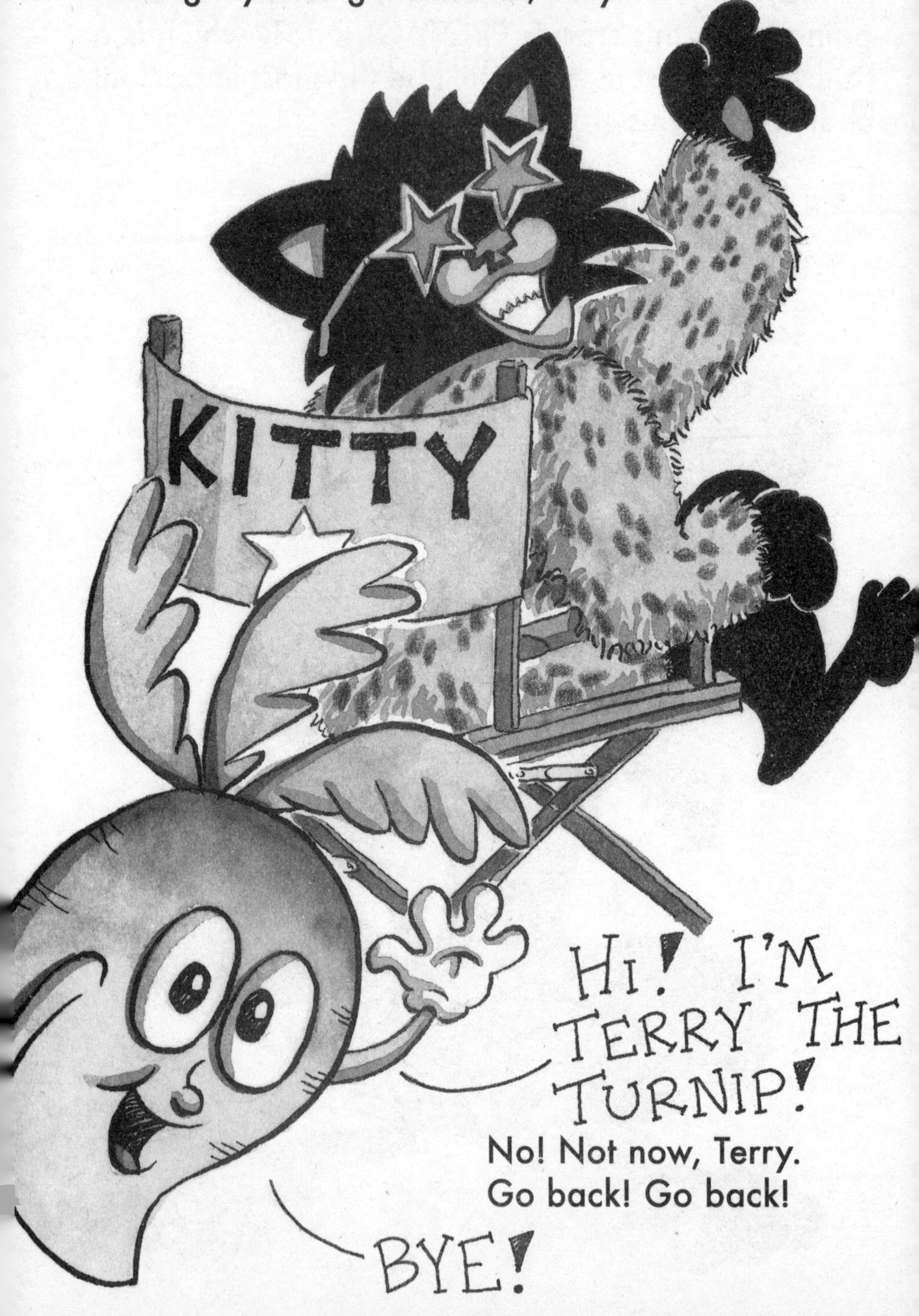
KITTY
HI! I'M TERRY THE TURNIP!
BYE!

No! Not now, Terry.
Go back! Go back!

Terry? Don't worry about him, Kitty. That was just a little FORESHADOWING, which is when a writer drops little hints about what's going to come later in the story.

But right now we need a SETTING, someplace where your story can take place.

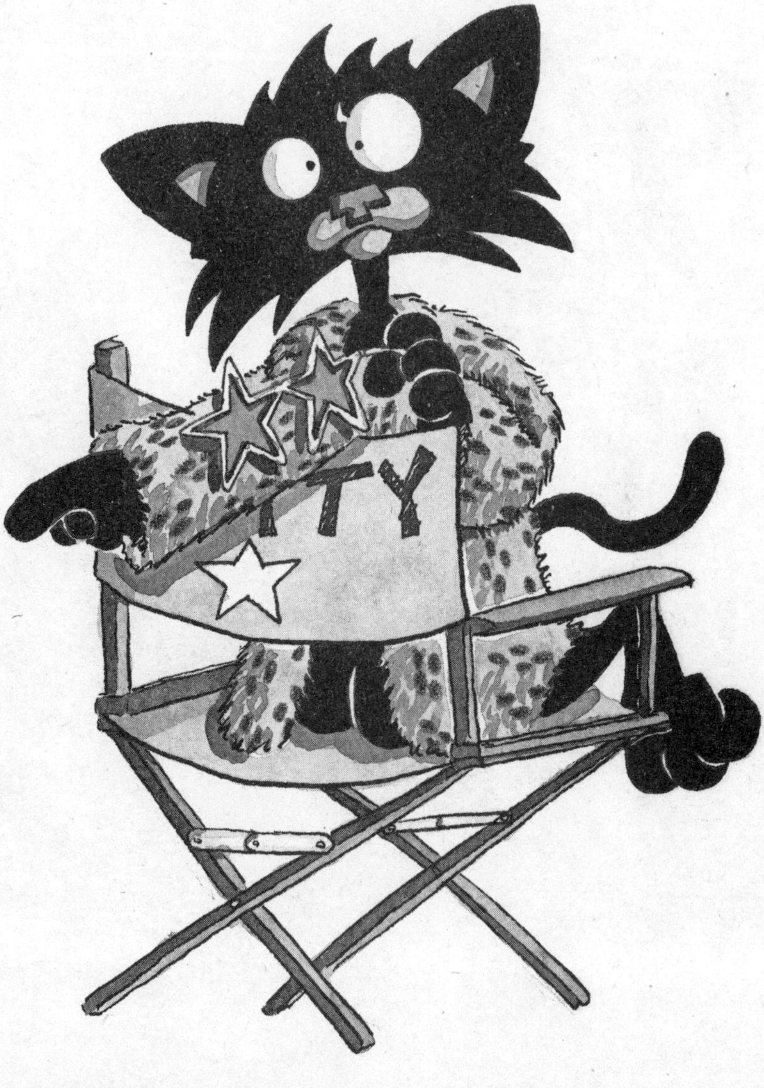

Deciding on a setting is one great way to start a story.

For instance, maybe our story will be a great pirate adventure! In that case, we might set our story in the middle of the ocean!

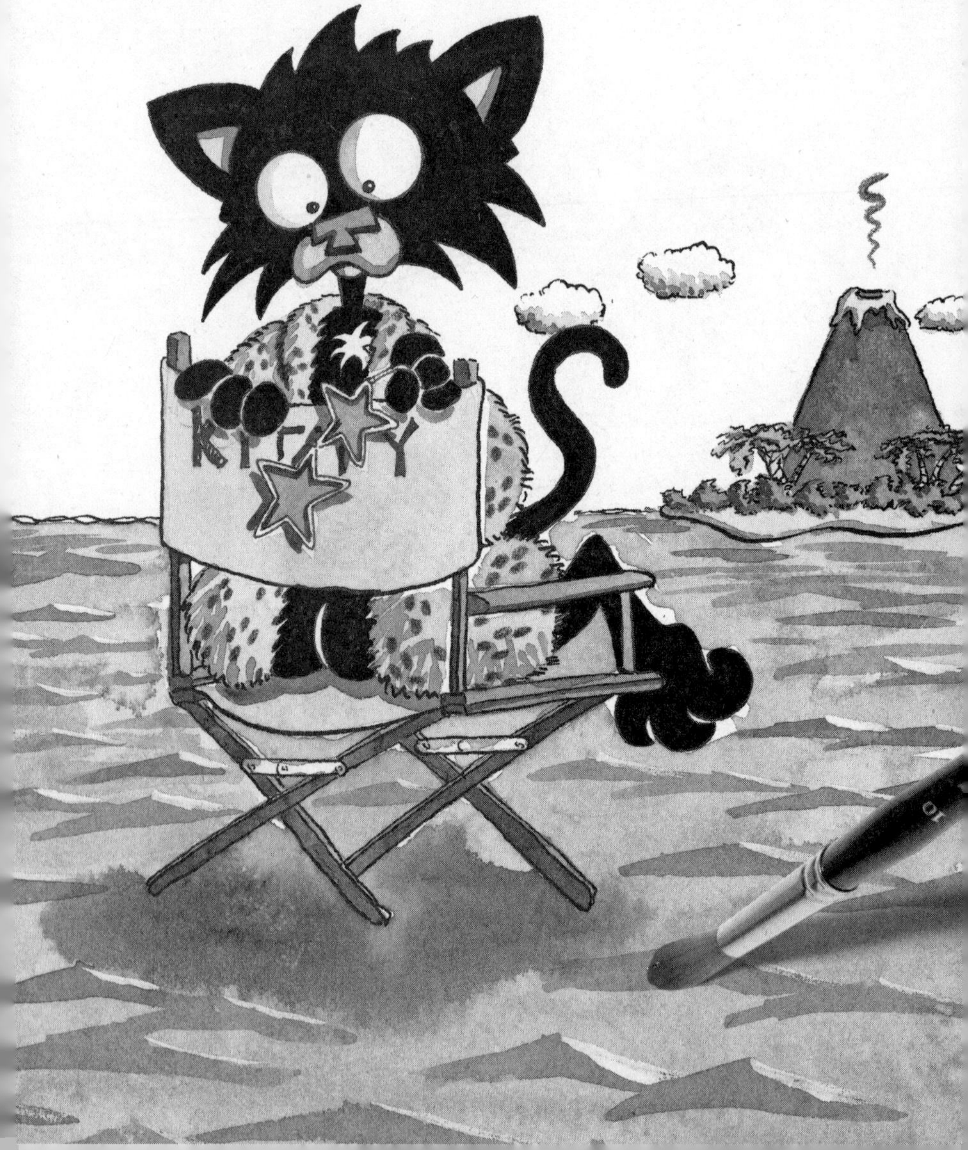

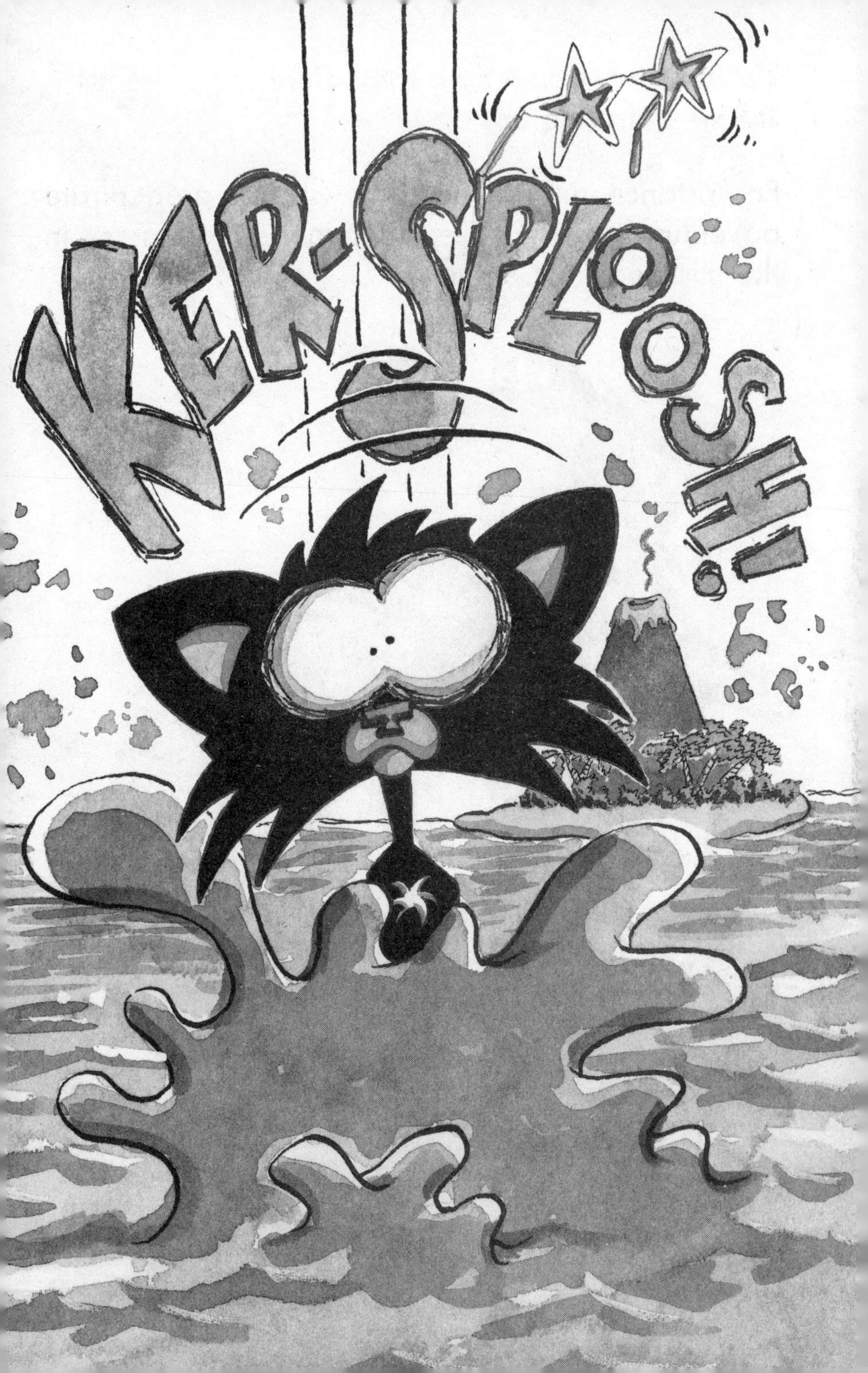
KER-SPLOOSH!!

Oops. Sorry about that, Kitty. Here . . .
let me help you up.

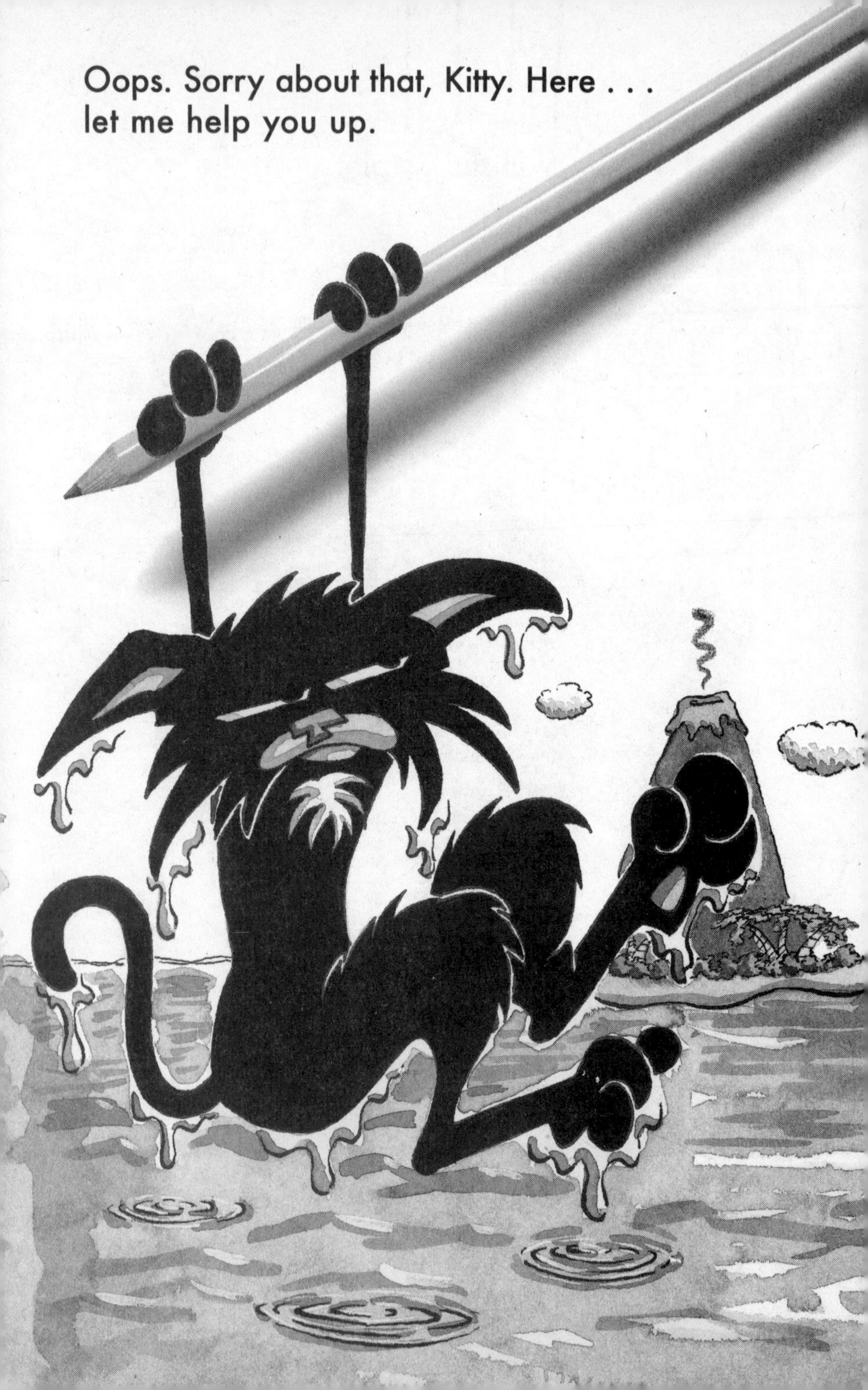

So ocean adventure was a bad idea. But don't worry, Kitty. We'll think of something. Maybe we could set our story in the jungle.

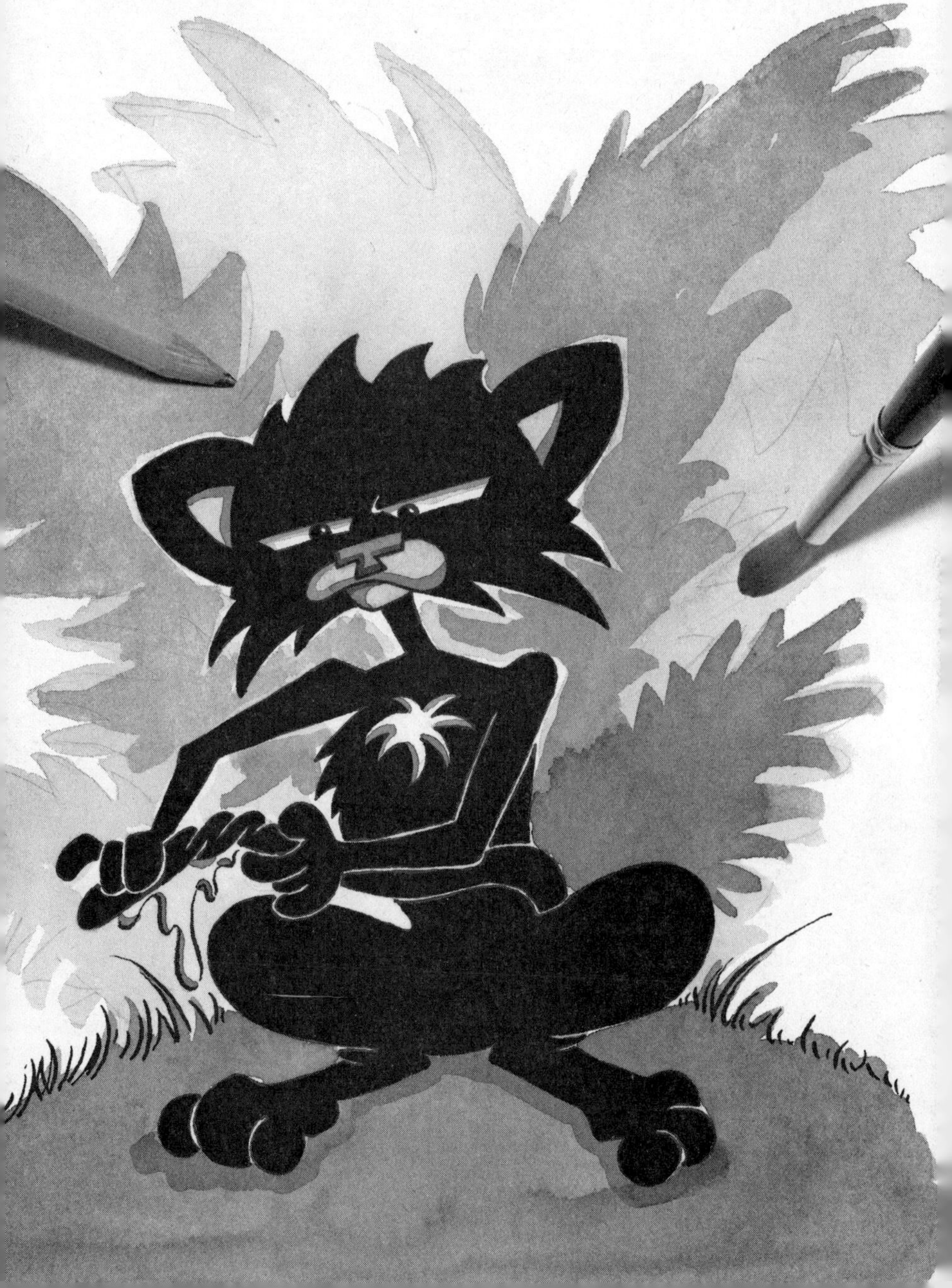

Sure! We'll make an exotic jungle tale set inside the wild, untamed forests of Africa with strange plants, mysterious noises, and huge, dangerous beasts of prey.

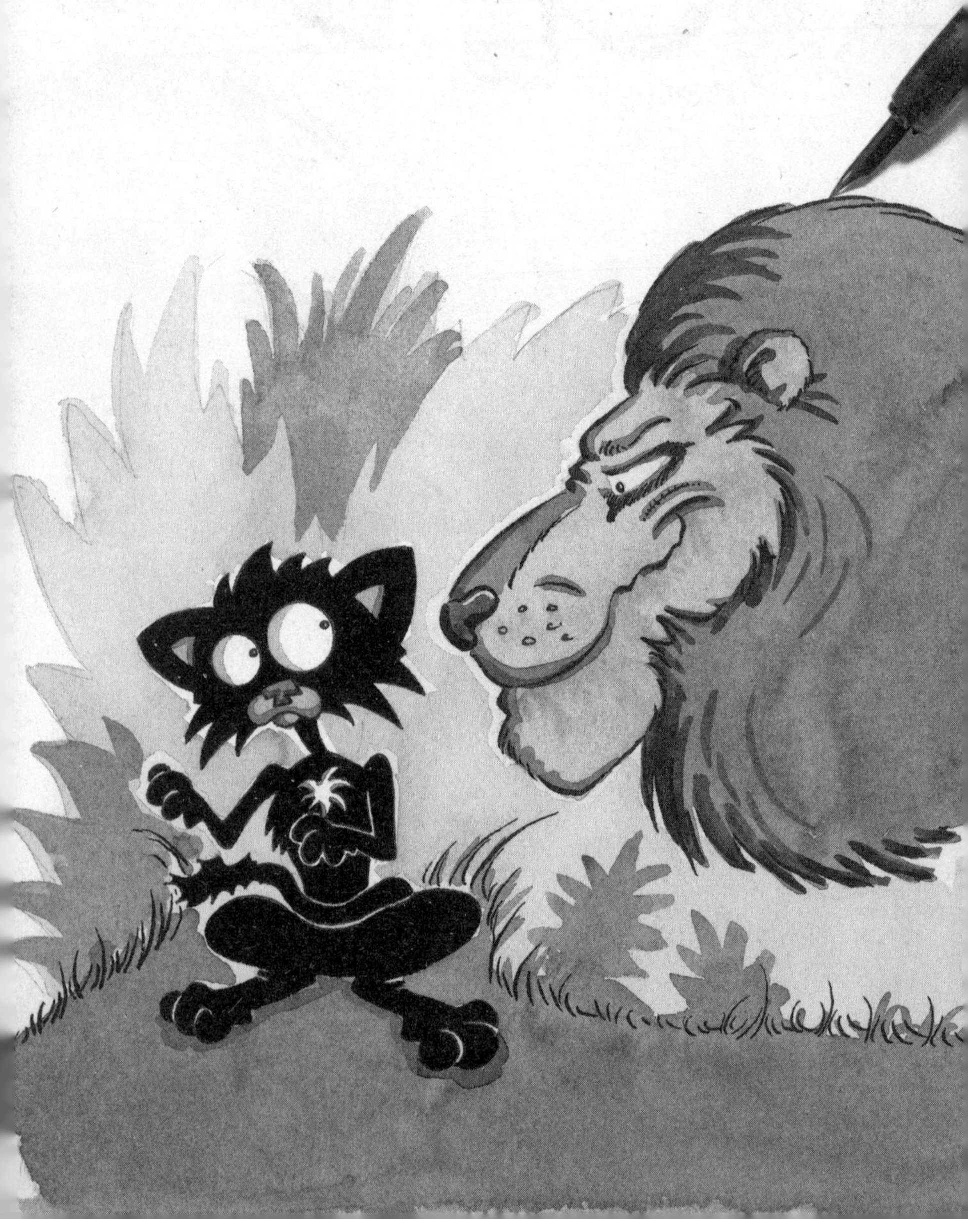

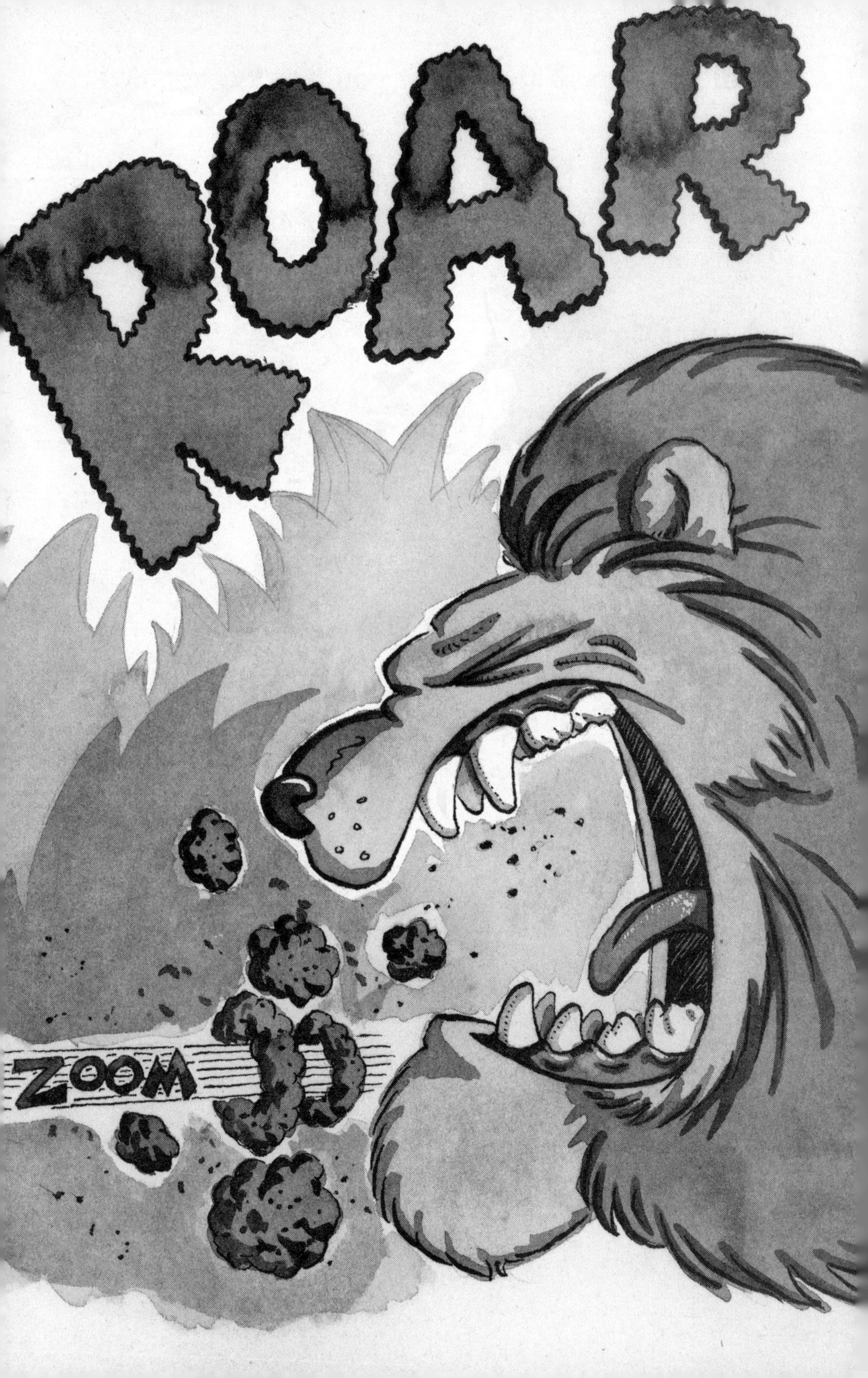
ROAR
ZOOM

What's wrong, Kitty? Don't you like this setting?

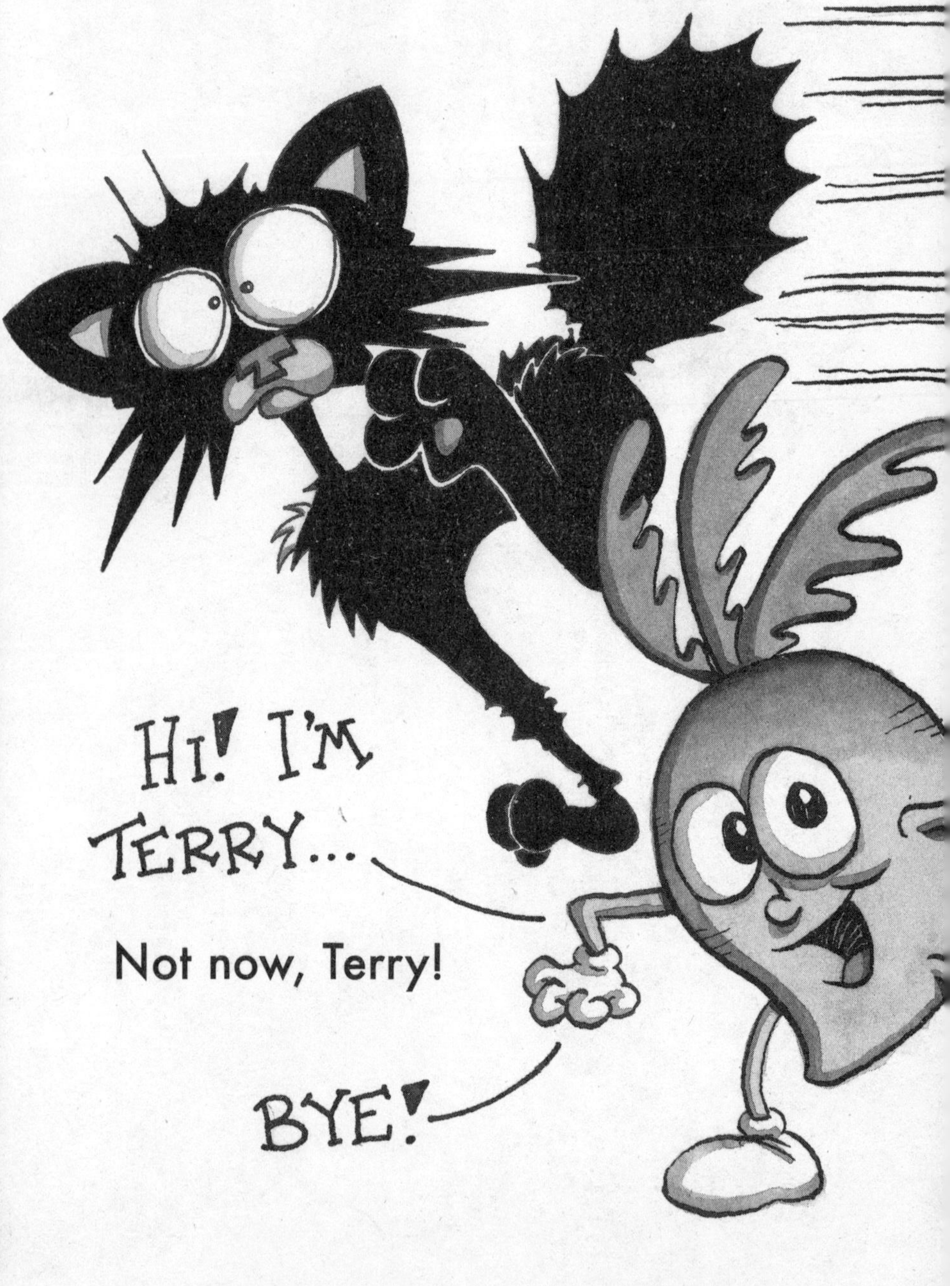
HI! I'M TERRY...
Not now, Terry!
BYE!